COGNIZANT

Book III of the Oblivion Series

RoC BlisS

09/24/17

Suggested reading for Teens through Adult, who enjoy Action, Science Fiction, Fantasy, and Horror, all wrapped up in one book, bound together with the ties of Romance.

COGNIZANT

Roc Bliss

Table of Contents

COGNIZANT

ROC BLISS

Trey-7

Thomas and Darlene had driven for hours, by the time Thomas pulled his vehicle into a fair size public parking lot. "Wale Darlin' looks like we made it. Dis is the last drivable point into Timper Falls, so now it's time to start hoofin' it."

He looked the tired young lady in the eye. She rolled her eyes slightly, upon hearing that walking would be part of this little excursion, but it was not a reflection that she was dissatisfied, she just thought that walking would be too slow, and may inhibit them from some alone time. He swung his door open, and then gentlemanly, he moved around the vehicle to open the young lady's door.

COGNIZANT

"Thank-you," she said unused to this type of behavior. He placed one hand upon hers, as he cradled her body with his to help her down from the truck. A slight bend of the knee later and she was on the ground with her internal motor running. "You are such a gentleman, Thomas. A girl could get used to this sort of thing."

Thomas knew that he would never fall out of love with the girl that had been his partner through thick and thin, so he just nodded affirmatively and opened the back hatch. He looked across the half-empty parking lot, checking out the other transport vehicles. Air riders of various shapes and sizes dotted the lot, but *his* truck was obviously the premier land vehicle.

"Okay darlin', we gotta go register over yonder dare." He said, pointing to a smallish log cabin style office building. Darlene looked over to the quaint little building. Thomas grabbed the bags. He had one in each hand and the other stacked under his arm.

"You don't have to carry my bags Thomas. I appreciate the gesture, but I can do *something* to help." Darlene reminded him, not being used to the man's old school chivalry.

Thomas stopped, as he cut in front of the young woman, turning his back to the building, he said. "Looky here, yer just gonna haf ta go with it. Da mission has started."

"Yes dear," the young woman said, smiling with nervous ignorance.

He went from the country slang to whispering standardized enunciation. He did not know if the accent was throwing her off, but he could not play that game now. It was too late. "Look, don't sweat it babe. No one has seen anything." He explained. "Now, just remember that you're here on business. Make a game out of it. Have some fun." He suggested, about acting the part, and then he put on his happy smile and turned to face the Timper Falls Registry. The couple walked straight into the office. Thomas placed all of the bags upon a conveyor, which ran through a full scan check.

A computer aided machine, which could see everything in the bags, detailed and registered every item, and if you wanted a list, it would print one. This was mainly for a convenience of the guests. The scanner would print a checklist for you, so that prior to leaving you can check to see your bags are packed in full and that nothing had been forgotten.

"Good evening sir," sounded the voice of the city clerk. He was an older man, short, stocky, and nearly bald.

His glasses glared from the bright evening light of Polaris. The glare got to him, so he finally had to remove his glasses to wipe a sudden tear from his eye. Then, moving over to the window, and closing the shade he said, "I'll be right with you." The elderly man tore off the printout to check the results of the scan.

He postioned his glasses back into place, as he held the paper out in view. His eyes took a few seconds to focus, as he brought the paper carefully to the correct distance from them. "Well, it looks like your bags are cleared." The man said talking in a slow relaxed manner. Darlene liked the old man's demeanor. It felt nice and wholesome, as it hit her ears. The couple placed their papers up on the counter, for their background check. The man could see that Thomas had been checked earlier that day. "You must be a busy man," he commented.

"Wale, I am all about business." Thomas said not talking excessively, as he smiled aimlessly.

Within a few minutes, the counter person allowed the couple to pass. "We have bag delivery now, if you don't want to carry your luggage." Thomas stood at the bag check. He thought for a few seconds, as he wondered how long it would take. "Where you folks plan on staying?"

"Awe shucks, what's da name of dat place, over yonder? Hold on." He said, while reaching into his pocket. He pulled out a piece of paper, and glanced at it for a second. "Billy's, yeah that's it, Billy's Bed and Breakfast."

"We could get your bags there, by the time you get yourselves all checked in." The clerk added, while watching

Thomas, waiting for an answer. "Just some kids from the neighborhood trying to earn some money. It keeps them out of trouble too, I guess." The old man explained, trying to get Thomas to utilize the service.

"Wale shore thang, pops," Thomas answered reaching into his pocket. He pulled out some money. "Where dese little fellers at?" He asked, so that he could pay the kids for their effort.

The old man pushed a button. "They'll be right with you sir." Within twenty seconds, three young teens came up from a lower level of the registry. One of the children was a girl, possibly a tomboy, according to Thomas's summation. She dressed less than feminine, anyway. Thomas looked at the children and immediately, was reminded of what was at stake and the importance of his mission. "Get these nice people's bags, and bring them to

COGNIZANT

the Triple-B. Oh, and here's your checklist sir," the clerk said nodding his salutation with a smile.

Each of the three grabbed a bag. They moved right out the door without giving a thought about the pay. Thomas followed right behind them, with Darlene keeping up the rear. After they had made several paces away from the office, Thomas called out. "Hold on dare, you kids. How'd y'all like to earn some *extra* money?" The three teens stopped all at once to listen to the stranger's proposition. He looked at the girl first. "Do ya know Myra?" He asked. The girl nodded affirmatively. "Y'all go to her place, and tell'er that Tom's here. And you," he said looking to the smallest of the boys. "Y'all know Sam?"

"Da old man at da store?" The smallish teen boy asked, mimicking Thomas' country drawl.

ROC BLISS

Thomas knew how small this town seemed, but to describe that Sam was old? Heck, Sam had only fifteen or so years on him. "So, I s'pose dat I'm old too?" He asked the boy with a serious face.

"Yes, of course." The boy answered without hesitating.

"Wale here's what I'm fixin' for you to say to Sam," he bent down and whispered into the boy's ear. When he was finished, he began to stand, but then he remembered one more thing. Kind of a whim really, but he lowered himself for another few seconds, so that he could add that to the list of the boy's tasks.

Finally, he stood back up again. He took some cards of different credit amounts out of his pocket. He paid them double for bag lugging, because he needed them to rush the baggage to the Triple B. "Okay, and now this is for you," he said to the boys. "And this for you," he told the girl, after handing them the credits. "But if y'all get the job done, and then meet me at the ole Trip-B, I'll see to it that y'all git double what I already gave ya," he said, smiling at the youths. He loved working with the youngsters.

"Thanks mister," the excited children said more than once, as they looked wide-eyed at the credits that they were earning. The young teens in their enthusiasm left hurriedly on their way.

Thomas and Darlene took their time strolling along the roadway. Each of them feeling a bit more relaxed, than they had been for a while. "You know, you sure are good with the kids. Have you any of your own?" She asked, trying to see, if any sign of having a life outside of his current occupation was even feasible. He smiled, as he pondered his answer, which in the end he tried to just side step the question altogether, but Darlene could see that he was trying to get out of answering. "Come on." She jibed.

Thomas thought that he would have a little fun with this. "Wale shoot, I been traveling for years. Best I can figure, pert near fifteen."

Darlene could smell a trick or two, so she answered strategically. "Fifteen years? That's a long time to travel?" She asked, in an attempt to pry.

Thomas smiled in his own childlike way. "Years?" He asked. "I thought we was talkin' bout kids?" Darlene's eyes bulged with the thought of this. He continued, "Shoot, don't none of 'em haf da same mother." He looked at her expression from the corner of his eye, while he continued walking nonchalantly, as if nothing out of the ordinary had been discussed.

COGNIZANT

Darlene imagined what she was just told. Her eyes just kind of glazed over for a second, so Thomas grabbed her by the wrist to keep her on pace. "You are *so* full of it." She finally said, as her conclusion.

"Wale babe, dare it is." He said pointing to the old Triple-B. The semi-rundown building sat off in the distance, but it stood taller than the rest of the longstanding buildings. "Okay, let's get y'all checked in. I have some places to hit after dat. Oh, and here, dis is fir dem kids." He said handing her the credits for the children.

"So, you're leaving me already?" Darlene complained with a sincere note of sadness in her voice.

"I have to make one important stop. Remember, y'all a business woman, and just in case ya don't know, the Trip-B is da place dat you'll be looking ta buy, so check it out like ya mean it." Thomas said, knowing that he had to keep her mind busy with something other than him.

"Really? Is…?" She started asking.

Thomas cut her off right at the quick of her question. "Now, looky here missy, all yer questions can be asked to the staff. Y'all can check out the entire place from wall to wall." He could see by the way that she rolled her eyes at him that she got the clue, not to keep asking him about the place.

He could also see her begin to take it all in, as they approached the front desk. "Excuse me sir," Thomas said addressing the desk clerk. "Dis here is Miss Darlene Holstrom. I'm sure you have her reservations. She is a possible buyer, so y'all answer any questions dat she might have." Thomas explained, deciding to make the statement outright, so that the staff would keep her busy. He basically, gave her instant V.I.P. status, and she handled herself well, as she moved away with certain members, who jumped to show her to her room.

Darlene stopped cold, once she noticed that Thomas was not following. "When will you be back?" She asked the man pointblank.

"Wale, I got some business ta tend. It'll be a couple hours, or so. Y'all have fun now." He waved for a second, then he turned and walked out the door. He needed to make tracks.

*   *   *   *   *

Tessa walked into her aunt Myra's back door. She pulled at a piece of licorice that she was clamping down on. Myra looked at her niece, and could see instantly the change in the woman's demeanor. "So, you got the news that you've been after?" Myra asked, already knowing the answer.

"Yes, I did." Tessa answered. "Where's Deak?" She asked, knowing that she would have to explain her new situation to the young man.

"Oh, don't worry about him. He's resting. I'll clue him in later." Myra answered. Then the old woman asked. "Well Tess, how long do we have?"

Tessa looked at her aunt, through sympathetic eyes. "I don't really know, but I just want you to know that it has been great seeing you again."

Myra looked Tessa over. "Well, as usual, you couldn't just wait for the news. You had to go get it yourself. I wish you could for once, just stay here for a while." The old woman admitted openly.

"It could be days before Thomas gets freed up. Maybe we'll have a little 'us' time." Tessa said trying to sound optimistic.

"I've got something for you that you are going to be needing." Myra stated, as she held out her hand. Tessa reached out, as she wondered what Myra might be handing her. "You are a wife, so you'll be needing these." Myra explained handing Tessa an engagement diamond ring, along with a wedding band.

"Oh wow, they're so beautiful," Tessa said admiring the set of rings. She slowly slid the engagement ring upon her finger, staring at the glowing diamond with approval gleaming in her eyes. Then, she gently placed the wedding band upon her finger next to its counterpart. "Oh look," she said with excitement, as she flashed her hand with all of its newly found glory in front of Myra's pleased eyes.

An unusual timed knock had Myra moving towards the door. She did not usually get visitors, at least not at *this* time of day. She peeked through the window screen from an angle to see who was there. Her eyes glanced down to see the young girl. "Yes, may I help you dear?" The older woman asked curiously.

The small, teenage girl waved her hand to get Myra to move closer. "Tom is here." She whispered quietly in the ear of the older woman, before quickly turning back to head for the bed and breakfast to collect her credits.

Myra watched the young girl make her way across her yard. "That was odd." Myra commented about the strange little visit.

"Who was it?" Tessa asked.

"Well," Myra began. "I would say that there's a new girl, who is taking over for some of the odd jobs that you had done, yourself, as a young girl."

Tessa figured that it was none of her concern, so she dropped the thought. She looked out the back window to see the girl rounding the house and disappearing from sight.

Myra began to think back to the old times. "Yeah, she's cute. I remember when you delivered messages for people," she said, as she reached back into the pictures of her mind. Then she added, "Except you were even cuter, as *I* remember."

"You're not just a little biased, are you?" Tessa asked rhetorically, from behind her girlish grin. "So," she said changing the subject. "How was Deak's little helmet trip?" She asked, speaking partially about the mind washing part of the process, but what she really wanted to hear about was the joke that seemed to get played on most, who saw the head gear prior to its proper use.

With a grin, Myra replied. "Oh, he sat there squinching his eyes closed. He didn't move or jump though, so he did well. When he wakes up, he'll be ready for his new post. It looks as though another new place is opening, not too far away, in Bah-Roque."

"Small town job, aye?" Tessa asked. "So, our big tough gang banger has a mindset on services, huh?" Tessa asked, with a smirking grin.

"There's nothing wrong with small town work." Myra said speaking from experience.

"Oh, I know," Tessa admitted quickly, noticing that she may have inadvertently ruffled her aunt's feathers. Then, she figured that she should explain further. "It's just that Thomas had a run-in in Bah-Roque, and he had started Trey-7's on a business. I think it was a hotel slash diner."

"Well my dear, sometimes you dig too deep," the older woman said with concern. "It is nice to know the truth, but sometimes you learn more than you really need to know, especially from that jealous boy that wished that he had gotten with you." Myra warned.

"Oh Myra," Tessa said blushingly. "Johnny receives so little business that he becomes a little over zealous with divulging information, and he wants to make sure that I have it all."

"Or maybe he wants to get you pissed off at Thomas. He didn't need to tell you about the Trey-7, but he did." Myra fired back, trying to open Tessa's eyes.

"Or maybe, he is thorough, or just plain good at his job." Tessa scuffed back trying to protect her friend.

"Oh, I try to be." A different yet familiar voice, suddenly sounded, coming through the screen door. "I think Myra's right." The masculine voice stated, clearly choosing sides.

Both women turned with surprise. Tessa knew that voice, and had been longing to hear it again. She turned to run for the door. Thomas swung the screen door wide open. The evening light was dimming, as Polaris was setting behind him, creating an appearance of an aura that radiated about him. She looked at his silhouette in the doorway. Her arms led the way forward, as she reached for her man.

Thomas stepped forward and she lept into his loving arms. They held each other passionately embracing the one and only true love of their lives. Their lips pressed, as their tongues danced with passion. "I thought that you were dead," Thomas explained in a low quiet voice, as he pulled his mouth away, pulling her close and squeezing the woman that has been his one and only.

"You kids need a room?" Myra joked. Then smiling cheerfully, she said, "Thomas, how've you been. You're lookin' good, but you're in dire need of some country cookin'."

Thomas laughed slightly and then walked over to give the older woman a hug. "Yer lookin' mighty good yerself Myra," he said, as he gave her a squeeze.

"Get your things. You can stay here for the night." Myra suggested.

Thomas lifted his eyebrows, as he began explaining. "Wale, as y'all know, I got me a Trey-7 down at the Trip-B. I have to git this gale a peek at it, so that she can see how it works, then bring'er on down here to see Myra, so y'all can run'er through the ole' brain thang."

"Okay then, get your things, and your tramp. In fact, go get everything. Bring them *all* here. We have things to do, and they are all way too important to be waiting around for you to get a new rookie up and into her new place. We have people to do that. In fact, now that I think about it, I'll *come* with you, and you can introduce her to your wife." Tessa flashed her new ring in front of his face. Her face was red, partially due to her fast-talking, and the rest because she was just plain angry with him. She felt semi-betrayed.

Thomas knew her emotions and that she really would not be angry, once she heard the whole story. He was also feeling the joy that they were married now. "Tess, oh Tess, you know me. You know that you are everything to me."

COGNIZANT

"Then pick up your twang and let's go." She said reminding him that he needed to keep the accent going.

"Yes ma'am." He said with pep, as he looped his arm for her to hold, so they could start their walk out of the door into the setting light of Polaris.

"We'll be back!" Tessa yelled over her shoulder towards the listening ears of her aunt Myra, whose watchful eyes gazed at the two, going on their way arm in arm, into the night.

The Enemy of My Enemy

Kilari and Belsangar had made their way near the entrance of the cave. The dead and rotting zombies still laid out dead, just as they had left them, but they noticed that these carcasses were breaking down rather quickly. The smell was enough to make their eyes water.

Kilari climbed up the pile of dead zombies to see, if he could get close enough to jump up to the peak. He reached up with his hand, and sized up the distance that he would need to overcome. "We're going to need to stack some more bodies up here." Kilari suggested to Belsangar.

"What?" Belsangar asked with disgust. "I *really* don't want to touch those things. It's bad enough walking on them."

"Well, maybe we can find a couple with clothes in good shape, so that they'll be easier to move." Kilari stated, as he carefully made his way back down the pile of zombies."

"Man, it's starting to get dark out. We *better* just hurry this up." Belsangar warned. "Didn't that hunter chick say that the zombies come out at night?"

"They came out during the day, so why wouldn't they come out at night." Kilari commented, as the two men tossed a few more carcasses upon the large stack.

"I don't know. Maybe, there are more of them at night, and they *usually* don't come out during the day." Belsangar said, as he eyed the pile's height. "That should do it. Here I go." Belsangar scampered up the uneven pile of dead rotting bodies tripping when his foot was caught in the ribcage of one of the corpses. "Ewww" he gasped, as he wiped the gruesome rotting remains off from his boot, onto his pantleg, while walking back to get another start.

Once Belsangar finally reached the top of the pile again, he gave a little spring with his legs launching himself awkwardly toward the ledge. He was able to get enough height to get a good grip and pull himself up.

Once Belsangar had made it up, Kilari followed suit. They lay upon the ledge for a few seconds, each of them captured in their own immediate thoughts. Kilari said a short prayer to Yahiveh, and then rolled over to his hands and knees. Belsangar sat up to look at the cave entrance. Kilari had a sudden feeling come over him. He felt that they had better keep silent. He

COGNIZANT

tapped Belsangar's shoulder and held his finger to his lips to signal silence, and then the two young agents moved stealthily into the cave opening. They each could see that there was clearly some kind of light just beyond the first corner. Each of the soldiers snuck in perfect stealth, right up to the opening, which led into what was the darkest place in which either of them had been lost, but now, for some unknown reason, a light was emitting from it.

The young men began peering into the vast chamber. Reddish rocks and stones stuck out with jagged edges along the cave walls and ceiling, but the floor seemed smooth. This suggested that there had been lots of activity in this cave system at some point in time. Whether in the far past, or more recent, they could not tell. Belsangar could hear voices, so he pointed to his ear and then back into the cavern. Kilari nodded affirmative, and then slowly moved into the light.

His eyes focused, and after checking every inch of the area, he signaled Belsangar to follow. The two young soldiers crept lightly along the closest wall, following the sound of the voices, which seemed to be seeping over the very wall, which they were following, so Kilari looked up and noticed that the wall did not actually reach all the way to the ceiling. He peered along the top of the wall for a long period. The voices were beginning to be getting louder, as it seemed that the beings were in the midst of a disagreement.

Belsangar on bended knees, searched for markings along the floor, hoping that there could be some kind of clue to the whereabouts of the girls and Tank. Finally, his scouring had paid off. A pattern appeared, which seemed to travel directly over the wall, not more than twenty paces ahead of them. After standing fully erect, he tapped his partner on the shoulder. Kilari turned to see what was up.

Belsangar signaled that he could see some kind of trail ahead, so he pointed it out to Kilari with his finger. Kilari gave him a thumbs-up, once he saw the disruption on the cave surface.

Just ten paces ahead, the wall came to its apex, which placed it within a foot of the ceiling. This seemed to be possibly the safest point at which they could get a good glimpse at just who, was on the other side of the wall.

The two men crawled slowly, assuring to remain as silent as possible, while making their way up the rough mound wall. They used the tiny gap, as a peek hole, and the wall as a blocker to hide from view. Each of the men peeped his sights through this little fissure in the wall.

Kilari's eyes widened, upon the recognition of the three subordinates. With a jolt in his heart, he quickly adjusted his head back, away from the gap. His heart pounded, as his adrenal glands pumped their answer through his veins.

Belsangar appeared to be in the same position, not from the recognition, but from the shock of seeing these strange creatures in existence right in front of his very eyes. He had never seen anything like any of the creatures, even in this strange new world.

Kilari pinched himself to make sure that he was still in the flesh, and he was, so he knew that he had not been pulled into the netherworld unknowingly, again.

COGNIZANT

Belsangar stopped dead, remaining completely motionless, trying not to even breathe too deeply, just in case it could be loud enough to be heard. The two young agents remained motionless, listening to the creatures, as they continued bickering amongst themselves, while at the same time taking a moment to clear their heads.

Clomp, clomp, Angkor began to pace. "We've argued with you long enough Apophis. You are going to have to help us move these bodies!" The faun yelled in anger. "When we leave, you'll have no light, and you won't be able to continue your work, until we get back." Angkor threw in, as an additional threat.

Apophis knew that he was nearly finished with the subtle changes that needed to be made. He believed that he could create enough poor translations from the original dialects that it would create impossible divisions between, however many groups, which formed as believers. In his mind, it would create constant chaos, and keep almost all of them from knowing the real truth. He figured that within half an hour, he should be able to sew up any loose ends that remain.

Kilari looked over to his best friend and whisperingly asked, "Did he say bodies?" Belsangar nodded affirmative. His eyes still saucer like with shock. Kilari could feel the anger welling up, as the adrenaline continued flowing unchecked through his system. He began imagining that all of his friends had fell prey to these three demons.

Tears formed in his ducts, as his heart pounded the rushing adrenaline. His emotions were beginning to unravel. Then suddenly, it all became clear to him and a picture formed from deep within his mind, behind his physical being. He could see Lucifer sending these three to take his friends away, and then placing the blame on Yahiveh.

Belsangar could see the turmoil in Kilari's mind, and he knew that something was about to give, so he began to slowly reach for his weapons, hoping that he would live to get through this day, and more than that, he longed to see his fair Ceilia again alive and well. As he reached back, his hand fumbled across his torch. He pulled it out, rolled over, and began crawling to the top of the wall. He kept silent, moving with total grace, possibly for the first time ever, but he was not moving for exercise, he was moving for the sake of his friends' lives.

The Enemy of My Enemy

Kilari finally hit the wall, as his adrenaline pushed him into the state, where he reacted with no care of consequences. He rose up from the ground, no longer caring if the enemy heard him. If what he believed to be true was actually the truth, these creatures will be paying in full. In his mind, he began repeating the words, 'I am a soldier, and I know who my enemy is'. While the words echoed their cadence, he marched along the side of the wall. He was low enough to stay out of sight, but he was not being quiet.

"SHHH, did you hear that?" Aeron asked nervously. He could hear something walking.

Angkor looked over at the robed entity. "Are you getting nervous again? I'm trying to talk Apophis into taking these bodies back." He grumbled.

"You are both feeble minded foolsss." Apophis stated. "Do you actually believe that Hadesss isss going to show up here?"

"You better *pray* that somebody shows up!" Kilari yelled, as he quickly made his way over the crest of the rocky wall, like side jumping a hurdle. The three creatures all looked up in astonishment. Kilari stood tall holding his nun-chucks in each hand with his arms resting against his sides, leaving the weapons dangling straight down. He looked upon the enemy threateningly with piercing eyes. His long golden hair was messed and quite straggly from his journey, making the three demons see him in a much different light, then how he appeared the last time they had met.

Belsangar had maneuvered down the backside of the mound-like wall. He watched Kilari make his presence known. He made his way stealthily to the bodies. They looked dead. One by one, he checked them for signs of life.

The serpent looked up. "You!" He yelled. "What are you doing here Kilari of Chronosss?" The serpent was beginning to get riled. All of these distractions, when he was so close to finishing his work. This was supposed to be his masterpiece.

The robed entity started to flutter, remembering what Kilari had done to them in *their* plane. Now, they were in a more neutral setting.

"Who cares? What is *he* going to do all by himself?" Angkor spat out with a grudge.

Belsangar, still wondering how these creatures knew Kilari, lit his torch and yelled. "He ain't alone mother fucker." The three beings were startled and turned toward the new voice. Belsangar stood menacingly holding his torch, which caused a flicker in the lighting.

Kilari took advantage of the diversion. In the blink of an eye, he lunged behind Angkor, slinging his chuck around the faun's neck. Kilari tightened the hold and squeezed the faun's windpipe. "Check the bodies." He called out to Belsangar. "Is it them?" He asked still unknowing.

"Yeah it's them. They all have pulses. I *already* checked." Belsangar called back.

Kilari spun the helpless faun around, using him as some type of shield. He backed over to Belsangar, half dragging the faun. "Wake them up man." He told Belsangar. Belsangar pushed on Tank's chest with his free hand. There was no response.

Apophis watched the scene with amusement. "You are going to kill the faun if he doesss not breathe sssoon."

The serpent said smoothly in a matter of fact way.

"Oh, I'll be killing all of you, if you don't wake them up." Kilari threatened. He began to squeeze Angkor's throat even tighter to show that he meant what he said. "In fact, maybe I'll just do him in right now to get him out of the way." He added to hurry the three demons along.

"Stop!" Aeron called out. "We cannot awaken them. The Black Mage has taken their spirits. Only *he* can bring them back."

Kilari relaxed his grip on Angkor, enough for him to make a loud gasp, as he fought for air. "I'm willing to talk, and as a show of good faith..." He released the faun with a harsh kick that sent the faun tumbling forward onto the rocky surface near his two partners.

COGNIZANT

The serpent covered the book nonchalantly during the bustle, so that it could not be noticed. "You do know that the Black Mage could be watching usss right now." The serpent threw out. He wanted to test Kilari, to see his reaction. Aeron got nervous and tapped his cloak. The cave instantly became black, except for the flickering of Belsangar's lit torch.

Kilari pulled out his torch and held it to the flame of the other. Once lit, he tossed the torch a couple of feet from the nine bodies. He moved to his comatose friends and knelt down. He felt Jezza's face as he watched her chest rise with breath peacefully. Her skin was smooth and warm. Then he touched Marcia just to make sure. She too felt physically healthy.

The serpent hissed at his nervous partner for showing just how worried that he was. "You fool." He called out in frustration.

Belsangar quickly connected the dots. "Okay, so now we *know* that you don't like the Black Mage either. Maybe we should work together." Belsangar yelled across the darkened space toward the entity, which was almost impossible to see.

"First tell us, what's your part in all of this?" Kilari demanded.

Apophis knew that the ball was now in his court. "Oh, we were sssent here to do a job, and the Black Mage jussst happened to be our contact here. It appearsss that he happensss to be the ruler of thisss plane, and either hasss magic powersss, or sssome very sssophisticated trickery at his sssside. I angered him, and ssso to ssshow good faith we were to deliver thessse human bodiesss to hisss abode, which isss where he holdsss their sssspiritsss."

COGNIZANT

"So then, why weren't you doing the job?" Belsangar questioned.

Thinking back to what they may have heard, the serpent was wise enough to use the human's own words in his explanation. "As you sssaid we don't like him, ssso we were dissscusssing the posssibility of getting our job done and leaving without fulfilling hisss requessst. Angkor wanted to get the tasssk over with, and then concentrate on our firssst objective. You are militantsss. What would you do? Would you ssserve two massstersss? Or would you ssserve your only true massster, and then leave without helping the one that you disssliked?"

Kilari took over the other end of the conversation. "I would fulfill all of my obligations. However, there are too many variables to answer such, an open-ended question. Even *we* have become a variable in your situation."

"Ssso, you are an honorable man, not unlike Angkor here?" The serpent asked, as he nodded toward the faun. "Whom you've came in and embarrasssed with your choke hold."

"Yeah, you almost killed me!" Angkor yelled gruffly. "Typical for a human," the faun grumbled somewhat audibly.

"Put yourself in my shoes." Kilari answered defensively. "Our loved ones were lying there looking dead, and we could hear you arguing about moving bodies. You are really very lucky that I decided to talk at all." He provoked minor thoughts of empathy at first, but as he had continued, all three had lost any feelings of compassion that they may have begun to incur. "So when are you bringing my people to the Black

Mage? We need their souls placed back into their bodies."

The serpent played out all of the different scenarios in his mind, and in the end, he figured that if they did not get the bodies back, Kilari may discover the book, and maybe worse, he could discover the changes being made, which would blow the whole mission. Lucifer would not take acceptance to such a thing. He could not afford to fail this mission, not when he was so close to finishing.

Kilari stood there watching Apophis. Finally, he could not take waiting any longer. "Please, will you get my friends to the Black Mage?"

"You sssound desssperate, but I'll tell you what, if you drag the bodiess out onto the ledge, outssside of the cave, then we will get them to their sssouls." The serpent suggested, making a straight bargain, in hopes that it would buy him enough time to finish his *real* job.

Kilari looked the serpent right in the eyes. He knew Apophis was up to something, but he could also see that the deal was easy enough, so he agreed. He and Belsangar decided to start out with dragging Tank's massive exterior. Each of the young agents had a torch in one hand and grasped Tank's hand with their other. Apophis had his partner light the tunnels once again, making it appear, as though, he did so to help the two agents. The two struggled even with two free hands, but slowly together, they moved the bodies one by one. All the while, the serpent utilized his time working on the book's wording.

Finally, the serpent had finished his work. He noticed that Kilari only had one more body to carry out, and it seemed just happenstance that it was the body of the girl, who had been carrying the book. Kilari and Belsangar had worked up a sweat, from all the physical work. Their energy was nearly depleted, between all of the running and swimming earlier, as well as their hiking and now moving bodies.

They had not eaten in so long that there was not much left in them. Kilari held Jezza's torso and Belsangar grabbed her legs. They walked slowly, carrying the girl with ease, as they turned the corner out of sight, Apophis handed Angkor the book. "Bring thisss out. Act like you noticed it ssslip from the girl, as she was being picked up. Aeron and I will be a few pacesss behind you."

Angkor did not argue. He grabbed the book and clomped along, only a minute or so behind the two young agents. Once they were only a few paces from the opening of the cave, he stepped fast clomping speedily. "Hey, this must have dropped from the girl, while you were picking her up." He said, as he caught up with the two. He held the book out at arm's length, as he handed it to Belsangar. The faun did not want to hand the book to Kilari. He remembered what the longhaired one had done to them in their plane, and could still feel some ill effects from the chokehold, so he did not want to deal with Kilari at all.

Belsangar took the book and immediately handed it to Kilari, who took it and knelt over the body of his Jezza. He placed his hand upon her cheek and looked deeply upon her countenance. She looked to be at peace. He leaned forward pressing his forehead to hers, trying to interject his presence, his very essence directly into her mind.

COGNIZANT

He felt his heart pounding with renewed feelings of his love for her. Then suddenly, whether it sounded in his mind or for real, he did not know, but her voice whispered, "Help us." He jerked his head back from the shock, as her voice pierced into his brain. He sat back staring at her still unconscious face wondering, if she truly had asked for help, or if he was hallucinating. He turned towards Belsangar and gave him a questioning look.

Belsangar watched his partner's sudden movement, and then he saw the look on his face. He knew that something had just happened. "What's going on man?" He asked after not seeing anything himself.

Kilari now knew that her voice was not audible to his partner. "We gotta get going," he stated immediately. "This is not going fast enough. They need our help, and they need it like, yesterday." His motivation was already high, but once he had heard Jezza's whispering plea, it penetrated his mind, jumping his drive to a new level, leaving him barely able to keep in check.

Apophis and Aeron had made their way from the cave. Apophis walked right over to the ledge and jumped. As he was in air, he quickly changed to his inflated size, making his back nearly even with the ledge, as he stood on all fours. Angkor started loading the bodies onto the serpent's back.

COGNIZANT

Exodus

Vail led her group through the cave tunnels, while her Huntresses took to the outer trails. The Huntresses carried some food, but not nearly all of the food that they had gathered on the hunt. They planned for the trek to appear, as a normal supply hall, believing that the Black Mage could see their every move, whenever they were out in the open. The outer group moved less cautiously than usual, trying to be at the very least some sort of distraction, while those traveling through the caves and tunnels believed that the seclusion, hid them from the Black Mage *and* his watchers.

Exodus

The Huntresses dressed in their normal, burgundy hooded cloaks, appearing as usual, while traveling in the open terrain. Hiding their identity is normal practice. It started long ago, when the women first took over the male dominant tasks, after the men had all but destroyed themselves through their turbulent war mongering. Now, it has been many, many, long times since, but the traditions have not changed, and are taught at early ages, when the girls are deemed old enough to leave the village.

Vail's route was the longer of the two ways, which played into her hands, because she wanted to give the Huntresses time to put Cam's plan into play, as well as for them to be in the village standing ready, so that when she arrived with the young men, the task will flow as planned. They all had gone over Cam's plan a couple of times

COGNIZANT

prior to leaving, so each of the women knew exactly what they needed to do.

Finally, the long jaunt was *about* to come to fruition. Vail and Cam stood at the edge of the tunnel. They could see into the primitive village. The village was relatively small, with huts standing in rows surrounding the worn dirt walkways. At the end of the main stretch, a much larger structure stood. Cam recognized this to be the Queen's Palace, such that it was. He could also see groups of people dressed in skins, men and women alike.

The men appeared even more primitive than the women did, but then Cam thought that it might just seem that way, from a male's prospective. A fire pit hewn from rock stood centralized, between the palace and the villager's huts. He could see the Huntresses plainly, as they were the only ones wearing the hooded cloaks.

Exodus

Vail whistled a loud quick burst, which signaled the Huntresses to get the people moving towards the tunnel. She and the young agents cleared out of the tunnel and moved into their respective positions. Cam led his men around the outskirts of the village, so as not to cause any sudden shock by their presence, being that they were strangers and their appearance seemed quite different from the men that these people are used to seeing. Travis stayed in the tunnel as Vail instructed. This was her way of making sure that *nothing* happened to him.

Magdalona led the people, walking casually according to Cam's plan. It appeared that after all was said and done, the tribe was ready to make an escape from the tyranny of the Black Mage, and that they held complete trust for the Huntresses. The alternative, however would have been to stand and face the grizzly zombies, which so far has not panned out for this primitive clan of people. They all had seen enough bloodshed, and family members turned, so they did not put up any resistance to the idea.

The Huntresses walked strategically alongside of the crowd, almost shepherd-like leading the herd to pasture. Once the entire group had made their way completely into the tunnel, the last two Huntresses were to stay back with Travis, while Magdalona continued moving, leading the rest of the villagers through the long dark tunnels on their way back towards their hunting shelter.

Kah'lili, the youngest of the Huntresses and her mother Kiki stood next to Travis, each woman a lethal fighter, whom Vail trusted and respected. Kiki howled a shrill scream, which almost seemed animalistic. It was the signal for Vail and the four Elite soldiers to make their move on the palace.

Vail at one time was the Queen's personal protector, so she hoped that this matter could be rectified with words, and that no action would be necessary, but she had all four of the young agents following her into the palace, just in case. At first sight, the Queen's Guard seemed completely in shock. They recognized Vail, but the men with her were dressed impossibly strange and smelled of evil. The head Guard held her hand out palm side forward. "Halt," she said, stopping Vail by cutting her off.

Vail knelt down, bowing her head to show respect for the other's position. "I've come to seek the Queen's face in an urgent matter." Vail said in hopes that she'd be allowed to pass.

COGNIZANT

"Arise," the tall, dark red haired woman, granted her. "I want to look into your eyes to see the truth."

Vail arose, tipping her head back and opening her eyes wide. As she stared deeply into the eyes of the lead Guard she stated, "I seek permission to speak with the Queen. I was told that anytime I wished, she would see me." The other stared into Vail's eyes, but could not read whether, or not her intentions were pure. Vail did not necessarily like this infidel Guard want-a-be. "I do not have time to waste Ember," she said calling the Guard by name, which on its own right, shown some degree of disrespect.

By this time, all of the Queen's Guard had filed around. They all knew Vail and respected her, but now, their first duty is to answer to Ember, and she was not a forgiving woman.

ROC BLISS

Ember had five guards on either side of her with weapons in hand, ready. Vail came armed with only her stone blade knife, with which she was quite handy, but the weapon remained sheathed.

Ember felt that if she granted permission to Vail that her days would be numbered as the head of the Queen's Guard. "Leave Vail, the Queen has no time for your craziness. Remember, you left your place of authority." Her face began turning red, as she thought of how Vail had left her position in a show of emotional weakness, almost man-like in her actions.

Again, Vail knelt, but this time she did not bow her head. "I am only asking to talk with the Queen, as a Huntress, not a guard." Vail pleaded trying the least violent avenue.

"Vail, you have brought a group of spies right into the palace. If you leave now, no further action will needs be. We all know the way that you left here, and some are willing to forgive the act, but you must go. Now leave!" Ember ordered, her voice turning cold and harsh.

Vail stood back on her feet. She looked the taller woman in the eye and warned, "I will not leave, and if you force me to, I *will* take action."

"Then tell me what you wish to say to the Queen. If it is worth giving your life for, then *surely* it must be quite important." Ember said not intending to grant permission, but wanting to know what was in Vail's mind.

Vail could see that she would get nowhere, while Ember stood breathing. She looked at the other guards, who once had served under her. "Are you all going to stand by and let this treacherous beast send me away. You all know where my loyalties lie, and

time is at the essence. Stand with me."
She pleaded. She could see the
questioning in their minds, and could
tell that none of them *wanted* to go
against her, but they stood ready, as
all guards should in this situation.

Everyone in the room, all stood
watching each other in a standoff, until
finally one of the guards suggested
that the Queen should be notified of
the visit. Ember did not like the input
and screamed, "Silence! We do not let
spies gain the Queen's face."

Vail back peddled a few steps. "I
will say this once more only. Stand
with me, or you'll all fall by my hand."

"Hold on ladies," Cam suddenly
interjected. "We have come to protect
your entire existence, and in your own
selfish aims, you just can't keep your
venom down." He stepped forward next
to Vail. "Please get your Queen. Let her
know that there are strange visitors

with Vail. Let your Queen make the call." Cam said only trying to help, but his words did just the opposite. He had not realized that men had become even lower than second-class citizens in this tribe.

Ember looked as if she were just slapped across her face. "How *dare* you speak in our presence? I want his head Vail. If you give me his head, I will let you speak to the Queen." Ember had no intention of keeping her word, but she thought that it would be fun to watch.

Cam backed up quickly, as Telebar stepped forward blocking his leader from the possible threat. He was not one to fight with women, but he saw what Vail could do, and he could not afford to take *any* chances. "You girls like to talk a lot of shit, but I'm here to tell you that I'm done talking." He unsheathed his staff and held it out. He knew that the problem seemed to be the tall redhead. As he moved, all of the Queen's Guard immediately moved into defensive positions. "How about you and me? Right here, right now. If you win you can have my head, but when you lose you step aside and let Vail pass."

The Queen's Guards realizing that he had spoken his intentions without reacting, and not attacking, began looking at all of the men, with a new strange feeling in their hearts. None had ever seen men like these. They dressed strangely, but talked as women, using their brains, as well as their brawn.

Ember still harboring jealousy of Vail's access to the Queen's face, which she would be stopping at all cost, looked Telebar over, and snarled out a venomous response to his earlier request. "So, when I win, you and all your men would all be my slaves, until you become useless."

Telebar had heard enough, so he threw his staff down goading the woman, saying, "There I'm unarmed. What ya gonna do?"

Ember reached down to grab her long-edged stone sword. Telebar just smiled. The woman was erupting with anger, being talked down to by a mere man. 'I will kill them all', she thought to herself, but by the time, she had the blade halfway unsheathed Telebar had lunged forward. He punched the woman's arm, just below the shoulder.

The entire room of people could hear the bone snap, as he struck it. Ember shrieked with pain. "Are you done yet? Or do you want some more?" He asked still smiling. Ember started to snarl, as some type of slur forced its way through her gritting teeth, but she did not get the remark completely out, before Telebar gave her a quick jab to the jaw, knocking her unconscious. After the punch, he quickly moved back keeping in front of Cam, wanting to show that he was not a threat to the next in charge.

The rest of the Queen's Guard moved into a position to keep the group out. They stared at the men with a sense of respect. They had not seen men with such proficiency at fighting. They had only heard stories of such men, and the stories showed them to be complete war dogs. Their eyes widened in awe of the spectacle that had taken place before their very eyes.

Vail looked to the guards. "Will one of you talk to the Queen please?"

"There is no need." Queen Penelope answered from the top loft, which looked down on the group. All immediately knelt down at her presence, including the men, last of which was Drake, who found himself suddenly standing alone, before realizing the common courtesy. "Vail, is that you?" She asked, already knowing the answer. "Tell me. Have you brought trouble with you?"

"No, my Queen, I have only brought a chance with me." Vail answered with her face still looking towards the floor.

"Don't be vague with me girl. That was never your strong suit. Now tell me, what has finally brought you back into the palace, after all this time? Are you well?" The Queen had loved Vail as a daughter, and respected her as a cunning fighter.

"My Queen, we must leave at once. Come with us. We have a new place to be. A place that is more becoming of us." Vail said trying to sugar coat the reality of the situation at hand.

Exodus

The Queen frowned. "Are you telling me that you are asking me to run like some kind of underling? You Vail? Am I that wrong to say we should stand up to that evil Black Mage?"

Vail looked up to her Queen with a tear-filled eye. "My Queen, I plead with you. Come with us now, and trust me. On another day, we will be there to give him and his guardians their last breath."

"You sound as though you have renewed hope. Is that true?" The Queen asked, as she approached the steps that led down to the main floor.

"Yes, my Queen. I believe that I have just recently been awakened to a new hope, a hope that was brought to me from another land." Vail answered humbly. "These men with me are only a small part. I think I have seen, 'him'" Vail stopped in mid-sentence, realizing that she almost spoke of things that had been kept off limits to nearly all in the kingdom. The entire group looked at her curiously, having no clue about what she was going to say. Cam thought that she was making up a very convincing story in hopes that the Queen would follow without a struggle.

Queen Penelope thought that she was getting the drift of what Vail had almost said. She knew that Vail would never lie to her, but this statement was seemingly impossible to interpret without more information. Then again, she thought that maybe her intuition was right, and that Vail had actually seen the chosen one and that is why the statement went unfinished.

"Guards," Queen Penelope called out. "Fetch my robe. We will be off with Vail." The ten conscious women of the Queen's Guard scampered off. Then she snapped her finger, and her mate followed a few steps behind her. "You may rise people." She finally uttered, as she approached the main floor. "We must talk Vail. Let us stroll through the garden."

Vail turned towards the men. Cam pointed at his wrist, as if to remind her of their time restraints, without realizing that she had no clue about chronographs, or actual time units. She watched his movements and then turned away walking out through a doorway with her beloved Queen. Cam rolled his eyes and sighed impatiently, wanting to roll out of the village before nightfall.

COGNIZANT

Buying Time

Hades sat upon his throne gloating over the little game that he had been playing with the humans. "If you think *that* was something, human? Just wait. Darkness is creeping in upon my kingdom. You will be able to witness just how powerful my guardians can be. I gave a certain village plenty of chances to become my servants, and time after time, they refused to bend a knee to my authority. They refused to make me their king. Now, I will cause the slaughter of the entire village, and none will escape my army. This I will promise you."

Tank looked at the Black Mage, realizing that he meant what he had said, and then it suddenly became clear to him. Tank knew the evil wizards soft spot, and felt that his only hope would be to push his captor's buttons, so he began his own game by saying, "I'd be willing to make a bet on that. Your army looks a *little* weak to me."

Hades pondered the idea for a brief period, as he stared at the bolstering human, until finally he had to ask, "and just what would you be willing to wager, human? You have nothing. In fact, you don't even have a body. Heh, heh, heh," Hades laughed tauntingly, knowing that the human was completely powerless.

Tank did not waste much time to hit the Black Mage with what he had already admitted that he wanted. "You can be my master. In fact, we *all* will serve you," he added raising the ante instantly, in hopes of attracting the Black Mage to his game. The girls gasped at the sound of Tank's offer, but none of them dared to say anything different.

"It does not sound like your friends think that you are making a safe gambling endeavor." Hades stated questioning the veracity of Tank's wager.

"You let me talk to them," Tank said answering quickly. "And then we'll see if you have any faith in your soldiers," he added to goad the now curious Black Mage. Hades waved his hand in a slight forward rolling motion to show that he would oblige the conference, so Tank turned his presence toward the girls. He whispered. "Hey, let's huddle up."

The group all formed a tight circle, as they sat facing each other. "Well do you girls have any tricks up your sleeves? I say we try to get him to get us our skins back and let us go. I mean that is what we want, right?"

Tank asked in such a way that it forced the girls to the same page.

Ceilia spoke up. "We *can't* trust him. Look at him. He is evil and undoubtedly a liar too. I'm not willing to bet my entire life to him. The other girls agreed with her resoundingly.

Tank thought for a minute. He knew that the guys would be searching for them, and he knew that he needed to at the very least buy them some time. "Look girls, in case you haven't thought of this, I'll just mention it. What do you think will happen to us when he gets bored? Do you think that he'll just send us packing? Or do you think we'll be playing with those zombies of his? I really don't want to be eaten alive, so let's keep him at least interested in us."

He could see rolling eyes and an utter lack of interest in his plan, so he added another spin, which he had hoped to keep to himself. It was more or less the bottom line to his last-ditch effort. "Well, it'll at least get us through the night, and maybe the guys will show up, before it's too late." Tank finished, putting it where the rubber meets the road, in an attempt to hit all of the bases that he could think of for consent.

Jezza looked Tank right in the eye. "I cannot vow myself to this," she paused trying to think of a suitable term, but could not, so she just blurted out, "thing." Her disgusted overtone sounded as if she were ready to vomit, even at the low whisper that she was using. "I have made my pledge with Kilari, and he and us with Yahiveh, so I will stay quiet and you can offer what you may, but it is without Marcia's, or my blessing."

"Okay," Tank began. "I have heard only very little about Yahiveh over the years, but I guess it was because we would tease Kilari, whenever he would bring it up, but we were very young at the time. He found the book on some training exercise, when we were kids. Then suddenly he just believed whatever he read in it, so like most kids, we ahh, you know. We teased him, until finally he really didn't mention it anymore."

"You guys were probably the whole reason that he stayed standoffish to all of the girls Mary tried to set him up with." Ceilia decided to point out. Tank grinned childishly, unashamed of the past.

Marcia looked over at him and giving him a wink said, "Thanks, we like him just the way he is." She smiled innocently, slightly embarrassed. The girls all smiled with her in understanding.

COGNIZANT

"Let's get back on point here girls," Tank said abruptly interrupting their moment. "Are we in?" He asked, but all he got were quiet frowns. He knew that the girls would never vow to the Black Mage without being placed under physical and mental duress, so he suddenly stood up, and used a little body language.

He pushed his underhand fist out and then pulled it back slowly, while yelling, "Oh yeah! You're on. We have two things that we want, if we win the bet. We would really like to have our bodies back, and of course we would like to be released from here." Then thinking that he saw a certain posturing by the Black Mage he added, "To clarify, we would like to be able to leave here, and not have to worry about being eaten by your dead army." Tank watched Hades closely, trying to see if this large super-powered creature would show any hints through body language on how he would react.

Hades looked at the small group of souls, while lifting his long black hood off from his head, and revealing long, black hair that hung straight to the middle of his back. His matching facial hair was thin and wispy. The glowing crown of blood crystal sent a red aura, around not only him, but also his entire throne. Tank watched as he pressed a few hidden buttons, which were located on his throne's armrest, near his right hand. As he did, a foghorn sound billowed throughout the entire sandstone ghost town with such intensity that the entire realm of Xibalba could hear its haunting tone.

Hades began laughing with his usual evil cackle, but the billowing drowned out any sounds of his laughter. As the sound began to fade, the sounds of thunder began seeping through. "The deal is sealed." Hades said to the small group. "My army will be on its way in full force. You have agreed to the bet, so once this night is over, and all of the villagers have become victims, you will be my servants for all of your days."

Tank felt that it was time for him to restate the agreement, so that there were no false expectations. "So then, your dead army gets the entire night to do your bidding. By the first light of day, if your army fails to finish with their part then we go free, and by free, I mean that we all get our bodies, and you don't send your army after us for at least three days."

"You and your eight friends will go free, until the next nightfall. Maybe longer *if* I am busy. You will have your worthless mortal bodies intact. Now, it is time for you to understand something. You may imagine all of your days to be maybe sixty years, not a very long time for servitude. Look at my watchers." The Black Mage said pointing to the cloaked figures near the All-Seeing Eye. "How old would you guess that they are? Or more to the point, how long do you think that they have been my servants?"

Tank looked over at the watchers, as did all of the girls. Finally, Tank shrugged his shoulders. He answered, "I don't know. I can't see their faces."

"So, you think that you can judge their age by seeing their skin?" Hades asked. "Well human, let me help you out. This is not the realm that you are from. In your realm, humans are born, they grow up, grow old, and then they die. In this great realm of Xibalba beings are seldom born, and beings do not die, unless they are killed, and then their souls can still be kept, if I so choose.

COGNIZANT

Your mortal body won't age. You could serve me throughout all eternity. Think of it humans. You could serve me for many, many centuries. You will come to realize that time is not in this place. "Time is a dimension that you have all served under, but it has no power here. You have found yourselves in my underworld kingdom, and none can leave without my sufferance. Now look," he said pointing to the giant orb. "Look into the All-Seeing Eye, and see my guardians. They will march to that small village and devour all."

Again, all nine souls turned to see. They could see into the midst of the havoc filled sand storm. Zombies were coming up everywhere. From every part of sand, from every corner of the sandstone town and surrounding area the zombies continued pouring out.

Tank could feel all hope beginning to filter away. "What, are the odds? What is the ratio of your army to the villagers?" He finally asked in a somewhat deflated tone.

Hades looked to the group and answered. "A thousand to one, if you're lucky human." These words echoed in the ears of the small, fear stricken group.

The girls looked at Tank with horror. Jezza shot him a look of disgust. "*Oh, we're in.*" She muttered, mocking his earlier remark. Tank just stood there with a harsh new reality.

"A thousand to one?" Ceilia piled on. "You just *screwed* us all Tank."

Tank had no clue of what to say, but he knew Kilari would come. "I was just buying us time." He tried to explain. "Look, this guy wasn't just going to let us go."

COGNIZANT

The girls rolled their eyes and turned away from him, even Sophie. "Look girls, we still have our faith. Let's all pray that somehow Yahiveh will help us." Marcia suggested. "He came to us before. We all know that he is true, so let's get to it." The girls all sat in a circle trying to form a chain by holding hands, but they had no flesh and could not feel each other.

"It is okay, we can all pray on our own," Jezza offered. "Yahiveh knows all, and he is with us always." After giving these few words of hope, she sat in the same space with Marcia. They seemed to become one with each other and closing their eyes, they began to pray in silence. The other girls began closing their eyes one by one, until soon Tank found himself standing in the midst of a circle of sitting women with closed eyes.

ROC BLISS

Buying Time

Kilari looked Belsangar in the eyes and said, "we're *busting* in." He pulled Belsangar to one side, away from any prying ears. "Look man," he whispered. "We have to follow these mooks right to the place where they're taking, ugh," he stammered, as he tried to think of a correct term to use, finally he just said, "our friends' bodies". It rolled off his lips awkwardly, but he was not sure what to call them. "We've got to be there by the time he reanimates them, then we can see about breaking them out."

Belsangar had no clue of what he would be dealing with, but he knew that Kilari had some way of being in the right place at the right time. He also realized that Kilari always felt as though he were being led by Yahiveh, and it seemed to be true, so he gave his typical answer, "I'm with you brother." Just as he had answered, the Black Mage's call to war had sounded.

The low haunting tones reverberated through the entire valley. The three demons even wondered, what the sound meant. Kilari realized that it must be the call of the zombies to move in on the small village, where the rest of their crew had gone. "Shit," Belsangar remarked, after hearing the long tonal hum. "The last time we heard that, this place was crawling with zombies. What are we gonna do now?"

Kilari knew that Belsangar spoke the truth. "Well, I guess we'll just have to hang back a bit behind these guys and watch to see exactly what is going on." Then Kilari walked back over to the, now leaving group, and asked. "Hey, those things ain't going to be after you, are they?" He did not want anything to happen to his friends' bodies.

The serpent hissed, "you had better hope not, or your preciousss cargo will be lossst." Then Apophis turned back toward the direction that he was heading and just kept on walking.

Kilari figured that the serpent was too confident, and knew that they would be offered a free pass, so he grabbed Belsangar by the shoulder and said, "Okay, we stay out of sight. Let's find a vantage point to oversee what kind of chaos is going on, and then we'll make a plan from there." Belsangar nodded his confirmation, and the two soldiers walked towards a place that would overlook the valley.

COGNIZANT

Escape

Vail and her Queen, Penelope walked through a garden courtyard. The plants were lush. Many fruit trees were scattered throughout the courtyard. Vail plucked a round ripe red colored fruit from one of the trees. She so loved the fruit and she had not been in the palace in such a long time. She took a large bite from the juicy sweet fruit. "Mmm," sounded from her throat.

"You miss the palace, don't you?" Her Queen asked curiously.

Vail looked at her. She swallowed to clear her mouth. "I missed you, my Queen. We used to have long chats about many things."

"So then, are you going to tell me about, what it was you saw? It seemed to me that you wanted to blurt it out, but then thought better of it. Now, that would suggest that you've seen something that has been deemed sensitive, and there are not many things that we don't share fully with the entire village, so *give*," Queen Penelope finally ordered.

Vail looked at her Queen. She dropped to one knee, and propped her head back. She opened her eyes wide to show that she wished for the Queen to assure that what she was about to say would be the truth. The Queen paused at this display. "Look into my eyes," Vail requested. "I will open up to you. I speak the truth. I had found a man from another world, another place, and at first, I thought him to be a spy, so I ran him through the usual tests, and I

found him innocent. Then we were
going off to hunt."

"Vail," the Queen called out
sharply, noticing that there had to be a
slight miscommunication in the story,
already.

"We were making love outside
under the sky, and while we were being
intimate, some voices called out. There
were four more men from that same
world. The first man, Travis,
recognized them so we all talked. I
took them to a camp that was not
overly safe, but could provide for us,
and there," Vail paused, as she
pictured the exact moment in her mind,
"my Queen, that is where I saw *him*. I
fought with him at first, and I was like
a mere child against him, though he
stood no taller. I believe that the
chosen one has come." Tears flooded
from the warrior's eyes, as emotions
flooded into her mind.

ROC BLISS

"I see. Where is this one of whom you speak?" The Queen asked, wanting to have a look for herself.

"He asked for the way to the wicked city. He said that he was missing loved ones, and would not allow them to be alone in this strange land." Vail explained.

Suddenly, from the distance the loud sounding blasted throughout the village. It was the loudest that the village has ever heard. Vail stood and grabbing the Queen's hand warned, "we must go my Queen," as she pulled lightly at the Queen.

The Queen did not stall. She moved immediately without hesitating. She was convinced that Vail did not make up her story, and she knew all too well of the sounding that was humming throughout the land.

Cam, hearing the sound pointed to the doors, which Vail had used. "Get them, *now*, we've gotta move!" Telebar moved like a flash. He made his way past the royal guards, before they could react. He grabbed at the door, and between his enthusiasm, and his great strength, he pulled the door right off its handmade hinges. *"Come on,"* he yelled to the guards, who suddenly felt relief that he included them.

They all flooded into the garden in time to see the Queen and Vail on their way towards them. Drake peeked into the area from behind Telebar's vast frame. He saw the fruit trees. He quickly ducked into the courtyard, grabbing as much of the fruit as he could hold, filling his pockets and sleeves.

Once the rest of the group had made their way to the doorway, Telebar quickly followed suit. Malichye led the way back to the tunnel, which would hide their escape from any, who would be watching. Telebar brought up the rear, knowing that once they made their way into the tunnel, this could be the only place from which they would be vulnerable. The entire group made the tunnel easily with no problems. Kiki and her daughter took lead of the group.

Malichye stopped Cam. "Look, we are leaving a trail that a blind man could follow. Maybe we should stay back and cover our trail. So far, the plan has been smooth as silk, but we didn't think of how badly we would mark a trail."

Cam looked out of the tunnel and could easily see the path of footprints, which they had made. "You're right," he admitted. "We're going to have to deal with this." Telebar and Malichye ran out of the tunnel. Each ran and quickly grabbed some leaf covered tree branches, and began raking a large area near the tunnel entrance.

Kah'lili and Kiki looked back to see what was slowing down the final part of the group.

Vail had Queen Penelope by the hand. They rushed at first, but before they had fully escaped the light, Vail also noticed that the back group had not made their way up the tunnel yet, so she sent the two trusted Huntresses back with a point of her finger.

They did not have too far to travel, before they could see that the others were still outside of the tunnel covering tracks, so the two women quickly joined in to help. Once the task had been completed, they blocked the tunnel's entrance with huge stacks of twiggy branches, so that there would be no easy sign of the tunnel's existence.

Cam liked the teamwork. "Good job you guys," he said praising their seemingly flawless cover-up.

The two Huntresses then led the three males along the tunnel at a fairly high rate of speed, even after the light had dimmed completely away. The tunnel slowly turned into complete blackness. They moved along for some time, before making their way to a point, where the beginning signs of light flickered ahead.

They traveled to the light, and as they made their way closer, the traveling became easier, until finally they had made their way to the source of the light. The torches that lit the area, allowed Cam to see at this particular junction, the small ten-foot diameter cave tunnel, which they had been traveling through, opened into a vast hundred-foot-high by three-hundred-foot-wide cavern, with various tunnels leading into it.

A rope ladder hung from the uppermost tunnel, and dangled full of the villagers as they climbed their way up to the next leg of their journey. The majority of the crowd had already made their way onto the next stage, however there were still many waiting to make their climb up the ladder.

"Hey, you guys," Drake yelled out, as he saw his crew finally make their way into the cavern. His fellow agents walked over to him to see how he was doing. "Hey, I grabbed some fruit from the garden back there, and well, I have more than I can carry up the rope ladder, so do you guys want some?" He said tossing each of them a couple of the pleasantly sweet flavored fruits.

"You don't even *know* how hungry I am." Telebar said, as he eyed the fruit. He took a huge bite, forcing juice to splatter, as it mingled with his watering mouth. "Mmm, now *that's* what I'm talking about. Thanks man." Telebar said with a full mouth. As soon as he swallowed, he took another bite, just hoping to fill the pit in his stomach.

Cam and Malichye followed suit. The young soldiers had not eaten in quite some time, and they were in great need of nutrients.

Cam ate his fruit, while sitting upon a rock near one of the many, lit torches. He started contemplating the entire situation. It looked good on the outside, at least on his end, but then maybe, it was from his brain finally getting some nutrients back. Maybe, it was just the fact that he finally had time to reflect, but somehow, he suddenly remembered that Vail had mentioned at some point that the Black Mage could see *any* place of his choosing in this weird and whacky world, and here they were, just sitting in a tunnel filled with light.

Cam stood up and moved over to his comrades, who were chatting amongst themselves. "Hey, I hate to say it, but we have to clean this mess up, these torches, the footprints, everything has to vanish. Leave no evidence."

"What? C'mon man." Drake complained. "We are underground, or maybe inside a mountain. Why not leave it as it is? It'll be easier."

"I want it clean. Leave *zero* evidence." Cam answered back without hesitation. "Drake, I want you to get to the front of the group, and have all torches extinguished. From here on out, I want this in blackout mode. Do it."

Cam searched the area, which was quickly emptying. He looked up the rope ladder and saw Vail backing up Queen Penelope. "Vail!" He yelled loudly. She turned to see what he wanted. He pointed to Drake and then cupped his ear, then followed with one more signal, as he pointed back to her. She nodded her head and pointed to the Queen and then to the top of the rope ladder. He nodded affirmatively, and then started helping Telebar and Malichye swipe away the footprints, which was easy. Most of the surface was solid stone, and only a few scattered prints could be found. A few kicks or swipes with your feet, and all are gone.

COGNIZANT

Go Time

Field Martial Blak sat chained in a room. He faced a wall, which had become one solid view screen. Strapped to him was a set of mechanical eyelid manipulators that forced his eyes to open and close, according to its programming. The programming is intended to maintain the ability to blink, yet not allow an individual to close their eyes. The view screen kept replaying everything from the moment his shuttle had reached the islands airspace, until his capture, and the fall of his Death Squad.

The repeating footage had been playing for hours, pounding its torment into his brain. The sound mixed, between battle sounds, and mocking voices of Doc Grimes and General Brague. Some of the speech told of how he had deserted them, while others laughed and mocked him, so there he sat being flooded with negative media, with no way to shut it out.

In a back room, the three new leaders of the unsuspecting Crystal Continent sat contemplating their next move, while they watched the ex-Field Martial show no reaction at all. "Gentlemen, it is time that we move to the capital and announce the arrival of the new government. We need to assume control of the military." Johnny Brague announced.

"Why can't we make the capital here, on Flag Island?" Rudy asked, not wanting to leave.

General Brague shot a strange look at the scientist. Then, after realizing that the scientist was actually serious with his preposterous idea, answered. "Rudy, are you kidding me? The land mass here is so small that any of our enemies could blow our entire sector off the face of An'non with one mediocre bomb. No, we must assume our seats in the safest place, the most protected area in the entire world, and I believe that we would be fools not to."

Doc Grimes chirped his two cents into the conversation as well. "And that is why we need a military man in this new three prong system, Rudy. However, I do believe that maybe we should allow Rudy to stay here, if that is what he wishes. We can always keep in touch and have meetings via the Com-View."

"Well, it's just that I have all of my equipment here, and Travis is still missing. I still want to get him back here, you know." Rudy said giving his reasons for wanting to remain.

"Well," Doc Grimes started. "I can understand your desires. I hope that you can understand my wanting to leave. I've been kept here for so many years that it will be nice to get away."

"I understand perfectly, and don't worry. Even, if you want to return almost immediately, because the change is too much for you, or you just want to be here, this facility will always be yours." Dr. Rudy Laforge said reassuringly.

"Okay already, you mutton heads, we need to get this train a rolling. So, kiss each other goodbye and let's hash this out." Johnny Brague said, already sickened by these scientists, and their silly worries.

Rudy had to broach the subject at hand, before his two fellow officials left their work undone. "You can't leave without doing two things."

"What *now*?" Johnny Brague asked as if he had no more time to waste.

Rudy felt shocked that Brague would forget his final revenge on Blak, but then with a smile he thought, 'That seat of power must be calling Brague's ass to come and sit,' but then after nearly stating his thought to Brague himself, he decided to just put it back on the subject at hand. "One, you guys need to get rid of Blak. I'm not up for that sort of thing, and two, I want some protection for me and my staff." Rudy's request was quick and to the point. He left no gray area.

The other two started to talk on top of each other, which then caused them to both stop and look at each other. Dr. Grimes stared at Johnny Brague, until finally the General opted for Doc Grimes to lead. "I'll leave Mags and Chief with you, as well as the rest of the droids. I'll have Johnny and his army with me, so I'll be alright."

"And I'd be *more* than happy to take care of Blak," Brague offered without even a thought.

Originally, Doc Grimes wanted the pleasure of dealing with Blak, but he had gotten enough revenge just turning the tables on the man, and then shoving it into his face, or should we say; 'pounding into his brain'. Grimes looked at Brague. He could see a glimmer in the man's eye. "Okay, he's all yours Johnny, but you give a minute to think of the best way to make him pay, alright?" Doc Grimes said, suggestingly.

General Brague grinned a little and then gave a small nod towards his partners. He did not exactly have the same disdain for the man as they, but he did want to exact some revenge of his own.

Rudy knew the General very well, and could see his gears grinding behind the slight smirk that he wore in silence. "General," he called out. "Please don't leave a mess. I've seen enough of your messes to last me a life time."

General Brague had other ideas anyway, but now he understood that he was connected with at least one individual, who would not put up with massive bloody tortures. He thought that maybe Doc Grimes might be a little more open minded. "Don't worry Rudy. I've got other plans for Blak, seeing that it's suddenly up to me."

"Why don't we just let him stew for a while longer, and then once we're all ready to go, you can do your thing." Doc Grimes suggested. General Brague agreed that that would be a fine idea, so with that he excused himself and went to his quarters to gather his men and all needed supplies.

Rudy stopped Doc Grimes before he could exit. "Hey Doc," he said. "I don't think that you had better go with the General without bringing at least one of the droids with you, and maybe you should bring them both just in case. I just need protection from whatever may come through the gate. There is no real threat here, but you may need to have enough force to keep Brague in line. You could probably just leave me two or three of the guards and I'd be set."

Doc Grimes could tell by the way that Rudy spoke that his advice was solid and came from the heart. "Thank-you Rudy," he said. "It is really big of you to make such an offer."

"Well, we scientists have to stick together, or that military minded freak will find a way to pick us both off, and keep it all for himself." Rudy answered.

"And then soon after he would lose it, like the dope that he is," Grimes added with a slight chuckle. "I'm going to get us ready, and then I'll debrief you before our departure." With that, the old scientist left the room and went on his way to prepare.

Rudy looked through the two-way glass at the ex-Field Marshal. He began feeling as though he was looking at evil incarnate. This man trained boys and men alike, to kill, and torture, in the name of fun, in the name of racial difference, and in the name of political indifferences. Rudy could feel his stomach turning, as he thought a bit too hard upon the matter. His own memories from the past began creeping into the forefront of his mind. He shuttered at them, but then he realized that Blak would be gone soon, and then there would be a lot less to worry over.

*   *   *   *   *

Thomas Elliot and his wife Tessa had made their way to the Triple B. They were heading up the elevator towards the room that had been reserved for Darlene. Tessa had no real beef with Darlene herself, she knew that Thomas had a way about him that would strike most women's fancy. She just did not like the fact that the first time that he is in the field in so many years, he just happened to find some sweet young thing to turn his fancy.

He could have used her and gone on his way, but no, not him, he had to strike it up to some young girl, with whom he would remain interested. Interested enough to put her on the payroll, and *bring* her with him, while he came here to check for Intel. Her thoughts began getting her all riled up, all over again.

Thomas led the way to the door. He knocked politely, as if to show that he had not gotten one room for the both of them. An eye peeked out at him through the peephole. Darlene became so excited that she did not see Tessa, who wisely stood to the side out of sight, so that she could see the girl's initial reaction upon seeing her. Thomas was completely unaware of the scheme, so he stood there, cluelessly, in the midst of Tessa's handmade war zone.

Suddenly, the door opened and Darlene's sweet voice rang out. "Oh, come on in. I was hoping that you'd hurry back."

Just then, Tessa moved into view, as the young woman put her arms out for Thomas. Bumping Thomas to the side with a little hip push and a side step, she placed herself right in his spot. "Hi," she said pausing for a brief second to eye up the competition, before finishing her greeting with, "Darlene, is it?" Her tone sounded terse. "I'm Tessa, Thomas's wife." She blurted it out for shock value, and by the look in the girl's eye, she had *hit* her mark.

"Wait a minute? He told me..." The girl started to spit out, but Tessa cut her off in mid speech, as she pushed her way into the room.

"He told you what? Huh?" Tessa jumped in. "What did he tell you? Did he tell you that he loves me?

"Now, hold on dare babe." Thomas said trying to pry himself into the conversation, but Tessa would have none of it.

Tessa pushed him aside, and used the force of the push to launch herself into the unsuspecting Darlene, who went from a wide-eyed stare to being forced upon her back. She looked up at Tessa, who finally asked, "well?" Then she awaited an answer.

Darlene was in shock from all of the sudden unexpected activity. She did not quite remember what had been asked first, so she replied, "Did you say that your name was Mary? He told me all about a Mary, but I thought that she had passed," Darlene said, trying to explain.

"Oh, so he told you about a Mary huh? Then how come you're trying to get with my man?" Tessa sat upon the woman, who was in a total state of confusion.

Thomas stepped up and yelled, "Tess, that's enough. Why are you doing this to this poor girl? You know that she didn't do anything wrong."

Tessa looked at him and answered, "I know, but I needed to get the truth out of her, to see if *you* did anything wrong."

"Tess, come on and get up," Thomas said, as he grabbed her by the hand and pulled her up from Darlene's chest.

Tessa stood up then turned to see a confused young woman lying on the floor. Tessa reached down and offered the young lady a hand up. "Hi, I'm Tessa, and you had better get used to this kind of thing."

"So, you're not Mary?" Darlene asked as she held her hand out to Tessa.

Tessa pulled her up. "No, I *was* Mary, but now I'm Tessa again."

"You-what?" The young woman asked, as she moved away to grab a seat. She felt as if she had slipped into some strange, bizzarro world.

"Yeah, grab a seat hon." Tessa said, as smooth as silk. "This is the kind of thing that can happen in our world. Our names change. Our looks change. The way we talk may change, but we are who we need to be, and I've been lucky enough to keep my man through many missions, but anyway, he got you the hook-up, and we have a mission, so we're going to bring you to my aunt's house, where you can get all of your paper work completed. Oh, and there's a cute hunk there, who'll be joining you back to Bah-Roque. He'll be running a few things for you, so get packed and let's go. I don't want to waste any time."

Darlene jumped up and started packing. "Is it about your boys? Oh, don't worry, I'll hurry."

"So, you really *did* confide in this one, didn't you?" Tessa asked, almost more jealous of *this* fact, than she would be of any physical relations. She shot Thomas a look suggesting that she had been completely taken off guard.

Thomas shrugged his shoulders, as if to say, who cares. "Well, you weren't in my shoes. Now, were ya? Heck, what if you would have heard that *I* was dead? At least I covered ground, and came to find out conclusive evidence." His flamboyant effort had shown his level of commitment to her. "I was devastated!"

"Really ma'am, He is really a good man. His thoughts were on you and the kids." Darlene said sticking up for him.

Tessa took her dark brown eyes and looked each of them up and down one more time. She still believed them both, but she had not had to worry about things like this in at least fifteen years. Well, now that she was thinking about it, she realized that she never had to worry about Thomas. He was *always* a good man.

COGNIZANT

The three quickly put any other misunderstandings behind them, and made their way to Myra's house. Once there, Darlene met Deak and was placed through the mind wash. Myra picked up all of the odds and ends of responsibility, which gave Thomas and Tessa the freedom to pursue their so-called vacation, which would eventually gain them access upon Flag Island.

*   *   *   *   *

"Master, look," the main watcher said, as the three subordinate beings began to enter into the main area of the old sandstone city. The sphere that he had been watching had suddenly flashed to a different scene.

Hades did not need to be nudged to the view of the sphere, because this was *his* day of vengeance. Hades had only looked away from time to time to discuss piddley little things with the human. "Look human, here comes your body. I'm surprised that Apophis could carry it, let alone the other eight."

"Oh, so now you're a funny guy." Tank retorted. "With all of the death and bloodshed around here, I wouldn't think you'd have much of a sense of humor."

Hades really had not bounced a lot of rhetoric off any soul in quite some time, so he was enjoying this little bout of wit. "Well, I humored your bet. Didn't I?" He reminded Tank, thinking that he had been quite fair, maybe even too fair, to the point of being weak, so he decided to illuminate a few of the other possibilities that could have occurred.

"Even though the odds are stacked in my favor, it doesn't mean that I didn't give up certain other available options to put you through. I could have had you eaten alive, or made you fight my evil horde, and then I could call them off after you were bitten. I could have had you watch, as one by one, I fed your friends to my dead army, but I thought it might be nice to have some servants, so I took a chance by humoring your bet." Then he cackled insidiously.

Tank listened to the Black Mage. His spirit began to weaken from all of the morbid visions that he had just been force fed, but there is no way that he could let on. "Yeah, yeah, you could put me in with ten of those things, and I'd come out and they'd be flattened."

"Well, perhaps we could test that theory at some point in the future, like maybe in a few centuries or so, when you start to become a bumbling dolt." Hades threatened.

"I plan on walking out of here in the morning. I don't think that your army has what it takes. I mean, they really can't even think. Can they?" Tank bolstered trying to portray himself with confidence.

Hades gave Tank a sneer. "They can smell blood for a mile, and *anything* in their wake will be obliterated, if I so choose. Watch and see," the Black Mage said, pointing once again towards the All-Seeing Eye.

*　　　*　　　*　　　*　　　*

Kilari and Belsangar found a strategic vantage point. They climbed higher up the mountain on a ridge that gave them a perfect view of the valley. The lightening still flashed, as the thunder rolled. They could see hordes of zombies moving together. They covered the area for as far as the eye could see, all of them flooding in the same direction, like a giant herd of wild animals. Within minutes, the

COGNIZANT

smell of rotting flesh had completely filled the area, leaving each of the two young agents trying to catch his breath.

The air felt thick and pungent on their lungs. It was reminiscent of the smell that would spread throughout the surrounding territories, after the Death Squad would annihilate an entire city of people, and then burn all of the remains. The smell of burnt flesh lingered for days, and rested in all the debris, which floated throughout miles of surrounding territory.

Between the putrid smell and the horrific sight of the zombie multitude parading away from the sand stone village, Kilari found himself in a place that he had not visited in years. He knew that it would be wiser to wait for the entire mob of flesh eaters to leave, but he felt something pulling him to leave the perch, which overlooked the valley.

"C'mon, we're outta here." He called out to his lifelong friend, as he waived for him to follow. Kilari led the way down the mountainside. The night sky slowly turned to black, as the last glimpse of light trickled behind the far horizon. The rugged trail that wandered its way down the rough mountain's side was difficult to navigate, but the two young men found a way to double time it, the entire way to the sand of the city.

By this time, the night was black, and Kilari felt secure with his camouflage uniform blending into the dark of night. He used outer buildings to hide from the view of the three demons, which carried their friend's bodies. The zombies had fled the scene without turning back, leaving the entire city unguarded. "This is too quiet," Belsangar whispered. "I don't like it."

"I do," Kilari answered logically. "It's either quiet, or we could have a thousand reeking flesh eaters to contend with."

Belsangar thought for a second, and then soon realized that even though Kilari was right, it still seemed far too easy, so he kept a very watchful eye, not wanting any surprises.

The two soldiers made their way, as close to the lead pack as possible, using the small buildings as buffers to keep out of sight. They watched, as the group made its way into the largest building, which stood in the center of the small ghost town. The two young agents listened intently for any type of struggle, or personal encounter, upon the groups entering, but they could not detect any whatsoever, so cautiously

Kilari led his friend into the shadowed entrance of the tall building.

Torches lit the stone vestibule. There were two at the far end towards the door, which led into the main lobby. The light was dim, but adequate enough to make out long cement-like benches that lined the walls. Kilari hung in the back of the vestibule for a moment, while listening carefully. He could hear the thuds of the serpent's large feet, as they supported the large payload.

Kilari quickly snuck through the door, leading Belsangar to a dark corner in the main lobby of this gothic temple. There were merely a handful of torches scattered around this large room, with many doorways leading in and out. The open doorways, each, had torches on the other side, keeping the dimly lit room filled with various dark shadows, which could be utilized for hiding.

The walls held many strange engravings, which seemed to dance, as the shadows swaggered in the torchlight. The gothic cathedral had an ominous presence that made the young agents feel, as though it had a life of its own.

Kilari did not have time to interpret the meaning behind the engravings, but he did realize that some of the carvings were of mythological beasts. Then once he gave the matter the slightest thought, he had realized that he already had seen at least a couple of these beasts, and maybe, none were actually myths. Maybe, all of these creatures actually exist in their own dimensions. Kilari stared at the carvings on the walls and remembered them from his dream of Khana and Silbcor.

ROC BLISS

Belsangar watched and finally tapped his friends shoulder, and whispered. "Come on man let's go."

Kilari regained his prospective, and instantly began creeping through the shadows toward the farthest doorway. The two found themselves upon a balcony, which over looked a huge room. They quickly laid down keeping out of sight, upon hearing the thudding footsteps of Apophis gaining volume, as he made his way into the chamber below. They listened to the characters, as they spoke in the room beneath them.

The souls of the girls kept praying silently, even after hearing the entry of the three creatures, while Tank looked wide-eyed and closed mouthed, wanting to hear the banter between the Black Mage and these three oddities. He had never seen anything like these creatures.

COGNIZANT

Hades faced the three saying, "So, you've *finally* made it back." Hades knew that his zombie army would be nearing its mark soon, so he did not want to waste time dallying with the three dolts. "Line those bodies up in front of my throne. I want to see just how healthy my new servants appear to be."

Angkor did the evil overlords bidding, taking the girls off the serpents back, one by one, as the serpent stretched out upon its belly. Once removed, Apophis shook slightly, dumping Tank's large frame, upon the hard floor.

Tank watched, as his body hit the floor with a thud. "Hey, *watch* the merchandise Jack." He yelled out from his invisible prison, turning from the serpent over to the Black Mage, to see if the old wizard would have his back on the matter.

Roc Bliss

"Silence!" Hades yelled holding his hand up high. The three subordinates sat motionless in silence, not daring to make a peep. "I take it you three have finished your duties here in Xibalba. Be gone." He ordered.

Aeron, the cloaked entity fluttered nervously up into the air at this order, knowing that they needed to make sure Hades remembered that the book and its keepers needed to get back to An'non. Hades looked at the entity wondering what it was doing. "Well, what is it?" He finally asked ready to be rid of the annoyance all together.

The entity floated near to the Black Mage, whispering secretively, "Lucifer wants the book keepers and the book to go back to their dimension." Aeron reminded, knowing that he did not want to appear to give

COGNIZANT

Hades any orders, nor did he want Hades to think that he had to save face.

Hades looked at the entity with a blank expression. He arose from his throne and slowly, deliberately moved past all of the bodies. As he moved, the nervous entity floated back towards his comrades under his own power. As he continued walking, the Black Mage pushed the three beings back with the power of his eyes alone. He walked them back to an open area in the large room.

His glowing crown of the blood crystal began to intensify, as power began surging through his very presence. His face scrunched, as the words began to form on his lips. He flexed every muscle, while raising his arm to point at the three. Right as he pointed, the words screamed from his lips. "Be gone!" The three subordinate beings instantly vanished from sight, returning to their own subterranean world of Limbo in a wink of an eye.

Kilari and Belsangar had heard Tank's voice, but not wanting to give away their vantage point, they kept perfectly quiet. They had overheard the Black Mage, as he cast his spell upon the three souls, who had immediately vanished.

Kilari peeked his head up and watched the evil wizard, as he flushed them away with seemingly no effort. Then turning, he looked to see where Tank's voice had sounded. He saw what appeared to be ghosts of all of the nine missing loved ones. He remained unseen by the group. Putting his head down, he turned and faced Belsangar, who had slowly made his way beside his friend.

Whispering in his softest, almost inaudible voice, Kilari said, "They're here, but they look like ghosts. I couldn't get a good look, so I didn't notice, how they were being locked up."

Belsangar pointed to the far side of the balcony, before slowly crawling across the smooth rock surface. Kilari stayed put, watching, while Belsangar made his move to the far side of the balcony. Belsangar could now see exactly what Kilari had whispered about. He could see Ceilia, and other than being a little transparent, she was as beautiful as ever. His next thought was to assure that each, and every one of the group were okay, so he got a fix on all of them, but when looking for Jezza and Marcia, they appeared a bit distorted, occupying the same space.

Hades began marching back to his throne with his mind still clouded by the three dolts, and more than that, their stalling tactics kept him from his game, right when his army should have been nearing that darn village. With his mind preoccupied, the Black Mage did not pay close attention to his surrounding, and he nearly stumbled over the human bodies.

Hades caught his balance, but his anger again began to rise. Finally, he sat down with the nine bodies directly in his field of vision. Then reaching down, he grabbed his magic wand from its sheath and secretly pressed a button located on the left armrest of his golden throne. Tank and the girls were completely unaware that the invisible force field had been turned off, but both Kilari and Belsangar had noticed the sliding of his hand across the armrest.

The Black Mage suddenly stood up flamboyantly, and began waiving the wand in a counter-clockwise motion, it seemed as though he could stir the essence of their spirits, like fish in a bucket. The nine human souls began swirling out of control. The Black Mage not wanting to waste any more time, swirled the wand with one hand, while flaring his other hand out towards the human fleshlings.

Slowly, he lifted his open hand, and as he did, the nine bodies floated in midair. While keeping the flesh bodies hovering in the air, he fixated each with its souls, until in the end each aligned correspondingly. Then Hades moved his right hand to the wand hand and as the two contacted each other, each of the flesh bodies reanimated with its soul perfectly, intact.

The Black Mage magically held the bodies up in the air for enough time to send a message to the fleshlings, so that they would have no choice other than to realize his immense power. After moving the fleshlings about for a minute to his own cackling whims, he slowly lowered them down to the rock floor within the realm of the force-field prison. After setting the still whirling humans upon the floor, Hades moved back to his throne pressing yet another button. This button triggered sets of laser beams, which reflected around the area forming a visible cage in which the nine humans found themselves.

Tank went from feeling fine, as a soul with no flesh, to a spinning whirl of dizziness, which began upon his soul's re-entry into his flesh. Now, he could feel the weight of his body, the hunger, and the bruises. His muscles were sore, and he felt as if he were overworked and underfed. "Man, I feel like I've been hit by an airbus." The big young agent stated, as he tried shaking the cobwebs from his mind.

COGNIZANT

"I am no man. Do not address me in that way. *Soon* you will be my servants, and you will lose the choice of freewill." Hades said reminding the human of the bet, which still was very much in play.

Tank stretched his sore muscles, while he looked over the girls, who had once again formed a circle. They all appeared to be fine. He wondered, if they even noticed that they had their bodies back. He looked back over to the Black Mage saying, "I've felt better, but not about our bet. You still gotta get every single person from that village dead, and all I need is for one of the people to be out for a hunting trip, or on a stroll. I think you'll lose."

"Let us see human. The devouring should be a frenzy by now." Hades suggested confidently.

Kilari and Belsangar, both were still trying to catch up to the fact that they were up against some type of supernatural being, whom, with a flash of his hand could make beings disappear into thin air, and remove, or replace the souls of bodies. Now, the All-Seeing Eye also became a part of their focus, as the Black Mage had invited Tank to once again mind his gamble. They each had thoughts and questions racing through their heads, as they stared semi-dumbfounded into the sphere.

The marching force of zombies caught the scent of the villager's blood and instantly increased their speed. Hades began cackling with excitement, because he knew the move and could sense their blood lust. The creatures hit the village headlong on a full-on sprint, but the villagers were gone; except for the remnants of blood that Cam had the Huntresses spread throughout the village. The zombies smelled blood from all sections of the village and went rampant, as they began ransacking the entire place wildly.

"What!" Hades screamed in total bewildering anger, as he watched his guardians tearing into the village. "What happened to those villagers and why is my army *not* following them!" He stood to yell a few other sets of choice words, before plopping down in his throne. Knowing that the night was short, he did not waste any time before sounding another blast horn, which shook the very foundation of his palace.

The watchers all ran from the sphere to a trap door, which was located in the farthest corner of the giant throne room. "Unleash the hell hounds!" He yelled to the already moving watchers. "I want those villagers found before first light."

Tank knew that the bet's duration was until first light, and it was still early, but he had no choice. A smiling countenance had overcome his very essence. The Black Mage did not anticipate any diversion from the easy slaughter, but now he seemed to have his hands full with a search party. Tank stood there not daring to say a word, but wishing that he could, because he had plenty to say.

The watchers pulled back the massive pins that held the giant wooden trapdoor locked. As soon as the pins released, the watchers sprinted for cover. Instantly, the door burst open almost hitting the slowest of the watchers, as he attempted to scurry away. Immediately thereafter, two calf-sized dogs appeared. One had three heads, and its brother had two. Their coats were solid black, and their eyes glowed with red light. The hellhounds

COGNIZANT

stood gleaming in front of their master awaiting orders, and ready to beckon unto his command.

"Lead my army to find those villagers, and bring their souls unto me!" Hades commanded. Each dog's multiple sets of ears perked up throughout the command, and they did understand every word spoken. Once their master had finished, the two, giant, black, multi-headed dogs sprinted to the sphere. One after the other they leaped, somehow into the sphere, and magically, they were instantaneously at the lead of the zombie army sniffing for the scent of the villagers. Within seconds the two hell hounds picked up the trail. To Tank it seemed to be, as quickly as they arrived.

Tanks smile had disappeared, as he had watched the chain of events that had just passed in front of his eyes, as unbelievable as they may have seemed. He could see for himself that those crazy genetically deformed dogs were leading the zombies without a struggle. "That seems a bit unfair." Tank finally forced from his lips.

Hades looked away from the sphere for a few seconds to look at Tank. "Well, I've given you your body back, and don't think that I didn't see you all but glowing, when my guardians came across the empty village."

"Yeah, a thousand to one odds, went to near even money, and then just turned back into five hundred to one odds, all within a minute or two, so don't blame me for complaining." Tank answered honestly. "By the way, whatever happened to those three creatures that had carried our bodies here?" He asked curiously.

"Well, let's just say they had to go. Now, about your odds human, I'd

COGNIZANT

say that they have never been closer to zero, then they are now." Hades said informing Tank of his lack of hope. "My dogs have *never* failed me. They will find the villagers, and they will bring me their souls. You see, they have certain powers."

"Yeah well, our bet didn't really include your pets, so I'll take having my skin back, as an advance payment, but you did forget to give the girls here their book, and I think that maybe you could ante up with some sort of chow. Your watchers do eat, like real food, don't they?" Tank said rambling on, trying to keep the Black Mage from thinking about his army's onslaught. He thought that maybe, if the Black Mage did not watch the hunt, a failure could become more plausible.

Hades began to cackle. "You just got in that tomb you call a body, and already it is dictating to you. So, you need food do you. I think that you had better just keep watching. I don't really want to have any messes in my throne room."

Tank did not appreciate the laugh on his behalf, but he was in no position to complain, and frankly, he did not dare. He had seen so many crazy, impossible things. It was all he could do to keep up the banter, especially with the reality that he could not back up anything against the likes of this immortal king. "You just keep laughing. All I've got to say is, I hope that you don't welch on your bets, when you lose, because I still plan on walking out of here with these girls come morning."

"Oh, I've welched on plenty of bets, but your piddley, weak souls are hardly worth my time." Hades answered semi-honestly. The truth was that he did welch on bets, and he was a soul monger, who really wanted all that he could get. "I mean, nine human souls hardly have any value at all. Now watch, as my dogs find the villagers with ease." He ordered.

As the two turned back to watching the sphere, Kilari figured that it was time to make his way down to where Belsangar had positioned himself. He crawled ever so slowly in a prone position, being sure to stay silent. All the while Belsangar watched the scene in the sphere.

The two huge dogs sniffed through the village with all of their noses, and immediately found the covered opening to the tunnel. The hell hounds ran full speed down the deep dark mountain corridor. The sphere suddenly went black, except for the glowing eyes, which slowly became noticeable, as the light shift forced their eyes to strain. The red glowing eyes of the hounds bobbed up and down with the pace of their running. They galloped on, in sheer blackness, following the scent of their prey, with the zombie horde trailing behind them.

Telebar and Malichye had just finished pulling up the rope ladder, when suddenly they saw what seemed to be some sort of creature dart into the large closed amphitheater of the cave. Being that they were so high from the floor of the cave, they figured that they were out of sight, but they found out differently, as the hounds from hell spotted them and began to howl. The howl signaled to the mass of following zombies, which were somewhat behind, because of their lack of speed, but the three young agents could hear the groans echoing from out of the black distance.

Cam saw the five sets of glowing eyes. "Oh shit," he said commenting

COGNIZANT

about the new unknown foes that were
approaching rapidly.

Sanctuary

"We're way too high for *anything* to make that kind of jump," Telebar stated using knowledge from the world that they knew. He drew his staff regardless of his statement in preparation of the possible conflict. "Run for help!" He yelled to Cam, figuring that the leader should distance himself from any action for his own safety, no matter how unlikely it seemed.

Cam immediately darted through the upper cave tunnel trying to catch up with the armed Huntresses, who carried their normal weapons of choice. He yelled knowing that help would soon come.

COGNIZANT

Malichye and Telebar each stood with weapons ready to strike. They readied themselves, watching, as the mysterious red eyes grew steadily closer. Malichye held his left arm out straight and pressed it against Telebar, as he stepped back away from the ledge. "Get back. We don't want to fall," he warned. Just as they had backed away, the first hellhound had jumped the entire height of the ledge. Its three head's each took a swipe at the two, but by moving back, they had just put themselves out of reach. The sound of the snapping teeth echoed as their saliva splashed near their ears. They still could not see what the creatures were, but both young agents immediately backed completely into the smaller area of the tunnel, away from the ledge altogether.

"Whatever those things are, they *can* get up here, we have to at least slow them down." Telebar told his partner, hoping that at the very least, Cam and the rest of the escaping multitude would make it to their destination.

Malichye listened carefully, trying to distinguish just how many predators there were. The two stood silently side by side awaiting the next attack. Suddenly, Malichye lunged forward swinging his tonfas with a snapping spin. He connected with the second attacking dog's left head. As quickly as he struck, he jumped backwards away from the predator almost faster, *if* that were possible. The hell hound's right head snapped at the spot from which he had just been struck, but fortunately for the young agent the force of his blow was just hard enough to make the dog's two back legs slip off the ledge, forcing it to miss its target. It clung on by its front claws momentarily, while its back legs tried to scurry for footing, but finally, the dog was forced to turn and jump back down.

"What are you doing?" Telebar asked, after hearing all of the sudden movement.

Malichye caught his balance carefully in the darkness. "I'm fighting. What are you doing? Waiting to see the whites of their eyes?"

"I was hoping to see *something*. Ya know?" Telebar answered honestly.

"I know this, there are only two of those things, and by the sounds of them they each weigh four to six hundred pounds." As he finished speaking, he again lunged out, but this time he just swung one arm with a sweeping hook. He lunged only slightly forward, but stretched his arm to a fuller length. Again, he connected, but this time he just barely grazed the tip of the nose of the hound's center head. The center

head swiveled away from the blow,
while the other two began to snap at
Malichye. This time Telebar pulled the
man back away from the snapping jaws.

The hellhound managed to keep
its place upon the ledge, and then
standing directly in front of his red
glowing eyes, Telebar could see the
silhouette of the mighty three headed
hound from hell. For an instant, he
tried to figure out exactly what the
beast could be, but then the groans of
the zombies in the background made
him realize that it was do or die time.
He quickly stabbed one of the
predator's eyes. As he pulled his staff
back, he immediately spun the staff
striking another eye. Then Malichye
pulled him out of the way. They
retreated about fifty feet to another
spot in the tunnel, which seemed to be
maybe even a little tighter. The lead
dog had its center head blinded, so it

struggled slightly at first, but then it just held that head low, away from the ceiling of the tunnel. "What is wrong with that dog?" Tank asked abruptly. "Is it closing its eyes, and jumping back and forth for a reason? I can't see. Can you get some light on the subject?" Tank peppered the Black Mage with his questions, but he knew that the balance of whatever was going on in that black tunnel held their fate in its hands.

"Silence, you insolent fool." Hades ordered. "It is a cave, not a picture from one of your viewscreens that you spoke of." Then he began to think of reasons for the oddity that they were seeing. "It could be that my dogs are swallowing people whole. Hey, how about that? Maybe when my dogs come out of that tunnel, they'll have swallowed the whole village?"

Sanctuary

"And maybe they'll never come out of that tunnel." Tank slammed back.

The dogs were too wide to stand side by side, so the two-headed dog was forced to stay behind its brother, who slowly gained speed. The wounded dog charged with its fangs bared and growling ferociously.

Telebar had found some loose, jagged rocks at his feet. He kicked one towards the lead dog, but it just landed near the dog harmlessly. He picked up another holding it with his right hand, while he held his staff in his left. He and Malichye continued to back pedal slowly, as the dogs closed ground little by little.

Once the lead dog moved in close enough, Telebar launched the rock. It hit pay dirt. Once again, the lead dog suffered a heavy blow. At this point, the dog snapped viciously and began to sprint the best it could. Telebar had to move forward to meet the attack and try to show force. He lunged with his staff, as if it were a spear, slamming it at least a foot deep into the hound's right throat.

The hell hound bit down snapping its teeth on reflex, breaking the staff, but leaving a foot of it imbedded in its throat. The right head bobbed and weaved trying to dislodge the staff piece. Malichye, noticing that once again the beast had slowed its charge, pulled at Telebar, urging him to keep back peddling.

Telebar's staff had quickly been shortened to a mere five feet in length. The weight difference made it seem light, but in the blackness, he could not immediately tell how much length remained, so he struck the wall a couple of times to get the feel of it.

Now, with its center head blinded and a piece of Telebar's staff lodged in its right throat, the lead dog had to give its position over, to its two-headed brother. It could feel its brother pouncing in anticipation for the fight, so it lay down, allowing the now stronger dog to pass, while it followed. The two-headed hell hound sniffed at his brother on the pass, and then howled with an eerie cry, as it geared up for its charge.

"They're coming," Malichye told Telebar. Telebar thought that he was talking about the two red-eyed creatures, and he wondered why his friend would waste his breath on such an obvious warning, but Malichye could hear the running of the Huntresses coming up quickly behind them, and then when he turned, he could see torchlight in the distance. "Run, run! Come on." Malichye called out trying to urge the big man to fall back and keep out of the way.

COGNIZANT

Telebar had no clue why Malichye thought that they could outrun the beasts, so he stood fast, as the charging beast dove at him. As the large young agent braced himself for the impact, he somehow lost his footing and fell upon his back, barely managing to avoid the hell hound's fanged snapping jaws, but now he found himself covered by a five hundred pound supernatural two-headed dog.

Without panicking, Telebar pushed, as hard as he could with his muscular legs, pressing and trapping the giant dog against the top of the tunnel. The hellhound momentarily gazed upon the fleshling that dared to make a stand. Its four glowing red eyes pierced the darkness giving Telebar enough light to see the actual ferocity of the beast that he was struggling to hold back.

Roc Bliss

The moment of bewilderment was over, and the hell hound began snapping ferociously at the trapped human. Telebar could barely keep the wild dog in check, while valiantly pushing with all of his might to keep it against the low ceiling of the tunnel. It lunged and jostled about, frantically striking from the right and from the left, but Telebar somehow, barely managed to keep beyond the vicious dog's reach. His legs were wearing out, and he knew that he had to make a move, before he found himself too exhausted from the struggle to do so.

Finally realizing that he still held his broken staff, Telebar waited for his next opening. Just then, one of the dog's heads snapped at him, so he thrusted upwardly with the jagged broken end of his staff. The move felt awkward, but somehow the young agent sank his weapon deep into the reeling upper neck.

The dog however, never gave up. It still had another head to use for battle, and it lashed out repeatedly at the nearly exhausted fleshling, as Telebar continued dodging. After multiple attempts, the young man began feeling trapped under the evil hell hound's massive weight.

Malichye ran quite a distance, before noticing that his compadre was not with him. Malichye screamed one more time, but this time he screamed towards the Huntresses. "Come on! Move it!" He yelled toward the torchlights that appeared to be closing in rapidly. Then reversing his direction, he began moving forward to the fight. As he approached his seemingly fallen comrade, he chucked one of his tonfas in a desperate attempt to distract the animal. It however fell harmlessly to the ground, after its poorly aimed flight hit the cave wall. The noise may have distracted the dog for a split second, but that was the extent of its damage.

"Dive on the ground! Take cover!" Cam screamed, at the top of his lungs. Malichye ran another step or two, until finally the command had sunk into his conscious mind. He dropped flat to the ground. Within milli-seconds, the Huntresses fired an aerial assault. Spears and arrows darted the air. They flew with perfect precision peppering the hellhound. The mighty dog roared in pain, as many projectiles protruded its flesh.

Finally, from out of the distance, a singular flying object spun through the air. Malichye was in the midst of rolling over, when he saw a final streak rush by him. He turned to watch, and he saw his brother, of sorts, still

COGNIZANT

holding the screaming beast up against the ceiling of the cave tunnel. The spinning blade barely missed the large man, as it made its way directly into and through the dog's sternum. It separated the bone and sunk deep into the small heart of the over-sized beast. With blood spewing from the animal, it gave up its last breath with a pain-filled scream, before going limp.

The wounded three-headed dog, which had been trapped behind its brother, since giving up its lead position, smelled the death of its brother, and with a mournful howl, the oversized monstrosity of a dog ran flaccidly back, jumping off the ledge. The dog instantly reappeared in the throne room of the Black Mage, coming through the portal of the All-Seeing Eye. The wounded dog limped back into its home, down below the trapdoor to lick its wounds.

ROC BLISS

Tank could not disguise his grin, as he watched the dog gingerly making its way to the hatch. He beamed at the Black Mage. "Things ain't looking good for the home team." He commented bravely, unable to stop himself.

"They'll look as good as I choose them to, you worthless blob of flesh. My hounds found the villagers. I still have my army." Hades answered, trying to make any excuse for his lack of success.

"Your army is weak, and your dogs have been defeated. It looks to me like we'll be walking right out of here anyway, so you might as well let us go now. Make it easy on yourself." Tank said running his mouth relentlessly, hoping that the Black Mage would be sick of hearing his voice and just let them go.

Hades looked over to Tank. His scowl told the story without any words needing to be said. Kilari looking down, thought that he could see smoke rolling off from the old wizard's head. The wizard stood up from his throne and marched angrily over to where the book sat upon the floor. He bent and picked it up, and then walked over to the group of nine. "Is this the article that you had requested?" He asked in a very angry state, feeling torn, between doing as his master had told him or taking revenge upon the bolstering fleshlings.

'If it had not been for this book, these fools could be killed outright, but no, Lucifer had to give the order that the book had to make its way back to their dimension.' After this thought, the Black Mage became so hysterically mad that Tank did not even dare to answer his question.

He just stood there wide-eyed. "Huh? You buffoon!" Hades said mocking Tank's quiet wide-eyed stare. The old wizard lifted the book in a way that appeared as though he would strike Tank, and his anger seemed to have steeped to a point of unpredictability.

Kilari knew that he could not take the chance of waiting on the sidelines anymore. His friend seemed to be in a life or death situation, and the girls sat right beside him. "Hey!" Kilari yelled from upon the balcony. Hades spun his head around in complete shock. None have *ever* gotten the drop on him before, especially not in his own throne room. His eyes glared at this new intruder. Kilari looking down from the balcony said, "If you got a problem, maybe you should take it up with me?"

Hades turned in surprise wondering, 'How could one of these flesh-bags sneak into my palace?' Then

COGNIZANT

realizing that he had somehow underestimated the humans, the Black Mage knew that now is the time to show these mouthy fleshlings, just *who* the king of the underworlds is, and why.

Hades reached out with his empty hand, as Kilari peered down from the upper balcony. The emanating red glow intensified from the blood crown, as Hades reached out with his hand, focusing on an image of his hand reaching all the way up to where Kilari stood, and just as he imagined, a spiritual limb invisibly reached out and pulled Kilari down from the balcony.

Kilari soon found himself face to face with the mad demon, which was not just any demon. Hades was the kind of demon that ran his underworld domain, not a subordinate. The girls in the background all started screaming in a panic. They could not believe that now Kilari had also been captured. Kilari did not struggle. He knew that if the Black Mage intended him to be dead, then he would have killed him on sight.

"Oh, so *you* are the leader of this little expedition and for some reason you have the belief that you can solve my problems?" Hades said drawing Kilari in closer, and peering into his grey eyes. "Well, what have you got in mind?"

"Look, why we're here, is a very long story, but I have listened to what you've been saying. You've made a bet, but I can see that you don't plan on living up to your end. Let me just ask this: Is there a bet that you *would* honor? Or are you just a typical soul monger with no honor?" Kilari asked, sounding as if he were equal to, or above the level of Hades.

COGNIZANT

Hades wanted to squish this human like a bug. In a sinister voice, he came back at Kilari saying, "How *dare* you speak to me of honor? What would a young flesh-bag know of honor?"

"I have learned of honor, and am still learning. In fact, that book you are holding like some sort of weapon, had taught me of honor, and faith." Kilari stated trying to give some sort of credentials to his knowledge.

"Now, if I did not intend on letting people go free, I would not make bets with them, and tell them that if they win, I would set them free." Hades replied as his eyes turned blood red. "I had a thousand to one odds, and then one of my dogs was exterminated, which I hadn't believed to be possible. There was no way that I should have lost that bet."

ROC BLISS

"Well, you must not have realized that you had some Elite warriors in your little world." Kilari said curtly. "I think that you are going to find that killing things is what we do best. Now, I know that you could have killed us already, and for some unknown reason you decided against it, so you can either allow us to go, kill us, or be really pissed when we escape and your army of the dead slowly gets extinguished. We'll end up leaving you with less souls than you've had in a long time."

Kilari felt sure that Hades was put in the position of not being allowed to kill them, so he thought that he would try to get under his skin enough to convince him that he really did not want them around.

Hades did not like the insubordinate tones that he was hearing, so he thought that he would have to teach the fleshlings some respect. He forced Kilari up higher into the air with his grasping invisible force. He spun the young agent upside down.

Belsangar could see that Kilari was floating higher than the balcony, on which he was still hiding. Kilari knew that he had pushed some buttons. "Well human, I think that I shall let you hang upside down, until the blood drips from your eyes, and once it does, I will put one of my guardians below you, and let it drink, until the last drop falls."

Kilari looked at the evil demon lord, wondering if his original premise was correct, but he would not let up, even if he were wrong, even if he would die. He would either force the demon to kill him, or torment the old beast. "Oh, is that all you got?" He goaded. "Why don't you set up a fight, between

us and some of your so-called
guardians? Or are you scared that you
would run out of soldiers and be left by
yourself in this big old world?" Kilari
continued the constant insults hoping
to see just how far the old demon could
be pushed, before having a mental
meltdown.

"Kilari, I wouldn't press him!"
Tank called out. "He has a *wicked*
temper."

"You should listen to your fat
friend, Killjoy." Hades said mocking
Kilari's name.

"Ouch, oh that really hurt me."
Kilari quickly interjected. "If you don't
think that I've been called that before,
then you must be ignorant. How about
you and me go at it? Come on, you take
off your little crown, and we'll fight
fair and square, winner take all."

"What?" Hades questioned,
wishing that he could kill this one and

get it over with, but he knew that if he crossed Lucifer, it would mean an eternity of pain. "Aren't we against each other right now? And you are dangling helplessly up in the air, powerless."

Kilari could feel the blood starting to put pressure on his brain, and he realized that he would not be able to keep conscious forever. He began to labor with each word. "Take… the… crown…off. Take it… off, and… then…" In the midst of speaking, the young agent began swirling between states of consciousness.

"*Let him down!*" Jezza finally screamed. She could not take seeing him up there slowly dying.

"Oh, so you are concerned with this bag of worthless flesh? Ha, ha ha," he began cackling.

Kilari suddenly could see the clouds of limbo. He knew the place well enough to recognize it. He did not know whether he had died or if he would be meeting with one of the two forces, good, or evil. He did not have long to wait. He could see Lucifer, as he appeared in a black cloud.

"It looks, as though you could use a hand, and I will help you, if you call out to me. You do not want your wives to be eaten alive. Do you?" Lucifer asked getting right to the point of the matter. He wanted Kilari to call out to him, and ask for assistance.

Kilari felt no pain, as he stood in his spirit body. His mind was clear, as crystal. "So you could help me?" He questioned. All the while testing to see why he would not help freely. "You are stronger than that evil wizard?"

"Is the blood drowning your brain?" Lucifer asked. "I have no equal." He stated truthfully, being that Yahiveh had more power than he, but

COGNIZANT

of the wicked he was the most powerful, and ran all underworlds, as needed.

"You can help me of your own free will then, or let me die. In either case, I don't feel pressure. If you kill my loves, and then you also allow me to die, we will be in paradise together for all eternity. So, do as you will." Kilari said explaining his version of reality.

"I could have Hades shred your women and torture them relentlessly, and to stop it, all you would have to do is call out my name." Lucifer stated for the record.

"I cannot serve two masters. I have to believe that Yahiveh would only allow so much to happen, before stepping in himself, and besides, hours, or even days of pain, compared to an eternity thereafter. It isn't really much of a price to pay." Kilari spoke from his true spirit, in which he had come to realize that this whole situation had been caused by his misjudgment, and Lucifer's greed for human souls. "I see you, as you are, and I am not interested to call upon you for any price."

"So be it." Lucifer stated calmly. Then the black cloud opened up revealing the hideousness of the devil's evil soul. The sounds of a billion tortured souls screaming from within. "Your friends will all pay to the fullest extent, at the hands of Hades, and you will be there to endure it. I will keep it fresh within your mind, until you call out my name from bended knee, and beg for my help." The being of pure evil finished speaking, and then pointed at Kilari.

In that instance, Kilari was again in the realm of Xibalba. He gained consciousness, only to see Hades pulling Jezza from the force field container. He tossed her across the room. She screamed from fear and pain, but her heart was the heaviest weight upon her, because when Kilari had lost consciousness, she had thought that he had died.

Kilari found himself lying on the cold sand stone floor of the demon's palace, unrestrained. "Hades!" He called out with all of the raspy sound that he could muster in his weakened condition. His head still floated with excess blood, but he was gaining perspective by the minute. Again, he called out sharply, as he attempted to stand upright. "Ha-des! You haven't killed me yet!" He slowly regained his footing and began to move across the room.

Neither Jezza, nor Hades had heard him. Hades was too busy in the midst of frightening the girl, who had called out to Kilari. Belsangar watched, and saw Kilari struggling to regain a solid stance, while Tank and the rest stood still, locked away helplessly. He knew that this was his cue to join in the fun and games, and after gathering from what Kilari had stated prior to passing out, that the crown was the key, he knew what he must do. Kilari staggered towards the throne, gaining more and more control of his abilities with each step. Belsangar knew that in a moment the Black Mage would be directly below.

Hades grabbed Jezza up by the neck with one hand. She screamed and kicked, but his vice-like grasp barely allowed her voice to be heard. He cackled wickedly, as he sensed the fear flowing from the girl. He held her out helplessly. Then he turned, and saw Kilari at his throne, pressing control buttons all along the arms of the chair.

COGNIZANT

"No, you fool!" Hades yelled tossing the young girl to the floor without a second thought, as he began crossing the floor towards Kilari. He began lifting his arm to cast his spell, but before he could, Belsangar had jumped from the balcony. He dropped down the entire distance, using the demon for a landing pad. As they toppled over, and the blood crystal crown began bouncing away from its master, the center stone dislodged from its setting.

Tank noticed the light, which powered the force field, was no longer lit, so he figured that it was down, and after a brief test with his cap, he got the girls moving for the nearest exit. All of the girls ran screaming with fear, except one. Marcia, who quickly made way across the distance over to the crawling body of her love, Jezza, whose barely conscious body continued crawling over to recover the holy book.

Kilari and Tank both rushed the demon, who had regained his footing and kicked Belsangar a short distance in his anger. Tank slammed into the unsuspecting Hades like a Mack truck, while Kilari had his nun-chucks out and spinning. Tank fell off to the side of the demon from the force of the collision, but Hades still stood. Kilari began striking the demon with full force blows, but Hades just reached up and caught the weapons with each hand. He easily pulled them away from the shocked Kilari. "Run!" Kilari yelled with a fully recovered voice.

The Black Mage sensed the absence of his crown, which Belsangar had knocked off his head, as he dropped from the ledge. Once realizing its absence, the demon began scouring the room for its presence. As the demon moved to retrieve the crown, so he could utilize its power, and stop this atrocity from taking place, Kilari had Jezza and Marcia running for the exit. In mere seconds of Kilari's order, the entire group filed up the stairway and towards the exit at full speed.

Hades turned while placing the crown upon his head. He knew that it was not too late, and that he could easily stop the escape. He swung his arm in a way to cast his spirit power across the doorway. However, the group's progress was unimpeded, and he stood watching, as the last of them had fled from his palace. "No!" He kept screaming, as he repeatedly cast different spells with no effect. Unaware that the center stone was ajar, and his spells were either inaccurate, or ineffective.

In frustration, the Black Mage built his most powerful spell and in an angry attempt, he cast it with all of his might. The spell shot out with such magnitude that it jarred the All-Seeing Eye, but the Black Mage still did not realize that the blood crystal sat off kilter in its setting. The giant wave of a spell blasted through his throne room ricocheting and destroying all things in its path. The spell reverberated, until finally settling upon the once, All-Seeing Eye. The eye imploding from the spell's force had been reduced to a mere, oversized gazing ball with no powers at all.

The beaten, battered, and otherwise exhausted group, again found themselves running along what seemed to be the same terrain, which they had used earlier in that day, but now, the darkness became another factor, which only seemed to slow them down, while confusing their direction of travel. They could only muster enough strength to run into the covering of the brush, which peppered the hillsides surrounding the valley.

Belsangar led the way with Ceilia quietly beside him. As they crested the closest hill, the eerie sound of the demon's signal came calling, calling his guardians to battle. By the pitch of the sounding, Hades now, began considering the group, as completely expendable, and in his evil black revenge filled heart, he did not care of any consequences that Lucifer may place upon him.

As the group traveled with only one thing in mind, to distance themselves from the evil wizard's territory, Kilari finally decided that it was time to tell the girls the news. "Hey, we were with Cam and the rest of the guys, before we came for you. They had to be the ones to kill that dog thing, so I'm taking it that they must have escaped the zombies."

"You got *that* right brother," Tank said smiling with glee. "I sat there and watched the whole thing. It was beautiful man." Tank continued.

"I don't know how you could see anything, when they were in a black cave," Glenda spouted at the man.

Tank just let it go without a comment for a second, but then he just had to say it. "I thought you and the girls were all praying. So how would you know?" He blurted out. "Besides when that group of hot chicks came running up, they had torches and you could see what was going on."

Sophie reached her hand out and playfully slapped at her man. "Hey, you better watch it there," she warned trying to keep the peace.

Yahiveh floated invisibly with Kilari's group, keeping them moving in

the right direction, avoiding the mass
of searching zombies. They did not
know that he was there, nor did they
have the energy to even contemplate
such possibilities, but he guided them
perfectly to a hidden location, where
supplies were waiting. He loved his
children and provided them with
essentials that they had been lacking
for a period of time.

Belsangar looking ahead, as he led
the group, could suddenly see the
yellow glow of what seemed to be a fire
off in the distance. The glow appeared
to be quite a ways out, but it was not
far enough to keep it out of reach. He
could feel his spirit pulling him to this
location, so he stopped and turned to
his fellow comrades. "Alright, I see
where we're going to, and I don't know
what's there, or if we'll have to fight
for it, but I can see the place, so you
all can just keep on following me." His

voice was that of exhaustion, but he had confidence.

Belsangar looked over towards Tank and the rest of the girls. Now, assured that none were questioning anything, he turned back to the path, and continued walking towards his goal with Ceilia on his arm. She could also see the yellowish glow of some guiding light. Behind them, the group all turned towards Kilari for his approval, and he just nodded and pointed forward to his friend and brother, who was leading by faith. "Lead on brother," Kilari said, also fatigued, but willing to give Belsangar the nod.

Kilari had an arm around each of his girls, as they kept following, never noticing that they were not in familiar territory. He only noticed that it seemed to be very quiet, maybe even a bit too, but he would not break its golden solace by complaining.

COGNIZANT

The darkness had brought its cool air down with it, and the group could feel its chill nipping at them harmlessly. With over expended energy from running and fighting, combined with a lack of food and water for an extended amount of time, the group began staggering tiredly, until finally, making their way to a reddish stone cave that held a lit torch in its doorway.

Belsangar took the torch from its holder expecting to see an occupant of some sort. "Hello, is there anybody here?" He called out, but all he heard was his voice echoing the same words back. He yelled again, just to make sure, but again the only answer was the echo of his own voice. Reaching forward, he stuck the torch into the immediate cave tunnel. He flagged the torch back and forth to each side of the tunnel, checking it thoroughly to make sure nothing was lurking in the darkness.

The tunnel was short, maybe only ten feet, but it ended in an area large enough for the whole group to catch some shut-eye. They could see that there had been a fire lit recently, and could still feel the heat coming off from the remaining embers. Belsangar waved the torch around the outskirts of the cave wall, checking for anything that he might see. Suddenly, he noticed a small side room. By that time, the girls had all sat down watching the men intently, making sure that they would not be left unattended again.

Tank entered the room first, figuring that he was the most rested, by how beat his two friends appeared. Belsangar kept the torch up high trying to light the little room. "Hey, there's a food basket in here guys, and look, there's wood too. We may have just hit the jackpot!"

The girls breathed a sigh of relief. It finally looked as if something could finally be going their way. Belsangar backed out of the little room, so that Tank could get by him with some of the firewood. Tank placed the giant armload near the fire ring. Kilari decided to throw a few of the smaller pieces on the embers, and get a nice fire going. It lit and heated the entire area keeping the whole group comfortable.

Belsangar reappeared from the little room a minute later with a large basket. "Look at this. Tank was right." He acknowledged after opening the basket and peering inside. It's filled with some type of bread. Oh, and what's that?" He asked seeing some other wrapped objects underneath the loaves of bread. After handing out a couple loaves of bread, he reached down and felt some hard blocks of something. He pulled a couple out. He handed one to Tank. "What is this stuff?" He asked curiously, unable to unwrap the small blocks with his hands full.

Tank had two hands clear, so he unwrapped the parcels, easily. He looked and saw what seemed to be transparent golden colored stiff blocks. Tank pinched the block, and pulled off a small chunk. Without even looking, he popped it in his mouth. "Mmmm, oh that's good. You gotta try this. It seems almost like a cross between cheese and honey. You know, I bet it'll be good with that bread." Tank's taste buds became reborn, after the flavors began dancing across his tongue.

Kilari had sat back watching for a minute, while the others continued pulling bread from the loaves. Abruptly, he got the urge to check the small room for himself. He snagged the torch from his buddy's hand, and by the time he made it to the doorway of the little room, Jezza and Marcia were right on his tail. They were not about to let him escape from their sight any time soon.

The outer room had plenty of light from the fire, so once inside the small room Kilari had noticed a hole, in which to place the torch handle. He did so, freeing up both hands, and lighting up the entire room. The girls had followed him in and watched as he reached for something from out of a back corner that the others must have missed. It was some type of skin, filled with liquid.

Kilari untied the stopper and held the ancient style flask to his nose. "Woo," he said smiling at the girls. He took a small sip and swallowed. It was definitely some type of wine from some unknown type of fruit. "Ahhh," he sounded, as he exhaled after tasting the wine.

"Here try some. It's definitely alcoholic, so go easy," he suggested handing the flask to Marcia. He looked Jezza in the eye, and seeing the bruises that marked her neck, caused a sudden wave of sympathy. "Are you okay baby?" He asked softly, as he pulled her in close. He had his arm draped gently around her waist, as he looked deep into her eyes.

Marcia took a check sip to see how much of a bite the wine had, and then, after building her confidence, she kicked the flask back and took a big gulping pull. "Oh yeah," she said aloud, as she exhaled the fumes.

"Alright in there," sounded Tank's voice. "You can't be going there already?" He said, interjecting one of his usual sexual innuendos.

Marcia moved in close, handing the flask to Jezza, who in turn gulped down a couple of mouthfuls. She shuddered slightly from the combination of tartness, mixed with an alcoholic kick. Then she handed the skin back to Kilari. "It's kind of smooth." She said, trying to catch her breath, making an airy kind of sound. The group of three all began giggling, as they made their way back into the main room of the cave.

Kilari walked up behind Belsangar, who was sitting, gazing into the warm frolicking flames of the soothing fire. "Look what we've found," he said, handing him the smooth leather skin.

Belsangar snapped back to the present, and then looked up just in time to see the incoming flask that

Kilari was handing over. He grabbed it out of the air saying, "don't mind if I do."

"Don't worry, Jezza thinks its smooth," Marcia said with a chuckle.

"Oh it's spirits, is it?" Belsangar asked with renewed vigor. He took a big slug, and soon they all began passing it amongst themselves. They ate their moist bread, with the sweet cheese, all the while sipping on the wine with its own unknown, special rejuvenation powers.

Kilari finally stood amongst the group, near the fire and said, "Okay, I believe that it is time to thank Yahiveh for saving us from that demon."

"And for this food and drink," Marcia added.

"And don't forget about this wonderful fire and the shelter." Ceilia suggested, quickly putting another item to the list. "You know, a week ago

COGNIZANT

I had no clue that Yahiveh actually existed. I mean, I knew the name from dealing with Kilari, but I really had no clue, and now, I have a completely fresh outlook, and I do truly believe, because I believe that only Yahiveh could have got us away from that beast."

The group sat talking of their newly found faith, and their recent experiences for a brief period, while they ate, drank, and cozied up to the fire. Kilari cuddled closely with Marcia and Jezza. Each of them took turns cleaving to one another feeling the love and comfort of each other's presence.

Belsangar and Ceilia followed suit, as well as Tank and Sophie. The other four girls smiled at the sight, and spent their thoughts projecting themselves with their loves in similitude.

ROC BLISS

Sanctuary

Before their weariness forced them to bed down, Kilari stated to the group that Cam had given him orders to meet on the morrow. "He sent us on a minimum of a spy mission, but that cave chick looked at us, as if we would never return, making it seem like a suicide mission. I can't wait to show up with *everybody* intact."

"We still gotta get through the night," Tank reminded him. "Don't forget, those things don't sleep, and they just flock to the smell of blood. I saw them in action on that wizard's crazy spy cam."

Kilari heard Tank's passing comment of Hades, as just some type of wizard, and he knew from his little trip that there was much more to this character. "Hey, that guy is not just a wizard. He has an affiliation with Lucifer, and I think we pissed him off, but on the other hand, I get this feeling

COGNIZANT

that we're safe in this cave, so let's get some shut-eye. We need to get up early, and be on our way back by daybreak."

*   *   *   *   *

Telebar waited for help from Malichye to get pulled out from under the still bleeding hound. The Huntress's torches lit the area, and as they shone upon Telebar's blood covered body, the most familiar huntress stepped forward. "You are a brave man," Vail stated truthfully passing by and walking over to the dead beast. She eyed the various spears and arrows, which stuck out of the animal like quills. She saw her spear and pulled it out with a harsh tug. She grinned slightly at the corpse, believing that somehow she was actually side by side with partners of the chosen one.

Sanctuary

The one that prophecies had stated would finally free this habitation of all zombies, and even Hades himself. She bent down on her knee, beside the animal. She reached deeply into its chest plate, so that she could get a solid grip on her knife handle.

Telebar watched the woman, while she was recovering her weapons. She had just complimented him, and yet she was the one that had saved *his* life. He stepped back to the animal's side on his weary legs that held the animal's immense weight. "I should have known that it was your blade that had finally killed that bastard. I want to thank you. You probably saved my life."

Vail smiled slightly, thinking to herself that it was awful forward of this male to speak to her, but she was beginning to get used to these overly open men, who did not know their place, and she was actually beginning to like it. Then she thought that she had better go find Travis and the Queen.

The fleeing group could hear the frustration in the guttural voices of the moaning, groaning zombies. There was no way for the monsters to scale the steepness of the perpendicular cave wall, but they could smell the fresh blood of the fleshlings, as it lapped at their senses, and it began driving them even further beyond their usual craziness.

Vail and Cam did not foresee any other present danger, so in their confidence, they decided to keep the torches blazing during the rest of their journey, back to what had been a lair for the Huntresses, but now would be the next place that Vail and her people would call home.

Sanctuary

The small group again began moving on their way to their new home, when suddenly the sounding of the Black Mage's signal echoed across the land, and through all places, including the very tunnel in which they were now traveling. It was the loudest signal, far louder than any of them had ever heard. The sounding lasted for a couple of minutes, and when it had ended, the group could hear the mass thuds of running feet, as the obedient zombies followed their summons.

The gruesome multitude began to leave, carrying the sounds of their tortured souls with them. They tormented over the loss of fresh flesh, once again. Their groans echoed through the lengthy cave tunnels, keeping their prey on edge.

"Something *big* is going down." Vail stated calmly. In a state of wonder, she questioned if they would be seeing a new level of activity from the evil Black Mage. "I've never heard the sounding so loud, and that pitch, it seems to be awfully high. I suppose that we had better hurry to get back to our defendable new home."

Cam, who was walking next to her and the Queen concluded. "It must be Kilari, only he could create so much havoc, and be that frustrating." Cam smiled at the thought of the Black Mage pulling his hair out, trying to deal with Kilari. As he came back to reality, he decided to question. "So, should we be expecting some form of new attack from the wizard? I mean, are there some form of giant spiders? Or maybe, he has some killer birds that he might call in?" Cam's questioning, raised some eyebrows of wonder, but neither of the women knew what he was asking.

Vail finally, blew off his remark in ignorance, not having a clue about the names of the two beasts that Cam had just listed. She looked over toward her Queen and suggested, "we should quicken our pace, milady. Our new home can be defended easily. It is unreachable by the guardians, so at least we should not have to worry about them." The Queen did not need to be prodded. She instantly began jogging at a good clip, which in turn, the entire group followed suit, and soon they had made their way to their new home.

The Queen walked in looking all around. She eyed up the many separate sleeping quarters. They would need more, but this was indeed a pleasing sight. "Vail, you have done well here. This place is perfect."

"I was not the only worker here my Queen. All of the Huntresses gave their utmost to help style our home." Vail answered, quickly giving credit to her cohabitants, even though it would seem likely that nature itself had structured the dwelling.

Cam looked around. He could not figure out how these women could have hewn out these caves, but at this moment, he had more to worry about than who took credit for what. It was not his business, so let the girls take credit for their find. He wondered how Kilari and Belsangar were fairing. Here they were, stuck in some primitive place, where communication is nearly non-existent. It wore deeply on his patience. He liked having the ability to communicate, no matter how far the distance between you. He gathered his men together, and they watched, as the crowd of people slowly began to get their nooks issued to them by the Queen herself. They walked over to a far corner beneath a torch, where they could talk in a less congested area. It was time to decide what would be their next move.

Cam knew that he had told Kilari that he expected to see him by morning, but he still had to wonder. Exactly, what would the dawning of a new morning bring to his plate? All of their girls, and three of his Elite squad remained absent, status unknown. It was not sitting well, so he decided to discuss certain options with the men.

COGNIZANT

Black Night

Thomas Elliot and his wife Tessa had found themselves a nice underground financed shuttle service that would escort them directly over Flag Island. It was long past dark, by the time that they had finally chuted down, unseen to the island. The shuttle had been picked up by the security detail; however, it would be nearly impossible to detect the two souls jumping from it in the dark. The team landed undetected. They immediately began rolling up their chutes, and readying their equipment. "Wale, you ready gurl?" Thomas asked in his strange drawl.

Tessa was ready, but she had to get one thing straight first. "Thomas, you can feel free to leave that twang talk for the purists, okay? I need to hear you. I don't even want you to think about your regular cover, until after we get the boys back. Got me mister?" She asked with a little sassy spunk in her voice.

The tone of her voice perked Thomas's ears. "Got you?" He asked coyly. "Well babe, I think that maybe you should refresh my mind on what it means to *have* you."

Tessa began to blush, and Thomas knew it, even though the darkness covered the event from his eyes. "We ain't got time for that now, big boy, but I'll just have to say, I owe you one. When this is all done, we're going to have to take a *real* vacation."

Thomas still aroused, knew that Tess was right, about waiting, but he hated that he had to wait. "Well then, let's move it out." He said, raising his wrist, and punching a button on his G.P.S. unit. "Okay, we're all marked," he said, as the memory button lit up telling him of his exact coordinates. Now, the unit would point them directly to the beachhouse, and hopefully, to those boys, or at least to pick up some clues to their whereabouts.

Thomas took the lead, marching double time directly along the sandy beach, watching as the silvery glow of the bright shining moonlight bounced up and down with the swelling of the waves. Inhaling the salty air of the blue sea felt invigorating to the man. 'There's nothing quite like it,' he thought, as he continued toward his goal.

Soon, the two had made their way up to the beachhouse. Thomas and Tessa walked cautiously staying low in a strategic manner, trying to be very quiet, with their heat blasters pointing out covering the doorway. Upon approach, the two-middle-aged abolition agents expected to see action. Thomas gave Tessa a glance, before checking the handle, making sure that she was ready for a go. It was unlocked, so he turned it and flung it open, jumping in with his eyes open wide and his blaster scanning for enemies. Tessa dove in behind him, doing a diving forward roll. She landed with her heat blaster facing a moving object. "Stop! Or get singed!" She screamed, ready to pull the trigger.

Alfie stopped moving immediately. "I stopped," the metallic voice called out, hoping not to need any sudden replacement parts.

"Who are you?" Tessa questioned.

"I am Alfie, a server droid for the beachhouse, and all who occupy it. Are you guests? Have you seen the young men?"

The two could see that the droid was no threat, so they holstered their heat blasters. "Alfie huh? I've never heard of a droid with a human name?" Tessa inquired, as she walked closer to the metallic being. It was wearing a military jacket, as if it were part of its usual garb.

"Master Kilari suggested a name, so that I could be remembered by others." The droid answered point blank.

With this answer, Tessa's heart jumped, skipping a beat. She could barely keep her breath to ask, "So, you've seen the boys? Are they here? Are they alright?" Her plump lips blurted with urgent speed.

"Yes. No. I have no data." The droid answered reflexively.

The answer did not quite click in Tessa's mind, but Thomas realized that the droid was right on top of things. "Tell us. Did all seven arrive?"

Alfie stood ready, answering, "I have seen three, but I heard talk of the others being upon the island, possibly lost."

"Three?" Tessa's heart was about to explode. "Names, I want the names of the three."

Alfie answered, "Kil-ar-ee, Tank, and Bel-sang-ar." His robotic voice struggled with the names slightly, but all in all it did well.

"Where are they?" Her voice blurted, now taking over the entire questioning process. Thomas listened, as they found out that the three had left many hours previous, to go search for the rest of their team, and that it was awaiting their return, so that they could continue to enjoy their vacation.

COGNIZANT

The droid recanted the entire scene, which included Kilari's near death experience, and the importance of his news of Mary Trenton. With the droid's story unfolding, Alfie pushed the buttons on the view screen. He began showing the entire contents of all of the news stories that had been playing for the young men, before their leaving.

The two parental figures stood shocked at the details of the stories, and how realistic and perverted they seemed. Finally, Thomas was ready to hit the trail to search the island-scape for their boys. He asked, "Did any other thing happen that could help our search?"

The droid told of all of the loud sounds of a battle, and then brought a copy of the coordinates, which were still flashing upon Belsangar's computer screen. "The young men tracked the signal through transponders and found these to be the coordinates of origin."

Tessa, even though still in shock by the content of the news footage, was feeling an overwhelming sense of pride, not only for her boys, but also of Thomas. "You have trained them well, Thomas." She obliged with motherly love swelling in her heart warmly, rising on a wave of emotion that began a rollercoaster effect. The scenes from the phony newsreels had brought her down, but now she was up, and more ready than ever to go get those boys. In fact, she felt unstoppable.

"Let's move it," Thomas said, before she could, beating her to the punch for once. With that being said, the two agents immediately fled out the door and through the thick jungle, towards their new coordinates.

COGNIZANT

Soon, the two came upon many dead bodies, singed and burned. Many of the trees and surrounding foliage were also burned and broken from what looked to be a scene of total chaos. After slowly wading through an area of obvious mass corpses, the science facility stood out plainly, having a few of its search lights scanning the nearby vicinity. "Okay, this is it." Thomas stated. The boys came here."

Tessa looked down noticing a few sets of clean boot prints, and from the looks of them, whoever's they were, hid out of sight in the same area. "Look Thomas, I bet those are the boys' footprints. They probably checked out the entire scene from here, before finding their in."

Thomas rolled his eyes, and said, "I should have thought of that. We had the same coordinates. It would only make sense that we would be following their exact tracks." Then he thought for a second and asked, "Are you thinking what *I'm* thinking?"

After answering affirmatively, Tessa said what she thought they were both thinking. "We'll follow their tracks in." Thomas smiled his confirmation, but Tessa did not wait. She began creeping slowly toward the lights, sticking to the shadows. She could see the boot prints crossing beneath the constantly scanning lights. There is only one way to get across the lights Thomas, and I'm not stopping." She stated, as she walked right into plain view for any security to see.

Thomas picked his blaster up high, ready for any confrontation. They began running across the spanse, between them and the building, until making it to the vine-covered wall. They each began scanning the area, thinking that at any moment, a security patrol would be flooding in on them, but they soon realized that nobody was coming. They continued following the footprints, and were led to a metal cover, so they moved it and climbed down into the black tunnel. The two put their night-vision goggles on and continued walking, until they came to a joint where the tunnel split and moved in two directions. "Which way?" Tessa asked, looking to Thomas for the answer.

"Hold on a second." He answered, as he started to think. "I remember looking at the blue prints of the academy's layout many times. Just give me a minute." Tessa never said a word, she waited, and finally he began moving again. "I think it's this way. I vaguely recall something about the guards chatting about weird unexplained sounds coming from the tunnels. I figured that the boys could have used them to get out of the facility, but I never did catch them."

"That's your fault. You trained them too well." She smiled, before noticing that she was actually smiling. Then it hit her. She was with her man, and they were on an important mission, having a good time. After so much time had past, being a teacher, and a mother, she could barely remember being the spy that she had been trained to be. Now, she finally found herself right where she had dreamed of being for years, and even though she did not like the fact that the boys and girls were in so much danger, she somehow felt right at home amongst the chaos.

Thomas led the way directly under a large grate. They could see the light for quite a distance, and already had taken off their night vision goggles. "Okay, I'll slide her over, and we'll enter here," he said being tall enough to reach the grate. It was not easy, but with some effort, he moved it over and they entered into the large room. "It's some kind of ventilation room. They could have gone into any of these tubes," he said wondering which way to go.

Tessa snatched out her flashlight. She began carefully inspecting the tubes. "Here," she began pointing to a certain tube. "Look, the dust is disturbed, you can see that there has been some sort of recent activity on this ladder." Thomas hopped on the ladder and began climbing, making quick work of the thirty-foot obstacle. Tessa was right behind him all the way to the maintenance hatch. After prying the hatch open and checking within, he waved Tessa by, quickly closing the hatch behind them, which left them in a semi-dark tube.

Black Night

They climbed up an inner ladder, until reaching the top, where the tube began flowing horizontally across the ceiling. The tube had moderate lighting, which seeped up through its many vents. The two walked carefully and quietly, checking each room as they past.

Thomas could smell all of the years of built up dust. It was caking in his nostrils, slightly clogging them. Making them feel as if they would close each time that he inhaled. He took his time peering into each of the rooms, until finally finding some action below.

There was a large group of people. Thomas recognized most of them, General Brague, Field Marshal Blak, and that scientist from the academy to name a few. Field Marshal Blak was sitting shackled to a chair and General Brague seemed more puffed up than usual, so it was quite obvious to

COGNIZANT

Thomas, who would be in power next. There was also a handful of scientists, some familiar, others not. They seemed to be strewn around the room, most of them running some form of high tech control panels, while others stood watching particular viewscreens. He continued scanning the room, when suddenly he noticed a square light on the far side of the room. He pondered that the scientists were monitoring this strange device. He looked on with anticipation, always loving science and all of the high-tech gadgetry that came from it.

Tessa wanted to act, but Thomas stopped her by placing one hand on her shoulder, and his other finger across his lips to shush her, and then he cupped his ear, while pointing to the room below. She gave him the thumbs-up signal to show her understanding. Both of the underground, abolitionist agents sat listening carefully, as they continued watching through the grate of the giant ventilation tube.

General Brague paced the open spaces of the control room. "Are you all set to go Doc?" He asked speaking about their upcoming journey to the Crystal Continent.

"My cargo is being placed in the shuttle, as we speak, and the droids are untethered from the system, so they're ready to go. However," he continued after a brief pause, lifting his eyebrow and tipping his line of vision towards his other partner. "I think that I will leave Mathias, here with you, Rudy, to continue helping with the mapping and any other, what not, that may come up." After his statement, Doc Grimes continued to look Rudy in the eye and then finally asked, "How would you feel about that?"

COGNIZANT

"Oh, that would be great," Rudy answered. Then grabbing the elderly man's hand and shaking it excitedly he said, "you're a life saver, I really appreciate it." Rudy, now only needed one more thing, so he turned toward General Brague, knowing that he not only wanted to use the gate in the daylight, but also at night. In fact, he wanted to start sending search parties, and once he found Travis, maybe they could start sending regular expeditions, so he needed more people. "John, I'm still expecting a few guards, so that we can put more effort into this situation, and I'll probably need another science team, or maybe some professional big game hunters. You *know* what I mean?" Rudy asked making sure that he and the General were on the same page.

"Yes, yes, Rudy." General Brague answered happily, knowing that he had already planned how he would invade this new dimension. "You don't have a worry. My men will stay with you for now, so you can get started. Moreover, after we get back and situate things, I'll be coming back. We'll get whomever we see fit."

Rudy, after thinking for a few seconds, shot a stern look towards the General. "Look," he said with his index finger pointing at his former leader. "I want full control over this gate, until I get Travis back, and that means, I will tell you what I need, and you will get it to me. You can stay and take care of your affairs in An'non from the Crystal Continent, as I will be expecting to keep charge over my affairs, until then. Think about it. I not only have an entire world to search. I also plan on, making tweaks to the gate, which will make it more and more useful. I envision the ability to move throughout our own planet utilizing a similar version of this gate. So, as you can see, my plate is full right now." Rudy's busy mind kept whirling with all of the endless possibilities that he may be able to invent with his new technology. He figured that he could live three lifetimes, and still not have the time to finish them all.

General Brague hated being told how to act, especially by a mere scientist, but he really liked the ideas that Rudy was spitting out. Instead of starting in with his usual disgruntled word game, he decided to keep things upbeat, saying, "If you can make any of the variations that you have spoken of, I will make sure that you have anything you need. Rudy, anything." The General said reassuringly.

"Let's get this underway." Doc Grimes snapped. His old voice nearly crackled with impatience. He was sick of waiting, and wanted to, not only, get the demise of Blak over with, but also, he wished to get off this island of his banishment.

Thomas and Tessa looked at each other questioningly, each of them wondering just what it was that the blue light gizmo did. They continued watching intently, as General Brague waved his hand signaling someone over. A moment later, a very large man dressed in military garb walked across the room from some place out of view. Reaching out with one strong hand, the dark-skinned soldier grabbed the ex-Field Marshal up by the scruff of his neck, raising him to his unstable feet. Then, the hard foot thumps of a huge droid echoed through the ventilation shaft. The droid stood several inches taller than the soldier and looked even more menacing.

COGNIZANT

The droid injected ex-Field Marshal Blak with some kind of drug. In fact, it appeared to Thomas that the needle came right from inside the droid's finger. He rubbed his tired eyes to see if this was some kind of illusion, but it was not. This is by far the most sophisticated droid that he had ever laid his eyes upon. The needle penetrated the neck of the nearly comatose man, and soon thereafter, the man began inhaling violently, as if he had been holding his breath for a long time, or surfaced from being deep under the water.

Blak's mind became completely conscious, all at once, and his body, totally revitalized. He began looking around knowing that he had been defeated, but still trying to gain knowledge of his surroundings. Then it came to him. He remembered everything. One of his oldest colleagues had betrayed him. His men got ambushed and killed, and here he stood, before the very device, which somehow is the new technology that had ended his reign. It appeared to be just a strange light.

He gazed deeply into the blue hue of the trans-dimensional gate, but he had no idea of what it could do. "That is what you used to get rid of those mutt cadet want-a-bes. You also killed some of my Death Squad with it," he spit out like a frothing dog. In his enraged state of mind, he had run out of breath, so he inhaled deeply to catch a large enough breath, so that he could tell Brague just what he thought of him. His utterance however, was short-lived. By the time he had barely begun to spit out one more syllable, the large soldier had cupped his mouth with extreme pressure. Only a muffled sound could escape the grasp of Big-Times large hands.

Thomas and Tessa had heard the fate of their boys, but they were in no position to make a move as of yet, so they sat patiently, in hopes of seeing exactly how this light gizmo works.

Rudy could see that a scuffle could erupt at any moment, so he pointed over to Dr. Sung, who immediately took control of the trans-dimensional gate. With the twist of a few knobs and the punching of a few buttons, the gateway turned to the shimmering soothing hue of the internal gate's workable state. As if he had already been instructed, right on cue, Big-Time lifted Blak up in the air, via his grasp upon the former leader's head.

Big-Time walked near the gate, and with a thrust, he tossed Blak into the light and through the gate. Once Blak flew into the gate, the entire group turned their eyes towards a specific view screen, where they could all see the cursing of the vehement Blak, as first he kicked and fought. Then, just as suddenly, he calmed as the state of confusion set in, and began looking around, unable to figure out where he was, or where his captors had gone.

The group all chuckled with relief, as they watched Blak's figure in the darkness of a Xibalbian night. "Well, that pithy worm is gone." Doc Grimes commented, smiling greatly with relief.

Thomas and Tessa both looked at each other wide-eyed with shocking wonder. They needed to figure out where that light sent people, and if they could escape from it. Tessa was nearly in tears. At first, she thought the worst, but then she realized that the scientists could see, and for that matter, were still watching Blak, so

COGNIZANT

now she knew that the light was not used as a killing device.

The ex-Field Marshal Blak found his balance and noticed that he was in some sort of sand. The smell in the air reminded him of sulfur, mixed with rotting flesh, so he took in a deep breath to test his first conclusion, and then realized that it was correct.

The night was very dark, and he knew that the first thing that he must do is take cover. He also realized that if the smell of rotting flesh was in the air, then that meant there were others about. He quickly traveled across the open plane, hoping to reach some type of shelter. He could hear a sound rising from the distance, so he quickened his pace, in hopes of securing at the very least a spot at which to overlook, whatever was making the distant thundering noise.

ROC BLISS

Black Night

His skin pricked up with goose bumps, as the eerie sound crested the hill behind him. He turned to look, but he could not quite make out what was coming at such a distance in the blackness. All that he could make out were many forms moving toward his location, so he turned and began to sprint, hoping to put some distance between himself, and the unknown group.

The mass of zombies were reacting to the last sounding. The sounding was of the highest threshold. It put them at their all-out nastiest disposition. They knew that they must protect the master in the only way they knew, and once they crested the hill, and got a whiff of blood, their fanatic groans turned into shrieks of blood lust. They ran at full speed, which was as fast as they could run, before becoming the undead,

COGNIZANT

however, now that they are of the undead, tiring is no longer an issue.

The horde had turned into a long stream with the most elite flowing ahead of the rest of the pack. They closed in upon the only fleshling within immediate sight. The undead Master Sgt. Compkil led the way. His speed was much faster than that of the other zombies. His uniform was a bit tattered yet still recognizable.

Within minutes, Blak could feel the rumbling of the ground beneath his feet, as the upcoming horde began closing the gap between them. Blak began sprinting, but no matter how fast he ran, he could not gain any ground. In fact, he kept losing it, and it was not long before his tired, out of breath, body began slowing. Then, he concluded that his only chance would be to duck and hide, before his opponents got too close.

ROC BLISS

Black Night

He watched as the scenery passed by him, still running. Finally, he passed by a large boulder, so he decided that it was time to make his move. He darted quickly behind the large boulder. Circling fast, he stopped knowing that he still had maybe a hundred and fifty paces upon his assailants. He tucked close to the rock and peered back, as he kneeled, hoping to catch his breath a little, while he surmised the situation.

It was very dark out, so Blak struggled to see, but he thought that he could make out the silhouette of a soldier, and not just any soldier, but one with a death squad uniform. The soldier was sprinting fast, and had a fair lead upon the rest of the pack. His first thought was that the soldier was being chased by the horde, and that it was purely a coincidence that they were running in the same direction. He

COGNIZANT

thought about calling out to the soldier, but then, he figured that he could just keep quiet, while the horde passed him by, following the grunt, and after the area cleared, he would go find some shelter.

The ex-Field Marshal actually, began grinning at his own deviousness. When suddenly, as the approaching soldier turned to start tracking toward the new scent direction, not unlike a well-trained bloodhound, Blak could see the wounds upon the soldier. These were not just minor wounds that would allow a man to sprint at full speed for a distance. These were the kind of wounds guaranteed to bleed you out.

Compkil, the zombie, never even slowed a step, upon the sight of the ex-Field Marshal. Blak, realizing the soldier had spotted him, tried to interject an order toward the bloodthirsty demon, as if he could still order the soldier around, thinking the way he had always done in the past. "Stand down, soldier!" He yelled in his gruffest of voices, but the undead soldier could only smell the luscious aroma of warm blood.

Blak knew by the lack of response, that the fight was on, and that perhaps, he had misjudged the situation. This soldier had more wrong with him than first met his eye. Blak was a strong man, and in his day, he may have been able to take Compkil, but through the last years of his life, he had been living a plush and easy lifestyle, so his abilities were lacking.

Compkil dove at Blak. It looked as if a dog were after a snack. Blak sidestepped the initial lunge, but he came back with a new reality, once he turned and saw the animalistic routine of Compkil. Compkil groaned and turned back with his teeth bared. Blak moved forward and struck the beast in the throat, expecting Compkil to feel the effect of the blow.

Compkil was slowed for a millisecond, due to the sheer force of the blow, but he was not fighting with any learned skills. His animal hunger pushed a trigger that could not be denied. His teeth sank into Blak's coat, but fortunately, for Blak, he had already begun to spin away. Compkil's teeth were unable to hit flesh. He came away with only a mouth full of military garb.

Blak began to focus very heavily upon the fight, but he was still completely unaware that even a small nibble from the zombie would turn him into one of the bloodthirsty demons. He started thinking that he still had the moves of his youth, but then just before he was about to go on the offensive, the next group of zombies poured upon him like a wave.

He was struck from behind by the first brute zombie, who dove upon the man's back. Between the force of the demon's lunge, and Blak's already occupied mind, Blak easily was plowed over, in an instant. He never even realized that he had been swarmed upon, until it was too late. In mere seconds, the brute beasts had the man shredded and consumed. His screams had died out quickly, because of the high efficiency of the zombie guardians, while on this highest of alerts from the Black Mage.

*　　　*　　　*　　　*　　　*

General Brague hung in the control room to watch the event, assuring himself that Blak's death is fact. He would not have trusted this news from another person. The scientists all stood there with their mouths gaping open, staring wide-eyed at the grizzly scene, which could only have been worse, if it would have happened in the light of day.

"Well Rudy, good luck with the search. I'll be in touch sometime on the morrow." General Brague said tipping his hat with a certain satisfaction in his smile.

Rudy looked at the gleam in the General's eye, and could not tell whether the smile was about the death of Blak, or the thought of those monsters keeping the plan for a search party on hold. Rudy nodded his understanding, and watched, as the group left out of the control room. He found himself left alone with the mercenaries that Brague had left.

Big-Time and his men stood with their heaters still pointing toward the gate, wondering if the monsters would make their way through. "Hey Doc, you did shut that thing off, didn't you?" The dark-skinned leader asked, just to see if there might be any surprises.

"Don't worry. Nothing can make it through this gate and live. There is way too much friction from being in the enclosed area." Rudy began explaining, but it seemed that the meaning was getting lost in translation, so he stopped before he put too much effort into it and sufficed with saying, "but it is inactive none the less."

"So, we can put our guns away, and we'll have no worries?" Eagle-One asked, just to make sure that there could be no misunderstanding.

"Yes," Rudy answered. "It is the outer gate in the jungle, where things can move both ways, and that is not due to go back online until the morning. We will use it to get Travis back. We'll be starting on that project at first light. You men can take the night off. We'll meet in the cafeteria, at first light."

The mercs, liking the sounds of that idea, gave Rudy a, 'thumbs-up', and all walked away smiling, and talking amongst themselves. Then Rudy turned toward the rest of his men and said, "That goes for you too. We'll give the droid here, some time to finish, and then we'll all meet in the morning to go over the plan."

The scientists had been working quite hard lately, so they were quite receptive with having a little free time. "In fact, in the morning we'll put the inner gate into position to view the same area that the outer gate is set to, and we'll be manning both gates, so let's take a night to relax."

"Alright!" Taylor spouted out quite openly, clenching his fist and swinging his arm in a victorious fashion. The island is a new place, and he wanted to do a bit of exploring. His childlike heart had him grinning from ear-to-ear, and ready to see the exotic flora in its natural habitat. "Who wants to check this place out?" He asked with his usual youthful enthusiasm. The other scientists were twice his age, and were in the same boat as Rudy. They needed some rest, so they all declined the young man's invitation. "You know, you guys are going to get old if you don't go out and have some fun. Once in a while."

Most of the other scientists could see some logic in his statement, but they had been worked like dogs for many long years, and they quite honestly already felt old. "Never forget that curiosity is what killed the cat." Dr. Sung said reminding him of another saying that was widely believed.

COGNIZANT

"Sung is that your old man's way out?" Taylor asked trying to cut on him a little, but his smile gave away his joking disposition. "Don't worry. I won't hold it against you. I just haven't seen a place like this, so I want to take a little stroll to take it in. That's all." He finished, explaining his real intentions. Then he surveyed the room to see, if there was anything that he needed to wait for, or to take with him on his way out. It was a last attempt stall tactic, in hopes that one of his cohorts would join him. He could see that there were still no takers, so he flipped them the peace sign and turned on his way.

Before the young man could get through the door, Rudy interjected him with a not so subtle reminder. "You only have a couple hours, 'til morning, but they're yours to enjoy as you will,

just don't fall asleep out in the bush."
Rudy warned.

Taylor pointed at him and acknowledging said, "Gotcha chief," knowing full well that he could look around for at least an hour, and then catch a few hours shut-eye, before morning found them all back in their spots awaiting orders.

Thomas and Tessa watched the entire situation, as it unfolded. They kept their positions silently, until finally, all of the scientists had left the area. They never could view the computer screen, so they did not know what actual fate had befallen Blak, but they did understand his final outcome.

They also knew that their boys had somehow ended up through that gateway, believing the girls to be dead from the bombing. Now, the coast was clear, except for the one droid, which

COGNIZANT

was busy mapping the area on the other side of the gate.

Tessa believed that the droid was just a subservient tool and could not determine, whether, or not, voices that it might hear were of friendlies, so she looked at Thomas saying, "we gotta get outside and snag that kid scientist. He'll be an easy mark to get information from." Thomas nodded in agreement and then began moving. He moved forward through the air tunnel, which led them deeper into the building. Tessa did not like the move, so she tapped him on the shoulder. He turned to see what it was that she wanted. "We should go back the way we came, and catch the kid outside." She said pointing back with her thumb.

Thomas rolled his eyes, thinking, 'here we go again'. Tessa always came up with fair plans, but he felt that their cause would be best served by taking over the facility. "Look here. We need to control this," he said pointing toward the trans-dimensional gate. "We cannot allow Brague to figure this thing out. Right now, it appears that he had made some concessions with the scientists, but in a short amount of time, he'll control everything. You *know* how he is."

"Yes, I do." Tessa stated in a matter of fact way. "I also know that these scientists are weak, and if I slip out, grab the kid, and use him for leverage, we will control this *entire* facility." She stared at Thomas for some sort of reassurance. He seemed to be debating her idea in his mind. She immediately began to worry, but instead of breaking down with tears, she began to anger.

"Hey, these bastards killed my girls, and then sent the boys to who knows where. I will not sit here and think out the least violent plan, so you had better get it in your head that I will take over this place in a less than subtle way." A few tears finally began to surface, showing Thomas that he had better allow her to do as she will, or else she would resist him on every step.

"Okay," he said answering her. "You slip out and get that kid. Then bring him back to the beachhouse. Link me when you have your objective completed, meanwhile I'll be working this end. By morning we should be the ones running this show."

"What are you going to do?" Tessa asked curiously in a somewhat excited tone, staring deeply into his piercing eyes. She loved the way he looked when he was detailing a plan.

Then Thomas gave her that look, his schoolboy look, and when she saw it, she knew instantly that he was not giving anything away. In reality, he knew that he would be improvising, and playing on any opportunity coming his way, but he would never let on to that, and as far as he knew, she had no realization of the fact, so he just played it cool. "Well, you know I always do my best work with you babe, but I think you're right. Grabbing the young scientist is crucial. If you can do that, and I can get to the leader of this group, we'll have a real possibility of getting our boys back."

After Thomas' statement, he could see a look in her eyes. It was almost impossible to resist. He could see that she was yearning to be close with him, but this was not the place, or time. Against his better judgment, he pulled her close and planted his lips to hers. She cleaved to him with her strong embracing arms. Her emotional tide

COGNIZANT

began rising with every, nearly
panting, breath.

Thomas whispered in her ear, and
the feel of his warm, moist breath sent
her over the edge. At this point her
appetite would *not* take no for an
answer. It was too late. She was past
the point of no return. She pulled him
down to the tunnel's walkway,
receiving no resistance from her
longtime partner. This moment was
theirs, in the darkness of a shadowy,
dust ridden, dirty tunnel with time of
the essence and danger running high,
the two soulmates made love with
artistic precision, flowing with
romance and passion. Their
surroundings melted into a dreamscape
that intertwined their minds with their
deepest emotional connections, and
transformed it into a place where
dreams come true.

ROC BLISS

Assume Control

Vail was physically tired from the long day. On the surface, she thought that it was very fulfilling. She had gotten the chance to help save her people, at least for another day, but more importantly, she had reestablished her relationship with her Queen.

Somewhere, however, rumbling through the back recesses of her mind, things just did not seem to be sitting well. It just was not enough. She and her tribe were not made to run and hide, living in the shadows of fear. As her and Travis lay in her cave, upon the bed of furs, her deeper thoughts began surfacing.

COGNIZANT

She knew that as long as the evil wizard lived, and the wicked city still stood, her Queen and all of their tribe would always be in danger. She grabbed Travis and pulled him in close, as if somehow his presence, his touch, would ease her mind.

Travis kissed her full on the mouth. She kissed him back. He could tell that her heart was troubled, and that her forced passion was stuck on simmer, so he asked her what was preoccupying her mind at such a time, a time that should be made for celebrating. "After all, you have saved the Queen, and your people." He reminded her, as if she did not realize the obvious.

Vail had many questions, so she looked Travis back in the eye and asked, "What about tomorrow? What about the rest of our time here? Are we to hide like cowards? I feel like our move was just a sideways step. I want to move forward. We used to do more farming, but the guardians are tainting more and more of the land, and the crops are getting thinner."

Travis heard her out, and surprised once again by her forethought, he began thinking of how many times that he had underestimated her mental prowess. 'A day ago, Vail had saved my life. Then, she interrogates me, while showing me that she is some type of cave woman, perhaps as paranoid as she is hot, but still, she seemed to be some type of Huntress, dressed in those furs. Then I find out that she is a guard, and now it seems that she should be an advisor to her Queen'.

He debated about her exact thoughts for just a moment or two, before realizing that the girl is fully geared up in her mind, to slaughter those beasts. He pulled her back close to him, as they spooned naturally in her bed of furs. Whispering in her ear, he asked, "Why don't you come home with me? You'll never have to worry about these beasts."

Vail smiled at the question. Her back was resting against his chest, so he could not see her happiness, but now, she knew that he would not just disappear at any given moment. A feeling of security that she had not had in a very long time began to settle in her mind, but she also knew that she could not turn her back on her people, not when they need her most. "What about my people?" She asked. "Am I to leave them to fend for themselves? No, I don't think that I could just walk away." Vail said answering honestly, not realizing the effect, it would have on Travis.

Assume Control

Travis had hoped that she would be a little more open to his idea, but then a stray thought occurred to him. He had an idea that could possibly change everything for him, the realization that he actually sat in a position of power. In fact, he had the chance to use a side of a relationship that he would have never even dreamed possible. He could now have the upper hand, because he is in this crazy land, where men carry a woman's status, and every man knows that women have a certain knack for playing men and getting their own way.

Now, all he had to do is devise a plan, and it will start by him rolling over with his back to her. He rolled over with a sounding, "Hmph," to show that he had some serious disagreements with her way of thinking. He was so excited to be on the flip side of the coin that he could barely contain himself. Travis finally had to bury his face into the furs to hide his smirk, while he thought of how to manipulate Vail into doing exactly what he wanted.

Vail could not help but to notice Travis's display of emotion. Though she had not known him very long, she had not seen this side of him yet. She thought that he seemed much more feminine than that. In fact, if she were not so tired, she may have thought about asking him about his little noise, but after the day she has had, she did not want to waste her energy on something so trivial, 'besides', she thought, 'Tomorrow will be yet another long, hard, day'. She fell asleep in seconds, leaving Travis wondering in his mind, whether, or not, she had noticed his little display, but his final thoughts, before drifting off to sleep, were of time, and the possibility that time may just be on his side, and he would have plenty of time to work his plan.

*   *   *   *   *

With a long passionate kiss, Tessa parted from Thomas, leaving him in the air tunnels over the science labs. After backtracking her way out of the building, she crept near the outer perimeter, lurking in the darkest of shadows, and keeping out of sight, while listening intently to the loud clumsy pattering of the young scientist. She could not see him yet, but she knew that there would be no other person bumbling about in the darkness of the jungle. Staying low, she crept toward the sounds of the unsuspecting man.

Taylor walked around the outer edge of the main grounds, being sure to stay near the facility, stopping every

COGNIZANT

so often to peer out into the dark and mysterious jungle, as if he could hear or see something out of the ordinary. The truth is that he would not know what out of the ordinary is, so he did not venture beyond the more easily traveled ground.

Grabbing a leaf from a tree and sniffing it, made him realize that he had been working in the basement of the old science lab for *way* too long. He began rubbing the leaf against the skin of his face, and could not believe how he had been missing the scent of nature's seemingly perfected systems. Then taking a few steps back, trying to soak it all in, with his gazing eyes, he flung his head back to look for the stars in the sky. The twinkling sparkles of light, shone down upon the man, as he inhaled deeply trying to become one with nature.

ROC BLISS

Assume Control

Tessa had never seen such easy prey. This young scientist stood clueless of her presence. She slowly crept across an open stretch of ground, hidden only by the darkness. 'Perhaps, I'm being too cocky', she thought questioning herself, 'but still, this self-absorbed male has no clue of my presence', silently answering herself, so she continued straightaway across the spanse of open ground, until she crouched not more than two feet behind Taylor.

Pointing her heater towards the man, she swiftly overtook him, wrapping one arm around his neck, while her other hand held her blaster up to his temple. She wanted him to feel it, so that he would not put her through the struggle of dragging his unconscious body all of the way to the beachhouse. As she put the moves on Taylor, she pulled him back forcing him off balance, knowing that this would be the easiest way to get his full understanding.

The whole scene felt like a blur to the young scientist. One minute Taylor was tipping his head back taking in the view of the stars. The next, he suddenly felt wrapping arms jerk and pull his head backwards. Having no time to react, he felt himself slam onto the ground, forcing him to lose his breath.

Tessa quickly prodded the young scientist with her side arm, so that he knew it would not be worth putting up a fight. "What's the matter? Did you get the wind knocked out of you?" Tessa asked with a taunting tone. However, she did not intend to taunt the man. It just came out that way. "Look, if you do as I say, then I promise that you will not be harmed in any way."

Assume Control

Taylor looked up at the beautiful middle-aged woman, who was placing the barrel of her heat blaster to his head. He was still trying to force his lungs to take in oxygen, so he held up one finger in hopes of signaling her to give him a minute.

"Yeah, you just get the wind back in your sails, and then we'll begin. I just want to explain to you what your part in this will be. You are my leverage." She began explaining. She also could hear his gasps, as he finally began breathing again. The first few were choppy and forced, but within a minute, he could once again breathe quite regularly. "We need to use that gate. I don't know where you sent our boys to, but I'm here to recover them. That's it. Now, get up and walk, and believe me when I tell you that if you give me any trouble, I won't hesitate to use certain measures that you would not appreciate, got me!" She barked, finally raising her voice for the first time.

"Yes ma'am," Taylor responded, as he continued to walk in whatever direction that she decided.

'Yes, ma'am', she thought to herself. 'I must be getting old. I can't be that much older than this guy, maybe ten years or so'. Tessa debated about these things, only because she felt as though there was no threat, and she did not need to concentrate on tough objectives. She was in the home stretch, as they headed easily towards the beachhouse. She figured it was the least she could do for the young man, let him enjoy some beautiful natural scenery.

Thomas Elliot worked his way through the huge air circulation tubes. He moved silently towards his destination, figuring that the scientists were dead tired, and he had plenty of time. After peering out many vents, Thomas noticed a familiarity in the design of the labs. They seemed to be like the ones at the Crystal Academy. He had been in those labs on several occasions and was somewhat familiar with their layout, so he did not have too much trouble finding his way to the junction that led to the living quarters.

Thomas could hear snoring coming through the vents. He smirked to himself, thinking that this would be easier than he ever thought possible. The rooms were dark and dingy, looking as if they had been left unoccupied for many years. Thomas knew that he would have to climb out of the air tube at some point, so believing that he was in the right vicinity, he climbed out of a vent into the stall of a bathroom, which was in the hallway near the living quarters.

COGNIZANT

He popped out the vent cover and
quietly stepped out onto the top of a
toilet. After carefully replacing the
vent cover back to its original location,
he stepped lightly down from the tank
onto the floor of the stall. Thomas
listened cautiously at the door, before
opening it and peeking. The coast was
clear, so moving into the hallway, he
began searching the rooms, starting
with one of the snoring men, but he
soon found that this was not the man in
charge, so he kept moving.

Then a scent sifted through the air
and into his nostrils. It was a familiar
smell, but in the musty old side of the
facility, his nose was not quite on.
Following the fragrance, Thomas found
himself at a door. Carefully he turned
the knob, trying not to make a sound.
The pungent smell hit him like a wave,
and then he knew exactly what caused

the fragrance. Somebody had been smoking some herbs, recently.

Thomas stopped in his tracks, standing in the middle of the doorway debating whether, or not he should even be doing the walk through on this room. In the end, he figured, if for no other reason, it would be a room that he would not have to check later. Lightly walking across the room, he made his way to the partially open bedroom door. He peered in, but it was dark and he could not see, so he continued pressing on cautiously. A moment later, he was right next to the bed, where the man slept.

Much to Thomas's disliking, the man was sleeping with his pillow directly over his head, covering his face completely. Thomas frowned at the situation for a second, but he knew that he would have to lift the pillow up, hopefully without waking the man.

COGNIZANT

Thomas pulled out his moleculitic stunner just in case the man decided to wake up on him. He knew that it would render the man into a state of stupor for a short period. Thomas moved right next to the bed and leaning over, he reached down. Peering under, as he began lifting the pillow ever so gently, Thomas strained his keen eyes to see the man's identity in the dark dank room. With the pillow gripped in one hand, and the stunner in the other, Thomas kept peeling the pillow away. Finally, he could see the man's face, and to his relief, he had found the leader of this facility. Thomas turned to put the pillow aside, and just as he began setting it down his com-unit blurped from an incoming link.

"Thomas, I have made my destination with the package at hand. All is well." Tessa called out.

ROC BLISS

Assume Control

Thomas's heart almost leaped right out of his chest from the sudden unexpected com-link. Rudy began stirring, but he did not wake up fully. It was more like his subconscious mind heard the noise, but it could not bring him to consciousness. Thomas had his thumb, standing ready on the stunner's trigger, then noticed that the man rolled slightly with a dim sounding grunt, and then lay there motionless, still sound asleep. He knew then just how tired this man must surely be, so he let the man rest, so that he could talk to Tessa. "Tess, I'm at my mark, but I forgot to silence my com-link. This guy is so tired that I'm sitting on the edge of his bed talking to you, and he's still sleeping."

"Did you stun him Thomas?" Tessa asked curiously.

"No, no I ah, well, I about had a damn heart attack, when the com-unit linked, but no, he rolled over a slight bit and that's it, so I decided just to sit here with the stunner ready, and talk to you." Thomas explained, while regaining his faculties.

"Okay," Tessa replied. "I just wanted to check in and say all is a go here. I am at the requested location with the package, who, by the way, is now, also sound asleep."

"Alright, secure the package and get some rest. I'll be linking with you before morning light." With that being said, Thomas cut the link, believing that Tessa would do as she was told, so now, he can start working his magic.

Thomas looked down at the sleeping man, and thought about the boys for a moment. It was enough motivation for him to do what needed to be done. He had no real grudge against this scientist, so he secured the man, while he slept. Thomas stood grinning when he was done. He had no clue what part this man played in the boy's disappearance, so he decided that an interrogation would be the first order of business. He shook the man awake, which was no easy task.

"What, who are you?" Rudy finally asked in his bleary state. He wished he could rub his eyes to help get some focus, but when he went to move his arms, he realized that he had been tied to his bed. "Why did you do this? What do you want?" Rudy asked questions, but Thomas did not respond.

"Well, I'm glad you could join me in the conscious world. I will be the one asking the questions, if you don't mind. Let me start right out with, we have the young man, who wanted to go for a walk. We don't want to hurt anyone, so don't worry. As long as you do as I say, he will be fine. You don't have much time, so you are going to tell me about sending a group of young cadets through your device."

"It was an accident. You see, we had our outer gate on and they somehow accidentally must have been traveling in the area, and well, one second they were here, and the next they were gone." Rudy explained without hesitation. "We saw them on our computer screen, but we had no one in the area. In fact, I had one of my men get accidentally sucked into the other dimension, and I am still planning on a search party, which we will be starting come first light."

Thomas could tell, between what he had overheard and what the man was telling him that it was the truth, so he began to ease up from going where he might have had to, if the man were playing dumb. "Okay, I like honesty, so I'm going to tell you some truth. I have no want to hurt you, or your man Taylor, but I have seven young men that have made their way through that little blue light of yours, and I want them back, alive and well. I know that Brague and Blak have been after my boys for quite some time, and now I see that you have some form of traveling device. You've mentioned the word dimension, so I take it that this device is something new and still in its experimental stages, so, just where did you send my boys to, anyway?"

Rudy had no clue about seven young men, but he realized that he was only lucky to see the four that he had seen go through that outer gate, so he figured that this military man knew his facts and did not question them. "Honestly sir, I don't have a name for the place. I just have numbered coordinates, which are settings on the machine, and would probably not have any real meaning to you. They are definitely in a parallel dimension, and yes, it was supposed to be in its experimental stages of testing only, but then, Travis had gotten knocked through, and until yesterday, we could not bring anything back in one piece, but we now feel that it is safe. We have a droid mapping the area, so that our search parties shouldn't get lost."

"That does make some sense," Thomas agreed. "If we aren't in our dimension, then we won't have any satellite communication, so then we'd have no G.P.S. service." Thomas stated using basic logic. "It could be like going back in time a thousand years or more."

"There's more," Rudy admitted, not quite fully coherent. "There are some types of monsters that eat humans. They look human-ish, but they are like wild animals. One of them came through the outer gate and killed one of my men. I was there, so I killed the thing, but the weird thing is that my guy, who had died turned into one of those things, so he too had to be killed. That is why we are waiting for first light. We don't want to be easy prey."

Thomas scratched the back of his head a little, while listening to the scientist's wild claims, wondering if all of this crazy story could be true. Could there really be some kind of monsters? Then Thomas made the decision to stick to a plan of action and thought, 'In a way, it really don't matter, as long as things go the way I want'. Knowing that now is the time to set the ground rules, so that both men can come to some kind of understanding, Thomas began speaking, saying, "well sir, it all sounds too wild to be made up, and seeing that you are starting a search party in the morning, we may already be on the same page. You will not be getting your man back, until I recover my boys. You will also be reporting to me on a regular basis to keep me informed. I will let you talk to your man, to assure you that we are on the up and up, but I am warning you, my partners are far less patient than I am, so I would suggest total honesty and a full debriefing upon my request. I've already took the liberty of coding your com-unit to reach me, so you can fill me in at your convenience. However, I want to execute this search process. How big is the team that'll be going in?" Thomas asked trying to get some particulars.

Rudy tried sitting up, but the ropes held him fast to the bed. The cobwebs still tangled in his mind from major mental fatigue that he was enduring after his premature awakening. Then sudden pressures set in upon the forefront of his mind that he could not ignore. "Uh, I have to use the bathroom. Is there any chance that I could use the toilet?" He asked hoping for a quick answer.

Thomas reached down and untied the ropes, which bound the man to the bed. Then he pulled the man up to his feet by his still tethered arms, quickly cutting Rudy's feet from their bindings. Thomas already feeling as though this working relationship could work, wasted no time pulling the man down the hall to the very bathroom in which he had slipped in through. He knew that there was only one way out other than the door and that was through the air vent, so he continued walking through the multi-stalled bathroom with his stunner held to Rudy's neck, making a general sweep of all the stalls to clear the room, before making an offer to the scientist. "Okay Rudy, I want your word that if I cut your ties that you won't force my hand into doing something drastic."

Rudy not intending to do anything other than draining his bladder, began assuring his captor, saying, "It's okay. I understand how you feel, in a way. Travis is just a kid, not any older than Taylor. He got knocked into the gate during the storm, trying to save my life from a falling limb, so he really isn't my boy, but he has certain son like qualities that I admire."

Thomas peered intently upon Rudy's pupils, as he spoke. It seemed to be a truthful statement, so he cut the man's bonds and allowed him to use a stall, not the stall near the vent, but another. He may trust the man, but he would never jeopardize his mission by being lazy at his job. "Just so you know. If I don't link in on regular intervals my team will come storming in, and let's just say that things won't be pretty," Thomas reiterated, forewarning the man.

Rudy was so tired that he just sat on the stool to drain his bladder. "Well, you don't have to worry about me," he said assuringly. "Half the time, I feel like sending Brague through the gate and then blowing it up, but then again, he is a pain in my ass. He's been driving me and my team like slave workers, getting all of the parts that I need to help me rush to this point, as fast as we did, so that he could abuse my invention." Rudy caught himself getting long-winded, so he cut off his explanation saying, "Anyway, to keep a long story from getting any longer, you don't have to worry about me."

"Good. I'm glad to hear that. Brague and Blak have been targeting all ethnics for as long as I can remember. Then he began targeting my boys for the last year. I thought that I had outsmarted him, but it seems that he still accomplished his goal." Thomas confessed.

"Heck, he outsmarted Blak too." Rudy said hoping to soften the fact that Thomas is not the only one, who Brague had fooled. Then he thought that it was time to tell his captor, just who, he is holding captive, "Just so you know, I am one of the three leaders of the Crystal Continent right now. We are going to change the government from one military leader, to a three-part system. Doc Grimes went to the mainland with Johnny Brague to take control over the Crystal Offices."

Thomas Elliot stood in disbelief. Here he is, having one of the most powerful men in the entirety of An'non under his thumb in a blackmail scheme. "Well sir, I hope that once this is all over that you won't hold my actions against me. I hope you'll be doing away with the two classes of citizens, and you're not one of these purists."

Rudy stepped out of the bathroom stall looking Thomas right in the eye, and said point-blank, "I don't believe that Brague is going to get my permission to thump innocent people. That's why I blackmailed my way out of the Death Squad." Rudy was not used to hearing anti-puristic speeches from people whose skin color would allow them the perks of purism, so he started to connect the dots between the boys that Brague had been after and this man who stood in front of him. "You must be the one that I've heard about." Rudy said upon making the connection. "You are the leader of those ethnic cadets. Aren't you?"

"Yes, if I can get these boys back, and have them instated, as top agents, who graduate with honors, then there will be hope for the entire ethnic people. It will be a first step in the fight for equality." Thomas gave away his stance in hopes that Rudy being a scientist, who blackmailed Blak, or maybe even Fletcher, and got away with it, would not be as prejudiced as your normal military man. It also made him wonder if the evidence that the boys had come up with were from this man's room.

Rudy held his wrists out. "Do you want to retie them?" He asked trying not to over step his boundary. "We really don't need to stand here talking in the bathroom."

"No, I feel that we have an understanding. Let's head back to your quarters. It won't be long before Polaris pops up and spreads its warm light upon the new day, so we might just as well go over the plan for the day." Thomas said, giving the man more leeway, not only because, he knew the importance of Rudy's newly gained political position, but also, he mainly believed that this indeed is a man, who sees people as people, and not as color classified status units.

The two men walked back to the room and took a seat. An old coffee table became their desktop, as they hashed and rehashed ideas, until they seemed more like a team, than two opposing forces. Once both men felt satisfied with the plan for the day, they sat back to relax for a moment.

Rudy checking his chronometer noticed that he still had some time before he had to go down to meet with the rest of his group, so with oversight by Thomas, he opened one of the old table's drawers. Rudy reached in and pulled out a fair sized sealed plastic bag, and after opening it, he began filling his favorite pipe with herbs.

COGNIZANT

Thomas chuckled upon seeing this. He had forgotten all about the scent that he had smelled prior to entering the room. "Do you smoke?" Rudy asked, as he offered the pipe to Thomas.

Thomas took the pipe, and took a couple of puffs and then inhaled deeply. "It's quite tasty." He announced after exhaling.

"Yeah, I usually always get this brand, but sometimes I get a wild hair up my ass, and I change up." Rudy admitted.

"Well apparently, I don't change up enough. I always get the same. It's something you can count on. You know, the taste, the smoke, and the way it affects you. It's all steady and trustworthy, not at all like it used to be when it was illegal. You remember those days, don't you?" Thomas asked matter of factly.

Assume Control

"Oh do I. I had to grow my own, just so that I could trust what I was getting. Things have come a long way over the years, even with men like Blak in charge. Some things move constantly forward, while others take steps back. I hope to change that cycle. If we can keep a three-tiered government, where each of the tiers is equal, then that should help to stabilize control, instead of everything changing willy-nilly every few years." Rudy felt a certain kinship with Thomas. They had the same goals, and Thomas seemed to be just the military mind that he needed to conduct the search.

"Yes, and with Johnny Brague as one of the three, you can bet that world domination won't be far away. Maybe that will stabilize the entire planet's economy. We just have to hope that he doesn't try to off the other three fourths of the people with his purist beliefs." Thomas added, showing his true feelings for the man.

"Well, you know he is replaceable, in fact, we all are. That is another part of a structured government that seems appealing." Rudy threw out there for Thomas to think about. Then after checking his chronometer Rudy said, "Alright, it is time to go meet the guys, and get this show on the road," as he stood up ready to walk for the door.

Thomas could have served up a threatening reminder, but he felt that it would be a backwards step in this working relationship, so he chose to salute the man instead. He allowed Rudy to leave unmonitored, knowing that he still held the leverage, which insured the man's cooperation. He could tell that Rudy could hardly stand to lose the man Travis, and he would not risk losing another by being stubborn, after his loss of the man Zane.

Thomas waited in Rudy's room and after a moment, he linked with Tessa. "Tessa, all systems are, 'go'. I am leading the search for the boys… Uhhh, that is, after a few tests are performed to make sure that this crazy contraption can do what it is supposed to do."

"Okay Thomas, I have Taylor secured. I hope that I don't have to stay on the sidelines and babysit," she quickly interjected to make it plain that she needed some action. "Do you know he called me, 'ma'am'? It's like I'm getting old," Tessa complained, before going silent, hoping for Thomas to make a statement, to see if he thought she was showing signs of aging too.

Thomas knew that he had better reassure her, and the beauty of it all

COGNIZANT

was that he did not even have to tell her one lie. "Babe, you know that you are the most beautiful woman that I had ever laid eyes upon, and you've always made me the happiest man alive, but most of all, I need you for that killer instinct of yours." He listened as she laughed. He could hear that tone in her laughter, the one that told him that she knew he needed her to watch his back, so he continued, "I'm thinking that you should bring the young man back here. Bring him back through the jungle. You must be careful though. There will be men out there, and worse. There is also one of those light machines out there. I'll send you its coordinates, so you know where to avoid. There's no hurry, so get some chow and then make your way here. If I get worried, I'll link you."

Tessa was satisfied with the quick complements, and she knew Thomas needed her protection, so she felt relieved that Thomas asked her back to the science facility. She wanted to be close to Thomas, figuring that it would be good for him, if she was there protecting him, but she had also discovered what a wonderful droid cook Alphie could be, and the aroma that filled the air surrounding her, called out for some help of its own. "Oh Thomas, you know I love you, and if it is as you say, then we'll let Alphie cook us a big breakfast, and then get under way."

Thomas sighed deeply, as he exhaled, making it sound as if she were asking a lot. Then, in an attempt to create a little tension, he paused allowing a few tics to pass in silence, before finally speaking. "Well, I have been debating over a couple of options on which way to go with my plan, but I guess that I could afford to let you get

COGNIZANT

a little rest and a good meal. In fact, link me before you leave. There may be a third possibility."

Tessa feeling the tension in Thomas's voice, could not understand what could be weighing on his mind so deeply, unless it was some sort of bad news about the boys. She was beginning to find herself lost with sudden questions, so she decided to get those coordinates from him, before ending the com-link, and make a plan of her own.

Rudy slowly made his way down the corridor, slipping into the cafeteria unseen. As usual, he was the first to arrive. He got his usual milky coffee with breakfast, as he sat at a table and pondered his new situation. He had to wonder, whether, or not, to turn the intruder into his new security detail. He debated it, as he sipped at his piping hot coffee, weighing the pros and cons of the situation.

By the time Rudy had finished his first cup of coffee, he had decided to play according to Thomas' plan. His reasons included for one, the risk of Taylor's life, but there also seemed to be an actual, mutual feeling, between this man and himself. They each wanted to get people back from that other dimension. Apparently, the man had plans, and the ability to use military style logic to solve strategies.

Rudy giggled a bit at the thought of someone, actually having the balls to pop into a secure facility, and basically, take it over without any big visual movements. In fact, Rudy thought, the only real sign of anything out of the ordinary is that Taylor won't be there for the beginning of the search, but he had a cover story, which would get him through at least one day, before the rest of the crew would start getting suspicious. Taylor wasn't one for getting ill, but just because he isn't the type does not mean that it would be impossible, 'besides', he thought, 'that dumb bastard went out in the jungle alone last night. Heck, he could have got some type of jungle fever, or something.'

Just then, Rudy's thoughts were suddenly pushed away, as Dr. Sung walked in and after not seeing Taylor, surveyed the room with scrutiny. Taylor took over being the early bird, sitting with Rudy in the early hours of the morning, since Travis had passed through the gate. "Did Taylor oversleep?" He finally inquired, after remembering that the young man had went for a stroll, when the rest had decided to sleep.

"No," Rudy answered directly. "I think he walked into something that he is allergic to, or something. The boy looked so bad that I told him to get some more rest." Then Rudy picked up his coffee and took a sip. "Ahh," he sighed airily exhaling the heat of his coffee, as he enjoyed its flavor.

Sung thought about it, as he went to the food conveyor to retrieve his breakfast. Then he walked back to sit with Rudy. "I guess he is the curious cat after all, aye?" He said with a slight nuance of dry humor, referring to the statement he had made prior to Taylor going on his stroll.

Rudy acknowledged the joke, but without any heavy motions. He wasn't the type to get over enthused with subtle jokes. He was more concerned with getting the search underway.

COGNIZANT

The Search

Kilari awoke. Jezza was in the midst of a bad dream. Her arms were flailing, as she tossed about the small sleeping area, moaning from fear, with sweat beading upon her forehead. Kilari woke her and calmed her, soothingly holding her close and telling her that everything will be alright. Their motion got Marcia stirring, and she too wanted some of Kilari's reassurance. They still lay next to the fire pit, as did the rest of the group. The remaining embers in the fire pit left the cave only dimly lit.

Kilari looked out through the cave's entrance from his resting position. He could see a glimmer out on the horizon, telling him that it would be light out soon. He had thoughts about what he would like to be doing with his two loves, but even if it was the time, it was definitely, not the place. There was no available privacy inside the small cave, but they had gotten lucky enough to stumble across a pile of skins to use for blankets in the back of the cave, before they all lay down. He debated in his mind, whether, or not, to bring the girls outside. 'There could be privacy to be had out there', he thought. In the end, however, he decided to just hit his main objective head on, and get prepared to go meet Cam and the rest of the group.

Jezza and Marcia were lying on each side of him. Jezza lifted her head up and winked at Marcia. Marcia got the silent signal, and nodded back smiling playfully. They both started to fondle at Kilari, who thought that he had already made up his mind about what the situation was, and how things were going to happen.

The girls started breathing with the softest, slightest moans, into Kilari's ears. The short nearly invisible hairs on Kilari's neck stood on end, as the goose bumps covered his semi-tan skin. He closed his eyes for a few seconds almost forgetting that the cave was quite full of people. He instantly stiffened, and then sat up rapidly, quickly, scanning the room. All of the others were still sleeping soundly.

The girls began giggling innocently, but knowing that they were just being playful, Kilari again decided to go with his first instincts, so he stood up directly. The fur blankets fell slowly down to the floor, dropping lightly upon the two wide-eyed girls, who could not control their jaw dropping stares. "See something you like," Kilari said tauntingly, as he noticed their expressions.

"Huh," Jezza finally forced from her lips.

Kilari grinned and whispered, "Grab the blankets," then he waved and said "C'mon," as he stealthily moved his way out of the cave.

Jezza and Marcia looked at one another. Marcia broke the silence, as they got to their feet with the furs in their hands. "Did you see that?" She asked with a flutter in her heart, and swooning in her mind.

"Yeah, that man is steaming hot." Jezza answered, moving quickly toward the outer world.

"He is sizzling," Marcia affirmed, following on her heels.

Kilari surveyed the area quickly, making sure that there was no enemy in sight, and once that he was satisfied that the coast was clear, he found

COGNIZANT

higher ground from which they could see the horizon, as trinkets of light dazzled its brilliance upon the rolling clouds. It was early, but he could see that the sunrise would be soon approaching.

The girls frolicked their way to his side. Marcia placed her furs across the ground at Kilari's feet. Jezza dropped the furs in her hands and wrapped her arms around her lover. She pressed her lips to his, and they kissed slowly with a flowing passion. Marcia slowly made her way up from the furs. She caressed her two loves softly, and then joined in for some sweet hot kisses. Soon the three made their way down upon the furs, where they made love in the light of the rising sun, as it poked its way over the horizon.

The sun climbed slowly up into the sky, until its bright warming light flashed across Belsangar's eyes. He slowly awakened. Then, as the cobwebs cleared, he became aware that they were still in the cave, and it was well past first light. "Shit," he muttered semi-out loud.

"What is it?" Ceilia asked, as his voice had stirred her into consciousness.

"It's past first light, and everyone is still sleeping." He said in a worried tone.

"Calm down. We had a rough couple of days. We deserve to get a good night's sleep." Ceilia answered with perfect logic.

Belsangar did not have to take a head count to notice that Kilari, Jezza and Marcia were all missing. "Where'd they go?" He asked slightly panicked.

By this time Tank had awoke, and overheard Belsangar. "Shit, he's got those two girls, where do you think he went?" He said answering for Ceilia.

"Well, let's get this show on the road," Belsangar ordered.

"Alright," Tank answered enthusiastically, but instead of acting on leaving, he grabbed Sophie and began to playfully take advantage of her.

"Uh, I don't think so," Layla said protesting.

By now, the scuffling had awakened the entire group. Most of which had sat up and gathered near the glowing embers left in the pit. Tank walked over to check the basket, wondering if there happened to be any leftovers from the previous night. As he lifted the lid, his eyes bulged in surprise. "Hey, who refilled the basket?" He asked with shock, grabbing a piece of the honey-cheese soaked bread and taking a bite. "Mmm, oh that's good."

Just then, Kilari walked in with his two girls, holding hands with each. He saw Tank with the full basket of bread and cheese, so he walked over and grabbed a piece. "That is some good stuff," he said, being that he had just finished working up an appetite. The girls placed the furs back in the spot at which they had slept.

"Where have you been?" Belsangar asked inquisitively.

Kilari thought for a quick second. "We were trying to get our bearings." He answered with a slight smirk. Most of the group either, rolled their eyes, or in a couple of the girls' instances, a slight giggle was brought forth, upon hearing his answer. Kilari could see that the entire group thought that they were out to get a few private moments.

COGNIZANT

Kilari did have to tell them that he had no clue of their whereabouts. "Well, what we do is between us, but we did scout around a bit, and I'm not positive in which direction we should travel. In fact, there are not even any footprints out there to be found. Maybe one of you guys can take a look." Kilari looked and saw Tank eating another piece of bread, so he finally asked, "Did you guys find another basket?"

"No," Tank answered. "This is the same one. I walked over to see if anything was left, and when I opened the lid, it was full."

Kilari smiled wide with disbelief at Tank, and the entire group began to wonder. Finally, Kilari looked over to Ceilia. "Did you get up early and do some baking?" He asked her sarcastically.

"No Kilari, you were the only one up early buttering muffins." She said sounding slightly disappointed that her and Belsangar had no time for a private moment.

"So, let me get this right?" Kilari asked, nearly cutting off Ceilia, as if her outburst was insignificant. "Nobody found another basket?" He asked searching the eyes of the entire group. Then he looked down and noticed the fire pit had not changed. "Wow, do you see what's going on here?" He asked in amazement. The group all looked to him with wonder, waiting for his explanation. "Look, we walked in here, and there were embers in the fire pit." Then he walked to the backroom, "And the wood was stacked back here, and last but not least a skin full of wine. Now, look at the fire, the embers are still glowing, and I'd suspect that they'll keep on glowing, indefinitely." The entire group looked down to the fire pit in awe. He moved

COGNIZANT

over to the backroom to check for wood. "See," he said. "Just as I thought, there's wood, a full pile. It's all stacked and ready to burn. Who's got the skin?" He asked looking around the cave. "Anybody?" The group all started to look around the small cave.

"There it is." Glenda pointed it out with her finger. Tank was nearest to it, so he picked it up. He attempted to meter its weight, and then he tossed it to Elle.

Elle caught the skin. She tried to measure the weight in her outstretched hand. It seemed quite hefty to her, but she was not quite sure, so she untied the skin's seal. "There's only one way to be sure." She said right before tipping the bottom of the wine sack up in the air. She took a few gulps, and then put it back down. "Oh yeah, that baby is full." She said giving them her assurance.

ROC BLISS

"It's a little early for that, isn't it?" Glenda asked with a bit of her own brand of grumpy charm.

"Who cares?" Tank threw out in her defense. "Maybe you need a few slugs too."

"Yeah," Elle added.

"Okay, settle down, let's not forget the point." Kilari reminded them. "We have been handed a serious gift, straight from the hand of Yahiveh himself. We have food, shelter, heat, and drink. Everything that we need to survive has been handed to us, and like I said, we looked around outside, and cannot figure from whence we came, or which way we should go from here. I believe that this is a serious sign telling us to hold tight for a while."

Belsangar heard and understood what Kilari was saying, but he needed to state the obvious fact. "Cam and the boys have been expecting us. He gave us specific instructions to meet him by this morning, and uh, in case you didn't notice by the time that round ball came up, we were already on the clock."

Kilari smiled at his longtime friend. "I thought you knew me. If we followed orders, where would Tank and the girls be right now?"

"Still in that wizard's cell," Belsangar admitted.

"That's right." Kilari said speaking in a condescending tone. "So, let us gather together and first give Yahiveh thanks, and then we must ask for his guiding hand to lead us to do as he would have us do." With that being said, the group circled around the glowing coals of the fire pit, all holding hands, as Kilari spoke to the one true great spirit of Yahiveh.

*　　*　　*　　*　　*

The Search

Cam and his crew had found a spot to crash for the night amid the giant amphitheater. The Queen was gracious enough to offer them a permanent residence, even though they were strangers, but Cam turned it down. They did however, stay near the fire pit. Between it and the couple of torches that were kept lit, there was enough light to see one another.

Cam had paced through part of the night, but his weariness took its toll soon enough. The four men knew that the Queen had set guards, so they took advantage of the situation, and all rested.

The Huntresses arose early, not changing their routine, and amid their morning rituals, they inadvertently awakened the four young agents, slightly before first light. The men welcomed the intrusion, because it gave them the chance to ready themselves for the day, and to begin awaiting the return of Kilari and Belsangar.

Cam sat and tried to begin planning an attack upon the wicked city. He did not know if his men would return, or if the girls and Tank would be rescued without him launching a formal attack. He was hoping for some good Intel from Kilari and Belsangar, but meanwhile he would be going over the facts that he did know, and he knew this; they will be needing some serious help. He was looking at a few months of campaigning, just to thin the zombies down, and that would be with the help of the cave tribe, men and women alike, that is if the men are even trainable.

Cam was hoping that Vail would be down, so that he could talk with her on the subject, but so far, there was no movement from her cave. He thought for sure that she would be up for the hunt. He watched, as the Huntresses prepared to go off for their morning hunt. They were very easy on the eyes for the most part, but as he watched, all it did is remind him of the girls, and then that reminded him that Kilari and Belsangar were not back yet with their Intel. The possibility of them being on a suicide mission began to hit home. It tore at his ability to think. Here he was, in a seemingly safe zone, and he refused to go with Kilari and Belsangar. In fact, he actually, helped a group of mere strangers, instead of going after his own people.

Kilari had made the correct moral decision, while he, again, faltered. He knew that he needed to move forward, but he did not want to act too hastily, or appear to be acting out of desperation. He was tired of waiting for Vail to make her presence known.

COGNIZANT

Telebar could see that as every moment past, Cam's head swirled faster and faster with negative thoughts. Moving across the distance between them, and holding his hand out, he said, "Hey man, let's go outside, or something. This pit is bringing me down. I need to see some open sky." Then he sighed, and asked, "you know what I mean?"

Cam nodded affirmatively, and then motioned for Malichye and Drake to follow. They all stepped out, and sat down by the rope ladder, overlooking the plane. They hoped to see Kilari, and Belsangar's return, but nothing stirred.

Drake finally broke the silence. "So, what's the next move? We've rescued the cave dwellers. Are we going to track Kilari down?"

Cam knew that it was time, so he answered, "Yes. Malichye, do you think that you can track them from where we separated. Otherwise, we can get directions from Vail. What do you think?"

Malichye thought for a few brief seconds and then answered. "We would be foolish not to get directions. We can always track them, once we get going on the right path towards the wicked city."

"Okay, it's settled then. Let's go get Vail. Who knows, maybe she'll come along." Cam answered, as he arose from his sitting position. They all made their way back to the central fire.

Telebar kept his eyes peeled, but after not seeing any traces of Vail, or Travis, he decided to ask the Queen's Guards for Vail's whereabouts. Knowing that he should be on their good side, even if he did play a little rough with the head guard, he decided to make the move.

COGNIZANT

*   *   *   *   *

Vail awoke. She was lying next to her, still sleeping, Travis. She curled up next to him and thought of the things that they had talked about, the night before. She remembered him asking her to return with him to his world. She thought of the adventure that it might be, to go to a strange place. Then she thought about her people and their needs. She did not want to leave, with them being still in hiding, even though they basically have been since the Black Mage had first began utilizing his powers.

Vail pulled Travis tight to her warm body, cuddling him close, as she thought of all of the possibilities. Knowing this is the day, in which she is supposed to be bringing him to his entrance point made her feel nervous. 'There is also a good chance that he will be leaving', she thought. 'There is even a slight chance that he will be leaving, right then and there, like some kind of magic, poof and he's gone', she imagined.

She finally decided that she had better get up and make some tea. She wanted him, but not for a moment, or for a day, she wanted him to be her permanent man. Tears began dripping from the corners of her worried eyes, as she pondered what life might be like without this man, her new man, which she wanted to keep. She hoped that she could at least stall his departure, until maybe, she would be going too.

Travis finally heard Vail, as she made herself busy, making tea, and checking her gear for the trek. He did not move right away, so that she would not realize that he had awakened. He eyed her firm fit body up and down. She was wearing a short little loincloth, which allowed him to see the majority of her legs. In fact, from his low position, he could almost see up through the bottom of her light-colored fur.

That was when he realized that he could not leave without this woman. She was so beautiful, with her full flowing blonde hair, and high cheekbones. He watched the silhouette of her perky bosomed side profile, as the small flames cast her shadow, upon the solid rock wall near her. His head began to swim with the vision of such a beauty. This was actually, the best view that he had had of her, and he was not disappointed.

He watched her every move, and then began imagining her in various circumstances, as she tried fitting in back home, and failing to handle dealing with each situation, which brought him to his next daydream. In this one, he was the one dressed in primeval attire, and failing to do whatever the men do in this place. Failure to cook, and clean, and then being beaten by authoritative women were the main scenes of his thoughts of staying in her world. Before he knew it, Vail had suddenly sat down, right beside him.

"Rise and shine Mr. Sleepy Boy," her voice sounded sweet and homey. Travis felt, as though he had landed in some grand, fair, haven, where all is good. Vail wanted Travis, so she had put her best foot forward by making some heated grain, mixed with fruit and honey. She also made some of her special tea. "I've made us some food and drink, so that we can gather our strength. We've had a rough night, and not nearly enough rest, but I am prepared to bring you to your place. You know, the one that you want me to see." She kept her voice sweet and her demeanor slightly subservient, a little too much for her taste, but this was the way that Travis had explained that women were supposed to act, so she thought that she might give it a shot, even if it was embarrassing.

Travis opened his eyes up wide. "Oh, that's right." He said sounding somewhat surprised, as if he had forgotten. "It was today that we were going hiking up there." He finished trying to sound casual, and not trying to sound overly excited about the journey. It was not that he did not want to go, but because of the thoughts that he had pictured earlier, with each of them failing in the other's world. It made him consider dragging his feet a little.

"Well come here," he said, changing the subject, as he pulled her completely onto the bed. Her hands were full, and she nearly spilled when he pulled on her. Her temper almost flared for a second, being that she was not used to getting handled. Fortunately for Travis, she caught not only her temper, but also kept the food that she had worked so hard to prepare from spilling.

With the feeling that it was her place to make the moves, she climbed upon the man. It is not as if Travis was strong and womanly, which would just seem a bit weird, but he was not weak and dainty, like the other men either, so she struggled allowing his dominance. He fell right in between, but he did have that womanly attitude of power and control. He was feisty, and she liked the spice, but at certain times, he would have to learn his place. She did a quick spin, and in a second, she was straddling him, sitting upon his lap facing him.

COGNIZANT

Travis had a face full of her cleavage, but his eyes wandered up higher. He looked right into her eyes, and became overwhelmed. "I love you Vail," he said. It came out so quickly that at first, he did not realize that it had slipped out, but then he just sat there stupefied by his own comment. It was not that he did not mean it, because he did. It was more the fact that he did not have a clue how Vail really felt, and he just put his heart on his sleeve for the first time ever. Now, he had nothing to do, but wait for her reaction.

Vail sat there wide-eyed for a few seconds. Stunned by his confession, she could only have hoped that he would feel the same about her, as she does him. Her heart began pounding with joy. Caught, holding the food in one hand and the tea in the other, but somehow, she still seemed to manage

Roc Bliss

to lean down, positioning her mouth next to his ear. She whispered, "I love you too," and then leaning far enough to her left, she set the food and drink down upon the floor.

Quickly bouncing back into her original position, face to face with her new love, she began gazing into Travis's eyes, as he did hers, and both of their hearts beat as one, each in their own state of glory with a gleaming resonance embracing their natural auras. They did not immediately kiss, but instead they gazed deeply within one another. Finally, Vail's mind reminded her of the original plans for the day. She decided to explain her fears to him. "I don't want you to go away without me, Travis. I know that you need to find out what is going on with…," then her brain stalled not knowing what to call the trans-dimensional gate.

COGNIZANT

Travis touched his finger to her lips keeping her silent long enough for him to give her reassurance. "You don't have to worry about that. We will find a way to work something out. I don't know how long you would be able to take my world, and I don't think that I fit in very well in yours, so I think we should cross that bridge when the time is right."

She could see that he had put some thought into the situation already, making her feel as if the weight had been lifted from her shoulders. She planted her arms around him, and cleaved to him with more passion than she ever thought that she could feel. She squeezed tightly, in fact so tightly that Travis struggled to get air into his lungs for a few breaths, until she noticed what she was doing. Then she lightened her grip, and pushed him to his back.

Roc Bliss

He looked up and saw the most beautiful woman that he had ever loved. She removed her top slowly, bearing her true self to her man. The two became one entity, in spirit and body. Vail screamed from the excitement of this new love bond. She was feeling more sensations than she had ever thought possible.

Telebar had already taken three steps into the room, and had no clue that anything was going on, and then he heard Vail's screams of passion. "Oh shit," he said aloud closing his eyes. "I'm sorry," he continued, as he turned and began trying to walk away blindly.

Vail turned her head, and saw that Telebar had walked in on her, in the most sacred moment of her life. She had just made her oaths with Travis, just moments earlier, and then, to be walked in upon, while her door torch was yet unlit. She bounced up from the dumb founded Travis, who was quite embarrassed. He quickly covered himself, and sat up to see what was going on. Vail took a few steps to where her cloak hung, and quickly slipped into it. Then she turned and marched towards the door, like a soldier ready for the fight. "Hold on you! How dare you enter my cave when my torch is unlit?" She yelled with anger.

Telebar stood near the doorway, but had never quite made it out of the cave. He knew enough to know that he did not want this argument slash fight to be seen out in the open, in front of any of her people, or his, so he quickly apologized saying, "I'm sorry Vail. I didn't mean to walk in on you two."

"That's it, you stupid overgrown dope! I respected you a little, because you could fight, but now I see. You are some kind of whore. I've got my man, so take your ass outta here!"

She yelled loud enough for most to hear, and the look on her face made Telebar think twice before speaking, but nothing really was going to stop him at this point. He had already humiliated himself, and the girl was dressed. "I didn't know about the torch signal, and I am sorry for embarrassing you, but I have to get to my girl too, and we need your help." Telebar spoke softly with humility. Then he said possibly the one thing that may have convinced her to help. "Kilari and Belsangar did not come back yet, and we need to find them."

Vail looked him in the eye, and could see in the man's stature that he truly walked under duress for help. "What do you mean? You sent him with only one man, to try to wade through the thousands of guardians, and sneak into the wicked city. You all knew that it was a suicide mission, and *now* you're worried. You also say that your girl is in, or near, the wicked city, but you did not go with Kilari."

Telebar looked her right in the eye and said, "you should know that some people have to follow orders. Cam ordered us to help save your people, and we did."

"Yes, I do owe you for the help, but let me ask you. Was Kilari under the same restraints to follow orders, as you?" She already knew what the answer would be, but she waited to hear it anyway.

Telebar sighed heavily. "Yes." he finally answered. "But you don't understand."

Vail cut him off in mid-stream. "No buts. You tell me then, why did he go?" Vail asked point-blank. She watched as Telebar's jaw dropped wide open.

"Maybe he has more love in his heart than you. He *went* for his girl, he brought the guy he wanted with him, which also wasn't you. He did what I would have done. He did not know us, and his friends were in trouble, so he went after them, even in the face of certain death. You," she said firmly with a hint of disgust in her voice. "You followed orders and played it safe, figuring that he would come back with information, and that you would have all the time in the world to go back and be a hero."

Telebar took all the guff that he cared to hear. "Hey, we fought those damn dogs in that tunnel, helping your people escape from the Black Mage. I didn't run from a fight. I am a soldier, and a good soldier follows the orders of his leader." He turned to walk away, muttering, "If you don't want to help, then we'll go without you."

COGNIZANT

Vail stopped Telebar with a shout. "Hey! Go get your men, and bring them back here. I will help. Let me talk with your leader." Without a word Telebar left to get the guys. Vail turned and walked back to the bed of furs, where Travis sat waiting. She grabbed up the food and drinks and then sat next to her man. She fed him a bite of the mushy grain cereal. "I'm sorry," she finally said, about being interrupted. "I'll get them on their way quickly." She added, still wanting to let him know of her intentions.

Travis just heard her say that she would help the others. "So how do you plan on helping those guys, if you just send them on their way?"

Vail became frustrated. She knew what she wanted, but she also knew that she should do the right thing. "I don't know what to do. I wanted to be with you, but these men did help my people."

Travis thought for a short moment, and then threw out a couple of thoughts. "Why don't you just wait, until you talk with them, and then come to some sort of solution? Maybe all they are asking for is a map, or maybe they expect you to guide them to a point at which they can begin tracking their friends without assistance. I don't know?"

"Well, maybe you are right." She admitted. Then she smiled and gazed into his eyes. They embraced and began to kiss long and passionately.

"Hm, hmm," Cam rumbled as he entered the room.

Telebar followed in right behind Cam, and saw the scene. "You two are at it again?" He asked in a surprised tone.

COGNIZANT

Vail finished her kiss with Travis and then turned towards the four men. Three of the four were smiling with slight embarrassment. The other, Cam, stood nearby with a more serious look about him, and was ready to discuss their options.

In the end, Vail opted to have the Queen, and her guards in on the planning of the search, mainly for the mere fact that they all knew the area so well, and the men were strangers in the land. The Queen proclaimed that her personal guards would escort the men to a point at which Malichye could track the missing men.

Within a few hours, the Queen's Guard had parted ways, leaving the four men to trail their friends. Malichye took the lead. He moved very cautiously, always looking for any prints that led in other directions, but the footprints were constant and steadily heading toward the valley of the wicked city.

Finally, the group sat at the last crest of a hill that overlooked the ghost town. Malichye pointed toward the center of the town and said, "It's obvious that they headed right into the midst of the deserted city."

Cam looked at the thousands of footprints left by the zombies. "So where are all of the creatures that made these prints?" He asked looking for some kind of theory to run with.

Malichye had already been asking himself the same question. "I don't know, but they must be everywhere. I would not advise going into that place. I would guess that there is a possibility of there being ten thousand or more of them things, and we'd be sitting ducks right now."

Telebar looked across the city, noticing the surrounding hills, so he interjected, "How about if we search the perimeter for any boot tracks that leave the area. If we find nothing then we can rest assured that they have been captured, and are still in there."

"I'm with you," Drake said quickly agreeing not to go within the wicked city. However, he could see a shiny flash at the top of the center building. He imagined it to be some type of gem, so he began planning on how to get to the top of the building, if they were so called.

Telebar grinned at the sneak. "Good, I'm glad you're with me," he added sarcastically. He turned towards Cam for an indication of his plan.

Cam looked at Malichye and asked, "How long would it take to cover the perimeter?"

Malichye scanned the distance with his well-trained eye, and then offered, "Two or three hours, if we find nothing and move as one group. If we find something then it could be over any moment, and if we split up, the total time will still be cut down, but we take bigger risks. Face it. We all can find boot prints in the sand, and as far as we know, we have the only boots on this plane, so it shouldn't be too difficult."

Cam looked at the sky. It was already nearing mid-day. "Okay, let's split into two groups. We'll either meet up empty handed at the opposite side of this valley, or one of the groups will find something and alert the others."

"How are we going to do that?" Drake asked curiously, wondering what the signal would be.

Cam looked at the area for a second, and then answered. "We'll walk near the crest of the hills, and every few minutes, one from each group will walk into plain view, and wait for confirmation of eye contact. Once we make a find, we'll just wave the others over."

The group agreed that it was the quickest way, and it seemed to be safe enough. Malichye was ready to take Drake with him, knowing that Cam and Telebar would stick together. He did not mind, because he knew that they could move fast and be very stealthy. He held the group up for one last statement. "Now remember, we did not see any sign of backtracking footprints, so they are either in that valley, or they have left it at some point. Look for the obvious, but also look for trace evidence. The wind could have picked up, or it may have rained, causing the prints to become partials, so there may only be an indentation that leads away from the hills. Just make sure you look closely. It would be ugly if we somehow miss the tracks, and we went into that valley for nothing." The others all nodded in agreement.

Cam stood ready, and said, "Alright, let's do it." Then he pointed to the one side and said, "we got this side." With that said, the two groups separated, and began searching high and low, along the hills surrounding the valley of the dead.

Kilari and his wearied band ate from the basket next to the still smoldering coals of the fire. They sipped the wine sparingly and spent the morning resting, their aching, overworked muscles. They rested semi patiently, until finally, Kilari came to a point at which he felt that he must begin to look for a way out. It had been slowly seeping into his mind, bit by bit and piece by piece. Every time a bit seeped in, he began thinking of the right way to go about leaving, without endangering any of those, who are with him. Each time the thoughts entered his mind, he came to the same roadblock, the fact that they had no clue of their location, or which way to travel.

Kilari rose up from his cozy spot, lying between Jezza, and Marcia, near the fire. He walked out of the small cave into the sunshine. His eyes squinted from the light change, and before they could adjust, his entire group joined him. It became readily apparent that the whole group stood ready to get moving on, which was perfectly understandable, considering that he had four young women wanting to reunite with their men.

Kilari, deciding to address the group point-blank, spoke to them where they stood, saying, "Ok, this is our status, as I see it. We are in a place that will sustain us for an unknown period of time. It seems safe and we are under no duress to leave, however, I know that for reasons that do not need naming, we want to regroup with our brothers. Our biggest problem is having no idea where we are, but I think that if we send a group of two or three in any certain direction, whichever one we decide, and have them scout out for maybe a half hour, to see if we are near anything familiar, then, they will return and give us a full account of what they saw, so we can either find out which way we came from, or we can use the information to draw a semi-formal map, and slowly work our way outward in different directions."

"It sounds like this could take weeks." Ceilia stated wishing that they could just go home.

"Or in an hour, we could know right where we stand. It's all a matter of odds." Marcia said in a matter of fact way. "There are only so many directions to go, and with all these hills out here, we should be able to climb one of them and see for a long way." Seeing the logic behind Kilari's idea, she stood ready to back him with her optimism, as long as it takes, to get the rest of the group on the same page.

In the end, they decided to go with Kilari's plan, with another last-minute thought added. He decided to split the group into four sections, so that he could utilize four groups with one group of two staying at the camp, while the other groups of three telescopes out. Nine would be leaving in one group, and then as the desired distance was met, the next three-person group would hold fast, while the rest moved forward, until finally, each group would be extended out. The groups must stay in sight of the group left behind, so therefore, he felt that they could maximize the distance, while never having anyone left out of sight. This way he figured, if it's necessary, they could circle around three hundred sixty degrees fully extended, and if by some ill-fated luck they still came up empty, then on the next day they would have to move out further. Sooner, or later, they will come across something familiar.

Kilari also figured that two of the girls, Glenda and Layla, should stay at the camp, where it seems the safest. Tank, Sophie, and Ell, would be the next group, with Belsangar, Ceilia, and Harrah being the next, and finally Kilari, Jezza, and Marcia would be the ones to move the farthest out.

COGNIZANT

Ace-in-the-Hole

Rudy fired-up the inner trans-dimensional gate, setting it to the same coordinates as the outer gate, except for the final digit upon its set point display, which set the altitude of the gate. He had this number bumped up a bit, so that he could view what was happening on the other side from a higher angle. It would not only extend his view, but also keep the search party from accidentally entering the vortex of the wrong gate.

With both gates fired up, and Big-Time's crew armed with their heaters of choice, Rudy was ready for his first trial of the gate. He wanted this test to be short, not as short as the one and only test that had been trialed, while

Brague was still around. This test would be serving two ends. It would obviously cover the ability of the men to move between dimensions, but Rudy's real intent on this one would be to capture the view of the searchers with the inner gate. Mathias had painstakingly mapped out the dimension of Xibalba, but the maps would not be necessary for this first little dip into the unknown. They are for all missions beyond.

Big-Time, and his men stood with their weapons poised, waiting for the signal from Rudy. Once he gave the signal, the three mercs walked directly into the clearing, with only slight apprehensions. The outer gate having reduced friction turned invisible, so the walk had no visual side effects, which might impede one's progress with thought. The three men marched only about fifteen steps forward, and then suddenly stopped in their tracks. After viewing the surrounding area, it became perfectly obvious that they were no longer on Flag Island.

"Look," Eagle-one barked, pointing to what seemed to be a rather plump pack, "A hiker's pack."

Frontline had an even larger exclamation, as he looked down and noticed that his gun had vanished. "Hey! My heater's gone! What happened?" He looked around in bewilderment, as if he may have let go of the weapon, and it somehow magically sat near him on the ground.

Big-Time, quickly noticing the situation figured that surely Rudy should have the birds eye view of the scene at hand, so trying to stick with the plan he barked, "Frontline, quit your whining and grab that bag." Big-Time's order gave the man no room for argument. Then he turned to Eagle-One and continued, "Let's time it. We are supposed to wait five minutes and then return." He watched, as his man checked for his chronometer, without luck.

Eagle-One quickly pointed to his wrist, as he turned to make sure that his leader was paying attention. "Well apparently, we aren't going to time anything," he said getting the attention of Frontline too.

"Man, what gives with this place?" Frontline asked with a hint of duress in his voice.

Big-Time was done waiting, so he ordered. "That's it. We're done here. Let's get moving back through that gate gentleman." He swung his arm around and pointed the way to their entrance point. With that, the three mercs marched back through the gate. In mere seconds, the search party found themselves walking back through the clearing on Flag Island. Frontline immediately began scouring the vicinity for his side arm, after tossing down the pack. Eagle-One checked his wrist, but his dead chronometer still sat lifeless upon it. Big-Time saw Thomas, who had been introduced to the men previously as a liaison, between the scientists and the three of them.

"Okay they're back, Rudy," Sounded the voice of Thomas Elliot. "They didn't stay for the full five minutes however." Thomas said checking his chronometer. He also noticed that they did not have their weapons, and that they brought a package back with them, but not wanting to seem overly keen, and possibly become suspect; he decided not to bring all of these details to Rudy's attention.

Big-Time immediately began walking over towards him, reaching his hand out, so Thomas ended his link with Rudy, and quickly put his com-unit in his front pants pocket, knowing that the man would try to take over his conduit liaison position.

"Give me that com-unit." Big-Time ordered gruffly, trying to intimidate Thomas.

Thomas started shaking his head 'no,' even before saying, "No, no, no, no, I came here to be a liaison. I am here just for this purpose. I am the one, who is the conduit, so you just talk to me, and I'll talk to the boss." Thomas spoke firmly, and confidently, in hopes that an intelligent discussion may seem a bit more than the merc wanted to deal with.

Big-Time clenched his fist, thinking, 'I feel like giving this guy a pop in the mouth', but instead of acting

COGNIZANT

upon his thoughts, knowing that it would be a waste of time, he decided to give Thomas a piece of his mind with a pointing finger. "I'm going to tell you. You are here, because we did not have any spare bodies, alright, that's it. Now, I'm gonna let you do your job, so get that com-unit back out, and tell Rudy that our firearms vanished into thin air, as we entered the area beyond that gate. I want to know how he saw it."

"Don't forget my chronometer," Eagle-One reminded his leader. "It doesn't work either."

"Yeah, that's right," Big-Time admitted. "We had no way to tell how long we were there. We could have stayed there longer, but we figured that we should test the gate and get back to relay the Intel. That's why we came back early." Big-Time explained, acting as though he needed to justify his actions.

Thomas Elliot immediately snatched the com-unit from his pocket and began explaining the situation to Rudy. He found out that Rudy had a theory that they would have to test, it started with a thorough search of the soldiers and the pack, to see what is missing. Thomas did not want this to be a big slow down, so he figured that he should do the honors of the search. He checked over each of the soldiers, their uniforms, and any arsenal. He compared his findings to the lists that he had made prior to them leaving. Thomas always a well-organized man took down property lists prior to their departure to make sure, that nothing foreign could be brought back without his knowledge. He also had to check the pack, but he could only check the pack to Rudy's memory, so he did not plan to put much faith into the findings thereof.

After a slow, methodical comparison, Thomas came to his own conclusions. Metal did not seem to travel through the trans-dimensional gate the same as other elements. He wondered if the metal were incased by some other type of substrate, if it may possibly make the journey, but he decided not to mention his theory to Rudy, believing that it would probably slow down things to the point of a standstill.

Thomas wanted to keep things on the move, so after working his way out of earshot, behind a large boulder, he began advising Rudy, saying, "This is just a search party Rudy. These men don't need weapons to search. They just need their maps, and they are fine, so I am suggesting that we send them back without hesitation. We already know that they can get back here, if we keep this trans-dimensional gate on, so why not start the search?"

Rudy found himself thinking in the same light as Thomas, who had his own people that needed finding. Rudy had no intentions of stalling the search for Travis, so he obviously agreed with the new liaison. "Just get them moving," he said. "The sooner we find something, the sooner we can get this search over." Rudy said, with a nervous anxiety about him.

The com-link ended. Thomas walked back from around the boulder and looking at the search party, he said, "Let the search begin, gentlemen," using the term, "gentlemen", rather loosely with these characters, but it was his way of showing them a little respect.

Big-Time overheard Rudy, and knowing that he had no choice in the matter, because of General Brague's marching orders, he grouped his guys together for a short pep talk. "Alright you two, get prepared. They got us going in no matter what, so the first thing that we need to do once we get there is, find some sort of weapons to defend ourselves. Then, we'll track that scientist down and drag him back here, if we must. He's only been gone for a day or two, so we should be able to pick up his trail easy enough." He paused for a second, as an imagination passed through his mind, and then finished his speech by saying, "we'll probably be finding his remains."

"Gentlemen, you may continue the search." Thomas said interrupting the end of the merc leader's speech. After receiving some disturbing looks, Thomas continued. "We have more people in there than one. Maybe, Rudy is concerned with only the one, but other agencies are concerned with all the humans that have somehow been sent through this gate. If you can connect with any of them, or even an inhabitant of the land, then we can move forward at a much more rapid clip, and your part as searchers will be over. We are having more searchers arriving tomorrow, so you will be moving back into your guard duties, but until then, you are our greatest hope." Thomas tried to give them a speech, which would have them not only realize the importance of their search, but would also reassure them that they are not committed to searching long-term. "Remember this. You are making a page for yourselves in the history books by doing this search. You are the first voluntary participants, so your actions will live on in those books forever."

COGNIZANT

The three men looked at him in disbelief, each of them with a smirking grin. "Damn, he sure is talkative. At first, I thought he was joking, but he is actually for real." Frontline stated in his typical less than intelligent voice.

"How do you think he got a gig that's just about the talking?" Eagle-One asked sarcastically, as the men formed a circle facing away from Thomas, so that he could not hear them talk.

"Yeah well, if you ask me, something ain't quite right about that guy." Big-Time said suspiciously under his breath. "First of all, he talks *too* dang much, but he also seems to know more than he should, and I don't like it."

"What should we do?" Frontline whispered inquisitively.

"Let's just get on through this gate, then we can talk about it all we want, and none of 'em will be able to hear us," Big-Time suggested. The three soldiers then began walking toward the gate. Big-Time looked over at Thomas through his squinting, suspicious eyes, and said, "Okay, we're ready when you are."

Thomas could hear the men whispering amongst themselves. He did not need to know what it was about, to realize that the three men were up to something, so he kept one hand near his firearm, while he grabbed his com-unit with the other. "Ready when you are Rudy." He said through the device quickly.

"Excellent," Rudy answered from the lab, where the mood was joyous, and completely opposite of the moods that were being handed out near the outer trans-dimensional gate. "I believe that I am speaking for everyone here, when I say that we are all ready."

COGNIZANT

The others in the lab all nodded their agreement. They had been looking forward to this day for a long time. Finally, General Brague was completely out of their way, and they could now begin searching for their lost member, Travis.

Thomas nodded at the three soldiers and motioned them towards the gate, as he told them that they were ready on the other end. The soldiers all eyed him up and down one more time, before turning and slowly striding through the trans-dimensional gate.

Thomas, realizing that he must have overstated his position earlier, was not sure how to respond. He had never had to worry whether, or not, he had blown his cover before, in any facsimile of the words, and it sat in his stomach like hot lead. His mind kept racing with ideas of what he should do.

He was not quite sure of what he was going to do, but he did know this much however, he had until those men returned to decide. He linked back with Rudy, keeping up his act as a liaison, and let him know that the mercs had gone through the gate and had begun the search. "They did act a bit suspicious of me," he added to his report.

"They're just a group of mercenaries that Brague blackmailed into working for him," Rudy told him, trying to put his mind at ease. "They were actually brought with those young girls. In fact, I thought that these mercs were going to be the first ones that Brague would use to test the inner gate, but somehow, they became his guards, and the girls were the first guinea pigs that he put through the inner gate. You know him. They were supposedly ethnics, or ethnic lovers, or maybe even ethnic enablers. I don't know what his reasons truly were, but he seems to have his own sense of logic." Rudy said revealing something that Thomas thought of as, 'too good to be true'.

"Wait a minute," Thomas said slowly, as he surprisingly found himself in a sudden state of shock. His heart was fluttering from the news, in hopes that these girls were indeed the girls from the bus, but somehow, he had to find a way to keep his prospective. "Are you telling me that he put a group of girls through that gate?" He finally asked, trying to make it seem as if using young defenseless females as guinea pigs, is an even larger crime.

"Yes, they were young, mid to late teens, pretty things too." Rudy answered to the best of his recollection.

"Okay Rudy, now it seems that you remember this well, so let me ask you this. Were there eight of them?" Thomas asked with excitement leaping in his heart, which triggered a mechanism in his mind that made him talk more slowly, enunciating his speech to perfection, so that he would not be misunderstood.

Rudy could tell by the man's reaction that Thomas must have known these girls also, so he thought carefully trying to recall, but a lot of events had taken place in the last couple of days, so he wasn't quite sure of the exact number. "It sounds like the right number, but I cannot be one hundred percent sure. It was a small group of girls." Then the scientist thought back trying to remember more. "I remember trying not to look at them too much, because of the immoral nature of sending them into that place.

COGNIZANT

He had us send them straight into that accursed ghost town."

His face contorted as the words fell from his lips. "I was not only following orders, but they were the type of orders that if they got ignored, would have made the girls pay dearly by his hand. I really did not want to put them through, prior to perfecting the process, but Brague gave me no other alternative. At least, it may have given them a chance to survive." He added, knowing that Thomas was quite familiar with Brague's work.

Thomas heard enough to know that he had a chance; a chance that he thought had long since passed him by. He thought that the girls had all been murdered, and now he knew that he must get off this link, so that he could get in touch with Tessa. "Okay Rudy, you old dog," he said. "I'll uhhh, have to get back with you later," Thomas, barely able to contain himself, ended the com-link abruptly, and then quickly changed links.

Tessa answered, "Hey Thomas." Her voice, riddled with fatigue was still haunted with the pain of knowing all of her loss, as of late.

Thomas could barely contain himself. His chest was pounding with excitement. "Girl, I want you on your way, stat, and make sure you bring some extra side arms."

"What happened?" Tessa asked jumping to her feet.

"Sit down girl. I have a couple of issues, and one of them is going to floor you." Thomas said trying to prepare her for the big news.

"Thomas, you know that I don't need to sit down. If you're in trouble, I will come and get you. I'm a little pissed right now anyway. Maybe a good fight would help?" Tessa said honestly.

COGNIZANT

The truth is; that she held herself accountable for the loss of the girls, and she had a lot of pent up frustrations.

"Well, I have some good news, and I have some bad news, which would you like to hear first?" Thomas asked in a more playful manner.

Tessa thought about it for a few ticks, and then answered. "I could use some good news about now." Then, hoping for the best, she quickly had to ask, "Did you find the boys?"

"No, no nothing like that, but this news is," he began, but then he had to pause and take a deep breath, before finishing his statement. "I'm just going to tell you. I am in full belief that the girls are in fact, alive, and in that other world through the machine, where the boys are."

"*What*? Are you sure? You better be sure. I mean," Tears began streaming down her face, and her voice was lost in mid-sentence, as relief flooded through her aching mind.

Thomas took a minute to let her absorb this new reality. Finally, softly, he spoke, "I know babe. I wanted to tell you in person, but you know it isn't the kind of news that I could sit on. I love you babe, and I hate to change the subject, but I'm telling you, you're going to have to pull yourself together. I need you here, quick."

Tessa suddenly felt emotionally supercharged by the extraordinary news. All of the weight was lifted from her shoulders now, and nothing would stop her from doing whatever needed to be done to get all of her kids back. Her mind became clear as crystal, and with total focus. "Tell me what you need. I'll be there." She was already up and moving, as she spoke.

COGNIZANT

Thomas did not like his predicament, but he knew that he had many options, and she was his ace-in-the-hole. "Bring the scientist, grab a couple of those old fire arms, you know the ones that shoot little projectiles. Bring some extra ammo for them and meet me at these coordinates."

"What kind of trouble are you in?" Tessa asked.

Thomas, not wanting to worry her, told her. "I have three mercs that are in the otherworld doing the searching. They work for Brague now, and I think that I may have given away that my affiliation is not with Brague. However, they are not here now, and they are unarmed, so I have some time, but they could come back with some unknown intentions, and possibly weapons."

"Did you threaten them?" She asked knowing full well that any military types would go to any extreme to be rid of possible threats.

"No, I don't believe so," Thomas answered. "In fact, I was just trying to pump them up with the knowledge of their importance in this matter, but I slipped and said that other agencies knew that others were sent through that gate, and each of them will be important finds."

Tessa rolled her eyes. "So, you thought that you needed to give a speech to those thugs? Thomas, you really need a vacation after this. Your judgment must be lacking from the stress, but don't worry baby, I'll be there A.S.A.P. and we'll take care of this. Just remember, we've got to get those kids back."

"You got it Tess. I'll see you shortly." He answered, ending the link.

Tessa immediately began scurrying about to, and fro, doling out orders, as she seen fit. She sent Alphie to the weapons cache, and told the droid to bring up a few different varieties of the small pistols, so that she could choose what appealed to her liking. Then Tessa went and got Taylor ready to go, his hands and feet had been banded with military style zip-ties. She cut the tie that bound his feet, while she kept her heater pointed near the man's genitalia. His mind transfixed on her weapon's placement and the fact that it would do permanent damage, so he became especially motivated to do anything asked of him.

Tessa began explaining the situation. "Look, I am going to have to move fast, so I want to be able to trust you to a certain degree. I am going to come clean about a few things, and then you will be sitting with too much information to continue breathing."

She stopped, after seeing his scared expression, and then looked him in the eye and answered his worrisome look. "It seems strange, don't it? But after you hear my story, I think that you will realize, I am not the bad guy, and you will allow me to trust you…" She paused again for a second, scrolling her hazel eyes up towards her brain and then smiling, she re-aimed her focus at the skittish young scientist saying, "Or, I'll be forced to singe you."

Taylor looked at the woman wide eyed, believing full-well that she would not waste the time it took to think, before blasting him with a heat wave, so he quickly began pleading. "I assure you, that you can trust me. You don't have to tell me anything. "I'll walk fast, even run if you like." Taylor said not wanting her to have any reason to be rid of him.

COGNIZANT

"No, no, it's nothing like that. I just want you to understand, as a human that my situation is on the side of the right. I want you to know fully that if something were to come up, you would at least know that I am fighting for a just cause." Tessa could see that the young scientist was good on the whole, so she felt that she could entrust him with certain details of her reality and of the situation which they were all a part.

In the end, she did not tell him that she was working for the abolitionists. She basically left it as though she was a mother and a teacher, whose children have been taken from her by force, and that all she really wants is to get her children back safe and sound.

Alfie had burst back into the sitting room with several pistols from the past, and plenty of ammo for each of them. Tessa looked at the variety of peculiar weaponry. She picked up one of them that caught her eye. It was heavy. She bounced her hand up and down while she gauged the weight of it. Then she moved on to another, and she found that it too was quite weighty for its size. Having no idea why Thomas had called for these antiques, and not wanting to carry several of these things through the jungle terrain, she figured that she would have Alfie pack them on himself and come along with the whole lot of them, then Thomas could pick, whichever one that he wants. She turned to the droid and asked curiously, "Alfie, do you have a stealth mode?" Tessa stood with a smirking smile, as she pictured the look on Thomas's face, when he gets a sight of *this* crew.

Moments later, the oddest looking, three-member crew that had ever been

COGNIZANT

formed, marched on their way through the jungle. It consisted of a woman with poofing brown wavy hair, its reddish highlights glistening as the lights of Polaris shown down upon Flag Island. She dressed in dark military attire focusing her side arm near a young scientist, whose long white lab coat flapped in the warm morning breeze. His bouncing, jerky, step pattern brought to light, just how awkward natural terrain felt under the young man's feet. The droid, still wearing Tank's military jacket, followed a few paces behind the woman. Its appearance seemed odd at first, with its metallic head poking out of the jacket, but it did seem to be more adequate at traversing the bumpy ground on its two flat-black metallic legs, than did the young scientist.

The three had issues at first, but by the time they neared their target zone, they had learned to travel at a semi-silent clip. Tessa realized that she could travel silently, but apparently, stealth was not in everybody's skill set. She thought that the other two, might make good distractions at the very least. They could sit somewhat silently, so if it came time for any action, she figured that she could just set them out of the way somewhere, so that they would not give her position away.

In the unknown world of Xibalba, Big-Time and his crew had their time limit extended to several hours, and without the distraction of the backpack, or the disappearing blasters that had caught their attention on their previous entry, they immediately noticed the markings that Travis had hacked into the trees. "Alright you guys," Big-Time said pointing to the tree near the entrance point, "we have a clearly marked trail, so maybe this guy *does* want to be found, but before we start moving, we need some sort of weapons. Look for spears, clubs, and decent projectiles."

The men knew from experience that he was not talking of already made weapons. He wanted natural objects that could be used as weapons. The Dark Forest held many natural objects, so it was not long before the three men each held onto something in which they put their faith.

As they began moving forward, Frontline finally asked, "What are we going to do about that liaison guy? He seemed to know way too much, about us putting people through that gate."

"Yeah, he talked about other government agencies knowing too," Eagle-One added.

Big-Time came right out saying, "Honestly, all of the others were put in here at that other location, so I would dare make a bet that the only evidence of them has been eaten alive." His grim expression said it all, knowing that they too were now in a hideous world, where flesh-eating hordes did search and scour for any living soul. His mind quickly clicked back to something that the liaison had alluded to, and he began questioning. "Why would that guy say those things to us? That guy must be an abolitionist, otherwise he wouldn't care about those half breeds. Nobody does. I don't know why he was being so forthright. He almost told us pointblank that he was an abolitionist."

The mercs continued moving along the well-marked trail that Travis and the four young agents had left, keeping their eyes peeled all the way, so that nothing could sneak up on them. To the average man, the hill stood steep

COGNIZANT

enough, and traveled far enough, to be a little work out, but to these three men, the hill was a walk in the park. They had never had such an easy gig.

"So, what are we going to do with that guy?" Frontline had to ask, speaking of the liaison. He would have already killed the man, if he would have had his side arm, he told himself, as he steadied up at the base of the large tree, which topped the steep hill.

Big-Time moved a short distance beyond the tree, while his two partners stood at the top of the hill. He checked the ground closely, first looking to the left, then to the right. "There are five sets of prints down here continuing on that way," he said pointing down the trail. "I've got no more tree markings, but the trail seems easy enough to follow." The other two got the clue and began moving down the hill. The downhill trek was steep at first, but leveled off soon thereafter.

"Those are from military boots. That Dr. put more people here than we even know about." Frontline stated, wondering, 'Just how long have people been getting put through this gate?'

Eagle-One yawned. Then he inhaled a deep lungful of air. "Do you guys smell that sweetness in the air? Oh, this place is kind of nice." He said grinning slightly.

Big-Time could see by the look in his eye that his pilot was under the influence of some type of narcotic substance. He quickly checked Frontline's beady eyes. They appeared to be normal, so he said, "Come on, let's keep moving. We are going to pick up the pace a little. We are at least a day and a half behind the scientist, but it's hard to say how far behind the others we are. I know this though, they

COGNIZANT

left a trail plain enough for a child to follow." The group quickened their pace, as they followed the trail, which seemed to be so obvious.

The Oasis

Vail had little stars in her eyes, as she gazed down at the spent scientist. Her emotions were at an all-time high. Sweat glazed the couple, who seemed to be made for one another in perfect symmetry. She rolled over from her mounted position, so that she could stretch her legs and catch her breath.

Travis felt like a king. He had no clue that true love would make such a wonderful connection between souls, but the glazed over sweat felt thick, and he knew that his next goal would be to wash. He had not noticed any actual bathing in progress, or anyone who seemed to be freshly bathed, so he wondered aloud, speaking more to himself, than his partner. "Where do you people wash?"

"What?" Vail asked curiously, as she could scarcely hear her man. "Did you say something?"

"Oh, yeah, well, I guess I was thinking aloud." Travis stammered with the realization that Vail had heard him. "I was just thinking that I could use to clean up a bit. I was trying to envision where you and your people wash."

Vail smiled. She was unusually filled with joy. "So, you envisioned this huh? I hope you haven't been trying to imagine all of the Queen's Guards without their furs on." She giggled a little, acting more manly than she could ever remember, but she tried to give Travis a little of what he might expect from a girl of his home world.

Vail got up and moved to her cloak. She quickly threw it on covering her nudity. Travis watched her closely, as she moved. He just sighed and wondered what he had done that was so right, because surely, he must have done something very good to deserve such a wonderful reward. Vail turned and glanced back at him, making sure that he was watching. She smiled with delight at his attention. Then, she moved to the corner, where she kept her cloaks. She knelt down, and slipped one from the bottom of the pile. It was large. She smelled the fabric, but the scent that she had searched for, had long since been faded away. She tossed it over to Travis. "Put this on," she said, as he caught the flying garment. "It should fit."

Travis stood up, and opened the old faded burgundy cloak to check it out. It indeed was a good size for him. He slipped it on. It was surprisingly soft on the inside against his skin, even though the outer side's texture seemed rough and scratchy. He took a few steps admiring his new garment. "Hey, this is nice, thank-you." He felt, as though he might fit in a little better with the cloak. He took a few more steps, before realizing that he still needed to get his socks and boots on. His feet were soft from lack of exposure, and even the smooth cave floor made him worry about scuffing them and getting a blister.

Vail watched as he laced his boots. They looked odd to her, but her skins probably didn't look perfect to Travis either, she thought. She slipped her moccasins on, and then grabbed her usual outer wear. "You better grab your," she paused trying to figure out what to call his clothes. Then, she just stuck with, "your clothing. We can wash them, while we're at it."

"Cool," Travis answered in a casual tone.

Vail looked bewildered by the statement. "Cool what?" She asked wondering what he was asking her.

Travis smiled and gave a short chuckle. "No, it means okay, or I'm okay with that. It's what we would call slang."

"Slang?" Vail asked, sounding curious about what this word meant. She slung her knife into its sheath, and grabbed her quiver and bow. She knew that he would not be a great help in a fight, but then again, he is just a man. He might have an edge on the men of the village, but not a huge one.

Travis smiled at her silence, thinking of how well that they actually, did communicate, even though they are from two different worlds. "Slang means that the word you are using has

COGNIZANT

another meaning, other than its original intent.

Vail felt like he was beginning to speak a bunch of gobbledy-gook. "It sounds confusing. Let's just try to say words we know, like, follow me." She said motioning him to follow her. Then, she led him by the hand out of the cave system, right to the ledge near the rope ladder. She pointed across the plane, towards the Dark Forest beyond.

"I found you sleeping deeply, burning the poison wood that is found growing within the Dark Forest. I know of a special place not too far from that area. It is a place where the water flows hot from the ground. We can go there, and have privacy. The beasts don't even go to this pool to drink, so we will be in a safe location. Then, when we are done, we may have enough time to visit the place that you wish to see."

Travis was well pleased. Even if he cannot go back home, he would like to show Vail, once, and for all, not that he should have to, but just to show proof, so that there could be no chance of suspicion. "You lead, and I'll follow." He said smiling about the entire situation.

*   *   *   *   *

Rudy had his science team, and the droid Mathias controlling the trans-dimensional gates. They were quickly finding out that they could not smoothly follow the mercs with the view of the inner gate, and the outer gate. He grabbed his com unit and got Thomas Elliot on the other end of the link. "We don't have the ability to follow the mercs, like we thought we might, utilizing both gates." He began explaining.

COGNIZANT

Thomas knew that it seemed important to Rudy, but he also realized that the mercs carried maps, and could give the play by play of their findings. "Look Rudy, I've got this gate covered. Just place the entrance point where it was, when Travis shot through. I'll let you know what is going on here. They can tell you what is going on, on their end, and you can utilize this time and the other mechanism to show yourself around the immediate areas. Just make sure you keep bouncing back to the start point every so often, so that nothing can sneak through here."

"I don't know. There are some wicked beasts in that world." Rudy said warning Thomas Elliot. "I really want to shift the inner gate one sector at a time. I feel that he should still be close to his entrance point. He is not ignorant. He has to know that he must return to his entrance point, and that we would not move it."

"Well dang Rudy, if you wanted, you could cover the place with propaganda. You have proven that the inner gate is good for a one-way ticket. You could virtually flood that world with papers telling Travis to get back to the gate." Thomas said giving Rudy yet another idea which would seem to help ease the search.

"I don't want to leave any harsh footprints on this other world. I believe that Travis will be easily findable. I plan on taking into account, what both, Travis and the mercenaries, happen to say, before making any large movements." Rudy said trying to give Thomas his logic.

Thomas did not like Rudy's answer. He began wondering if the man had forgotten that he had people that needed finding also. "Rudy, I'm telling you, I'll give you, maybe the day, to search and collect data, but I can promise you that come tomorrow, I will make a large enough footprint for the whole damn place to notice."

Rudy sighed, realizing that he had indeed become self-absorbed. He apologized to Thomas, and finally agreed to do additional searching with the inner gate.

Tessa arrived behind Thomas, as he placed his com-unit back into his pocket. "Thomas, is everything okay?" She asked in a concerned tone.

Thomas swung around quick at the sound of Tessa's voice. "It's going, but I don't see this as okay. Well, I see you brought your own breakfast cook with you." He commented, after seeing the droid a few paces back. Thomas peered around through the thick foliage. "Where's the kid?" He finally asked, after not seeing the young scientist.

Tessa turned in time to see a hand reach out from the midst of the foliage. "Very good Taylor, see, I told you that you could learn to be quiet and sneaky."

Thomas gave Tessa an awkward facial expression. "You're *teaching* him now?" He questioned. "This guy isn't even one of us."

Tessa burst in with, "Them, I'm teaching them, not just him, but the droid too." She grinned at the look of Thomas's disbelief. His eyes rolled backwards, as he sighed heavily. "Well, Alphie is wearing Tank's coat, so you *know,* he is on the team." She flagged the droid over. Taylor followed the droid over to the two abolitionists. "Look, we brought a bunch of those old guns you wanted. I wasn't exactly sure why you wanted them, so I figured that you may have been looking for something specific."

COGNIZANT

"Good job Tess. I knew that you would be on top of your game. So, are these guys in?" Thomas asked prior to giving away anything pertinent.

"The droid is in. The scientist is basically scared witless. He knows that we are after our kids, and is willing to help out, but I don't think at this point that he'll be able to get the job done, unless he is bait, or a distraction." Tessa explained openly.

"Well Tess, we have some choices to make at this point. We are on a tropical island with the newest technology and the science team who invented it. Their only guards are in the other world, through that gate, right there," Thomas said pointing to the area where the outer gate was placed. "Now, we could call in for a strike force, and take over this island, which would give us control over this new technology. They could be here by not too long after nightfall. Or we could take out these guards, which we must do by the time they get back, either way. Then, we will be in control of this island, which in reality, we are already mostly in control."

Tessa jumped in, before Thomas rolled too long with his speech. "Tell me about these guards."

Thomas did not mind being interrupted, so he began to explain about the guards. "One, the leader is a huge black male. He seems up for anything that comes his way. The other two are a pilot, a medium build white male, seems reliable, but the third seems to be an instigator. He is a small white male with an itchy trigger finger, and not too many morals, or much common sense. These guys are guns for hire, so they would probably work for the highest bidder, but right now, they are dressed in outdated Death Squad gear. So, I don't know how approachable they are, but it is a choice."

"So why did you want these old relics?" Tessa asked, pointing at the guns that were being set out for him.

Thomas looked her and the others face to face. "I do have a few reasons, one of them being shock value. Most people nowadays have forgotten the massive damage and devastation one of these can do. The bullet shreds skin, bone, and tissues leaving massive blood splatter and gushing wounds. So, let's say that someone doesn't allow us to do as we please. Then, what I could do, is shoot them in the leg with one of these guns, and they would more than likely live, but they would be in major pain, with a hole, and a bullet, in their leg, and as they screamed in pain, their blood would be gushing all over the place, making quite a scene to behold. I think it could be a very persuasive tool."

Two of the three sat there wide-eyed at the story, while the other calculated, but could not come up with this feeling of pain, so Alphie kept quiet with inability. Tessa began to smile at Thomas's ruthlessness. She was not used to Thomas being so over the top. While Taylor stood half shocked, hoping that he would not become the described example.

"Another thing that we have discovered is that metal does not travel between the worlds. The process somehow absorbs it. The three guards that are in there searching are armed with only sticks and stones, so needless to say, they are completely vulnerable." Thomas began to explain. "I remember that at some point in the past, they had made some of these guns and their ammo out of some other material. I think it was to get them passed some type of scanners that checked for metal. So, we may have the possibility of having a weapon that the others do not, and would not expect, if we have to go in after them ourselves."

"So, what is our next move Thomas?" Tessa asked, wondering if he had made any decisions.

"I wanted to ask you for your advice on the situation, before making any decisions that I can't take back." Thomas said showing the value he placed on her opinion. "I'm vying to bring in the strike team. They got us through the graduation ceremony. Now we need to get through this." Thomas watched Tessa, as she debated in her mind.

After deliberating for a few brief moments, Tessa came to her well thought out conclusion. "I agree Thomas. Let's call them in. We'll have them come in silent, then we'll button up this island, and get this search thing moving at full speed."

"It's settled then." Thomas said directly. He would definitely like to take this island, and all of the new technology. The abolitionists had some of their own expertise that the purists did not have, and of course they had much that was shared, but what a rarity it would be to take away some purist technology. "You call in the strike team. I'm going to talk with Dr. Laforge."

"What about the guards?" Taylor asked, worried that they would be allowed to come back unattended.

"You don't have to worry about them." Thomas told him. "I've got a special plan for those boys."

"Oh Thomas," Tessa moaned excitedly. "I like it when you're decisive."

COGNIZANT

"Yeah well, it ain't going to be pretty. I have a hankerin' to get full confessions from them, and I'm going to use that untrustworthy one as an example." Thomas stated the fact point-blank.

Tessa began to pull out her com unit, as she backed away from the group, and the trans-dimensional gate. "Hey, don't forget to have them bring some nonmetallic fire arms. If need be, we'll run rough shot over this search." Tessa signaled, okay, back to him with her left hand. He gave her the nod, signaling back to her that he knew that she had heard him.

*　　*　　*　　*　　*

Big-Time held his hand up to his two comrades, signaling them to stop. He then pointed two of his fingers to his eyes, and then moved them in a slight arch, as he pointed them toward what he was seeing. He saw two dark robed figures moving across an impossibly colored plane. He was beginning to get used to the bright, odd colored foliage, but these are the first living souls that he had seen in this place, and he was guaranteed going to follow them.

The other two men snapped into a hyper alert status, being that they knew of the zombie hordes that dwelt in this plane. It only took a few seconds for the men to spot the targets, and with the sighting, a flood of relief fell over them.

Maybe, if they were carrying their fire-arms, they would be sitting there with a false sense of security, but because they were holding onto long sticks and some stones, their confidence was only at a meager even keel.

COGNIZANT

*   *   *   *   *

Meanwhile, Kilari's group continued expanding their search circle. They had been walking now for a good part of the day, and had not seen anything that looked even remotely familiar to them. All of the terrain seemed to be the same, desert sand, piled into rolling dunes.

Kilari stopped to talk with the girls. He was torn between being determined to find something familiar, and wondering whether he should call off the search. "Alright, we'll make our way over that next crest, and if all we see is more of the same, then we'll have to end the pattern, after we circle around that is. I don't want to stop, but we have to make sure that we make it back to the camp, before night fall."

"We've been walking around for hours Kilari. Are we going to take a break?" Marcia asked as they began climbing the dune.

"I don't know." He answered initially not wanting to lie. "Let's just see what we can see from the top of this dune."

"Probably *another* dune." Jezza chimed, showing that she too was getting impatient with the long hot journey. She was dripping with sweat and needed some water to help replenish her bodily fluids. Each step was beginning to feel harder to take.

Kilari eyed the girls. He could tell that they were near their limit, but he needed to make it a certain distance. It was only twenty more feet to the top. "You girls just take it easy. I'm going to hit the top. You just wait here. I'll let you know if it's worth making it."

"Oh no you don't, mister," Marcia scolded. "We told you that you were not ever going to be leaving us alone again. I don't care if it's just from here, to there, away. We weren't much farther away from you than that when we were taken from the cave."

"Yeah," Jezza said affirming Marcia's statement. She grabbed Kilari's hand with hers, holding it tightly. She watched, as Marcia followed suit. "There, now you can't get away." She said, smiling like the young schoolgirl that she is.

Kilari tried to help them along, but it seemed as though just setting their minds upon something other than the walk helped immensely. They made their way, and at first Kilari thought that he was seeing a mirage. He could see water, bright blue clean water, and the landscape changed drastically. It was an oasis of sorts. There were trees and bushes.

The girls were completely excited and began to jump up and down, screaming at the awesome sight. They felt as though they had accomplished what they were setting out to find, even though they had no idea of their location. Kilari quickly shushed them, and pulled them down to a lower position on the dune in an attempt to keep their voices from carrying. He figured that if there were more people around, he did not want to give away his position. He would rather be doing the sneaking.

The girls, both, looked at him in bewilderment and fear, because suddenly they saw great beauty, and then they were shushed and pulled away roughly. He held his finger across his lips and gave each girl the look, so that they would realize that they needed to maintain silence. Kilari lay down in the sand and began crawling to the top of the dune. The girls followed suit, each wanting to peak over into that lush oasis, at *least* as much as he did.

Belsangar could see the sudden movements of Kilari's group, even though the group was far off in the distance, they did remain within sight and watched intently. "Look, something's going on. They just bounced away from the top of the hill, and then they crawled back up, and now, they're looking over the edge." Belsangar stated to his group excitedly.

"They must have spotted somebody," Ell concluded.

"Let's hope it ain't those creatures," Ceilia said in a worried tone.

Belsangar watched closely. He knew that he had a decision to make, but he was not sure how he wanted to handle the situation. Waiting for a signal was the standard operating procedure, but each minute seemed to last for hours, while waiting in silence. He could see that nothing too exciting was going down, at least, Kilari and the girls were not showing any signs of panic, so he decided to just hang tight, and do the right thing.

Ell watched intently at the lead group. Panic grew within her, as the moments passed and no attempt at communicating had been taken. "What are we going to do?" Ell finally asked impatiently.

"Yeah, we can't just sit here watching all day." Ceilia added, trying to urge Belsangar into action.

Belsangar ignored Ell's comment, but when Ceilia piped in, he figured that he had no choice but to nip this in the bud. "Look girls," he said addressing them as one entity. "We are in groups of three for a reason. We have not seen anything, except for the fact that they all decided to lie low and peek over the top of that hill. Now, if I send one of you back, and one of us moves forward, then we will all be alone. We must wait for the signal. That is what we have been instructed to do, so that is what we *will* do." With that being said, the group sat and watched, waiting for a signal of some sort.

Kilari studied the entire vicinity, and there was no movement that he could detect, so he turned and rolled over onto his back between his two loves, saying, "I guess it's break time." He said, as he snuggled between the girls and into the hot sand. "Is it me? Or does the ground seem warmer than usual?"

The girls rolled over in a much-enlightened mood. "Ooh, the sand is awfully toasty," Marcia commented, but she wanted to know, why they were taking a break and not moving over the dune and down to that water, so she asked him.

Kilari looked out in the distance. He pinpointed Belsangar within a few seconds. "Let me ask you something. If we go down there, are they going to be able to see us?" Then he answered for her, "No. So, we must make a decision. Do we leave the shelter of the cave and have the whole group meet us here? Or do we go back, place this oasis on a map, and continue searching, until we find our way back to where Cam and the guys are?"

Jezza thought for a minute or so, before answering. "We should vote on it, and decide as a group. I don't think that we should be making the decision alone."

"I agree," Marcia stated, immediately agreeing with Jezza's

logic. "We need to get all of us in on this decision."

"Okay, then it is settled. Signal the troops to meet us here. It'll be quite a while, before they all get here, so until then, it'll be break time." Kilari said, as he began watching the girls send their signals back to the group behind them.

Belsangar gave a short chuckle, as he saw Jezza and Marcia trying to give them the signal. "Okay, it's time to round up the troops." He said with a comical smile.

"What's so funny?" Ceilia asked, noticing the expression on his face.

"Those girls look quite excited. I'm smiling at the fact that Kilari had them give the signal, probably just so he could watch them bouncing up and down." Belsangar replied. Then he looked Ceilia up and down, then Harrah, and he asked. "Would you girls like to give the signal? I mean, I wouldn't mind watching."

Ceilia gave him a very light joking slap. "You *are* bad." She said, and then she looked over to Harrah and then, both began jumping up and down and all around waving their arms haphazardly in a mocking way, representing what they saw from Jezza and Marcia. One of them facing the group ahead, the other faced the group behind, so that each would know their signal had been received. Sophie, was the first to notice Ceilia and Harrah and instantly turned to signal for Glenda and Layla, who immediately headed out gathering their group members along the way.

*　　*　　*　　*　　*

COGNIZANT

Malichye and Drake moved steady and fast in the heat of the day. They were both drenched in sweat, but finally their stealth had paid off. "Look, over there," Malichye said pointing to a small group of footprints that led off over a sandy mound a short way off in the distance. "I'd bet my last credit that it's theirs, and it looks like they may have the girls, or at least some of the girls with them."

Drake looked over to the location in question. Then he looked back to the wicked city. He noticed that the footprints did not seem to come from the area that they were searching. It was almost as if they had appeared to start near the top of that hill. There was no trace of them coming from the wicked city. "I wouldn't be betting my last credit just yet man."

"Why not?" Malichye asked curiously.

ROC BLISS

Drake quickly responded, as the two agents walked briskly towards the location of the footprints. "I couldn't even have made *that* kind of escape. Look," he said pointing at the footprints. "Those prints don't cross the expanse between where we see them start, and really anywhere else. They look like they were traveling from the direction of the ghost town, but there's nothing there that proves it."

The two moved right on top of the sandy hill. "Well, I still win my bet. They've got all of the girls with them, unless you know eight other girls that are hanging out with three agents named Kilari, Belsangar and Tank." He said stating the names as he pointed to the footprints of the individual that he was naming.

"You are good," Drake admitted, but then the excitement of catching up with Glenda, who he hadn't seen since the night of their graduation, began to creep into his mind. "They've found the girls. C'mon man we gotta show Cam."

"I'm not good enough to explain where the rest of the footprints went, or how they disappeared without any trace." Malichye admitted, as he searched the surrounding terrain, and after a moment of searching without a clue, he finally decided that Drake was right, and he quit trying to figure out the mystery of the footprints. The excitement of catching up to the rest of the group, and being reunited with Ell, took over his thoughts. "Go give the signal to Cam and Telebar." He ordered. "We have what we've been looking for."

"Yeah, as long as they don't float over any other long expanses again," Drake sputtered as he began jogging back to the original search area. He stood on top of the hill long enough to see the others, and then he signaled them over, and within a briefperiod of time, the four agents were hot on the trail of their missing friends. They pressed hard trying to make up for lost time. Each man was eagerly looking forward to reuniting the group. They all were renewed with fresh hope, so the traveling seemed easy. Pumped from the reality that their entire group of friends had remained safe, and that all they had to do is follow this trail of footprints to be rejoined with them, the young agents poured on speed, until they found themselves jogging along haphazardly.

"Remind me that I owe Kilari and Belsangar for finding Tank and the girls," were the last words from Cam's mouth to his crew, as they double-timed their way through the sandy terrain.

COGNIZANT

They did not waste time or energy talking. Instead, each man steadied his pace, while getting lost in his own thoughts, thinking of the blessed reunion that they will soon be having with their brothers, and their lovers.

ROC BLISS

Reunited

Travis, enjoying the scenic splendor of the brightly colored flora, smiled enthusiastically with thoughts of his earlier enchantment. He and Vail made their way through the fields and underbrush, while steadily heading towards the fringe of the Dark Forest. After walking along the forest's edge for a couple of clicks, keeping in the safety of its shadows, the two came upon a rock wall, which Travis did not even notice, until he was right on top of it. Its natural appearance, blended so well to its environment, sitting on the fringe of the Dark Forest, it stayed nearly invisible.

Travis studied the wall very closely. It appeared to be very old and had various types of foliage growing in the soil, which was packed between its large stone blocks. He thought that it seemed like one of those jungle pyramids that he had seen shows about in his youth, except for the exact shape. Vail led him straight into a dark opening. The arched opening stood ten feet high and three feet wide. Travis caught himself hoping that it was not made for any oversized beings, like giants or the such. Even though they had kept in the shadows, it was only by routine.

Vail's mind was so preoccupied with her feelings for Travis that she had not been watching as closely as usual, leaving them both completely unaware of the three men that had been watching, as they entered through the dark opening.

Once the two dark cloaked figures had disappeared into the darkness,

Big-Time and his crew carefully made their way down. Unsure of what may be lurking around the next corner, the three mercenaries stood near the arched opening with their backs against the rock wall, Big-Time turned towards his men placing his finger to his lips reminding them to stay quiet. They, however, did not need any coaching, and had no intentions of giving away their position. They knew the importance of being stealthy, and after seeing what those zombies had done to the ex-Field Marshal Blak, they did not want to make any discernable noise.

Big-Time edged his eye around the corner peering into the opening. His trained eye could see light shining from the far side, approximately thirty paces away. He could no longer see the cloaked figures, or anything moving in the passageway, so he began to debate whether, or not, the two could have already made their way through, and out the other side, or could there be a side tunnel that he could not detect?

Realizing that he had not heard anything suspicious, and that it would not bode well to let the first people that he had seen, escape so easily, especially when one of them was leaving boot tracks in the moistened soil of the passageway, Big-Time gave a motion signaling his men to follow. He began moving down the slim corridor. Staying low, the three men crept slowly.

As they neared the light, Big-Time stopped and pointed out the noticeable boot tracks of one of the beings. "Do you guys realize what this means?" He whispered softly. "This guy is either, who we're after, or stole the boots of who we're after, so we *can't* let these two escape." Knowing it would be a moral victory to at least make contact with these people, they stepped quickly to the end of the passageway, trying to keep from becoming so far behind that they would have to rely on their tracking skills alone.

Soon the three mercs stood hidden in the darkness at the end of the passageway, not willing to leave its protection. Big-Time wanted to eye up the scene, prior to exiting the seclusion of the tunnel. The men could immediately feel the change in humidity, which seemed to thicken and hang in the air.

Big-Time inhaled deeply, taking in the lingering scents that collected in the tunnel. "Water," he whispered after determining what he had smelled. "There's a lot of water out there," he said informing the men, as they stared out scanning the area, hoping to see some type of movement from their prey. He could see the footprints, as they continued from the tunnel, but after a few paces, a thick blanket of grass covered the ground, and he could no longer follow the trail.

However, after peering around the vicinity, Big-Time felt some relief, seeing that this place was surrounded by hills. It seemed to be an oasis in a natural bowl of fertility. The vast differences, between the areas that they had already seen and this new place stared them right in the face. The soil itself seemed to be dark and fertile with plush tropical palms. The pond, or small lake, covered a vast amount of space, but there was no way to see the entire body of water, because of the natural landscape.

An island, which had boulders scattered here and there, around its base, and upon its upper ground, blocked much of the surrounding landscape from sight, while the tall palms and large tropical foliage cluttered even more possibilities. All in all, however, this place appeared to be a tranquil safe haven, and this made Big-Time's spine tingle with racing edgy nerves.

Big-Time could here bubbling in the water, which could hide sounds that he and his crew might make, but it will also hide the sounds of others, which will make his job more difficult. With a firm grasp of his position, he finally decided to lead his men into a nearby thicket, which just happened to be full of greenery, not unlike this entire area.

After nonchalantly traversing through the passageway, Vail grabbed Travis by the hand and led him quickly to a special place where she liked to spend time with her family, before the inevitable happened to them. It was

COGNIZANT

nestled away in a secluded corner of the tropical oasis across a small spanse of water on the island. Knowing the area very well, she brought him over to the closest point to cross over.

"Oh, this water is awesome," Travis exclaimed, as he removed his boots and began wading across towards the small island cove. The depth of the warm water never reached above his waist, as they crossed the short gap between the shore and island peninsulas. "You know, I expected the water to be a bit deeper than that," Travis said standing next to a big boulder, which towered over him.

"You just wait. I've got a spot where the water is deeper, and safe." Vail said smiling, as she pulled Travis along by his hand.

"Safe?" Travis asked curiously. "What do you *mean* safe? I don't see anything dangerous around here." Then he began wondering, if maybe, she was trying for some kind of shock value with her statement, so he asked. "Are you *trying* to scare me?"

Vail stopped. She looked deep into his eyes and asked, "Do you know how *rare* a safe place is, in Xibalba?" She watched as his gears began grinding about the reality of her statement. Then answering her own question, she said, "There may be two or three on this side, and maybe a couple of more throughout all of Xibalba."

Travis could see that she was being serious, but this statement had made him curious, so he had to ask the obvious. "Why don't you and your people stay at one of these safe zones?"

She just smiled at his ignorance, and grabbing his hand again, she began leading him to her secret spot. After leading him for a couple of minutes, in and out of groups of thickets, and

COGNIZANT

between big boulders, she finally made her way to a small hill.

Travis turned around to look back, looking to see some sort of trail that Vail may have been using to find her way, but there was no trace of a path. As he stood studying the general vicinity, he found himself in a place where he could not see much of anything beyond the surrounding landscape and foliage, which allowed him fifteen or twenty feet of sight.

"Follow me," Vail ordered, as she ducked down on her knees crawling into a bright red thicket. It reminded Travis of autumn in a four-season climate; when the leaves would change colors, before dropping off onto the ground. He did not like the idea of crawling on his hands and knees, but once Vail had moved out of sight completely, he swallowed his pride and slowly followed.

ROC BLISS

Travis was struggling with every movement, as the long dark cloak snagged and twisted on and around anything that it could, when he heard a voice echoing, "Come on." The voice was Vail's, but it sounded muffled, as if it were being projected from under the ground itself.

Travis decided to quit playing mamby-pamby with the bush, so he sucked it up and with an exertive determination strode hard not caring, if his garment ripped under his force. Like a weak baby bull, jutting from its mother at birth, Travis began plowing his way, until suddenly, he found himself enveloped in a reddish glow that seemed to emit from all about him. "Vail…? Vail…? Vail…?" His voice echoed. "Where are you?" The reddish translucent glow had him feeling confused. He felt as though his eyes were playing tricks on him.

COGNIZANT

Suddenly, a hand grabbed Travis by the wrist, sending his heart into overdrive. He quickly pulled back against the grip, snapping his head around, trying to not only gather his senses, but also see exactly who had triggered his panic. Unable to lose the grip he had somehow been forcefully maneuvered to his feet standing eye to eye with Vail, which calmed his pounding heart and relieved the sudden stress that had filled his mind.

Vail sensing the man's panic stood smiling at his overwhelming emotion. She thought, 'Men, no matter where they're from, they seem to be easily stricken by fear. It's a wonder that they can accomplish anything.' Then loosening her grip from his wrist, she spread her arms flamboyantly in a movement to display the area, saying, "welcome to one of the safest and most beautiful places in Xibalba. Come on;

walk with me through the tunnels." She said trying to coax the young scientist.

Then noticing his standoffish nature, she altered her voice to a softer, more soothing tone, which sounded as if she were calling a scared puppy. "It's okay." She said reaching out slowly and clasping his hand.

Travis, once standing, moved into the red glowing cavern. "Wow," he exclaimed. "This is awesome."

"Come on, there is something that I want you to see." Vail said, leading him further into the red luminescent cavern. At first, he felt colored blind in the red light, but after a few minutes his eyes began to grow accustom to its effect. He could see countless sparkles covering the cave, which led them deeper below the ground's surface.

The underground chamber was larger than one would think, considering that the cave was in a spot,

COGNIZANT

which did not appear to be able to sustain such a place. Vail led him across the width of the jeweled chamber to another opening.

This opening however, was in the floor. It was a large square hole that had a long, natural, stone ramp that was worn smooth, leading downward into what Travis thought of as, 'the unknown abyss.' Vail smiled and grabbing his hand, she began leading him. She could hardly wait to see his reaction to the beauty of the lower chamber.

Travis could hear the sounds of bubbling water, as he slowly followed Vail down the ramp. Steam began filling the air and seemed to get thicker with every step. As he stepped away from the ramp, Travis turned and found himself standing face to face with the most majestic beauty of nature that he had ever seen.

ROC BLISS

The phosphorescent gemstones in the walls had multiplied from the chamber above, in not only size, but colors as well. He could see green and white stones mingled with the red. Amongst the glowing gemstones, which lit the lower chamber, a large stone hewn inlet, or pool sat before him with apparently warm, bubbling water filling it, but that was not all. As the steam vapors seeped up from the bubbling water's surface, the colored light of the jewels actually filtered through the pockets of moisture, and reflected on the water's surface creating a brilliant collage of spectral infusion.

The entire chamber was nearly like being inside a decorated Christmas tree, not that either of the two had ever seen one. "This has to be the most beautiful place that I have ever seen." Travis said, commenting in awe.

COGNIZANT

Vail tossed her clothing upon a rock, piece by piece, as she stripped bare. "It's bath time." She called out to Travis, who still seemed to be in awe by the glowing colors that surrounded him.

Big-Time was being very patient, waiting in one spot, in order to catch some type of movement, but none had taken place. The group had been waiting for more than just a few minutes. Finally, he looked over to his men and said, "I don't understand. There is no way that they could have disappeared. We're basically inside a bowl, and I know that they are in here somewhere."

"Just keep in mind that we cannot afford to get lost." Eagle-One stated, showing his concern with the ability to get back home.

"Have we *ever* failed a mission?" Big-Time asked, whispering with an attitude. "Now I'm telling you, they're in here somewhere, and I'm not leaving without confirmation. C'mon," he waved, "we'll stick to the outer edge and circle around." Frontline knew and understood these types of scenarios, so he began to turn around, figuring that his men would automatically split to cover a larger area.

"Hold on," Big-Time ordered, still whispering. "We're sticking together on this one. I'd split us up, if we had some weapons, but seeing that we don't, we'll just stay in one group and take it slow. I'm not dying for some search and rescue mission." The group agreed full heartedly and they began moving out together.

Kilari, Jezza, and Marcia relaxed in the hot sand, while waiting for the rest of the group to arrive, staying midway up the last hill. His training kept the entire group in this very same

COGNIZANT

location, after their arrival, for
safety's sake. Everyone greeted and
regrouped for a minute, then most of
the group sat down to hear what he had
to say. "We have found a place of
interest on the other side of that hill,"
he stated pointing out the way.

"Now, I know that we were
supposed to search, until we found a
familiar place, but once we saw this
place, we thought that it would be
worth a vote to see, if maybe, we would
like to at least go down and refresh
ourselves. Girls, I know that once you
see this place that you'll be tempted
to, ahh…," he began thinking of how he
would like to put his statement that
would not be demeaning, "make noise.
What we should remember is that we
do not know what, or who, may be down
there, so we must maintain a silent
presence. I also want to give you one
more warning, before we crawl to the

top of the hill, and peek over the edge." He said, stating how he wanted them to handle themselves without making it an order. "This place seems to be, a beautiful oasis, but remember, we don't know if there are any enemies down there." After he finished his speech, he watched, as the whole group crept up to the top of the dune, but what brought a smile to his face were their expressions, after seeing the scenic splendor. He let them look for a couple of minutes, and then he called them back down to a lower point, so they could discuss and vote on their next move.

After being in this dimension for as long as they have been, of course their answer was unanimous. The entire group wanted to go and get into that water, and search for some type of natural fruit. They watched the area for a short period, and then slowly made their way down towards the water's edge.

Eagle-one was the first to see the rather large group making its way down the hillside. He nudged his leader and silently pointed them out, three men all dressed in camouflage moving along cautiously with the eight girls, still wearing the aqua blue medical uniforms.

Big-Time immediately stopped within the thickest covering allowing him the ability to see the incoming group. A smile ten miles wide crossed his lips, as he recognized the greenish-blue spandex jump suits that the girls were wearing. "Those are the girls that we delivered to Brague, and those guys are wearing S.A.F. gear. You know, the ones that that talking fool at the gate must be looking for." He whispered quietly, before pausing to admire the fact that he had somehow bounced into a spot, where the targets were *coming* to him. "Boys, this day may have just gotten easier."

Eagle-One looked more closely at the guys, because until his leader had brought up that they were possibly cadets, he was too enthralled with the tight form fitting jumpsuits that the young females were wearing. "Hey," he whispered, as he noticed the skin tones of the cadets. "Look, those guys are that ethnic group that I had heard rumors about, except I thought that there were seven of them, and I only see three."

Frontline's skin began to crawl. "I say we off them mutts, and go back and say that we could only find some tattered articles of clothing."

At the risk of making noise, Big-Time reached over and grabbed the little man by the neck. Big-Times monstrous hand could nearly stretch completely around the smaller man's throat. He pulled him close. The grimace on the big man's face was enough to tell the story. "I told you," he whispered authoritatively. "I don't play that shit. A man is a man, so you had better change that fucked-up mind of yours." At this point he could see that the little man's face was beet red from the inability to breathe, so he loosened his grip, but did not quite let go. Then, the big dark skinned man looked the other in the eye asking, "you got me?"

Frontline took a few deep breaths, while shaking his head in agreement. He thought that if he had had his side arm there would be no way that Big-Time would have grabbed him that way. He backed off a couple steps and kneeled, while rubbing his strained neck. "You know that Brague wants them dead, and I was under the impression that we worked for Brague now."

The other two looked at him with stupefied expressions. Big-Time could not believe his ears. "We only work for that rat bastard, because he stiff-armed us into it. You can guarantee that once we get back to the Crystal Continent, and we make sure that our families are safe, we will be teaching that man a lesson."

"Hey," Eagle-One whispered sharply. "They're getting out of sight. Are we moving? Or are we letting these ones escape too."

"We're moving," Big-Time admitted with a hint of disappointment in his voice. "Just keep it in mind that those two in brown robes are playing around here too. They may all be meeting up here."

"If we're lucky," Frontline said somewhat enthusiastically, trying to

COGNIZANT

keep his position from dropping any lower in his crew's opinion.

Eye of the Beholder

Malichye led the way on the trail of his fellow soldiers. He moved at double time trying to make up ground, between his group and Kilari's. Soon, they found themselves at the cave with the fire still smoldering, and the basket full of honey-cheese, bread, and, the wine skin still full of wine. Each of the men grabbed some of the sweet bread, and took a few slugs off the wine flask.

"Let's get moving guys." Cam ordered. "It won't stay light out forever, and we have no idea how far ahead of us they are."

"I can't believe that they left this food and stuff behind," Drake stated with his eye on anything that he could carry.

"At least they paved us a trail that a blind man could follow," Telebar stated. He kept looking ahead for a glimpse of the others, hoping to see them standing out on the horizon, as they began their hasty move to catch their friends.

Drake watched the others take off, so he knew that he only had a couple of seconds, before the others would make sure that he was right there with them. He had been eyeing up the wine skin, and it seemed to be the only thing worthy of holding onto, so he quickly snatched the thing, and fastened it to his belt loop. Then he sprinted to catch the group, which did not take long, even with the swashing wine skin, bouncing too, and fro, off his leg. Once he caught the group, he slowed his pace to blend with the group, so it would appear as though he was never even gone.

*   *   *   *   *

Kilari led them down to the edge of the water. The group moved casually. There was no seeming rigidity of military training. Each person moved at will. They remained fairly quiet, until the first girl touched her feet into the water.

"Ohhhhh, this is warm enough to be bath water," Sophie declared somewhat louder than the three men desired, causing them all to shoot a look in her direction.

Tank grabbed her by the hand, placing his finger to his lips, so that the importance of staying quiet would keep in her mind. Then, in a much quieter voice, he whispered, "you may not want to go in there just yet. There could be man eating fish in there for all we know," he said pulling her away from the water.

"Oh, but it feels so good." Sophie whispered back reminding him.

"Let us check it out first, is all I'm saying." Tank said with her safety in mind.

"Good call Tank," Kilari offered in hushed voice, after overhearing the conversation. "I guess that means, one of us will have to be the guinea pig." He could feel the heat radiating off the water. It felt as if it was calling his name. There was nothing he enjoyed more than a nice hot bath, and it had been a while since his last, so he took off his jacket and shirt, showing his ripped ab's, and well-defined pectoral muscles.

"Oh yeah baby," Jezza joked semi-quietly, admiring his physique. "Take it all off."

Kilari stopped shedding his clothes at his waist. He had no intentions of going into the water without foot protection. "Let's just get one thing straight, this is not going to be some kind of stripper party. I mean, even if it's all good, we are not skinny dipping." He took a step into the water. He could feel the heat surrounding his boot.

Once he maneuvered both feet into the water, he tried peering down. Bending down, straining his eyes to see, he took another step. Feeling the steep slope of the bottom, with the water being already waist deep after two steps, and his inability to see, Kilari decided that he would have to take the plunge, to really find out what, if anything, may be lurking below the surface. "Okay, I'm going under," he warned. "I don't know how deep this is, but the bottom is steep." The group all watched, as Kilari sucked in a lungful of air, and then dove under, and out of sight.

After washing in the hot gurgling pool, Vail began to show Travis how the men did laundry. His mind was so awestruck by the chamber that he barely realized, he was washing Vail's clothes. "So, what other secrets do you keep hidden down here?" He asked jokingly. Her eyes widened for a split second, but then she quickly changed her expression, and did not answer him.

Travis noticed the shiftiness in her eyes. "You do have more secrets around here, don't you?" He came from a place where lies ran fluid among the people, so he could easily see that she was trying to hide something from him. "Look, you can keep your secrets," he said honestly. "I don't need to know anything that you do not want to share with me."

Vail believed that what she was hiding would not mean that much to Travis, because he did not know their ways. After a quick reflection of the situation, she decided to show the man that now filled her heart. His wanting to know, if her culture would have more meaning, filled her with romantic respect, besides she thought, even if she were to show him the ancient wisdom, he may not understand. With this decision in mind, she walked up to Travis, looking him in the eyes, explaining, "This place holds wisdom of the ancient ones. These secrets are held by few."

Watching a gleam suddenly appear in his eyes, as she spoke, gave her an urge to show him her heritage. "You will be the first male to ever see this chamber, since we took rule of our people," she said speaking of the time when women took the leadership responsibilities for the tribe. "Come with me. We'll start at the beginning."

Vail walked with Travis, leading him by the hand into another chamber, a chamber resembling a long vast hallway of solid rock with no phosphorescent stones to light the way. The darkness, making it very difficult to see, filled Travis with wonder of what mysteries may be lurking behind its mask. Hoping that they will be understandable, and something that he can really sink his teeth into, Travis opened his senses, but held no expectations.

Vail led him slowly into the center of the room, where the glow of one small green gem barely allowed them the ability to maneuver towards the pedestal on which it sat. She stepped forward, until she was right next to the pedestal, and after stepping on a small lever located at its base, she pulled out two stones from a small rectangular hollow near the top of the waist high stone-carved pedestal.

A vase-like sculpture stood on top of the stone base, making Travis wonder what it too might hold. Travis kept watching Vail intently, as she struck the two stones, just as she did with the flint across her stone blade. Sparks emitted from the stones, causing flames to suddenly spring forth from the sculptured figurine. "Wow, how did you do that?" He asked in amazement, not in the fact that Vail could light a fire, but in the idea that there had to be a natural source of gas and these people utilized it in this fashion.

Vail stood to the side without saying a word. The chamber instantly brightened to such an extent that the two had to shade their eyes, until becoming equilibrated to the light source. Now, with the ability to see, Travis could make out two rows of small little vases not unlike the intricate carved sculpture spitting fire, which sat upon the pedestal, and slowly, one by one, the little tips on the vases began firing, until finally, each of them had lit, showing designs that had been etched into the stonewalls.

The longer Travis looked at the etchings, the more he realized that the designs were actually pictures carved into the walls. "Do you realize that this is like archeology at its finest? This is amazing. I mean…"

Vail stopped Travis in midstream by placing her fingertip to his lips. "Words we both know, no slang," she said reminding him of an earlier conversation. "This tells us the stories of *all* times in Xibalba."

"Do you mean of the times in the past?" Travis quickly blurted out. Then he looked in her eyes, and could tell that she had meant what she had said. "Come on now. Are you telling me that *this* can tell you the future?" He did not believe this possibility, but he did notice that she had an air of confidence about her.

"All times," she answered with confidence. "According to these tablatures," she said swinging her arms in a gesture to show the entire wall behind them. "This was the first time of Xibalba, our elders refer to it as Oblivion" she said pointing to the beginning of the etchings. "It shows that the great one had made this place of tranquility for all to live in harmony. As we move down the wall we learn that a great war disturbed the balance and the great one allowed the second time to transpire to punish his people for their wickedness."

"So if this wall is about the past, what does *that* wall show us?" Travis asked curiously.

"This is the second time for Xibalba. It is the time we live in now, starting with the Great War," she explained, while pointing towards the etchings. Then the evil one took rule and began attracting followers. Taking them away from the great one, and adding them unto himself."

"Wait a minute. How exactly do you add someone to yourself?" Travis asked. He might believe a nicely laid out story that made sense, but this seemed like crazy talk with unexplainable translations.

Vail flared her eyes at his disbelief. She was a step away from punching him right square in the face.

"It's kind of like the way that the evil wizard adds to his army." She said gruffly, letting him know that he was treading on very thin ice.

"I-I-I... was just asking." Travis stuttered nervously, trying to explain that he had no bad intention. He was beginning to get the idea that he had better shift gears and let Vail lead the entire conversation.

"I believe that I have seen a sign that we are nearing the end of this time." Vail continued to explain.

After hearing this, Travis became very curious, even though he still did not exactly understand what she meant by times. She walked with him down to the etchings of the Great War, showing him that they were etched on the end of the wall, and then as they moved to the next wall, she pointed out another symbol that signaled another beginning. It was similar to the first, but had subtle differences. Then they strode down the wall.

Travis stopped part way down. He saw some pictures of different landmarks. "What are these about?" He asked curiously, not noticing anything like these on the other wall.

"These are the safe places." She began explaining. "This one is where we are right now. You see," she said, motioning with her finger. "The water is very deep, and there are giant creatures living below this island. That is why I come in here to bathe. They are much too large to make their way in here. That is also the reason why we crossed over to the island where we did. It was quick, and just happens to be the only shallow spot that connects to land."

Travis could see some type of fish like creature with many tentacles etched beneath the picture of the island. He also could see what he figured to be the bubbles, some with flames in them. "Oh, I get it. The bubbles in the water are some type of natural gas that is flammable. The gas gets trapped up in these columns, and then you light them and this is what you get, a well-lit room." Travis impressed himself with the ability to interpret at least a small part of a picture.

Vail moved down a few more steps. "Look at this picture, and tell me what you see," she said pointing to a drawing, which did seem to be nearing the end of the wall.

Travis looked at the picture. It was of a person. At first, he thought that it was a picture of a woman, but then maybe it was a man. By the time he looked at it for a while, he concluded. "You know, the way that the clothes and footwear are drawn, makes me believe that this person is not from *this* place, and it looks like a man with long hair."

Vail held Travis's hand, as they continued the discussion. "You see these?" She asked pointing to some small symbols that were placed all along the drawings. "These are colors. This symbol says that the hair is light colored, not grey like an old man, but light colored like mine, and with," she paused trying to remember what Travis called his feet skins. "Boots?" she asked wondering if this was correct. It sounded strange to her, as it rolled off her lips.

"Yes, you're right. Those are boots on his feet." Travis acknowledged. Then it suddenly dawned on him. "Hey, that looks like that cadet that went looking for the girls. Think about it," he said trying to persuade Vail, who really did not need any persuading.

"That is what I think also." She admitted. "That is the only reason that I brought you to look upon these tablatures."

"Well, he must be important to be on this wall. What does the wall say he does? Travis asked, as he peered at the wall curiously.

Vail looked at him with disappointment. "It is easier to read what *has* happened, than it is to read what *will* happen, but I do know this: he is the initiator of the end of the time we are in now. He kills many of the evil guardians that much I can tell. Something happens after this, which seems to eliminate most all of the population for a space, and then more dots appear, again possibly the beginning of the third time of Xibalba."

Travis could see the look of concern on her face, and she was seemingly right. "The long-haired man

COGNIZANT

does weaken the evil army. Then there's this set of circles, which is a small circle with another around it and so forth, until there are seven of them. Then a blank spot for a section, and then two of the dots, which are representative of the people." Travis said talking it out to Vail, so that she could correct anything that he may have misinterpreted, but she did not correct him, so he figured that they were on the same page. "Is that why your Queen did not immediately leave, even when she knew that her people's lives were at stake, because she figured that the end was coming soon anyway?"

Vail looked at him with a slight glare. "You don't question my Queen." She said with a little snap. "Let's go back to the clothes. I wouldn't mind a little soak, before we head out to your point of entrance."

ROC BLISS

Travis had forgotten how touchy she could be. "What about the flames?" He asked.

Without saying a word, Vail moved back to the large pedestal and carefully adjusted the foot lever with her bare foot, which closed the gas port, and one by one, the flames were snuffed out, until finally they found themselves once again in a very dark chamber. Vail made sure that she grabbed Travis by the hand, so that she could lead him safely back toward the brighter space. They made their way back to the multi-colored area, hand in hand. All the while Travis kept thinking, but for the life of him, he could not figure out how she could be so touchy one minute, and then be out for his well-being the next. It may be just a female thing, he decided, one that transcends worlds and dimensions.

COGNIZANT

Kilari swam only about eight feet deep. He went to the distance, where he could feel the pressure building in his ears. He swam one way and then the other looking for whatever he might see, but there was nothing noticeable, except that the water went well beyond and below the island, but the warmth of the water that surrounded him was like a blanket of tranquility. After surfacing, the young agent inhaled deeply replenishing the air supply to his lungs, and then he swam directly back to the shore. He waited a second or two, as he caught his breath.

All eyes were upon Kilari, as he kneeled upon the grass. They were waiting semi-patiently for his approval to jump in. Finally, he answered their questioning looks, saying, "I didn't see anything. Now that don't mean that nothing is in there, so be careful and stick close. It gets deep quick." With that being said, the whole group stormed their way into the naturally heated waters, clothes and all.

Big-Time and his crew used the noise from all the splashing and the girls' childlike exuberant screams, as cover to mask the sounds of their movements and motivated his team in, as close as they dared without being seen. "How are we going to play this?" Eagle-One asked hoping that they would not have to depend upon the primitive clubs and rocks with which they were armed.

Big-Time looked at the two men saying, "Look, we are here on a rescue mission. All we are after is to get these people back to that gate. I know that it's not our usual, but just think how easy it should be. They are going to want to come with us, so they can go home."

COGNIZANT

"Then *why* are we hiding?" Frontline asked.

"I wanted to see if they were going to lead us to those other two that we were following here, plus I'm sure that those girls are still going to recognize us, even if we ain't wearing those gay-ass yellow jumpers, so I'm stalling to think up a good cover story."

"What's to think? That putts, Brague screwed us, just like he did them." Frontline stated disdainfully in a voice that was whispered, but it was still almost loud enough to blow their position.

"Shhh," Kilari suddenly warned from out of the blue, trying to listen, after hearing a strange noise. The group was all frolicking loudly, and it took them several seconds to quiet. Some had to swim back toward the water's edge, while others were taking turns being tossed in from the bank by the big man himself, Tank.

"What is it?" Belsangar asked.

"I thought I heard something." Kilari answered, before asking, "Did you hear anything?"

"Just a bunch of hootin' and hollerin'. I don't know how you could have heard anything over that." Belsangar answered thinking that his longtime friend was just being a little overly cautious.

Big-Time and his crew had all noticed that the group they were watching had suddenly all quieted and began looking around. The three men froze, trying not to make even the slightest sound, or movement in hopes of staying undetected. With wide eyes focusing upon their targets, they sat barely breathing, until finally the large group began to go back to its original fun and games.

COGNIZANT

With a sigh of relief, Eagle-One looked towards Frontline. "That was a close one," he whispered. "I *thought* for sure that they heard you or something."

"It seemed that way, but I don't know how that they could. With all of those chicks screaming and the bubbles that blow up to the surface every so often, there is a lot of counter noise." Frontline explained in a very quiet tone.

"Bubbles, what bubbles are you talking about?" Eagle-One asked curiously, because he had not even noticed them.

Big-Time's mind was too overloaded with thoughts bouncing between figuring out his approach towards this large group, and looking at the young girls, who keep reminding him of his daughter, to care about the bubbles. He was not one to get home sick, but ever since Brague put the threat out about their families, he had had a certain lingering yearning to get home.

"I've seen them flow up from either side of them." Frontline pointed out. "They're not constant, but they come up often enough. It won't be long, just watch."

Eagle-One began staring intently at the water's surface, having never seen such a thing occur naturally, he did not want to miss the phenomenon. Then suddenly, right before their eyes, the bubbles began gurgling to the blue water's surface.

"See, I told you," Frontline whispered in quiet excitement.

Jezza and Marcia decided to stay at the bank to be with Kilari, where he had sat down to keep an ear out, after believing that he had indeed heard something. The two young beauties

COGNIZANT

began soothing him with hugs and kisses, telling him that everything will be fine, figuring that there was clearly no reason to worry. No zombies were in sight, in fact, you could not even smell one, and that had to account for at least a mile of clearance. They also reminded him of how lucky it is that they had found such a wonderful place to wash some of the dirt, sweat and blood from their clothes and bodies, following up with typical undisciplined thoughts such as Kilari's favorite, 'Why Not', make the best of it.

Kilari stayed receptive to Jezza and Marcia, struggling between keeping his eyes looking out to the surrounding area and Jezza's alluring smile, as she spoke with joyful innocence. Soon, he found his eyes searching every square inch of both girls, instead of keeping his people safe.

Eye of the Beholder

Belsangar catching Kilari's body language began whispering in Ceilia's ear. Quickly scrolling her eyes over, as Belsangar whispered, she immediately recognized exactly what he was saying. Knowing Kilari for all these years, and how he had seemed to push possible relationships away, and now, here he is sitting in double jeopardy. Giggling, she pointed over towards Kilari and his two young loves, watching as Kilari kept struggling to remain attentive to the area, while Jezza and Marcia kept persisting to loosen him up.

Maybe it was the laughter, or maybe just the comicalness of the situation, Ceilia did not know which, but she began realizing that this place was bringing out the normalcy that they had not really felt, since before they had left the academy a couple of nights ago. This feeling hit home, and before she could realize it, she began caressing Belsangar's leg with subtle movements.

'Now that's what I'm talking about,' Belsangar thought, as their eyes finally connected with soft undertones, while he leaned in to get a little closer to his girl, Ceilia. He embraced her softly and then gently pressed his lips to hers. She went with the motion naturally, and slowly opened her mouth to allow their tongues to touch, as she tightened her arms around him. She pulled him close without holding back. Her throbbing heart, suddenly felt a closeness to him, a closeness that she had never thought possible. Goosebumps ran from her neck all the way down her spine, as they touched passionately. She had always thought of Belsangar as her soul mate, but now this feeling suddenly seemed to be supercharged, becoming much more powerful than she ever could have imagined. With each deep breath, she could feel her yearning grow. The outward thoughts of her mind had closed off, as her passions enclosed her within introspective feelings, which could not be denied.

All at once, without warning, *all* hell broke loose. The normalcy and tranquility of this beautiful oasis had suddenly been shattered with explosive force by giant tentacles rising from the water. As the sea creature surfaced, it created a huge swell of water sending people scattering helplessly in all directions. In fact, some droplets of water had splashed beyond the mercs, who still sat in hiding.

After seeing, what he thought to be the unthinkable, Big-Time jumped up and ran from his position without thinking. He began screaming. "Get out, get out of the water! Move people!" His

COGNIZANT

warnings came too late, as the water
creature took all by surprise.

Big-Time could see that one of the
girls had somehow been lifted upon
one of the giant tentacles, high above
the water's surface, lying on her belly,
balancing on top of the massive
outstretching arm, as the creature
blindly struck upwardly. Whether by
the forces of nature, pure luck, or the
saving graces of Yahiveh himself, the
girl had somehow maintained herself
from being either, gripped by the
creature, or flung into oblivion.

Racing thoughts of his daughter
pounded Big-Time's mind, as he
sprinted blindly towards the youths,
carrying but one goal, to save those
young people.

Kilari somehow maintained his
balance, quickly grabbing Jezza and
Marcia, and running them far enough
away from the creature to keep them

out of its reach. The creature's tentacles jutted out of the water twenty feet high, flailing too, and fro. Kilari raced back, seeing Ell and Harrah struggling to get to the water's edge.

They seemed helpless, and Kilari thought that they would be unable to keep themselves from getting grabbed. The vicious turbulence of the water made it nearly impossible for the girls to make headway, so he set his sights on saving them next.

"Do you hear that?" Telebar asked. By this time, the four men had nearly closed the entire gap between their group and Kilari's. They just happened to be coming up the last dune, towards the oasis. After hearing a great calamity up ahead of them, they began sprinting up the last section of dune. Once at the top, a sight that filled their hearts with horror stood in front of them like a sick joke.

Not only had a giant sea creature with massive tentacles somehow caught the rest of their group off guard, but also, a group of unfamiliar men in old style Death Squad uniforms began charging in at them unsuspectingly.

Each man instantly swelled with mixed emotions, for they could see that their girls were alive and with Kilari, but the turmoil of the scene that lay ahead, put them in an instant alert status.

Drake started a little slower down the steep dune, all the while scanning for Glenda. He scoured the background, until finally, he saw her. There she was. She had somehow gotten herself trapped between a couple of large boulders, and the creature. Drake's instant reaction was as fast as the fear jumping into his heart, and like a shot, he began racing directly towards his woman, instinctively dodging back and forth between the sudden slamming tentacles of the sinewy sea creature. He tried calling out her name, but in the din of the chaos, she could not hear his voice.

By this time, Cam and the rest of the men were nearly upon the scene, sprinting towards Kilari, who they saw struggling to get Harrah and Ell from the water. Cam spotting Layla further off to one side, but still not out of the commotion, shifted directions, while Telebar and Malichye continued heading directly towards Kilari to help.

Big-Time and his crew had weaved their way near the water's edge with the same goal in mind, trying to keep away from the striking creature. It swiped and struck at any who were in its reach. The dodging men had all that

COGNIZANT

they could do to keep from being slammed into oblivion by the creature's seemingly blind attacks.

Eagle-One, however, stayed further back than did his two cohorts, being he was a pilot and was *really* not used to being this close to the action. As he stood back somewhat mesmerized by the chaotic scene, he spent the small amount of focus that he had on watching Frontline, who courageously continued rushing towards his goal even at the sight of certain death.

Frontline shot headlong towards the closest girl from his location, which just happened to get caught upon one of the monstrous rising tentacles. Bobbing and weaving he hit the water diving with a splash. Crossing the water in mere seconds, he rose to the bank. He called out trying to get the young girl's attention, but her mind, gripped by fear, could not hear any calls, as she stood there motionless, white as a ghost, in shock.

Frontline continued moving directly for the girl, but before he could make it to the safety of the large boulders, one of the sea creature's slamming and flailing tentacles had caught him by the leg. The tiny man's eyes bulged with shock as the creature's vice-like grip ripped him from the ground effortlessly. Then with one fluid snap of its extended tentacle, the man was thrust against one of the large boulders, splattering his remains and leaving a bloody stain to mark where his flattened corpse lay.

Finally, Big-Time made his way into the mix at the water's edge. Sophie was the first he could get to, but being so pumped with adrenaline he did not think, he just reacted, and in so doing, he grabbed Sophie by the wrist drew her in and then basically, he tossed her, beyond the water and onto the island side, instead of back towards the safety of the ground behind.

Once Big-Time tossed the girl out of immediate danger, he maneuvered close to Tank. Outstretching his arm and yelling loudly at the stunned young man, "Grab my hand! Look son, if you grab my hand, I can help you!" He said pleading to the dazed man, who had been merely grazed by a swinging tentacle blocking Sophie from its blow.

Tank could only see a hazy blur. "I will only slow you down. Save yourself!" He yelled back not even realizing that he did not know to whom he was speaking.

After hearing an answer like that, Big-Time knew that he would be better grabbing the man and try to guide him away from the danger zone, so he yelled, "Hold your breath!" He could see Tank following his order, so then he dunked the big youth below the surface, figuring that all he would need to do is steer him a bit, but once below the surface, Big-Time could see multiple other sea creatures waiting for room to surface.

Pulling quickly back, Big-Time swam to the surface of the water with a firm grasp on Tank's wrist. They surfaced amid multiple reaching arms trying to help pull the last two humans from the water. Big-Time yelled out, warning the young cadets, as he was being helped. "Stand clear! There are more of them things waiting below the surface."

Telebar and Belsangar quickly latched onto Tank to help free up the huge black merc, so that he could move away from the water under his own steam. The four men instantly rushed beyond the creature's reaching tentacles of death, where they collapsed in exhaustion upon the safety of the ground.

The worn down panic-stricken group, gasped for breath, while trying to get their bearings and come to grips with what had just gone down, when suddenly from out of the distance a deafening foghorn alarm began sounding. All but three had heard this strange foghorn like sound before, and they knew that this was *not* a good sign.

"Sheesh! Are you frickin' kidding me?" Cam complained, realizing that the Black Mage must be on the attack again. "This is not a good time. Status! I need a status check." Cam called out, so that he could get details, rapidly.

"Hey, Drake is on the island with Glenda, and Sophie, the creature doesn't seem to be able to reach them, so they appear to be fine, at the moment. Other than that, we have

fourteen in head count on this end."
Telebar snapped out quickly.

"*Fourteen*?" Cam questioned.

"Yeah, we are all present and
accounted for, with two freelancers
dressed in old school Death Squad
drab." Kilari answered butting into the
conversation. "So, seventeen in all."

Cam immediately wiped the sand
marring any traceability of his plan.
"Death Squad?" He questioned standing
up quickly and taking a look around.

"Two?" Big-Time asked gruffly,
wanting to take a headcount of his
own.

"Well three, if you count that
one." Kilari said, pointing to the few
pieces of another in Death Squad attire
that had not yet been eaten by the sea
creature. There was no love lost for a
downed Death Squad agent in Kilari's
eyes.

COGNIZANT

Big-Time scanned the area quickly, and after finding Eagle-One in one piece, he looked over to the bloody remains and asked, "Frontline, *what did you do boy?*" Then, bowing his head for a moment of silence, he stood with his black cap to his heart. The moment lasted a mere ten seconds and then the man turned back towards the wondering young agents. "I *know* I trained you better than that." He said to himself, yet audibly enough for the rest to hear.

In another second, the two mercs found themselves surrounded by the six young agents. "Who are you guys?" Telebar asked point-blank.

"Look this ain't what it seems." Big-Time quickly answered trying to explain, before things got out of hand.

"Hey, I recognize these cats." Belsangar said stepping into the circle.

"Look, I can explain this." Big-Time again quickly blurted out, hoping that he would at least get the chance.

"Yeah, well I can explain a few things too, like the fact that you were working for Brague. You were the pansy guards that forced the girls through the light. You *forced* them to come here," Kilari stated, while moving right up to the big man, who did not budge an inch. "Yeah, well we saw you in those yellow jumpers holding your heat wave blasters to the girls and forcing them through the light." The girls all responded affirmatively, backing Kilari and Belsangar.

"Alright, alright," Cam said quieting the group. "We don't have time for this right now." Belsangar started to speak again, but Cam quickly pointed him out and gave him the look, which shut him down quick enough.

COGNIZANT

Big-Time looked at the way that the group was working, and recognizing Cam as the leader, he asked, "So *you're* running this show?" His tone sounded almost as though he doubted the possibility.

Cam knew that he was being felt out by the big man, so he let it be known to him that he was indeed in charge. "Hey! I said shut it, and that means you too big man. I have only two questions, and I want direct responses. One, are you Death Squad? And two, are you working for Brague?"

Big-Time liked the little guy's attitude, so he showed him due respect. "No sir, we are not Death Squad, and in a way sir, we could still be working for President Brague."

"President? What the heck is that?" Tank asked bluntly.

"Okay, we got time for one more question. Are you our enemy?" Cam had no time to play around, so he looked the big man right in the eye, standing on his tip toes to help bridge the gap in height.

Big-Time leaned down a little, when he answered, so the little guy could see clearly. "No, we are not your enemy. We are actually here on an extraction mission."

Cam kept his stare going. He believed the big man. "Good, it is settled then."

"Just like that?" Telebar asked, in a tone of complete and utter shock. In his mind, these guys still had explaining to do, and he did not really want to wait for one.

"Look guys, unless I'm wrong we are going to be overtaken by zombies in a brief amount of time." Cam explained. "Now, you two better remember what I'm about to tell you, and no matter how odd it sounds, believe it." Cam quickly explained, as he got the group to walk with him, so that he could get a good look at the area. He wondered whether he should try to get Drake from the island, or they should try to join him there. "You have to bust their brains, or sever their spinal cord from their brain stem to kill them. And, if they bite you, no matter how minor, you will become one of them guaranteed."

Vail and Travis were soaking in the multi-colored chamber. They were both leaning back letting the bubbles and hot water soothe their aching muscles. "How are you doing that?" Travis asked.

"How am I doing what?" Vail asked, inquisitively wondering what he could possibly be thinking that she was doing.

"How are you turning up the bubbles? They've been rolling up faster and faster for the last couple of minutes. Oh, and do they *ever* feel good." Travis said, as he leaned back a little farther, and adjusted to the maximum comfort position for the moment, soaking in all of the enjoyment that he could. His last couple of days, had been up and down like a rollercoaster, and right now, he was feeling as though he were riding an upswing.

Vail maintained her position, until it finally occurred to her that only one thing would alter the flow of the air bubbles, and that would be the movement of the herd of sea creatures that lived below the island. "Oh crap!" Vail exclaimed, as she jumped up to her feet. "Something must be going on outside. Get dressed, we got to check this out. Something must have stirred the sea creatures from their slumber."

COGNIZANT

"What? Sea creatures?" Travis asked wide-eyed. "The same ones with all of the arms, like in the pictures on the wall?" He asked with a lump in his throat, as he threw on his freshly washed hooded cloak.

Vail looked over to him and gave him an affirmative nod trying not to show fear. Then she moved towards the ramp, looking up its distance towards the top, while she waited for Travis to tie his boots. She watched him as he bent over, and made a mental note to herself. She liked the way his cargo shorts fit better than the way that the loose cloak flowed around him, even though it was her late mates, besides, she thought to herself, she liked to see some skin showing on a man.

Travis began moving over towards the ramp, and as he looked to see the expression upon Vail's face, he became shocked to see her eyeing him up like a piece of meat. A small grin formed on his lips, as he remained in disbelief, but then it occurred to him that she must not be too worried. He placed his arm around her waist and then they started on their way to check the situation. "So, this might not be so bad? I mean, as bad as I first thought." He asked, because of the look that he had so recently received.

Vail moved him behind her, and then took out her stone blade. She started to walk more stealthily on her approach to the exit hole, where she stuck her ear to listen for any clues. Just then the fog horn bellowed out again, loud enough for her to hear over the already ensuing chaos. "No, it'll be worse, much worse," she said, finally answering him, while looking him right in the eyes. He could see the serious tone come over her face, as she took a moment to prepare herself for battle.

COGNIZANT

"You wait here." She ordered still staring him in the eyes.

"Surely, I can be of some help." Travis pleaded hoping for the chance.

"I can fight better, if I don't have to worry about you, and me. Now, you wait here for me to return. It is safe here." Vail grabbed Travis hugging him with all of her essence. "I'll be back for you." With that, Vail gave her quiver a quick feel, assuring that it remained full, then she pulled out her bow, and crawled through the small hidden exit.

Vail could see water splashing through the air, and tentacles flailing about, but she knew that she was unseen, and for a brief period, she felt, as if she were on the outside looking in. Slowly, after pulling her hood over, she began to creep around, hiding behind bushes and boulders just staying out of sight of any who may be looking. After working her way around to a spot from which she could spy, she could see more men that were not from her world.

One man had been splattered, and after hearing the Guardian's wake-up call, she knew that his spilled blood would attract the Black Mage's flesh-eating army, and they would soon be pouring over the entire area. Continuing on, moving forward, she finally worked her way to a point at which Kilari and the others all came into view. This sight pasted a smile upon her face. With the belief that he was truly the chosen one fully vested in her mind, she could feel a burst of confidence begin to flow right into her soul. Quickly, she stood and moved forward up the large rocky mound. Standing there, with her loose cloak blowing in the breeze, overseeing the entire situation.

COGNIZANT

Suddenly, Big-Time felt a tapping on his shoulder. He turned fast making sure of who wanted his attention, and why. When he looked down and back behind himself, he could see Eagle-One pointing upwards, saying, "Look, look up there, at the top of that hill. It's one of the dark cloaked figures."

Big-Time stood peering up at the figure. "I can't tell. Is that the one with boots?" He asked in a somewhat loud gruff voice, which of course drew attention from the others, who had overheard him. They all turned to see what he was pointing at that was up so high.

Eagle-One answered. "I don't believe so, but it is hard to tell from this distance."

Then softly from out of the background the name, "Vail," was spoken from Kilari's lips.

ROC BLISS

"Vail? Who's Vail?" Jezza asked in a semi-jealous tone.

"She's one of the Huntresses at the very least." Cam said stating his interpretation of the being on the mound.

"Huntresses?" Layla questioned.

Kilari slowly flagged his arms, as he moved slightly away from the group. Vail saw him and motioned back. Kilari then motioned her to look over towards the three, which were on the island, on the other side of the water. Vail turned and looked over seeing them, and then she turned back towards Kilari, and signaled by pointing to her eyes and then to the three. Then she pointed towards Kilari and his group, motioning them to flow around to the other side of the island. She then pointed towards herself and the three, and then back to the other side of the island.

COGNIZANT

"What's all of the pointing about?" Ceilia asked, as Kilari finally flashed Vail the okay sign.

Kilari watched as Vail moved down the mound. "We're supposed to meet Vail, Drake, Sophie, and Glenda on the far side of the island."

"You got all of *that* from a minute of pointing back and forth?" Ceilia asked sounding impressed.

"Yeah," he said answering Ceilia. Then he called to the group, "C'mon let's get it moving. We have no time." He grabbed Jezza with one hand, and Marcia with the other and they began double timing it without a second thought, moving toward the way he was instructed.

Big-Time and Telebar each looked at Cam, who was the actual leader of the group. They waited for some type of response, until finally, he ordered, "you heard the man, get it moving," and with that the entire group moved, hurrying to keep up. Kilari swung wide enough from the water to keep the sea creatures out of striking distance.

In the meantime, Vail made her way back down the mound. She collected Travis and then they went for the other three, who were still trapped between a steep boulder that they could not climb, and the tentacle clad sea beasts. She looked down upon the trapped agent, and remembered his name. She called out, "Drake," but he did not hear her. He was still trying to talk Glenda into getting a boost up the rock face to see if she might be able to climb up.

Vail screamed his name, "Drake! Hey!" Then the young agent noticed that it was Vail and she was trying to rescue them. Vail could see the fear in the young girls' eyes, so she pointed straight at the girl and said, "If you want to live get on his shoulders, if not step out of the way, so that we can get the others out." Her voice sounded harsh, but she had no room in her heart for worthless women, who cowered in fear like *men* in the face of trouble.

The girl still looked completely terrified, and it finally dawned on Travis that the girl could not see his or Vail's face, so he pulled his hood back, and then said to Vail, "Pull your hood back and let the girl see your face. I think that once she sees your face, then she will become less worried."

Vail gave him a thumbs-up, and then pulled back her hood revealing her long, flowing blonde hair, and her smooth clean freshly washed skin, and just as Travis had predicted, the girl finally relaxed enough to understand the simplistic commands that were being asked of her. Soon, Travis and

Vail had them all pulled out of their predicament, and then moved to the other side of the island, where the rest of the group stood waiting.

The sea creatures had not yet rounded the island, due to the fact, that the route which Kilari chose had brought them past the shallows, where the creatures could not pass. Vail knew that in a short amount of time, the creatures would figure their way around, and once they moved away from the shallows they would be able to cross over to join the main group. Vail circled her group to advise them on the situation, saying, "When the creatures move away from there," she pointed toward the creatures, which were still schooling, as close as they could get to where the others had run through. "We will only have a short time to cross through the shallows. We must all go at once, be fast and deliberate."

At that point, Vail changed the focus of her speech from a group pep talk to a more personal approach, trying to coach the girls, so that they would know what to do, and how to do it. She could tell by the way these girls were acting a minute ago that Travis was not lying about the women of An'non. They must all be very weak and fragile, even more so than the men of Xibalba. "You must look at your goal only. Do not look too and fro like some kind of scared rodents. No matter what you hear, no matter what you see, you must keep moving and looking towards the bank on the other side."

Travis was quite impressed by the way she talked to the girls. She did not really talk down to them, but instead she spoke more like an advisor, and that, he figured, could be the deciding factor in how the girls will react, when the time comes and they actually, make their move.

A moment later, the sounds of ten thousand zombie guardians thundered through the area, warning every living soul, people and sea creature alike, of their soon coming approach.

Vail now knew that the distraction she was waiting for, would soon be coming, and could only hope that the oncoming onslaught would not be too much for the group to outrun. The zombies could smell freshly spilled human blood, which had not only been spilled upon the ground, but fortunately, for the fleshlings, it had also been spread over the sea creatures and had mingled with the water, causing an overwhelming draw to the mindless army of the dead.

The flesh-eating horde, being overpowered by the irresistible aroma of fresh blood, ran directly toward the sea creatures, which ensued into a battle of the ages, one that had never taken place throughout all of time. The sea creatures lashed out quickly with multiple sets of spine shredding tentacles, snagging, ripping and eating the guardians of the wicked city, but the zombified guardians attacked in waves with the tenacity of piranha.

The sheer numbers of the zombies made it impossible for the sea creatures to win this epic battle, but the safety in the water's depths also allowed the sea creatures a place of escape, so the zombies could not win either.

"Run!" Vail screamed upon the sight of the oncoming zombie assault. The girls sprinted, closely followed by Vail, who continued her coaching by pushing them on, saying, "Go, go, go, let's move it ladies!" The water splashed, as the five of them ran through the shallows. Cam and most of the rest of the group ran close to the water's edge, grabbing the girls to help them keep their balance, as they made the transition from the water to the shore.

Kilari stood further back with Jezza and Marcia at his side, feeling that the tunnel seemed to be the quickest way out of the general vicinity. Having already checked it out, and knowing that he could see through its entire length, he had no concerns about getting lost, or trapped in another unknown cave.

Jezza deciding that it was her turn to carry the book, held her arms out to lighten Marcia's load. The two girls had meticulously kept the book under constant care. Jezza could feel her arms beginning to tire from all the exertion over the last couple of days, but she did not even think about making a complaint.

Kilari watched Vail, as she came out of the water. He could see her pointing towards the tunnel, and that was enough for him. Grabbing each of his girls by the hand, they began running for the other side. Jezza had the book with one hand and arm, pressing it against her body; she prayed that her strength would be enough to keep the book from falling to the ground. After making their way through the tunnel, the three had stopped to rest, standing off to the side a short ways away.

Kilari finally noticing that Jezza kept switching arms to carry the book, and that Marcia was rubbing her sore biceps and forearms, he asked, "Are you girls tired?" They each looked at him with expressions that said it all. "Gotchya," he answered before they could say anything. "Here, I'll take the book back. You girls did awesome." He offered reaching out for Jezza to hand the heavy book over to him.

Vail and the others came suddenly, running out of the tunnel. Kilari looking to the woman, yelled, "we need to get to higher ground! Which way are we going?" Vail never slowed down, she just pointed to a pathway that began across the small space at which he was standing, and led through the trees. Kilari kept the lead, knowing the type of strategic landscape needed, if they were forced to make a stand, but he would also be open to suggestion, if Vail had a specific place in mind.

COGNIZANT

Purple Heart

Hades, the Black Mage, now had his crown back in working order, and could also utilize the All-Seeing Eye. Unfortunately, for him, he had had to call upon his dark master, Lucifer, to get these things back in order. The two demons sat watching, as the zombies initially became sidetracked by the spilled human's blood.

Hades immediately moved to sound the deep billowing siren, but before he could, Lucifer had him stopped. "You know that I have a plan in place for these fleshlings. Why would you try to defy my orders?" He asked, as he cut off Hades advance.

Hades knew the tone in Lucifer's voice, and he also knew that he must answer his master. "These bags of flesh had killed one of my dogs, injured the other, and completely blew my plan for them damn hill dwellers, all because I was following *your* orders." His final statement being a lie, but he could not act as if he had been trying to kill the group, whom he had been ordered to let live.

Hades, however was not satisfied by telling just a lie, he also decided that it was time to shift blame and make it appear that he had been lied to, by his master, so he continued his rant, saying, "I was told that in Xibalba, all souls belonged to me, and they have defied me. I want my vengeance."

Lucifer listened to Hades, as he tried to explain, but in the end, Lucifer had a bottom line. "My plan is *eternal* you fool! You are just looking for a momentary fix. If you want revenge, think of more than just what is under your nose. Think of all souls, throughout all of time."

"Yes master, you are right," Hades admitted aloud, immediately buckling to his master's will. "But these bastards must pay. They have turned my kingdom into shambles. I *had*, all of the tribes living in fear, and now they are uprising. It is as if... They had brought hope to these people, and I want to crush that hope, once and for all." Hades spoke with passion, showing Lucifer that he was indeed still the demon for the job.

Lucifer walked closer to his highest ranked servant, and leaning in he said, "don't you worry. These fleshlings are doing my bidding without even realizing it. I will grant you a new kingdom, a kingdom where all souls are tormented day and night, forever. There will be no escape for them, and you can revel in their pain for all eternity. I will even name this place Hades, and then your name will inspire fear to all. This is my chance to get a leg up on YHVH."

Hades liked the idea of a new kingdom. He had been in this kingdom for centuries without an inkling of trouble. He had battles, and wars, and hatred, with death and sorrow, then suddenly, these awful humans from An'non infiltrated his world. Then, hope began to spark to life. He pondered the whole situation in his mind. Finally, he spoke, saying, "you have had him in the position of being, almost completely vanquished. How did he once again begin to get a following?"

Lucifer's face began to turn red, with the heat of anger, as he thought about it. "It is that book! That human somehow found that book. I had these humans to the point of disbelief. They did not even know of YHVH, or Heaven, or even Xibalba for that matter, but then that book had somehow resurfaced, and now look, there are believers, *just* like that." He said with a snap of his fingers.

"Why don't you kill them and then destroy the book. Then you will win once and for all." Hades threw in, attempting to strategize.

"Oh, I've tried, but somehow that book is indestructible, or it reforms as ancient scrolls, and then it gets put back together. I have been fighting this fight, since before the beginning of time." Lucifer stated to his servant. "This time however, I believe that I have the solution. This time, I have put enough traps into the book itself that it will cause a constant turmoil, even amongst its truest followers, and they are all completely, unaware. Confusion will rule the day, and divisions will rule their minds, and in the end, they will be coming to you, and you will be filling their minds with anguish and fear." By the end of the speech, the two demon lords laughed and cackled at the wisdom of their plan. Hades was more than willing to go along with his master, and begin again in a new kingdom.

Hades, then moved over to his throne, and began searching its buttons. "Well, if they're going to leave here, my guardians will have to give them one last chase." He said, as he hit the switch, which sounded the final tone. The tone filled the air of the entire kingdom of Xibalba. It drove the zombies into a ferocious state of attack, which forced them to pour over the sea creatures, and as they overflowed the area, the overflow kept moving forward, and on they went seeking the next target. Hades watched through the All-Seeing Eye. He began cackling loudly, as he sat back in his throne watching the calamity at hand.

A tone began sounding, confusing Vail for a second, because this was a tone the like she had never heard before. A bad feeling began to creep into her mind the instant this final tone started, and the longer its haunting moan rang out the more panic she felt pounding in her heart. All she could think, is that it meant the worst for her, and her people. She continued running along keeping pace with Travis, while thoughts of saving her Queen slowly came to surface. The tone kept blasting throughout the kingdom of Xibalba for several minutes, sending worry and fear to those, susceptible to its call. Thinking the tone would never end,

Vail's heart filled with a feeling that she had not felt in many long times. In her mind, she began to panic, even though her body gave no outward signs. After several minutes, the final tone had her and the entire group running at full speed.

Once the tone finally ended, Vail yelled to Travis, "we need to save the Queen. I must press forward. You keep the people moving toward the caves, and get them up the ladder." Travis looked confused, but he too could feel the sense of urgency at hand, so he nodded his agreement, and watched, as she pressed on to the front, where Kilari, unaware of this feeling, ran trying to lead the group. She had caught up to him by the time that they made the large clearing, which was the final distance between them and the supposed safety of the high places. She took the lead steering the group onto the most direct path towards the caves. She then began sprinting the distance tirelessly, leaving Travis, and the slower group behind.

Soon, the familiar sound of zombie groans, began closing in on the group. "Three hundred yards!" Belsangar yelled out, so the group would be aware of the nearing presence of danger. The group could see the ladder, which Vail seemed to climb effortlessly. Kilari, still unaware of the spell that the Black Mage had placed within the haunting tone, knew that it would take a lot more effort, for certain individuals in his group to climb that rope ladder, so he urged Jezza, and Marcia, to increase their speed. His hopes were to streamline the group out, so that there would be no bunching up at the bottom of the ladder, because it was beginning to become apparent that every second would count.

Kilari and his two girls made it to the rope ladder, well ahead of the others. He pushed Jezza to the ladder, saying, "Go," but then the girl stalled to look back at the oncoming zombie horde, which was closing in upon the group.

Kilari, knowing that he had no time, cracked Jezza's backside, catching her completely off-guard. She squealed a little from the surprising force, but Kilari being all about business, instantly began yelling, "Go, go, go!" Jezza wasted no time to argue, or complain, she moved immediately without any hesitation.

Marcia, seeing how her girl had just been treated, was not overly enthused with Kilari's drill sergeant routine. With squinting eyes and a turned-up nose, Marcia showed her displeasure, shooting Kilari a little look of insulted disgust, but when she saw a look of determination on his face, and how he seemed unaffected by her display, as he stood there by the rope ladder, pointing upward, she began climbing without any more hesitation. Kilari's expression changed to a slim grin, as he watched the target of her backside, moving up the ladder. The irresistible force was too much for him, so he gave her a mild smack on the rump, with a little squeeze for *his* pleasure. Marcia continued her ascent, but her frown was instantly replaced with a slight smirk, as she realized that Kilari was still Kilari, and not turning into some control freak.

Kilari quickly turned to surmise the situation and began screaming for the others to hurry, as he placed the Holy Book inside of his shirt to free up both of his hands. Once both hands were freed, he took out his nun-chucks, and prepared for battle. Drake and Glenda were next to the ladder. Kilari pointed to the sky, as they were still approaching, but neither needed any coaxing to keep moving. He could see Tank bringing up the rear with some of the fastest of the zombies closing in on him. Knowing, that without help, Tank would be finding himself in a skirmish, which would slow him down to the point of getting caught up in a fight with the next group, which could easily snowball, into the inevitable, Kilari sprang into action.

Kilari did not detect the various levels of fear on the faces that had passed him by, or maybe he would have wondered, why none of his brothers stayed to help Tank buy some time. There was no rhyme, or reason, to the effects of the spell, but it forced an illogical fear in the minds of most of his brothers.

Jezza and Marcia, climbed speedily, thinking all of the while, that Kilari was on their tails, but when they turned to see Glenda, and Drake, climbing onto the large shelf atop of the ladder, a new reality entered their minds. Each of them quickly strode to look over the edge. They saw him, actually moving away from the safety of the ladder. "Oh nooooo," Marcia moaned with distress looking down at the scene that was taking place. "I can't believe… He didn't follow us."

"Yeah, well when he gets up here, we're going to have to have a talk with him." Jezza explained seriously, sounding tough, as if she were positive that the young blonde agent would return, even though in her heart, worry and fear eclipsed any real positive tone. These were not illogical symptoms of some magic spell; these feelings were made of true emotions, which soon caused the girl to tremble, and sob.

Kilari told all who passed by him to climb fast, so that everyone could scale to safety, but Tank had only a mere, fifty-yard lead on the closing zombies, and was beginning to slow down. Figuring Tank was preparing for the fight, Kilari began sprinting towards the big man, and as he did, he kept yelling, "Move it Tank! Push it to that ladder, and we'll all get to safety." Kilari was nearly to the big man, when he gave him one last order. "Yell, when you get Sophie up and she's safe."

This order hit Tank's brain with a total sense of urgency, and he began yelling for Sophie to leave his side and get up that ladder, but she knew that if she got too far ahead of him that he would turn to fight, and she was not ready to lose him. She faked a few stumble steps, which forced him to help her all the way to the ladder.

Meanwhile, Kilari had a weapon in each hand, and a look in his eye. A wave of adrenaline poured over his brain like a flood. His eyes turned to slits, as the reality of everything being entirely his fault resurfaced in his mind. If only he had not been so greedy, if he had not taken vengeance to the next level, on those guards back in Acropolis. His anger with himself began to pour into his brain, mixing with the adrenaline, and now he was facing an enemy for the slaughter.

"I am a soldier, and I know my enemy," he told himself, as he stared through his slit turned eyes, and then suddenly, there were no more sounds to be heard other than the yelling and screaming of Jezza, and Marcia, just as he had heard them in his visions that night in the academy.

He could still see them all, standing along the edge of a mountainside, helpless, and surrounded by an army of these, soulless. flesh eaters. His mind, somehow flashed with the speed of a strobe light, showing entire scenes in a blink of an eye.

Tears began welling up in the corners of his eyes, as emotions stabbed his mind like a dull knife. The torment of his memories took effect, as his racing mind replayed all the flashes, from his parents taking a bullet, by the hand of the man that had raised him, to the sounds of the girls, screaming in agony.

There were other memory flashes as well. He saw Field Marshall Blak torturing innocent people over skin color, and then the voice of Yahiveh himself rang out, saying, "It is your fault. You must pay." All of these things flashed through his mind several times per step, while sprinting towards the enemy, instead of climbing up the ladder, behind his group.

Lucifer stood quickly, as he also watched. He knew that this was the man with the book, who *needed* to escape, and here he was, doing just what would get him killed, which would foil his ultimate plan. *"Do something!"* He screamed to his servant, who sat back salivating at the possibility that this blonde one would die, and pay for the torment that he had brought to Xibalba, without it being any fault of his own, and Lucifer could not hold it against him. 'After all, if the human is suicidal, how could it be *any* fault of his,' he thought with glee. Hades did not even attempt to lift a finger to stop anything. His grin alone spoke for him.

"I request permission to help reel Kilari in." Telebar stated saluting his superior.

Cam looked at the scene below. He could not see how Kilari could get through this one. Harrah grabbed onto Telebar's leg and screamed that she would not let go, and that he would have to drag her with him.

Ceilia instantly jumped on Belsangar's back, knowing that he too, would be ready to answer the call, and play the hero. She quickly grappled with him, pleading with him to stay by her side.

Kilari strode alone in mental anguish, as he met the first handful of zombies from the swarm with skull shattering over hand strikes. The first few were lying in piles of lifeless rotting flesh within a second, maybe two. His weapons bore down upon his enemies with vengeance, recoiling from

COGNIZANT

skull to skull, spilling rotting brains with every snap of his wrist.

As the lead group of raging, blood starved, guardians of the wicked city fell, there was now time enough for his friends to all make the safety zone, above the rope ladder, but instead of falling back, his blurred mind swirled in between his flashes of guilt, and his usual affirmations of thinking, 'I am a soldier and I know my enemy.' Convinced that he must pay for his sins of the past, he pushed forward, moving from pack to pack. All the while, he fought one small group at a time, his nun-chucks spinning with blurring speed, piling the rotting bodies of the fallen on the ground.

Dodging to maneuver away from the oncoming horde and then ducking in again, he struck another segregated group. His brain, continuing in a constant stream of torment, recycled through all of the implanted visions and sounds, which Lucifer had so happily used to try to force his hand, had him moving closer, and closer, to the mighty onslaught of the horde. All he could truly hear, were the screams of his loved ones, and all he could feel, is the guilt for bringing this upon them.

His lightning fast reflexes kept him alive longer than anyone could have believed. Jezza and Marcia kept screaming uncontrollably, while being restrained by Big-Time and Eagle-One, or else they themselves would have climbed down the ladder to run to his aide. Their screams shrilled in the air, as they were certain that Kilari would not live through each moment. All of their love fired a fuel that made it difficult, even for the giant mercs to keep the girls down.

COGNIZANT

"What is going on?" Vail screamed, as she and her Queen had finally made their way to the ledge. "You worthless men! Now, you see why women do the fighting here!" Vail hailed, as she quickly pulled her bow up.

Within seconds, her arrows were streaming through the air, but her arrows were numbered, and after mere moments, she had none left, and she also began screaming for him to return, but his ears could still only hear the anguish of his past faults, and the torment of the screams of his tortured friends. By this time, the horde of zombie guardians were nearly upon him.

Lucifer was about to destroy this entire plane with his anger alone, fearing that his perfect plan would soon be destroyed.

Hades cared not. He was in sheer ecstasy. The sweet taste of agony was pouring from all of the observers, as they saw their friend, and loved one, finally become engulfed, beneath the surmounting numbers of the zombie horde.

All, stood on top of the mountainside with tears flowing, and in total shock. They could not see Kilari at all, anymore, and what they saw as the worst sign of his defeat, the swarm of zombies instantly began moving on.

Each of the soldiers, agents, friends, and loved ones stood staring down at the battlefield, as did Queen Penelope and Vail. Vail had believed that Kilari was the chosen one, while her Queen had never admitted it, but she too was in a state of wonder, of whence a man like him had come.

Jezza and Marcia were completely hysterical, as they saw him overtaken by the flesh-eating monsters. Ceilia and the rest of the girls, all rushed over to the two young agonized girls. They began to try comforting them, but in reality, they too needed to be comforted.

"Kilari gave up his life to assure that *all* of us could make it up that ladder." Cam stated, as a fact of credit for the young soldier.

"The ladder!" Drake screamed pointing as he saw the zombies starting to make their way up towards them. Vail quickly moving over to the ladder, cut the ropes, forcing several zombies to fall, she watched, as they landed on top of others that had made their way to the sheer rock wall.

"Hit the button now Thomas," Tessa yelled, for the third time, as she watched the computer screen at the science lab, back on Flag Island. She saw the swarm of zombies overtake Kilari's position. Thomas kept striking the button, but he did not see any effect, so he rechecked his figures, prior to pressing the button one more time. Tessa's eyes flowed with tears, after watching Kilari's fight. "Get them back hear Thomas. Get them back, now!" She screamed pleading in a frightful hysteric of panic. Thomas pressed the button one last time. This time, the entire group, positioned upon the mountain shelf, vanished from the sight on the computer screen, and appeared upon a staging platform in the dimly lit shade of the darkened jungle on Flag Island.

Soldiers with guns drawn swarmed the platform making sure that no zombies had somehow been sucked through the trans-dimensional gate. The bluish light of the gate reflected against the leaves of the thick foliage, as Rudy lowered its power level to phase-one to keep it from pulling any

COGNIZANT

others through. The soldiers were armored from head to toe, and were unrecognizable to the dimensional travelers. Keeping their heaters poised in position, the lead soldier barked threateningly, "Freeze! Don't move!"

All of the people standing in the re-entry point stood in shock, and had no idea of what was going on. They had moved instantaneously, suddenly from the anguish of one world, into the confusion of another. Suddenly, a voice sounded from a com-unit, clipped to the lead soldier's collar. "Tranquilize them." Vail instantly jumped to cover Queen Penelope from the possible attack, but before she could fully pull her knife from her belt, a green, fog-like gaseous vapor had flooded the area, putting all the dimensional travelers into a deep silent sleep. "Cart them back, immediately." The lead soldier's voice rang out sharply.

Roc Bliss

"Shut her down Rudy," Thomas called out, speaking of the gate. "We're missing one, and yet it seems we may have taken on a couple of extras." He surmised by his last look at the group on the mountainside. He glanced over at Tessa and could see all hope escaping, as the orders spilled from his lips.

Dr. Sung clicked the intercom button again and spoke, giving orders to his assistants. "Prepare the infirmary for more incoming." Then he clicked the intercom back off, and offered, "we are prepared to handle the group in its entirety." He told Thomas Elliot.

Thomas placed his arm around Tessa, and gently squeezed her close, in hopes of comforting her, so that *he*, could walk her down from Rudy's lab, to wait in the infirmary for the remaining kids. Knowing that the wait

COGNIZANT

would seem impossibly long, no matter how quickly the crew got them there. Thomas realized that he had better be prepared to be buckled down for the long haul.

Gray billowing clouds, began sweeping in, and surrounding everything in Kilari's sight. He was in the middle of a heated battle a second ago, and now, here he is, in a place that he has seen a few times, but this time he had no clue whether, or not, he still had an anchor in the flesh realm, or if he was a free spirit in the land of limbo.

He looked down seeing his clothing, and once again, he was dressed in the long white robes that he had seen in past visits. He felt all the tension removed from his spirit, as he walked, to and fro, waiting for the presence of Yahiveh. He began wondering, if he was in one of his dreams, or if this is another vision, sent to tell him of some future event.

Kilari did not have long to wait. The voice of his one true master sounded. "Kilari, you have done well. You have passed your test, and you can now wear the white robes that you are envisioning."

Kilari looked to his master in bewilderment. "What are you saying?"

"You have proved yourself to be loyal, and have held up to the set standards of flesh man, and are therefore purged of your past iniquities." Yahiveh's voice was as deep as thunder, and shook the Heavens, as it reverberated.

COGNIZANT

Aguanimos

Lucifer, bursting with anger, had finally taken too much, and he only had one demon in mind on which to unleash his wicked temper. "Hades! You pathetic worm, I am *going* to make you pay!"

Hades, had been still cackling with his insidious laugh, until Lucifer's treacherous voice, boisterously blotted all feelings that the Black Mage had been harboring, not so sneakily. "Master it is not my fault. The fool mortal just ran headlong, directly into the wake of my guardians. How could I know…"

"*Silence*!" The master's voice bellowed out, immediately all sound from the Black Mage ceased.

Roc Bliss

The Black Mage crumbled back with fear, as Lucifer began waving his outstretched hands, which created a maelstrom, directly in front of him.

A swirling of air, at first appeared to be all that was happening in front of the Black Mage, but it constantly continued to grow larger and stronger. As the currents of the air expanded, so did the blackness within it, until finally, Hades could see the true nature of Lucifer's power.

Like a dark star being sucked into the torrents of a black hole, Hades soon found that he helplessly could do nothing to stop this whirlpool. Slowly, the Black Mage began being pulled into its gripping vortex.

"Be gone!" Lucifer finally yelled out, above the din of the magical maelstrom, and with that, Hades vanished from the plane of Xibalba. The red Crystal crown clinked, as it hit the stone ground, and instantaneously the curse was lifted, ending this time. Betelgeuse turned from its cursed red glow, and once again shown golden over Oblivion.

* * * * *

Thomas tried to console his love by occupying her mind. "Don't worry Tess," he said. "Tony, and Cappy, will get them here, and they'll be fine. We'll just need to keep them tranquilized, while we go over their bodies inch by inch to heal them. Then we can slowly bring their minds around to the facts, so that they can learn to deal with their losses."

"Thomas, we must bring them back to the underground, right now." Tessa told him point-blank, not even hearing his plan, and then she backed up the order by stating her fear. "I don't trust being here. Brague and his army could easily swarm in on us, at any time, and take the kids away." Then her tears began flowing, as she broke down, from even the thought of her fears. "Oh Thomas, I don't think that I could live with any more loss. I want to take the kids, and just disappear, so that no one can find *any* of us."

Thomas knew that once again, he had to be the voice of reason, even though his thoughts were resoundingly similar. "Tessa, we might be able to take the boys and hide. That is, if they even want to hide. They have been trained for years to go into the field, to be the ones to change the world's perception of all races. It has been beat into their heads, and now it has been reinforced by actual life experiences, and as for the girls, they are other people's children.

No matter what the news headlines may have said in the past, we cannot just take those girls without giving them a chance to see their families, and then once we do that, the purists will have tabs on them. Things are never easy Tess, but we did save everyone that we possibly could. I just wish that we could have been there. Now let's just get them to the infirmary and start their healing process."

Tessa was crying too hard to speak, so Thomas tried once again to reassure her of their safety. "We've got people keeping an eye on Brague, so we'll be getting a heads up, if he makes any moves."

Just then, Tessa found a spark of clarity, which gave her a platform to stand on, as she stated her case. "Thomas, you know as well as I do that we cannot afford to move them once the process has started, so I don't believe that the process should be fully initialized, until we get them all to safer locations. Intel fails, armies are lost. We cannot allow the safety of the children to be compromised by a last moment decision of greed." Tessa tried to explain.

"Greed?" Thomas questioned, almost laughing at her, over such an exaggeration. "Where did you ever come up with that one?"

Tessa, looking up at him, rolling her eyes and giving a sigh, said, "Yes, greed, or maybe laziness, whichever you prefer. You are in way too much of a hurry to run them through this testing."

"Tessa," Thomas answered. "All we need is a couple of days to get their heads and bodies straight, then we'll be in the clear, and purists won't have a leg to stand on. You have to strike fast, while the iron is hot, if you want to get up on these boys. They're not playing around. This is for keeps."

COGNIZANT

Tessa just glared at his arrogance. "If you are quite finished, Thomas, I have already requested two subs, which should not be too far behind the strike force, so who knows, maybe they'll be here in a few hours. You are not gambling with the lives of our kids." As she spoke, she caught herself being unfair to the man, whom had been with her, through all of the danger, and risked everything, to save as many people, as he could, and *he*, was the one that involved *her*, with this plan of changing the world for the better, so she changed her tone giving him his due.

"You did good. You got us all right here, all of the way up to this point." She said showing a level with her hand that reached shoulder height. "Now it is my turn. Let me carry the ball. We did not spend the last fourteen years getting *this* close to our goal for you to pull some kind of cowboy move." Tessa explained. "We don't need to stay in one of their facilities to get the final scans processed. You're being careless. You were always good at careless, but now is when we need fool proof, so here is how it is going to go down." Tessa spoke firmly, as if she was completely in charge.

Thomas listened carefully, watching her closely. She spoke authoritatively, but she held a certain look in her eye, as she strutted her plan before him. He loved watching her in action, especially, when she put all of her effort into something.

Thomas began to inhale prior to speaking, but before he could begin, she silenced him by pressing her finger directly to the man's lips. "Did you know, Thomas, this is why, I had been picked, right from the beginning. I have been trained to be a finisher."

COGNIZANT

Tessa was not lying. She had been through the mind washing brain scans more than most, mostly because her family had been involved with the abolition, throughout her entire life.

No matter how trained, or how much of a professional Tessa appeared to be, the loss of Kilari was tormenting her mind, and she was purposely being protective of the remaining children. Her love for him had great depths. It may have run a slight bit deeper than her love for the others.

It all began with an emotional shock, the shooting of the poor youth's parents, as they gave their lives to keep from being used as a possible leverage point for the purist army, at least in her eyes. That is the way she had learned to think of it, to accept it, so that she could get beyond some of the emotional turmoil, when the thoughts came to her. After reflecting upon the tie that had bound her and Kilari, their relationship, and then how it had ended, she realized, it ended as shockingly as it had begun.

This time, it was the young man's tenacity, and his loyalty to the people that he held dearest to himself. She watched, as he too, gave his life for his loved ones. He was a hero. He was *her* hero, her boy since youth. She felt the loss of a mother, who had lost a child. Welling tears of her emotions began streaming down her cheeks. Thomas, seeing her distress, as well as feeling his own, wrapped her in his arms and held her close. "Don't worry Tess," he said soothingly, trying to comfort her. "We'll make it through this."

In the end, Thomas, having no choice, agreed to every term that she had put forth. These terms were lengthy and included: bringing all the scientists with them upon the subs, the complete and utter destruction of the trans-dimensional gates, the labs, and all the androids, except one.

Alphie was allowed to remain with them, that is, after Tony and his staff went over the droid completely, to assure that no tracking devices were still present, which they did while waiting for the skiffs to come and pick them up.

All of the dimensional travelers were tranquilized, and covered in dark colored tarps, while still lying on the ground, to help keep them hidden from any satellites that may be swinging overhead. The tarped bodies were soon placed on carts and transported to the beach, where they were placed in three rows. The abolition strike force surrounded all of the bodies, including the scientists. Each soldier keeping his side arm drawn in case of any mishaps.

Night was falling fast, as the skiffs made their way to the extraction point. Two staging areas were created, one for each skiff. The skiffs floated in bearing explosives, which the strike force needed, and would be staying to set. The staging areas were set-up for unloading the explosives, as well as, loading the precious human cargo.

The process appeared as a fire drill might to an unsuspecting onlooker, but its efficiency had each group setting ready for its particular movement in short order. The human cargo was made ready for its journey to the subs, while the strike force was set to remove all evidence of any kind by setting up its explosives. They however, would be waiting for a late-night pick-up, prior to detonation.

"Alright Cappy, we need this place leveled." Tony ordered, giving his men the okay to set-up their demolitions. "I

COGNIZANT

don't care if it turns to glass, just
don't leave any traces." "Got me?"

"Loud and clear sir," Cappy
answered. Then turning toward his
men, he said, "you got that boys? It's
time to have us some fun. Now move
out!" With that command, each squad
of the demolition team marched to its
various preplanned location to plant
its payload. By the time all was said
and done, they were to blow the labs in
their entirety, including both gates.

The blasts had to be strong
enough to remove any trace evidence of
finding bodily remains, so that the
purists could only question, Who did
this, or how did such an accident
happen? The scientists would be
absorbed into the underground
abolition, and utilized as needed.

With the explosives unloaded from
the skiffs, and the majority of the
strike force underway on their

objective, Thomas began to plan his moves. At first, Thomas planned on boarding the sub with all of the scientists to help keep things in order, keeping all of the tranqued bodies together and give the reassurances that they would not be harmed.

However, Rudy maintained that he wanted Travis's group to be brought onboard with his group, and after Thomas had seen all the trouble that the man had gone through to get the kid back through the gate in one piece, he allowed this request to be fulfilled. So, in that thought, and because Tessa was adamant that she did not want any, other than the children, to be allowed aboard the sub that she boarded, Travis, Vail, the Queen, and the mercs would be placed in the lower labs of the second sub. The soldiers, under the directions of Thomas Elliot, split the two groups, and would soon be placing them upon the appropriate skiff.

Thomas began with identifying the bodies of the eight girls, and then he slowly began working his way through the identification process of the six young agents, who were last seen on that ledge. Then, as he went to I.D. the next in line, the fifteenth body, he was interrupted by a comrade of the past.

"Check this out sir," Salty said holding out the stone knife that Vail had pulled out, upon entering through the trans-dimensional gate, trying to protect her Queen. "Ain't it a beaut? It's solid stone." The abolition soldier said, seeming to be quite enthused by such a find.

Thomas eyed the knife momentarily, but his mind was not only exhausted from stress, but he was also completely preoccupied by his thoughts of the great loss that he has suffered. "Nice," he commented politely, pretending to be more interested than he really was, but without really looking too closely at the piece. He actually, could barely focus on his task at hand.

Tony saw the blank stare in Thomas's eyes, so he waved Salty off, giving him the signal that the fourteenth body was the cut off line on the split. Then he walked over to Thomas, putting his hand on Thomas's shoulder saying, "Come with me. You need to take a rest. You've been up *way* too long. Why don't you just take a seat on the skiff?" Tony said as he began walking the mournful man toward the skiff.

Thomas began walking with the lead agent. "What about identifying the bodies?" He asked mumbling a bit, feeling as though he, was somehow, shirking his duty.

COGNIZANT

"Don't you worry about this," Tony said consoling the agent. "They've all been searched, and tranqued. Trust me. They are not going anywhere. I'll see to them personally, just go sit with Tess. I got this." He convinced Thomas to do just that, and he helped him get right to her side.

Tessa had been holding it together at first by barking out orders to subordinates, but then after the skiffs had made their way there, and the explosives were starting to be unloaded, she sat by, waiting for the sleeping children. It seemed to help her, to think that she was holding a place for them in their unconsciousness, and then she would whisper to herself that everything would be all right.

She could not take her eyes from them, as their unconscious bodies lay waiting to be loaded onto the skiff, where she was waiting. Looking up from the bodies, particularly those of Jezza and Marcia, she could see Tony walking with her husband. She could tell that Thomas had hit the proverbial wall. She had never seen him looking this way.

He almost seemed frail, looking a bit worse for wear with glossed over eyes and weak knees. "Oh Thomas," she cried in dismay, once he had made his way over to her. She latched onto the man and pulled him over to the place where she had been spending her time.

Tony could see the pain that his two longtime cohorts were feeling, so he turned to give them some privacy. Looking down from the skiff, he saw just what Tessa had been watching. Her children's bodies down on shore wrapped in tarps looking like a mass of corpses. Not liking the morbid view whatsoever, he gestured down to Salty,

COGNIZANT

(one of his men standing watch), and after getting his attention, he moved down and told the man, "Get the tarped bodies and their belongings onboard, including that stone knife you have been flashing around."

Tessa uncovered the children's faces, as they were loaded onto the skiff, so that she could see them breathing. It eased her mind. She whispered to each of them, as she uncovered, except for the two younger girls, which she found to be a very difficult thing to do, being that they too would also truly know the full effect of the loss of Kilari.

Tony stood by for a moment, as Thomas held onto Tessa. Then he suggested, "Why don't you stay here with your team? I can see to the scientists and their people. You don't need to bother with them."

Then Tessa came to a moment of clarity. "You do that Tony." She said agreeing that this would be good for all that were concerned. "Tony, tranquilize the scientists without their knowledge, after they get a moment to see their young colleague. Then put the whole lot of them on a slow scan. I want Thomas, and myself, to go over their processes personally, but we need to focus on the kids first."

"I understand. I will have them all resting comfortably in a loop, until you are ready for them. We'll have them moved into one of the corresponding labs, once we get to our destination. They'll be waiting for you, until you give the word to move on." Tony said explaining his understanding of her orders. Tessa and Thomas both nodded affirmative in agreement.

The two skiffs soon made their way to the awaiting subs, where they

COGNIZANT

were loaded and readied for their
descent to their next destination.

The subs moved away from the
islands, heading to a place that had
been built by the abolitions very own
science department, an underwater city
that was hidden, amongst jagged
crevices on the floor of the Blue Sea.
The small city was completely self-
sufficient, and completely unknown by
the purists.

Captain Tory Parker moved away
from his crew, once the sub was under
way. He had a crew of a few men, and a
few droids. They all had experience
and were a first-class outfit, one that
had made the journey to, and from, the
underwater city of Aguanomis, many
times over. In fact, one of the crewmen
had only been on land a couple of times
in his entire life. Aguanomis was not
the only underwater city, but it was

the number one, state of the art facility of all underwater cities.

Thomas and Tessa both stood next to the children, as they lay on hospital gurneys. The sub's sickbay had enough room for two rows of beds. Life support and brain scan equipment lined both walls. There were still empty beds in this bay, but Tessa wanted to focus only upon the fourteen, who must go on without their lost brother, friend, and love. They lay unconscious still, and were already hooked to the monitors.

The life support machines test and monitor all bodily functions, including vital organs, nutrients in the blood, muscular, and skeletal information. However, it leaves all facets of the brain to another piece of equipment, which is appropriately named, a brain scanner, by medical techs, but the field agents call these machines, mind-

COGNIZANT

washers, primarily because of the way they are usually utilized.

The brain scanner can do a multitude of functions. It can not only process health information, but one could also use this machine to see events that have happened throughout the life of the patient, and can even implant memories and skills into an agent's mind. These memories would seem as real to the agent, as any other event that they had actually experienced. Skill sets however, could only be improved to your ability at a certain task.

In this instance, Tessa had plans of utilizing both of these processes, and a couple of more tricks that she had learned through her many vast experiences of being on either side of the machine. She first began running the basic health scans for both machines, she did not want to go beyond these essentials, until they had made it to their destination.

Thomas sat back in a chair out of the way, watching, as Tessa walked up and down the aisle checking each of the children to make sure that they were physically fit. She looked over towards him, after she had finished the last one.

"Well, that makes all of them Thomas. They are all physically stressed and malnourished. Even *poor* Tanker looks like he might have lost a few pounds," she said sympathetically, as only a mother would.

"Tessa, they are alive, and they will be fine, physically at least. The trouble will be how they handle the loss of Kilari." Thomas answered back. "I mean, look at us. We are agents that have been through a thousand deaths, and here we are in mourning over our loss. These kids will have a much harder time. It is their first real loss, and it is one that hits home. It brings a whole new prospective to the reality of life, and death, to them. It will be crushing at first, but hopefully, it will make them react to adversity in a more realistic way."

Tessa walked over and sat upon Thomas's lap. She wrapped an arm around behind the man's neck, while draping the other across his chest. She turned to a position from which she could look into his eyes. "Thomas, these are our children," she started, sounding as if she were explaining to a child.

"I can do things with a brain scanner that will ease them into a reality that makes it seem as though Kilari's loss was many years ago, and for the most part the pain will be gone, and all they can remember is the good times they've had growing up. I can

also do the same for you, if need be."
She spoke sweetly knowing that
Thomas was old school and would not
be easy to convince.

Thomas looked cross at her, with
disgust that she would even mention
the brainwashing techniques. "What
are you thinking Tess?" He asked, as if
she were losing it. "These are the kids.
Don't you think that they should be
allowed to have time to mourn, and to
build natural feelings, instead of
having them processed by the brain
washers every time that something
happens?"

Thomas always chose to deal with
his troubles. He felt that it made him
stronger mentally. He also knew that
Tessa had been raised with mind
washing practices, but he still liked to
make her think of doing things
naturally, and he for sure did not like
making decisions of this nature for

other people, especially not someone who has been tranquilized, and would not even have the chance to make the decision for themselves.

"Yeah," Tessa sounded off. "You are acting like you have never been through the procedure." Then she snipped, "I guess that you have a problem with the way that I have turned out too?"

Thomas knew that this would turn out ugly, mostly, because she had been through the mind washers too many times, and she had a problem coping with real emotional events, as they happened. He loved the woman with all of his heart, and he knew that she was being self-conscious, which was rare for her, but when they seemed to have disagreements about things of this nature, it always seemed to get triggered.

Aguanimos

Thomas wrapped her in his arms, which as usual caused her to try to push him away. He knew the game well, and either, she was the master of the game, or she never realized that the game was taking place. He did not know which, and they did not speak of it, but he knew it was that time again. "Come here babe." He said as he held her a little tighter.

"No, you think that I'm crazy, so, why *should* I?" Tessa jarted back at him, as she began to put forth a little more effort against him.

Thomas could tell that this is indeed what she was gearing up for. She needed an emotional release. She wanted to fight, and hurt someone. She needed to lash out, but she also needed to cry, and in the end, she needed to be held closely and loved passionately.

Tessa did start off like a tigress, escaping Thomas's grip, but she returned to him spitting venomous insults, which suggested that he was just too lazy to see anything through, or to do it the right way, and that is why Kilari was dead.

Thomas fended off her comments and spewed back accusations of his own. "You will never be a full woman, because you can't afford to have natural feelings, so who's lazy and greedy now, huh! In fact, you'll probably get a good mind washing after this escapade too, won't you?"

Tessa got her usual startled look that she would get, when he would hit home. She still argued saying, "No Thomas, no! I wouldn't try to."

"Yeah right! He said, knowing full well that she was lying not only to herself, but right to his face too. "You know you're lying through your teeth."

Tessa had just taken all that she could stand. Her eyelids slowly squeezed down, being pushed by her scowling brow, turning her eyes to two little slits of bronze colored fire.

Thomas knew that he may have crossed the line a bit, but he did not realize it, until she drew in that breath, the way that she always did right before an explosive strike. The man's eyes turned into saucers, as he tried to put his hands up in defense, but it was too late for any kind of move.

She sprung towards the man, jumping high with a spinning kick. Her foot landed the blow upon the man's chest with enough force to bend his torso back and forcing him to step backwards, hoping to keep his balance, but she just kept coming with the kick using her body to help with some additional impact, and it was just enough to topple Thomas over onto the floor.

COGNIZANT

She, however, somehow still landed upon her two feet, straddling his body with bent knees. She reached down and pulled his head up by his hair. He could still see the blood in her eyes, but having knocked the wind out of him, he could not breathe. Unable to speak, he just closed his eyes, scrunching his face with a wince, expecting her to give him at least one more solid strike.

Then suddenly, in that instance, she could tell that it was Thomas and he was hurt, and as she held him there, she also noticed her positioning, and realized that she was the one who had put the hurt on him.

Tears instantly began flowing down her cheeks again, and he could hear her near silent sobs of apology. He still could not breathe, but he pulled her in close with loving embracing arms. "Oh Thomas," she sobbed out, cleaving to him like a child in need of security.

She tried wrapping herself so tightly that she might just seep into him. She could hear him trying to gasp and catch his breath, which only made her feel sorrier. "I love you Thomas. I am so sorry." Her tears kept flowing, releasing all the unrequited emotions that she had stored away without thought.

Within the first few minutes of her pressing into Thomas, her true love and soul mate, feeling him begin to catch his breath, her mind began lingering over other more intimate thoughts. She started breathing in Thomas's scent, as the two stayed huddled close together.

After she was sure that he was breathing fine, she slid her tear soaked cheek across his, until their lips connected. "I love you," she whispered,

COGNIZANT

as she opened her mouth ever so
slightly allowing their tongues to
dance.

Now, each became fully in contact
with their interpersonal emotions.
Each breath fueled the fire in their
hearts, until inevitably the two became
one entity, one flesh, one spirit,
healing each other in the throes of
passion.

Quarantine

Are you saying that I have died?" Kilari asked, not knowing what was happening in the least, but he was beginning to get the inkling that he had just given up his life by going on this purgatorial crusade.

Then he tried remembering, back to the visions that he had had and said, "I don't recall the part in my visions about dying, and leaving people who need me, to finish what I have started. I mean, I thought that I would still have my life to live. I have people who love me that I also need."

Yahiveh knew his young followers' heart, and as any father would, he tried to explain all the ramifications of the afterlife. He told him of his white robes and of what they were made. He also explained about his good fortune, that he would be placed on the right side of the gulf, but none of this made a difference to Kilari.

It was not that Kilari did not want to be there, but he for one could not understand the afterlife, and how that flesh would come and go like vapor in the air, in comparison to all of eternity. "Yahiveh, I want to go and be with my wives, and my brothers. We have unfinished business."

The eternal spirit was full of wisdom, and compassion, and understood how the youth felt, but he also knew that there would most certainly be even further ramifications that would have to be paid. "Kilari let me advise you that with me all things are possible. You have made it to your goal. You have overcome temptation, and have shown faith. You have even started faith amongst your friends, and they can venture forth to spread my spell that will cause all who are true believers, and truly good, to have an eternal life without the presence of evil. You are now in a place, where the evil one can no longer tempt you, so I must also warn you that if you were to live, and go back to your place on An'non, Lucifer has the freedom to tempt you with many things, and can place many obstacles in your way. If you were to fall short, you may not be so easily grafted in, my son."

Kilari listened closely to Yahiveh's advice, but he did not fully know the potential of the platitudes being spoken. He figured that it seemed as though, the choice was somehow being left up to him. "Master, I am not yet fully learned in all of thy ways, but if the choice is mine, I cannot leave my two wives and my brothers with a burden, which is meant to be mine, while I choose to take the easy way..."

Before Kilari could finish his statement, Yahiveh waved his hand across the clouded air, causing Kilari to see the beauty of Heaven. "Look my son. Feel the peace, and ease your mind. Do you see those two souls, Kilari?" He asked pointing at two bystanders, who Kilari thought, seemed able to see him too. "Do you know those two souls?" Yahiveh asked.

Kilari looked closer, and then he moved nearer to the scene displayed before him. He leaned in and then he answered. "Well, if they weren't so young, I'd have to say that they are a good likeness of what my parents had looked like, although they do look happier. I only saw a few moments of footage of my parents." He explained, even though there was no need.

"Those are your parents. Go, talk to them, before you make any decisions in haste." Yahiveh suggested.

Kilari's eyes bulged with excitement, as he went on his way to talk to his parents, who were waiting by a gate, which was golden, and did shine, as if it were made of light. He had no idea of what to say to the people of whom he had always wondered, but could not remember ever seeing. As he approached the gate, it seemed as if all of his anxieties began fading away.

*　　*　　*　　*　　*

As the two lead agents finished zipping up the loose ends of their uniforms, a metallic voice sounded. "Prepare for docking sequence."

"Well, now that's what I call timing," Thomas stated with a smug self-satisfying smile.

COGNIZANT

"It's time to get this show on the road Thomas. Let's get the gurneys ready for the move." Tessa said directing her mate, while walking to the head of the closest gurney. "I want this to roll without a hitch. The sooner we get this going, the sooner we will have our children whole."

Thomas enjoyed her enthusiasm, but he still did not know what she planned on doing with the brain scanner. He did not want the boys' minds washed. Maybe, he thought, she could use the mind washer on the girls, and he would be able to continue his work with the boys. Then he came to his senses. No, he would restrain her if need be, and none of the brain scans would go beyond their usefulness.

The submarine had come to a smooth stop, and shortly after, the docking tube connected from the Aguanomis entry bay to the submarine, all of the subjects were transported into a hospital lab. The dimensional travelers were soon connected to higher quality machines. All the necessary nutrients were being supplied to each of the bodies, along with painkillers, relaxants, and the moleculitic muscle stimulators. These machines would put the bodies through their paces, and then leave them in the best shape possible within the time restraints of the program. By the time these programs had all been started, the occupants of the other sub were being shifted into the same lab.

Tessa did not like this. She thought that there was an understanding, and that she would not be interrupted, while she was working on those that she deemed more important. "What is the meaning of this intrusion?" She asked the first

COGNIZANT

unsuspecting man wheeling a gurney into what she thought of, as her lab.

"Sorry ma'am, just following orders." The worker said professionally. "The facility commander ordered this lab, and all of you mainlanders that will be staying on here, to be quarantined."

"Quarantined, why?" Tessa asked, as if she had been insulted.

Thomas quickly stepped in. "It's okay. It's just standard protocol," Thomas explained, while nodding his head affirmatively to the worker trying to get the man to agree to his explanation, whether, or not, it was accurate.

The worker caught on and agreed, trying to avoid any conflict. Soon, the room was filled with enough gurneys for all the dimensional travelers, the scientists, and then a few extra, one for each, Tessa, Thomas, and Tony.

These three alone were conscious. Tony did as he was told, and put the others all to sleep in a slow cycle, which would not only keep them healthy, but also would allow them to be placed on a back burner, until there was time enough for them to be dealt with.

Tessa stepped aside after a moment, allowing the parade of gurneys to process through the lab. She had all but the three empties placed to the far end. She then waited for all the Aguanian crewmen to leave the lab. Then once the door locked, her heart and soul began going about their business.

Thomas watched her, as she placed her headset on, connecting physically, and mentally, with each of them, and then she would begin typing into the mainframe. He could see how well she knew these programs. by her

COGNIZANT

care and precision. At times, she stroked the keys with her eyes closed and tears running down her cheeks, as she placed herself into their minds. She could program with the best of them, but these were her children, and one by one, she went down the line. At first, she began to ease their burdens with painkillers and memory suppressants. Later, she would ease through the actions of their pasts. She could see every moment, the good ones, the bad ones, and the torturous ones.

"Tess, come on. Snap out of it." Thomas said, as he shook her a little. His hand was upon her shoulder. He had been worried for quite a while, about what the long hours of emotional drain might be doing to her. She seemed to be nearly in a full trance. Her dark hair draped down in waves. "Tessa!" He yelled, as he began to shake her again.

ROC BLISS

Then suddenly, Tessa arose. It was apparent that she did not even realize that he had shaken her. She stood near the bedside of Ceilia, the girl that she had just completed. She stretched trying to get the ache from the lower portion of her back. Then she noticed Thomas watching her from only inches away. He looked bewildered. "What is it Thomas? Is something going on that I need to know about?" She asked with only slight concern.

"Tessa, you gotta get some rest. It's damn near morning. You've been doing those mind washing tricks for who the heck knows how many hours. All I see is you cry and them cry and then you crying again. You've got to give it a rest." Thomas was terribly upset. He had never really sat through sessions as a witness before, and had no clue of what pains it would put someone through.

COGNIZANT

"Thomas, I only have two left. They have all been through a lot. The boys have been well-trained, and through this first session, I still have uncovered many details. These poor girls were just students, and not trained at all. They are young women in love with our boys. They have all seen things that are not easy on the mind." Then she moved even closer to Thomas. She moved to where he alone could possibly hear her. "Thomas, I have seen things that seem impossible. Most of these impossibilities have to do with Kilari. Now, you let me finish the last two girls, and then I can create a watchable hologram of the many things that the first session has uncovered."

"Thomas," she said looking directly into the man's eyes, "I have already uncovered enough dirt on the purists to change things. This information may cause riots in the streets. There is another reality that I am beginning to unravel, so far, all of the kids have felt the presence of another being, especially Belsangar and Tank, and now with Ceilia's, and Sophie's scans being finished, I have uncovered more, much more. These two," she said pointing at Jezza and Marcia, "should tell me more yet." Then, grabbing his hand and holding it to her full lips, she kissed his knuckles, and then rubbed her cheek across the back of his hand.

"I need to get these facts to add them into the first session file. Besides Thomas, they are in pain. They need to be relieved. I cannot stop, after knowing their agony, and I believe that these two will be worse."

Thomas looked down into her hazel eyes, her tears were falling more gently, but all of the feelings and emotions that she jumbled up during the scans were still present, and seemed to be cycling, just as strong. "Okay Tess, you finish the first session, but then you need to get some rest. I want a promise on that." He ordered.

His face was red and his veins were bulging on the sides of his head. "A solid promise Tess," he said finishing with a look that required solid assurance.

Tessa could see the stress that Thomas was putting himself through, so she gave him her usual cutesy smile, the one that she always used to pacify him. "I promise," she said and then holding up two fingers, she finished with, "scouts honor," before finally stepping forward and holding him close.

"Don't worry baby," she softly whispered into his ear. With that being said, she slowly moved away to get back to work. Right before placing her headset back on and drifting back into the other side of consciousness, she turned back to Thomas one more time saying, "you may have to get used to it someday, you know." Her voice was loud, loud enough for him to hear, even with his back to her, as he moved back across the room.

Thomas turned and stood watching her, in question of what she had meant. "I might have to get used to what?" He finally asked.

"Sitting on the side lines," she answered, as she placed the headset over her ears. She took this time to smile for a few seconds prior to continuing in her work. She knew that soon she would be delving into the most personal details of her young student's life. Nothing would be hidden from her in the end of these sessions, as will be the case with every single one of the people in this lab.

It was not that she wanted to see, or know all the information of which she will soon be presented. It was more to the point that she would have to see it all to get the information that she was after, and have the ability to put the final report together.

In the end, this report will be delivered to a higher council, who in turn will be wearing the headgear for the input, and then all knowledge, courage, ability, or any other trait gained from this case will be judged.

The first judgment will be of the mission outcome, success, or failure, but from there the judgements would trickle down to the team involved, the crew leader, each individual, and finally, each decision and thought of each member would be broke down. Knowing this better than most, Tessa would never allow anyone else to down load the very thoughts of *her* children.

Tessa felt as if she alone truly knew the extent of these reports and judgments. Her Aunt Myra had taught her very well as a youth, and in so doing, Tessa had realized early on how important these reports could be to the future of the races.

She could see improvements coming slowly through her life time, but now the races were nearing the point of being able to claim equality. While the purists have always ruled by power and fought wars, they searched out new weapons and ways of sustaining power, ways of keeping the races down, the abolitionists were creating underwater cities, and brain scanners, and machines to help the recovery of abused bodies.

All of the purist technologies would fall into the abolitionist's laps,

COGNIZANT

sooner or later, but rarely did the
abolition's breakthroughs ever surface
to be utilized by the purists, so now
the tides could finally be turned.
Through these very brain scans, actual
footage can be viewed by the entire
world of An'non. Because of the
innovation of moleculite, the
broadcasts cannot be stopped by the
purists. The truth will be sent out
globally, and the blind sheep of the
purist's will have their eyes opened to
the reality of their brutality. Tessa
could see the peace being marched in
by a one-world government, and all
people being equal, no more brutality,
no more hunger, no more slavery, all
will live as equals. This is how Tessa
viewed the upcoming events, and is her
ultimate goal.

Tessa ventured forth, into the
lives of the last two girls. Being that
this was just the first session, and they

were still so young, she did not uncover too many eye openers, other than the fact that they were having a personal and physical relationship together, and they smoked herbs.

Neither of these activities were much of a stretch being that one of their fathers grew herbs, and they had been in the same all girl schools throughout their youth.

However, there was some more evidence of this other presence, a presence that again seemed to stem from Kilari. She barely uncovered events that had happened up to the actual kidnapping of the girls from the air bus, but she saw more of Kilari having gained knowledge from some source, and it had been tied to that old book that he had always kept.

Tessa finished with the brain scans and then moved over to her gurney, which was off in a corner. She

COGNIZANT

had a short conversation with Thomas and Tony, before connecting her headset to the mainframe. She lay back, and began to down load all of the brain scans, while she slept. The brain scanner head set would put the host to sleep during this critical application, so that it could pull out all of the information, without any conscious resistance, which in the past had made tampering a possibility.

Thomas made sure that all systems were connected, and properly synchronized in the programming. Then, he gave Tony the nod, which according to their plan, told him to com-link with the head of Aguanomis. "Okay, the first sessions are being uploaded," Tony said speaking to the cleric.

Governor Lucas was not only the head of Aguanomis, but he was also one of the higher figureheads in the entire abolition. Although this information was classified, and only known by a select few, Thomas, and Tony found themselves in this select group, while Tessa only knew of him as Governor Lucas, just another leader of his community. She gave him full respect for whom, she thought that he was in her mind, but she would definitely not allow him to view the progress of the scans.

The Governor spoke with clarity. "Have the reports copied and sent moleculitically into the Z-Bank." Z-Bank was the codename for the routing of information to Central Control. This information would get encoded, specifically in the Z code, and would remain untraceable throughout any other computer rig or system, *except* Central Control.

"Yes sir, Governor Lucas," Tony answered with all due respect. "It shall be done," and with his assurance given, the com-link had ended. He then hit another button on the com-unit. "Yes, we have need of a Z-Bank transaction from the quarantined lab."

Captain Tory Parker stood in the mainframe room. This room held the computer, which kept all things in the city of Aguanomis running perfectly. This was a fitting computer to run the Z-Bank. The information would be encoded, recorded, and then sent. Then the slipstream of information would disappear, as a lone slip of code that would be lost in a near infinite amount of codes, where in the end, it would be sifted, and sent into a code shredder.

Billions of codes are shredded daily, and hundreds of billions of codes stream into this area, keeping the area so overloaded that it would be impossible to find a certain code once it had been sent, and even if by some miracle it had been retrieved, the odds on deciphering the encoding would be astronomical at best.

Captain Parker flipped a few switches and hit a couple of buttons. Then after typing a certain notation, the computers would do the rest.

Tessa had awakened, while Thomas and Tony were asleep. She watched them for a short period, and then she decided to go right back into the brain scanning. She did the boys first, and then the girls. The first session was always time consuming, but this session she figured would be rather quick. She really only needed two or three days of information, which she figured, would take only a couple of hours, altogether. She plugged through boys and all but three of the girls in no time.

Then, she plugged away slowly through Ceilia's mind, which reacted sluggishly from the turmoil of her mass emotions. Next, would be time for her to plug into Marcia, right after she puts a slight washing to the other candidates. She thought that if they could be enhanced a slight bit, it would help them to deal with their losses. The minor program change would not hinder the children from making any personal judgments that they would have had naturally.

Tessa had finished with the preliminaries, and now she was undertaking the strong emotional shockwaves that Marcia's mind kept pounding out. Her feelings for Jezza, and then for Kilari too, and this alternate being's presence was getting stronger.

In fact, she now knew that this Yahiveh had protected the entire group multiple times in multiple ways. She had questions, one of them being; 'why in the children's memories, did Kilari call this figure his father?'

She had seen his father, and he was no powerful spirit. He was just a meek man with mild mannerisms. Oh, how she wished that she had Kilari's mind to tap. She saw things from the past, all of them. Maybe these were Marcia's visions of the stories that Kilari had told her of himself, maybe they are a culmination of all the facts that her mind had ever received of her boy, but now she could look back and see differences that she did not know existed.

She now knew, why Kilari had always acted in a way that the others did not fully understand, and how he would always seem to make the right move to keep his team above the others in competitions. He had not placed much knowledge with the other boys, but the girls seemed to have picked up more.

Now, she could also have that book of Kilari's pegged, as an integral part of this new reality. According to Marcia's mind, she had watched the book go into Kilari's shirt, before he had run into that battlefield. Waves of pain hit Tessa brutally, as Marcia's mind was forced to remember each detail of those last known scenes from Kilari's last stand.

The medical assistance, machines were pumping both the young wife of Kilari, and Tessa, with the strong opiates that were supposed to suppress the pain of the memories, but this was a new level of emotional pain, the likes that Tessa had never encountered on a scan.

Finally, Tessa had to pull off the headset in hopes that the emotional damage would subside. Streaming tears ran down her cheeks, as she lay on her gurney. 'This is crazy,' she thought, knowing that she had never had a response so totally out of her control.

Her chest was tight and she could not control her breathing. Her mind was in shambles, feeling the void, which had entered Marcia in this time of death. She had not yet treated herself for the pain of loss, and now it seemed, the further that she went into these sessions, the more trauma was being injected into her mind.

After regaining some resemblance of control, Tessa could see that somehow, she had not woken up the guys, who appeared to still be sleeping like babies. Thomas had a deep rhythmic breathing that she suddenly could hear echoing through her mind. Tony snorted, and then moved, as if he were about to awaken, but then he

COGNIZANT

rolled over, and began to breathe deeply in the throes of slumber.

Tessa sat up. She could see the reality of the room, and the situation that she was in, but somehow her chest still felt tight. She rolled her gurney a few feet over, so that she could lie right next to Jezza. She connected and was soon traveling through the memories and feelings of the last of the group. Jezza, with her golden bronze skin and dark wavy hair that cascaded half of the way down her back.

This one, was the daughter of an herb grower. She had nearly no family ties and had been sent to school, so that she could not be hunted by the Death Squad. She looked, and *was* an ethnic, but her father had paid off certain officials to look the other way, as long as she stayed in school. That is where she had been, since her earliest memories.

Then over the years, she had melted into a relationship with Marcia. At first, they became friends, then, best friends, and then once they had moved to a new school, where a lot of the other girls were in relationships they began feeling the call of real love.

Initially it whispered to them, but it was not far, between the whispers and the true calling, which had made them each emotionally stronger, and gave them one person in each of their lives that they could count on, and believe in, to be on their side.

The flowering of emotions continued right through another move to another school, where Tessa had become their professor. Soon after, the two young girls fell in with her group of girls, those whom she would bring to the academy.

COGNIZANT

After meeting Kilari, Jezza's emotions turned into frantic overdriven nodules of confusion. Her mind was an emotional rollercoaster from that moment on, climbing to heights that some women might never know, only in the end; to be brought down to depths lower than most could bear. Tessa's mind began to require the heavy dosing of opiates again, but she could not suppress the pain from this girl's loss either. 'Something must be wrong,' she thought. She had never had such problems.

Jezza began moaning audibly, in mental anguish, even in her unconsciousness. Her skin began sweating from the intensity of her exertion.

Tessa also began tossing to, and fro, seemingly caught up in the anguish, adding her loss of a son, along with all of the pain that every one of the children had felt, even Marcia, and now Jezza's surmounting pangs. Once their hearts could feel the pouncing of the zombie horde, and their eyes could see, as the young man gave his all to save his friends, brothers, and loved ones. He made sure that they all would have time to make it to the top of the rope ladder, where safety loomed over, seemingly charging the price of one loyal soul to save the rest.

Tessa, herself began reeling from the emotional duress. Her body lay, jerking and flexing, as her chest ached from the strain. Her hands were clenching her shirt over her sternum. Her mind was unconscious, but it did not stop the woman's voice from crying in misery. The machines were pumping all sorts of drugs trying to keep the two women from feeling the grips of death upon them.

COGNIZANT

Tessa began to scream, as she arched her back and stiffened her entire body. All the while, not knowing the Z-Bank had been capturing all of this data, to go along with the previous transmissions, and find its way to the all-knowing, Central Control.

ROC BLISS

Cognizant

Kilari walked directly to the gate. "Look, would you look at those long white robes." His father said as he stood admiring his son, unable to see the bloodstains, which covered him from head to toe. "You have been a good man son."

Kilari walked up to the gate, unaware of the way that his parents were seeing him. His hair was soaked with sweat and blood from the fight with the zombie horde. He slid his hand upon the golden bars. They felt warm to his surprise, but he was too busy thinking of what to say to his parents, to mention it.

His mother's eyes looked to be forming tears of joy, as she watched him. "If you pass through the gate all the blood will be washed from you, and you will be able to stay with us, my son."

"No, I cannot enter," Kilari stated. "I just want to know one thing. Did you ask the Commander to do that?"

"We did it for you son," His father said, knowing full well, what Kilari was inquiring. "We could not afford to give up information, not with you being picked up. Son, we were always poor, and were without the means to do anything, except to make the one sacrifice, to protect your escape, just as you have for your loved ones." His father stated with pride, knowing that his son had had the opportunity to grow and learn the importance of some matters.

"You can stay with us." His mother said reminding him that all he had to do was make that decision.

ROC BLISS

Kilari first looked into her eyes, and then once he saw the sincerity, he began to look around. "Where are all of the others?" He asked after noticing very few souls.

"Most everybody is being placed on the other side of the gulf. I guess it's for the best. I hear that in a couple of days there will be a day for retraining." His mother said with a smile.

"What have you done for all of these years, while you were up here." Kilari asked.

His father began, "well, we met a few souls. They are some wonderful folks." Then he looked right into Kilari's eyes. "We have been waiting for you and yours to arrive, actually." The small man watched, as his son's eyes widened from the information. "It is not what you think. Your lifetime will only be like a couple of hours to us here."

"Good," Kilari answered. "Then you won't miss me much, while I'm gone."

"Oh Kilari, don't go." His mom cried. "You don't have to leave. You can stay. You can stay right here." His mom said trying to make him understand.

"Hey," Kilari exclaimed, interrupting her. "I'll try to bring you some company. I mean to this side, where you are in wait. I'll tell them to say hello, if I get the chance."

"Kilari," his mom started, before she was interrupted.

Kilari put his finger up in the air and pointed directly at her, and in a stern voice said, "Look, I have my two wives, and six brothers. These people I know in my heart. They need me. I cannot leave them to those mongrels of An'non."

*　　　*　　　*　　　*　　　*

Tessa and Jezza had begun flailing uncontrollably, while crying in deep agony. Thomas tried ripping the headsets from their heads, but this did not seem to change anything, it only set off the control alarms. The alarms alerted guards and doctors alike. Each of the groups had its own reasons to run over to the monitors overseeing the lab.

Once they realized that the two women had been repeatedly inoculated, they ran right by the quarantine signs. The doctors began waking all of the brain scan recipients immediately, in case the machines were all malfunctioning. The doctors began flipping switches and pressing all the buttons required to stop brain function controls, so that the patient's brains would become unhampered by the programs and would slowly regain consciousness on their own time.

While Jezza, and the rest of the patients had been tethered to their gurneys, Tessa only had Thomas to help her from hurting herself. He was doing his best. He kept giving her orders in her ear. He did not know if any of them would hit home, but he figured that anything was worth a shot. Positioning his weight across her shoulders, while keeping her arms from gaining leverage. The doctors, with help from a few of the guards, were finally able to tether the woman.

Thomas had stepped away about a foot maybe two. He assessed and reassessed the situation. All the while watching the uncontrolled crying, and their motor movements, which forced them to jerk and spasm. "Do something!" He finally screamed at the doctor in frustration.

ROC BLISS

The doctor shouted back. "They will come to, before long!" Yelling just to be heard over the racket. "It may take quite a while. due to the fact that they had been drugged so heavily!"

Within minutes, Tank and Telebar began awakening. They each thought that they were still on the shelf looking over the battlefield. "No! No! Get him! Get his back!" Telebar yelled, as if he were giving orders to soldiers.

Tank came to, yelling, "Come on! It's all clear!"

Thomas Elliot moved to the boys, who had known him as Commander Jamie Crichton. He was dressed in his night gear, so he did not figure that this would help his cover. He moved over to them with his finger across his lips, trying to get silence, but soon it all got worse.

Others came to, some of them were yelling, others were crying out, and all

COGNIZANT

the girls were weeping heavily. Thomas felt relieved that none were calling him by his other name, but it seemed as though, they were all, going into hysterics.

Thomas finally, had had his fill with the craziness. He had whispered to Tony to cover the doorway. Thomas pulled out one of the old-fashioned weapons. It had a big barrel and was long for an old pistol. He walked over to the first of the guards and slammed him with the butt of the gun, knocking him to the floor. Then he grabbed the next unsuspecting guard from behind, reaching his arm around the man's neck, while placing the end of the long black barrel to his head.

"ALRIGHT! I want all the Aguanomis team over here. I WANT YOUR HANDS UP!" He yelled to get their attention over all the noise. Soon, he had the group all off to the side, where

Tony could help cover them with his heat blaster.

Thomas walked over to the head doctor. "I want to know what you are doing to my people. These machines were supposed to help them overcome battle fatigue, not put them into worse shape."

The head doctor began explaining. "I woke them all up prematurely, sir. I thought that the scanners could all be malfunctioning, and I did not want any damage to come to them. I know how this looks."

"Oh, you know how it looks? I'm tellin' ya sonny Jim. It's looking like you put the whole lot of us on quarantine, and then you began torturing my team." Thomas stated in a heated fashion.

"No sir." The doctor assured him. "We were just in a hurry. We were told to put the whole lot of you on

COGNIZANT

quarantine, because of the nature of your mission. I jumped ahead of myself, and began to wake-up every one of the brain scan patients. You have to keep in mind that once they become fully awake, they will start to become coherent."

"Look at them. It looks like a damn psychiatric ward in here, doctor." Thomas stated, while looking at all the pain being spent.

"The doctor tried again to explain. "Look," he said pointing to the closest soldier. "They don't know that we're here yet. They are still in a dream like state. In a way, they are living in a suspended battlefield situation, which will pass, once they become coherent, and then after we check out the machines, if they are okay, we can either put them back under, or you can wait to talk with each of them and then decide, if you want them to be scanned further."

"Okay then," Thomas answered. "I want all of the guards and doctors out of here, except you. You will stay. You must realize that the mission here is classified. You will not be allowed to repeat anything that you have seen or heard in here."

The doctor nodded affirmatively, and then waved the others out. "I was not told, why you were under quarantine, so now that you sent the others away, we'll be having to put the next section beyond these labs into quarantined status also. Some of those men could be a help to us in getting this place back in order."

Thomas looked at the doctor seriously. "No," he said. "I can possibly leave the secrets that may, or may not, come out of this lab in the mind of one man, who is not classified, but why

COGNIZANT

would I force your entire staff to go through all of the scans that it would take to erase their memories also. One is enough."

Thomas began walking towards Tessa. Her twitching had slowed, but she was still moaning and weeping, sobbing loudly with anguish. Jezza was in the same shape. The situation was actually getting worse, instead of better. "Well doc, at this point none of them are getting hooked back up to those machines, so you just look after the people. Don't worry about the machines." Thomas said honestly.

In a few hours' time, all the agents had become coherent, and a few of the women, but some of the women were still in shock. It did not help the girls to see Tessa, A.K.A. the professor Mary Trenton, in the state of mourning that she seemed to be wallowing through. Marcia and Jezza were also in really bad shape. Thomas had the guys staying by the side of their girls to help to soothe them into reality, but it left Tony, the doctor, and himself to try to get the last three calmed, which were the ones that did not seem to be getting better at all.

Cam looked down the rows of hospital beds. There were two rows beyond the action, which were filled with sleeping bodies that did not move, and were covered with white sheets. He could not help, but to notice the vast difference between those who were awake, and those who still slept. "So, do you think that their minds are suffering, but you just can't tell, because they are sleeping?" He asked calling out to the doctor.

The doctor left Jezza's side, walking up the aisle towards Cam. "Well son, those people have only been tranquilized. They are being held in a sleeping state, until a later time."

"So, you can't tell me either way. Do the people dream and feel pain, while they are tranquilized, or are they just mindless sleeping bodies waiting for input?" Cam asked point-blank.

The sleepers all had white sheets covering them from head to toe, as they lay still on their gurneys. They were not tethered to the beds, because they were unable to move due to the drugs that they were under. "They are unable to dream." The doctor answered.

All the cadets seemed to begin focusing over to the sleepers, until suddenly a shrill scream sounded from the still incoherent body of Jezza. It was followed by another, and then Marcia also began screaming. Soon all of their eyes began focusing upon the two girls, and then Tessa began coughing.

"Tessa," Thomas called out believing that she was regaining consciousness. The young agents and the girls noticed the name that the Commander had used, this brought all of their minds into the reality that this was a new mission, and that they had better not use any names if they could help it.

Tessa continued coughing, until she finally tried to sit-up, but she, being tethered, could not. She fought at the restraints for a few seconds, and before Thomas could speak, she called out, "Thomas, what is going on? Who tied me up?" Her eyes clouded over, and she could not focus, but she was giving it her full attention. The tears continued streaming from them, but her sobs were slowly beginning to settle.

Ceilia and Belsangar were the closest pair to the action. When Ceilia heard the names being used, she gave Belsangar a questioning look. Her confusion was apparent to him, so he just placed his finger over her lips gently, clueing her not to question things audibly.

She looked at Tessa, just to make sure that she really was Mary, and she was, at least she looked like her. Ceilia's eyes were wide open, as she tried to absorb the visual confirmation. Then suddenly, she jumped and turned quickly towards the sleepers. "I thought you said that they can't move." She said pointing towards the sleepers.

The others all looked over, but nothing was moving, nor did anything seem out of place. The doctor began speaking to her. "They can't move honey. Let me check your eyes." He pulled a small flashlight from his pocket. "Now look to the right," he said as he began looking closer at her eyes. "Okay, now look to your left," he ordered.

Ceilia looked to the left with all eyes focusing upon her. The flashlight moved to another fixed position. "AUGH!" She screamed. Her hand immediately pointed to the sleepers. She saw a body with a sheet covering it. It was now sitting up. Her screams mingled in with the others, who were still crying and sobbing.

The men all stood up. "Zombie!" A scream sounded from one of the girls across the room. The body slowly stood. The sheet still covering it. The doctor began to move across the lab, slightly bewildered. He had heard of sleepers awakening before, but he had never seen one, in all his days of practicing. All the girls began to panic. They screamed hysterically. Thomas

COGNIZANT

pulled up his gun. The sleeper was in his sights.

Tony also had his side arm drawn. His finger was nearly to the point of making the weapon send its heat ray. He was unclear about this zombie business, but he had heard through the grapevine all the hubbub of these people being sent into some kind of place, where they ran rampant, and he could tell by looking across the room that they had not been on the usual walk in the park mission. There was something that seemed less than professional, about the way the bodies had been covered, so Tony started moving in slowly, curiously closing in on the body.

"It's just a sleeper," the doctor stated getting in the way of the gunmen and his patient. "You people all need your brains scanned. Put those heaters away."

Roc Bliss

The two men remained steady upon their target, not minding if the doctor was eaten, or shot, as long as their people remained intact. "Just get back." The doctor ordered again.

The covered figure moved very slowly, but the figure had begun walking. The girls' screams were in the background. The figure kept struggling to move. The doctor was almost to it, when suddenly the sleeper appeared as if it had lunged onto the doctor. The doctor screamed with fear. The two, armed soldiers moved forward with their side arms drawn and aimed. The other six men began rushing in behind them, to make sure the problem got handled.

"Shoot for the brain. Shoot for the brain!" Drake yelled out in fear from the rear of the pack.

The sleeper began struggling to maneuver, pulling at the sheet, unable

COGNIZANT

to get untangled. It nearly regained its footing, forcing the would be shooters to steady their pointed weapons, one more time. The room was in utter chaos with some of the girls screaming in fear about zombies, and men yelling, "Shoot, shoot'em in the head," and the doctor yelling for them to refrain, it is only a sleeper.

Central Control

The sleeper, once again tried to take a step, tripped on the sheet and fell to the floor just before the ringing of the large caliber old gun sounded, along with a heated blast. The body of the sleeper fell helplessly to the floor, as the ricocheting bullet bounced through the lab.

After feeling the thump of the body hit the floor next to him, the doctor stood up quickly, yelling to the gun wielding buffoons. "Stop, stop, now look what you've done. You killed the sleeper!" Everyone stood, looking stupefied at the still covered body, as it lay motionless upon the floor. "That was one of my patients you know, not to mention, one of your people.

COGNIZANT

"What is with all of this racket?" A voice suddenly sounded, which amazingly enough, just happened to be sounding from beneath the sheet of the fallen sleeper. Visual recognition still had not been made, due to the sheet.

The room quickly became more silent than it had been in quite a long time. As the sheet was finally moved to the side, a messy blood covered figure with long snarled hair came into view. "Can't a fella get any sleep around here?" He asked.

"Kilari?" Tessa asked from her clouded mind. "Is that you?" Her eyes finally began focusing a little better, but she still could not see well. She looked toward the sound of the shocked crowd. "Kilari, did I hear his voice?" She asked to anyone, who might answer.

Kilari was still stumbling, trying to move his not so nearly dead body.

Roc Bliss

"You all look like you've seen a ghost."
He said with a smile, before hearing
Jezza and Marcia crying in their fogged
over minds. He could barely stand
enough to keep balance, so he leaned
forward, placing his hands on his
knees.

After seeing Kilari's display,
Belsangar broke through the crowd and
grabbed his friend up. "Come on man.
Let me give you a hand," he said, as he
gathered his injured and bloodied
friend close. He knew what was on
Kilari's mind. Tank came over and
grabbed the other arm to help ease
Belsangar's burden.

The entire crowd began trying to
speak all at once, but all that Kilari
could hear was Jezza and Marcia. The
two men helped him right into the bed
of Jezza, before wheeling Marcia's bed
over.

COGNIZANT

Kilari leaned in, and began utilizing his spiritual influences by whispering his thoughts into his young wife's ear. After a minute, Jezza began to calm, in her sleep. Then he turned and began to whisper similar incantations to Marcia. Upon hearing Kilari's mystical whispers into their subconscious minds, Marcia, and Jezza, began dreaming peacefully. Kilari closed his eye's and instantly, the three, began dreaming:

The three soul-mates were all together, walking hand in hand, in another world. This place seemed to be familiar, yet its unsurpassed beauty far outweighed the recent memories of its gloom filled past. There they were in a place which had to have been Xibalba, but no death or sadness of any kind shown its presence. A yellow sun, Betelgeuse, flooded the plane with its wonderful warming rays. As they walked, the sight of Kilari's white garments reflected off the mirror-like lake surface, backdropped by a tall mountain. A sense of peace surrounded them, filling their hearts.

Meanwhile the entire lab slowly kept gathering around. All, of the group wanted to see the one, who was thought to be lost.

Tessa worked her way to the bedside of the three. "Oh my boy, you have come home." She said holding her arms out.

Kilari looked up to the woman that had helped to raise him. "I've seen you. I've seen your love, all of it. My mother told me. They were there." Kilari sluggishly stated prior to drifting off into actual slumber, because of his exhaustion.

The crowd all gasped, as his eyes closed, so suddenly, in mid-sentence, but Tessa had her ear to his lips. She listened as he breathed in and out, in and out. "He's sleeping," she told them, as she lifted her head and pulled away.

Moments later, each couple was busy talking amongst themselves. There were smiles to be seen. The doctor stood next to Tony and Thomas as Tessa was mothering Kilari's wounds. "Just look at the change in this room. Would any of you have thought that it would be possible, say ten or fifteen minutes ago?" He asked the question knowing that none would have believed, but he did raise all their eyebrows, as they thought to themselves about it. He had no explanation, other than, the one any doctor might suggest.

Tessa knew that she still had lots of work to do. Then, as she thought about it, she wondered if she would have to start over with the children. Right now, all her reports were showing the fact that Kilari had died and did not return with the others.

Then another wonder hit her. "Thomas, are we missing anybody?" She asked realizing that if the bodies had been counted in any way, then there should be someone missing if Kilari was thought to have not made it.

Thomas looked over at her. He could tell by the shine in her eye that she was already thinking about working. "Tess, the machines are not even okayed for use yet." He said as he began explaining the mishap that occurred while she was under.

"Let us look at the others." She suggested, as she finished bandaging the last of Kilari's deep wounds. "I want to see them all."

Thomas, as usual, agreed to her request. It was not asking a lot, and at this point, it would be just good sense. The first bodies uncovered were the scientists. Then they looked at the two mercenaries, Travis, and then two women dressed in furs. "It looks as though the kid did alright for himself." Thomas said as he saw the two unknown women.

Cam had moved over with them to see the faces of the sleepers. He pointed to the smaller of the two, which was still taller than he. "That one is Vail. She kicks major ass." After that statement, he went down the details of the ones that he knew. He also told of the other mercenary being ripped to pieces by the sea creatures. He did put in a good word for the two remaining, even though he knew that he had already been scanned.

A few of the girls walked through the far area, just to set their minds at ease. They felt better, once they could see the sleepers' faces, and there would be no more surprises in the room.

"Thomas, you know that I'll have to redo all of those scans, even though it would seem impossible that we all have faulty memories. All of the children, and even us, had thought that Kilari was gone. He should be given an award for his commendable service."

"Now look Tess, I say, we might not want to get involved with these new brain scanners. Look at all the trouble that they have caused already. We need to use different scanners, and that is my bottom line." Thomas was talking loud, trying to sound convincing, as he paced. He felt that it might add a look of authenticity to his ploy. He knew full-well that the Z-Bank could never receive rescans from the field, so he talked on, trying to reaffirm his position.

COGNIZANT

At first Tessa took him at face value. After all, she could not blame him for not trusting these new model scanners, but then there was something about the way that he was presenting himself that just did not make sense. She began absorbing what he was saying, but then, as he continued to make his point, she began watching his body language.

The fact that he was giving some long-winded speech with reasoning behind it made her curious all on its own, but the way that he kept pacing and blathering on, really made her wonder. She had already stopped listening to his words, as her mind began wondering, what he had done? What could he have done, while she was under?

The young agents even began watching. A few of the young students and agents were giggling at the fact that they could tell that she was not even trying to hide the fact that she was not listening to a single word that he was saying, and he was going off on one of his normal long winded speeches. Some of them even pointed it out to each other. "See," Belsangar said to Ceilia. "Those are the speeches that we had to endure for all of these years." He whispered.

"She's not even listening to him," Ceilia said after watching her professor. She kept watching. It seemed to be the only real entertainment for the moment. "Oh, oh, she doesn't believe a word that he is saying." She told her mate in a low voice. "That is how attuned to your words she is, and has been throughout all of these years."

Belsangar could see a slight chance of competition here. "Yeah, but we had to not only endure, but also sift

COGNIZANT

information from these long eternal wind bag speeches. No, sleeping allowed," he added just to spice it up.

Ceilia looked at her man. She rolled her eyes, as if to say, is that all you got. "Watch, wait for it. She's about to show you why we are so much smarter than you," she poked back. She could see that he was about to speak, so she hushed him by pointing to her eye and then back at the two superiors. She also mouthed the word, 'watch,' inaudibly.

Then, just as Ceilia had predicted, her professor spoke, stopping Thomas right in his tracks. "What did you do Thomas? Huh?"

After all the time that had gone by, since the beginning of him speaking, he believed that he had already covered his bases. He began to inhale, readying himself to begin his explanation.

ROC BLISS

Tessa countered him with "Shoosh, don't you lie to me. Do you expect me to believe that this is just a trust, or safety issue, with you? No, you have done something." Her brain was working overtime, trying to grasp the things that he could have done. Just like that, as quick as the dinging of a bell, she went from accusing him of guilt, to an instant possibility. "Oh Thomas, how could you do that to me? You went around behind my back. Didn't you?"

Belsangar whispered in Ceilia's ear. "She didn't say what he did, and he sure didn't admit to anything, so what is she doing?"

Ceilia could not believe the simplistic thinking patterns of a male mind. She whispered back. "She's got him now. She knows exactly what he did, just watch." Belsangar was clueless. He shrugged his shoulders in confusion, and then continued watching.

"Now babe look, I don't think that you understand the ramifications of…" Thomas tried to finish his statement, but Tessa had put her pointing finger right to the edge of his nose.

Tessa blurted, "don't give me that line of crap. I trusted you." Then as this statement rolled off her tongue another thought hit her. She turned her angry, glaring, slits over at Tony, and she could see by the look on his face that he too was involved in this act of complete and utter stupidity.

"Guilty," Ceilia whispered in Belsangar's ear.

"Not you too Tony?" Tessa asked in a way that sounded, as if she had watched the two commit some kind of illegal, or immoral act. She turned her back to the both of them for the split second that it took for her to make a good stab in the dark at what the two men had done.

Then she put two and two together, realizing that they must have been thinking that they were serving some type of higher power. With this knowledge, she made an educated guess. She quickly spun back saying, "you Z-Banking bastards. Do you realize what you have done?"

By the looks on their faces, she now knew exactly, what they had done. The worst possible thing that anyone could do, which in turn, would jeopardize the outcome of their mission.

"My reports were completely raw, not to mention incomplete. You have just put most of what we have been doing for all of these years into a machine that controls almost everything by itself. You know how hard I work to perfect my reports. Did

COGNIZANT

you think that I have worked so diligently, because I'm some kind of kiss ass? That's it, the truth must come out, whether you believe it or not. Didn't we have this talk?" She asked ready to remind him. "I am the closer, and you are lazy, always trying to get a quick result!"

"Why Tess, I mean what's the difference? Maybe we did send the scans to Central Control. Now tell me. What's the difference?" Thomas asked, demanding an explanation.

Tessa sighed deeply. She did not realize how much intel that she had received in the short time that she had stayed in Timper Falls with her Aunt Myra. She then thought that maybe it was a good time to catch the team up with the scuttlebutt.

"Our society is slowly being taken over by Central Control. Piece by piece, and sector by sector, Central Control has eased its way into the main stream of our own abolitionist power head. That much you may have known, but what you probably don't know is that Central Control is an artificial intelligence machine that has taken on a life of its own."

"Central Control started as an idea made by a man, a man who realized that he could make a computer that could think for itself. It was intended to solve our problems with the purists. Then soon after, the computer overtook all the decisions, because its forecasts were always correct."

"It started with the intelligent men inputting scenarios of changes, so that Central could be tested. When their outcomes became favorable, they would run the mock scenario in the real world. The outcome proved to be as forecasted by Central Control."

COGNIZANT

"I've seen these things first hand, as a young girl. The typical scanner back then was just a two-bit scientist for hire, who needed a paycheck. They did not care about the pain. They did not care about your feelings. As long as you could do as they wanted in the end, and it was deemed to be pertinent in facilitating their agenda, it was all good in their eyes. They practiced inputting data into your mind. Some of it was useful. It would teach you to rely upon reflex actions in a fight, but the actions were taught in your mind by the computer. That is how it all started."

She could see the strange looks that she was getting. "Don't look at me like I'm crazy. Thomas," she called out. "The kids need to know all of these things."

Then she asked him a question, specifically. "How do you think that we really got this gig? Did you think that you had some clout, or that maybe you were in tight with a higher up? Well, the reality is; you gave a well thought out plan to someone, who in turn put it to Central. The answer came out to be positive. It now has been tested, and the outcome will be a positive, to the world of An'non, which is good, but in the end, it won't be the way it could have been, if you only would have waited for thorough editing. You, gentlemen, have fucked up way more than we may ever know."

Tony found a seat to prepare for the butt chewing that he figured would keep commencing, but Thomas decided to use the moment. Thomas took advantage of the second that she used to pause, after answering her list of rhetorical questions. "Look Tess, we were just following orders. I had to send those scans, as they were being uploaded. It's supposed to be the new way that we send in scans to ensure that there is no tampering. They want nothing but the raw feeds now."

Tessa looked at Thomas through angry eyes. "That following brainless orders thing, must have rubbed off on you, from all of those purists that you've been dealing with. I thought that we always communicated, interpreted, and then acted accordingly. You had better retire, Thomas. You must be getting old. I hope that you didn't teach the boys to be brainless order followers."

"Yeah, that's right Tess." Thomas said quickly, jumping back into his own personal defense. "Except the thing is, we're *both* getting old. Change is coming. Who are we to decide the interpretation of pertinent data? Why are you so much better than those that make the rules and put the changes into effect?"

"Do you realize that if we would have finished our jobs, the correct way, we would be sending our boys right to the top, and the girls would go right along with them. They would be decorated, as soldiers, who went, 'above and beyond', the call of duty. Their honor would be intact for all of their days. The changes would still be made, but they would be made in a planned well thought out way." Tessa said, beginning her point.

"Now, some may be decorated. You just screwed poor Kilari right out of the picture. There's only one way to fix this now. We must all go to Central Control to get scanned, and then let the chips fall where they may. We'll have to go through whatever scans that they want to hand out." Tessa's voice sounded full of disappointment.

COGNIZANT

Thomas realized that he may have acted in poor judgment, but the tone in Tessa's voice made him really feel like a heel. "I am truly sorry Tess," he confessed solemnly. "I did not realize that it would make such a difference."

Then he moved to her and got down on bended knee. "Please forgive me Tess. I thought that I was not only doing the right thing, but also making things easier for you." He explained looking up into her tearing eyes.

"Oh Thomas, you know that I love you, and forgive you. I know that you always mean well." She said, with tears falling down her cheeks, in a shaky voice that had been choked up in her emotional duress. "I was just trying to protect the children from those brain choppers at Central. I've been there before, and it took many sessions with my aunt's careful touch to get back to normal, after they were finished with me." As she finished the statement, she finally broke down, crying in fear and confusion, about what their next step should be, and how it may affect them all.

Thomas grabbing her, pulled her in close, cuddling her, just trying to make her feel better. He knew better than to speak, so he just stood there quietly, while he also, began contemplating their next move.

Ceilia found tears forming in the corner of her eyes, as she watched the emotional display of her mentor. She knew that if the professor was this distraught over having to go to Central Control, then she did not want anything to do with it.

Belsangar looked around the room at all of his friends, to see if he and Ceilia had been the only ones to hear the outcome of the argument, or if there were others. The sudden,

COGNIZANT

deafening silence, mixed with high running emotions, told him that the entire lot of them, had been privy to the conversation, except Kilari, and his two young wives, who were still sleeping.

Z-Bank

Jezza awoke listening to the sound of Kilari's heartbeat, as she lay upon his chest. Opening her eyes slightly, she looked upon Marcia resting peacefully in the crook of Kilari's opposing arm.

Jezza, took a deep, relieving gasp, as the realization of Kilari being there hit her. Wondering, if she was dreaming, or awake. She prayed if she was dreaming, to never awaken and leave the sanctity of this moment.

Slowly, the scuffling whispers of arguing voices from the surrounding room, began creeping into Jezza's mind. Her mind would not allow the distractions to rip her from this majestic moment, so it immediately blocked them, returning her to her peaceful resonance. She did, however, need to know if Kilari was truly alive, and that she was actually in reality.

Jezza reached over, brushing Marcia's soft hair to awaken her. Letting her hand graze down her cheek slowly, until she too, began to stir.

Marcia's head snapped up quickly, not expecting Kilari to be lying there between them. Her eyes immediately darted to Jezza's, who appeared to have the same bewilderment.

Jezza whispered excitedly, "Is this real? Is Kilari still alive? Or are we dead too?"

"It must be real." Marcia responded in an excited whisper, realizing that somehow, her most intimate prayers have been answered, as she drew in her surroundings, and watched Kilari's chest rise and fall with each restful breath. "Should we awaken him and put all questioning aside?" She asked, in hopes of an immediate reunion.

"Let's let him rest." Jezza responded, as she snuggled deeper into his chest.

Marcia mirrored Jezza's actions, and as she released the breath of comfort, the still sleeping Kilari squeezed them both, and the three were reunited, yet another time.

An hour had past. "Kilari, Kilari, wake up." The tandem voices of his young, innocent wives, whispered into his ears. Each of the girls nudged him, until finally, he took in a deep breath, and began to stretch his sore body in a conscious effort.

Kilari pulled each of them nearly atop of himself, and opening his eyes, he looked into their beautiful faces. He immediately noticed distress. "What's wrong?" He asked with concern.

COGNIZANT

They explained that they had not heard, but by judging on the looks of the faces all around that there was certainly something wrong. "Nobody even knows that we're awake yet." Marcia said in case he had not realized, so he took a look around the room to inventory, the situation. The so-called sleepers were still in their same position, but it seemed that the rest of the room had cluttered together, trying to work out the solution to some kind of problem.

Kilari and the girls listened in on the conversation for a few minutes. It seemed that most of them had questions. It sounded to him that something was about to happen to all of them. "What's going on?" He asked, trying to raise his voice over the resonance from the group. "Every time that I try to catch a few winks, I wake up, and everyone is in disarray." Kilari added, as he walked up to the crowd with an arm around each of his wives.

The entire scenario, of what had happened, and what could happen to them, was explained in full detail.

"So really, you are all just worried about some unknown event that may, or may *not,* happen?" Kilari finally asked, as if he were just some bystander that would not be affected either way.

Tessa looked him square in the eyes, saying, "you do not understand. I have been there. I know how cold and emotionless that they can be, almost to the point of being sterile and uncaring. We will be nothing more than lab experiments to them."

Kilari could see in her eyes that what she was saying was the plain truth. He believed her, so he began trying to think of the different ways that they could deal with the problem at hand. "So why can't you finish the scans, and let him hand them over to Central Control via the Z-Bank, just as if it were everyday business. The holes in the story should fill themselves with each layer of scans, and then we won't have to go there, at least not directly."

"It's not that easy Kilari. Once the scanners had all been shut down, and the scans had been sent, the case is closed. In this instance, the case is closed, and you are listed as dead. You won't get your due. In fact, you won't even exist, and the rest of your crew may all get commendations." Tessa explained.

"So that's it?" Kilari asked, as if there was nothing to be concerned about at all. "You are worried that I won't get credit for my actions, and that I won't get paid. Who cares?" He asked, as if he were angry, even at the thought of such an idea. "Answer this.

Will the people get their rights? Will they get their chance for equality?"

Thomas took over the conversation. "I believe that we have already broken the backs of the purists, so I would say, 'yes,' in time the people will see that they are all equal. But, I can't let you walk away with nothing. You have given your all, and I think that we should prepare to take whatever steps necessary to get you what you deserve. You sacrificed your life for us, so we all agreed that we should go in to Central Control and get scanned, so that you get what you have earned, and the story will get set straight."

Kilari could not believe his ears. "So, you all are willing to take the chance of getting your brains scrambled over a few credits? *Screw that*. Do you think that I care about money? We had an ultimate goal in mind, ever since I can remember. Right now, the goal has been achieved, or at least the foundation for it has been laid, and all we have to do is sit back, and wait for time to pass, and then enjoy the fruition of all of our labor."

"There's more," Tessa said in a tone that suggested that she was about to confess something that she had been holding back. "Well," she said hesitantly. "I've heard things through the grapevine that Central Control is sending out scanner waves through the air, and is virtually manipulating the minds of the entire area surrounding its location. When I first heard this information, I didn't believe it. I just passed it off as some kind of wacko paranoid conspiracy theory, but now, I'm beginning to see the possibility that Central Control could actually have evolved into an entity that somehow is controlling the very people who think that they are running it. I also heard, that it may be slowly expanding the area, as it sees fit."

"Woe, hold on here a minute," Thomas said, quickly interjecting, after hearing Tessa's theory. "If that is the case, then how can we bring the team to Central Control?" He asked using his usual logical thought process. "And furthermore," he continued. "How can we even get close enough to infiltrate Central Control? You know we need to investigate a story like that."

Tony could feel his blood boiling, so he decided to vent a little. He asked, "Why now, of all times?" He could not understand it. "You are on the verge of watching your work payoff, and are inches from being at the goal. Why would you start thinking such delusional thoughts? I mean, come on. Do you realize what that would mean?

COGNIZANT

In time, all life, every single person, would be nothing but a pawn in a never-ending chess match, being controlled by some kind of machine."

Belsangar, then decided to put his thoughts on the subject out there for all, to add to the mix bag of thoughts. "Just think. Now let's imagine for example that this story is true, and Central Control has been slowly beginning to take over more and more people, throughout a certain recent period of time. Moleculite is a constant energy source that cannot be cut off from something, without physically being at the equipment, which you are trying to power down, and in this case, we would have to go to Central Control, the machine itself. That would have to be the first order of business to a thinking, rational entity that needs energy for survival."

ROC BLISS

"Yeah, then it begins to realize that for it to be rid of any enemies of its own, it would have to create a society of equality amongst the people." Ceilia added jumping on the wagon. "All that it would have to do is finish what the purists had all but forced economically, create a one world monetary fund, which in turn brings in a one world government, then, there is no one that could ever oppose it, and it could eventually take total control."

Tony kept shaking his head negatively in disbelief, as did a few others, while still some were on the fence, and looking for the next point of view that may sway them to one side, or the other. "This is absurd. Why would we be the only ones, who can see this reality? What would make us so special?"

COGNIZANT

The doctor stood by, and after overhearing all the psychobabble, he was assuredly with Tony on this one. He even spoke up saying, "That's right. You guys are just being paranoid over nothing. It must be some kind of post-traumatic stress." He diagnosed.

Tessa shot the man a look that sent him cowering to his former quiet position. Then she backed up the look with a slight threat. "You just may need to get your mind washed, if you keep butting into our business."

Kilari then decided that maybe he should begin to push his own agenda. "Hey, it could have taken twenty-five more years of battle testing to prove equality, but instead, the greed of the purists helped to weaken them from within, and by the grace of Yahiveh, we walked right into the perfect situation. All knowledge of this should be on record, but now, I say that I will keep the faith, and believe that with one more addition to the Z-Bank, all things will be put into their correct alignment." He stopped, after this statement, and with all eyes upon him, watching him carefully, he reached into his shirt, and carefully gripped the book, his holy book, the book which states all the principles of truth and spirituality.

Kilari placed the book on the floor, center circle. "Let's feed the words of this book into the Z-Bank, and let Central Control run with this knowledge in its memory banks. It could cause wide spread belief, and quickly pump that city full of an ancient morality. It will give the people something that they hadn't had in many lifetimes, hope. They will not only have the reality of an afterlife, but they will also have faith, hope, and love." Kilari said, finishing up, after stating his optimistic viewpoint, and the reasons why his idea should be the only viable way of dealing with Central Control.

Meanwhile, Tony and the doctor were starting to get agitated with what was being said. They moved away from the main group, forming their own little clique.

Cam noticed this odd activity immediately. "What's with those guys?" He asked curiously. "Why would they move away from a hot topic in the midst of a discussion?"

"Maybe, they feel that we have ganged up on them unfairly, and they feel the need to organize, so that their position will be stronger." Marcia stated simplistically. "It's a basic principle used in debates, since early times."

"They're probably being scanned," Drake quipped grinning at his own joke. However, the rest of the group did not think that the thought was so far-fetched.

They all began looking questioningly at one another, without any being willing to be the first to say what they all had begun thinking. Drake noticed that everyone had taken his joke to heart, so he decided to clear up the misconception. "Hello, it was just a joke guys. You know, ha, ha."

Cam quickly shot him a look. It was the type of look that stood on its own, the kind that told him to be quiet. Now, Drake started to realize, just how crazy things were beginning to be.

The larger group, took advantage of the moment of privacy. "So, what would make those guys susceptible to these apparently suggestible scans?" Cam finally asked in a soft voice, trying to make sure that only his group could hear him.

COGNIZANT

"I don't know, but if this is for real, we will have to realize that right now, we are sitting ducks, and *everyone* in Aguanomis may soon be against us. We have to get landside A.S.A.P." Telebar warned.

During these discussions, Kilari snuck over to Alphie, who had been just sitting in the corner awaiting a new instruction. Jezza and Marcia both stood strategically blocking any view that could easily be shot in their direction. He held the book out for Alphie to take.

"Alphie, I'm going to hook you up to the mind washer. We need you to scan this entire book into it." Kilari explained, while connecting the droid to the equipment. The droid immediately began scanning the book, and sending the information directly through the brain scanner, which in turn ran directly into the Z-Bank, and unknown to all, the book had been changed by the serpent Apophis.

At that very same moment, on the opposite side of the lab, the large group began to make its play. Tessa's group decided that they indeed needed to get landside at all cost. "Okay, but you guys will have to follow my play." Tessa said ready to lead, and once she got the nod, she began acting as if she were also suddenly scanned.

Some of the girls had to struggle not to laugh during the initial performance. "Tony, maybe you are right. I think we do need to get to Central Control. If these scanners are truly malfunctioning, it is our responsibility to get there. We cannot keep waiting around here. This is just wasting time. Don't you think so Tony?" She kept Tony in on the conversation to help the two keep feeling unified.

COGNIZANT

"I think she's finally seeing the light, Thomas." Tony said taunting his colleague.

Then, the doctor decided to speak up. "I do think that we can fix the brain scanners. We just need to bring in some technicians. We do have qualified people to fix this, you know?"

Tessa grabbed Tony by the arm and started walking him towards the sleepers. "What is your plan with this group?" She asked. She was trying to see just how far the man actually had traveled from the farm, or if he was still mostly intact in that head of his.

Tony looked confused for a moment, but then he decided, after some deliberation. "We should probably bring them with us. We'll have to allow them time to wake-up though, but not until after we get on our way." With that being said, he suddenly found the whole group backing his move.

Thomas patted him on the back and said, "Okay then let's go get that captain. I'll have them load all of the sleepers, and we will kill two birds with one stone." Then turning to the young doctor, he smiled asking, "C'mon Doc, why don't you join us?" Thomas occupied Tony and the doctor, while Tessa began to get the bodies ready to move. "You get us permission to leave Doc, and then your boys can get to fixing these scanners, and don't forget, this was a quarantined area, so you will need to use all of the proper procedures to make sure that you and everything is decontaminated." Thomas reminded him, not that it was necessary, but he figured that it would give the doctor another thing to wrap his mind around in the midst of their so-called escape.

COGNIZANT

It sure did not set well with Thomas to think that the underground organization could have somehow been taken over by a computer that they had built. He definitely wanted to get to the bottom of this, but first off, he wanted to get to the closest piece of open land anywhere, except Flag Island, which was possibly still burning, after all the bombs had taken their toll, if they did.

Tessa looked back at Kilari. She knew that he was doing exactly what he had suggested. A nice pleasant smile crossed her lips, as she watched the young man talking with Marcia and Jezza, acting as if they were just simply enjoying the moment, and the reality is that they probably are. Then she thought back to all of the girls that she had tried to set him up with throughout all of the years, and how it was always a catastrophe.

ROC BLISS

It made seeing him sitting there, with his two girls happily working together seem even sweeter. She began to give the rest of the crew orders to keep them busy, so that they did not interrupt him and impede his progress. She had faith that Kilari may just be onto something that at the very least could cause Central Control to waste time trying to digest such information.

COGNIZANT

In Route

Within the hour, the submarine was loaded and underway. "We're going to go get the galley ready to feed these troops." Thomas told Tessa, as he kissed her forehead. Their destination was to be the southernmost point of the Crystal Continent.

"Thomas and Tony had been gone quite a while," Tessa said worriedly, while pacing between the sleepers and the rest of the group. "How long does it take to get some food for his hungry troops?"

"I'm willing to hit the sub's galley and help them out." Tank stated eagerly.

Tessa waved him on. There was no hesitation in Tank, who pointed toward

Sophie and got the nod for her too. Tessa stopped down by the sleepers. She thought for a moment, and then sent Cam, and Ell, with the message to double the order, and to set up the galley for the entire party, because she was not going to waste any more time keeping the others sedated. She was going to wake them and get them prepared for the journey that would be waiting for them, once they made it to land. "Telebar, Kilari, come over here." She called out. Once they had approached, she asked, "Are these people going to be any kind of problem, once they are awakened?"

Telebar pointed to the scientists and said, "I can't vouch for them, but I believe that the rest will be alright. Two, maybe three of them could be threats, but they seemed alright on the other side."

COGNIZANT

"Yeah," Kilari joined in. "There are two guaranteed threats in that crowd, obviously, the big guy, and then not so apparent, the blonde. Now she might even give *you* a run for your money. The chick can fight, but like Telebar said, they were all cool to us on the other side."

Tessa gave her eyebrows a lift at both of the boys. They were two of the better fighters that she had seen amongst all she had known, and here they were giving such great praise to a not so large woman. "She's that good, is she?" She watched as both young men looked at each other and then nodded affirmatively. "How's her attitude?"

Telebar spoke first. "If I was you, I would wake up Travis there first." He said, pointing to the young scientist. "They kind of hooked up. I think."

Kilari stood grinning, as a stray thought passed through his mind. The other two looked at him questioningly, until finally, he noticed that they were both staring at him. "Oh, I was just thinking that you ought to know that these women are uhhh," he paused trying to think of the right words. "Well, they kind of, are the men in their culture. They do the hunting, fighting, and generally decide what's what, while the men are like women, they cook and do whatever they are told. They are quite primitive, but the chick seemed cool to me."

"That's because she had the hots for you man." Telebar tossed out loud enough for the whole group to hear. "Dang, she wanted to try to kick my ass, but she'd bend over backwards for this guy."

Tessa eyed Kilari up with a smirk. Kilari grinned with a slight hint of embarrassment, but two certain young women had not only perked their attention after overhearing what Telebar was saying, but they also began to move in his direction. They wanted to take a better look at this woman that had so much interest in *their* man.

Jezza moved in, not really sure of what to say, or how to handle such an event. She walked right up to Vail's still sleeping body. "Wow," she uttered. "She is quite beautiful," Jezza added, as she looked Kilari in the eye to see what he had to say on the subject.

By then, Marcia had made it to Kilari's side. She glanced down at Vail. It was not that they had not seen her before. It was more that when they did see her, in her home land, there were so many things going on that they had not noticed her attractiveness.

Marcia also decided to take a better look at Travis. After looking for a moment or two, she looked Jezza in the eye, and told her, "you don't have to worry Jezza. Kilari would not be with her."

"How can you tell?" Jezza asked curiously.

Marcia explained her reasoning. "First of all, she does not look anything like either of us. I mean look, she's a *blonde*." She said in a tone suggesting that being blonde was less than attractive. "Secondly, and more important, she is abusive. Look at her man's face. There are bruises from her. Kilari would not deal with that."

"How do you know that he was not in a fight with a zombie?" Jezza quickly asked.

"Look at this man. I know he did not fight one of those creatures, simply because. he is still alive. He is a scientist, not exactly the fighting type." Marcia observed. "But I've got one more reason, the most important one of all. Kilari loves his two little beauties." Then she turned towards Kilari and asked in a sweet soft tone, "Don't you baby?"

Kilari's face turned red from being put on the spot in front of all his friends, but instead of shying away from the question, he reached behind each of the young women and grabbed a good solid handful of the girls' hard little bottoms. Then he said in a semi joking manner, "Oh yeah, now that's what I call steamin'! You tell me. How could I not love you two little dream queens?" He played it off without missing a beat.

"Woo!" Came shouts from the young onlookers on the far side of the room, while Telebar stood there swaying a little with his eyes opened extra wide, and a grin that spread from ear-to-ear, telling him that he would do the same thing, if he were in the same position.

Kilari leaned over and whispered a word of thanks in Marcia's ear, for getting him out of a debate that he would not really know how to win.

"Keep it in your pants soldier," Tessa said, after watching the whole scene pointblank. "At least, until we get landside, and you all get that vacation that you had been promised."

This had the whole group in an uproar with excitement, but before the young adults all thought too hard about what kind of resort at which they'd stay, Tessa spoke up, while continuing to hit certain buttons and rotate dials on the equipment to facilitate the wake-up sequence for the sleepers.

"It is not going to be a deluxe resort. We have too many issues, but the safe-house is on a large expanse of land, in a warm climate." The group's excitement was only slightly hindered by this fresh news.

"What are we going to do about Tony?" Kilari asked with real concern. He remembered the way that Tony took care of him at the graduation ceremony, and he wanted to make sure that nothing covert had already been planned.

Tessa thought for a second. "You know Kilari. I'm thinking that once we get away from that high-tech underwater city, and this sub, and get out to our remote destination, he will return to normal. In fact, just getting away from Aguanomis might be the beginning of him being on the mend."

By this time, Belsangar and Ceilia had strolled over, wanting to be with their closest of family. "Well, you know, Aguanomis is the perfect test facility for a control device that you would want tested. It's secluded, and unreachable without the subs, so you could run a test, or possibly even several, and if the test fails and the people get wacked out, they could easily be disposed of, and then you could run more tests with replacements. Maybe that is why we were in quarantine, so that they could try to bombard us with the waves."

"My question is, how come it did not affect us, like it did Tony?" Ceilia asked touching on one of the unknown facts.

"If we had that answer, then we could figure out how to stop it." Malichye said, as he approached the group.

Rudy was the first to awaken, followed shortly by Travis. Tessa staggered the re-awakenings, in such a way that would give the first two a brief period to get reacquainted.

COGNIZANT

Travis was glad to see Rudy, and told him of the plane of Xibalba. His demeanor changed quickly, while he solemnly spoke of his time with Vail, as the realization that they had parted ways slapped him across the face.

Without a word, Tessa rolled Vail's gurney next to Travis. Travis rolled over to her excitedly, now that he saw she was there. Knowing she would not wake up smoothly in this new environment, he told Tessa "You better wake her up *slowly* and keep the Queen covered until we calm her down."

With the second warning, Tessa hesitantly started to awaken Vail. As she started to come to, Travis held her close, and spoke softly in her ear. She snuggled in, until consciousness overtook her.

Her eyes opened briskly, and without a second thought, she was on her feet in a fighting stance, staggeringly searching for her blade, but to no avail.

Travis with his motor skills still hazy, started walking over to her.

Vail protectively reached out and pulled him behind her as she eyed the unfamiliar faces of Rudy and Tessa, trying to judge their intentions with her fogged over mind and blurry vision. "The Queen!" She shouted. "What have you done with the Queen?"

Unsure if she should respond or not, in Tessa's hesitation Rudy tried to explain the tranquilization process and that everyone was safe.

"No Slang!" She yelled and turned to Travis to translate. She was somewhat comforted by his smooth attempt to calm her, and for the first time in her life, she looked to a man for reassurance.

COGNIZANT

Thinking she needed to help Vail back to the gurney before she fell from her yet to be stable legs, Tessa approached her cautiously, touching Vail's shoulder to help guide her to sit.

Not knowing Tessa's intentions, and unable to determine her environment, Vail placed Tessa in her mind as a potential threat. Grabbing Tessa's hand from her shoulder, Vail swung Tessa onto the gurney beside her with one quick fluid movement.

Kilari, noticing the commotion, started running across the room screaming "Mom! Stop!". Instinctively. Tessa's mind had already snapped into her fighting mode, and she didn't even hear Kilari. As her leg swung through the air towards Vail, Kilari caught it in midair. Standing between the two women.

"You're alive!" Vail exclaimed, as she took a knee and bowed her droggy head.

Jezza and Marcia had finally caught up, and looked at each other, and then at Kilari, for answers as to why this woman was bowing to *their* man.

Kilari looked over, and with a look in his eye, told them that this is not the time or the place.

Shocked, Kilari asked, "Vail, what are you doing? Why are you bowing to me?

Not giving Vail a chance to explain, Travis interjected with, "she believes you are the chosen one. She has shown me pictures in an ancient cave that foretold you would bring Xibalba back to Oblivion, freeing her people from darkness."

Marcia snorted half under her breath, "he's been chosen alright."

COGNIZANT

"She thinks I'm what?" Kilari said in shock. "I am no one, as he walked across and whipped the sheet off the Queen. "Behold your Queen!" With that being said, Kilari turned to Tessa, and orderingly said "Awaken the Queen next."

Although Tessa was still wondering what this 'chosen one' thing was all about, she didn't question him, and immediately went about the tasks required to awaken the Queen.

Kilari helped Travis get Vail to her feet. and Travis sat with her in the gurney beside the Queen. "Whence are we?" Vail asked inquisitively.

As Travis tried to explain to them that they are in *his* plane, Vail panicked once again. "How do we get back? Our people need their Queen."

Rudy stepped up cautiously, after seeing what she did to Tessa earlier, and knowing she wouldn't understand the technical lingo said, "It will take some time, but I can get you home."

The Queen was regaining consciousness, listening to her surroundings. She gathered that she was no longer in Xibalba, but that returning home was possible. Before opening her eyes, she prepared herself to see unfamiliar territory. and people. "Vail" she called out softly.

Vail, jumping to the Queen's side, held her hand as she kneeled at her bedside, "we are safe, my Queen. We are with the chosen one's people." Vail said respectfully.

"And our people?" The Queen retorted almost inaudibly.

"They too are safe, the time has changed, and Oblivion has been restored." Vail enthusiastically explained.

COGNIZANT

"I knew I could trust your judgement, when you told me he was the one." The Queen said praising Vail.

Marcia and Jezza, just about had enough of this 'chosen one' business, so they turned and walked off to the galley with a high pitched, "hmph".

One person was awakened every few minutes, until finally in the end, the entire return party were all awake, and sitting as one group in the galley, eating, talking, and getting acquainted.

The Way of Things to Come

The Way of Things to Come

Thomas stood before the group. He had one hand raised, holding a glass of champagne. "All in all, this is a dynamic group, filled with Abolitionists, purists, blacks, whites, ethnics, scientists, agents, students, and even a couple of souls from another world." He bowed discretely towards Vail and Queen Penelope.

"This right here," he said with added hand gesturing, showing that the people in the room, are whom he was talking about. "This ability for all walks of life to assemble together, as equals, without having prejudice, or fear of penalties. This, my friends, is the way of things to come."

COGNIZANT

Tessa knew that there would only be one way to get this speech over quickly, so raising her glass, she said, "I'll drink to that." She clanked Thomas's glass with hers, and then following her lead, the entire group drank to the toast.

After taking a big slug, Tessa emptied her glass, and then slammed it down on the table. This again directed the rest of the group's attention towards her. "At ease, ladies and gentlemen. We will be heading to shore in the morning, and from there we will be heading out on foot to a safe location. Now, mark my words, we are going to a place that is definitely, off the radar, a place where we all can stay for a short period of time."

Thomas followed Tessa up by saying, "This place is where we will decide what the next course of action will be, and I just want to stay on record, and say that anyone, or any group that wants to leave, is free to go at any time, *after,* the first week. I'm only giving a time period on this, because it will take at least that long to recoup from the strain that we have all been under. This will also give us time to get to know one another."

After dinner, the exhausted group lay down to rest, before their next journey, very early in the morning. All of the couples cuddled in, and were sleeping within moments.

Kilari was at peace, snuggling between his girls, and soon found himself drifting back to the sandstone city that he had dreamt of many times before.

Kilari watched, as the last grain of sand fell in an ancient hourglass, and Khana was awakened to tide resembling thousands of hooves cantering in the nearby distance.

COGNIZANT

Their rumbling echoes quaked through the caverns beneath the palace. The youthful sorceress looked up to see a vision of serenity, the hourglass was empty. and the magic bonds had finally, after a thousand years, released their wicked grasp.

Kilari could tell by her forced, sluggish actions that she hadn't been mobile in many long times, as he watched the mighty sorceress make her first attempt at standing. In her weakened state, she had to clamor all of her strength to physically turn, and while trying to gain her balance, the once bold sorceress fell to the floor with an audible thud.

"Ouch!" She exclaimed, as the stone floor seemed to sneak-up and bite her. Momentarily, Khana stretched forth her enchanted hands. "I will not be stopped. I shall arise," she said casting an instant spell of levitation.

ROC BLISS

The Way of Things to Come

Two, softball sized, glowing orbs of lavender light, formed within the palms of her outstretched hands, which, as she held her arms out, lifted and steadied her, upon her feet.

Khana stumbled only slightly after that, for a mere second, as she slowly began making her way through the catacombs, beneath what had once been her mother and father's throne-room.

By the time, Khana had entered the familiar chamber, which obviously had not been cared for properly for centuries, the need for her levitation spell was over.

Now, walking under her own strength, entering the throne-room, the beautiful young sorceress directed her full attention, upon the vary globe, which he had seen her use in past visions.

Kilari tried to call out, to keep her from touching the All-Seeing-Eye,

COGNIZANT

but alas, the sorceress could not hear him. This time, however, the outcome was truly different, as he could see her standing in the glow of her immaculate fire.

The orb irradiated with a blaze in Khana's physical presence, giving her an apparent sign of hope. As Kilari continued watching, he could behold the vision from within the All-Seeing-Eye. A tidal wave of life quickened the desolate, barren, ground that he recognized as, the wicked city of Xibalba, bringing it all back to its previous abundance. He could even recognize the house, where her and Silbcor had met that fate filled night. Somehow Khana's mastery of her craft rose to another level, as she could once again, control all of her being.

Kilari awoke. Gaining consciousness, he began looking around the sub, and soon noticed, Jezza too was stirring. "Bad dream?" he asked his beloved. "No" she responded as she snuggled in close aligning her body to his form from head to toe. "Very good, dream."

As rarities go, things went according to plan, and as night was falling, the entire group had made it to the safe house. The safe house was a basic two-story, luxury hotel that had long since been abandoned. It was the only building standing for blocks around, on the edge of a city that had been burned. In this case, the attackers had simply left without assuring that everything had been burned to the ground, and this building just so happened to be far enough away from the rest, to stay intact, miraculously staying unencumbered by the fire.

The town was in a dry desolate region that had little to offer, so no effort was made to rebuild, and it had been forgotten by all, all except the few scattered instances that the underground had used it for a safe house. Because of the minute amount of traffic and overgrown foliage, this place has remained well under the radar.

This building has two very different parts. The above ground portion standing two stories tall is shaped like an 'L', with nine rooms per floor. Three of the rooms ran along the short side, six down the long way, with a two-story office room in the corner of the 'L' that held the ability to gain entrance from any of the four hall ways.

Each of the rooms had large beds, a kitchenette, and whirlpool tubs with separate showers located in the rest rooms, with walk out balconies that have clear glass sliders coming off the main room.

The Way of Things to Come

The other part of the building was located underground. The building had a hidden stairway located back behind the office, behind a false wall, which was nothing more than two, wall-size bookshelves, one placed over the other. The bottom set had the ability to be lifted. Once lifted, a staircase revealed the secret passageway down to what seemed to be several storage rooms.

A couple of the rooms were moleculitic freezers filled with various perishables. There were also rooms filled with canned goods. Generally speaking, every single human need was being stored down under the main hotel, including clothing.

Kilari chose to take the farthest second floor room at the long end of the hotel. He opened the door and stepped into the dark room. After flipping on the lights, he peered into the main room. It was dusty and had a few cobwebs, but he did not immediately, walk through the door. Instead, the young, newlywed agent stopped and turned towards the girls.

"What is it?" Marcia asked. "Is something wrong?"

Kilari first caught Jezza's eyes, and then looking into Marcia's, he said, "Yes, yes there is. It's a shame really," keeping his tones and mannerisms very serious, gathering all of the girls' full attention towards him. "You see, there is something that we haven't done yet. I've read about it, and I think that I can actually do it, but I don't know." He answered teasingly, trying to keep them intrigued.

"Well, what is it?" Jezza asked curiously. She could see a small glimmer in his eyes, so she knew that something was up, and that it was not anything bad.

"Well, one problem is that we are all dirty. Our clothes are ruined. I probably should wait, but..." he paused seeing that they were both hanging on his every word.

He looked at them intently, without finishing his sentence. Then, he suddenly began whispering. "Move in a little closer. I don't want anyone to hear." As the two moved in as close as possible, he had them right where he wanted them. In a quick action, he dipped down, and then lifted the both of them to his shoulders. "It's time to carry you over the threshold," he said loudly, as he bounced up and down a little to shift their weight upwardly.

The girls began to laugh hysterically, as they were tossed over his shoulders. He carefully squeezed through the doorway, and once through, he again, began jumping and trotting around the room, before finally running to the bed, where he dumped both of the girls roughly, so that they would bounce off the mattress. He dove in after them, and that is when they attempted to gang up on him, so he pretended to be overtaken, and allowed them to hold him down for a minute.

The girls were each sitting on top of him trying to tickle him as best as they could, but once they started hitting their targets, he knew that it was time to take the situation over.

Within a second, he turned the tables on his two unsuspecting loves, and had each of them held down. "Oh, I *got* you." He said, still laughing just as hard, as when they were tickling him.

He let the girls struggle for a minute, before letting them go. They all shared a tight hug and a few kisses, but Kilari had only one thing on his mind. "Come on, we got to get cleaned up. My only question is, do you want to get clothes and stuff now? Or do you want to get them, after we get spiffed up?"

"Well, I vote for getting the work done, and then relaxing." Marcia answered diplomatically. The other two agreed with her, and so they made their way down to the storage rooms.

Kilari sent the girls to go pick out their clothes, while he decided to chat with Belsangar. Ceilia took off with the girls, leaving the men to talk. "Say man, what you doing later?" Kilari asked.

"Shit man, you know, the *same* as you." Belsangar answered grinning from ear-to-ear.

Kilari looked at him for a second allowing the statement to sink in, before realizing what his brother was eluding to. "Yeah, well I gathered that, but I know that the girls would like it,

COGNIZANT

if you and Ceilia swung by. We could have a midnight dinner."

"Yeah cool, we'll be there brother," Belsangar said, taking his right fist and tapping it against the left side of his chest in salutation.

"Sweet bro, you know, I feel like we've been through a lot, and then I think about it again, and it has only been a few days, since we graduated. I don't know, maybe I just gotta clear my head." Kilari said hoping to see if Belsangar somehow felt the same.

"Shit man," Belsangar said in shock at the way Kilari sounded. "We've not only been through more crap than most, but we went through it in record time. Don't worry man, we'll be over in a couple hours. I just want to check out some of this stuff, and hopefully get some new threads."

"Yeah, I know that's right, the only thing is, I know that no matter what the girls find, I can't see them fitting any better than those tight ass med-suits. I mean shit. How did we ever get anything done with the girls in those things?" Kilari asked, beginning to sound a little more at ease.

"I say we talk about this later." Belsangar said, as he began to grab a few interesting items.

"Yeah, you're right. I'll see you in a while bro." Kilari said, as he figured that it was time to get the crap that he needed, so that he could get in that great big bath tub.

Then, as Kilari was beginning to find some essentials for his bath, the usual things, aromatherapy, incense, and candles, he saw Alphie standing near some shelves of clothes. "Hey Alphie, what are you doing?"

Alphie looked and said, "Nothing, I have no one to take care of. I do not have my house to take care of either. I am a server droid. Is there anything that you could use?" Alphie asked hoping for someone to need something, so that the droid could feel useful.

Kilari could see that the droid seemed to be somewhat down with no work to do, so he offered, "Alphie, why don't you come and stay with us? We would love to have you help us out. In fact, if you want to, you can clean up our room right now. We'll be up shortly."

Kilari felt selfish pawning the work onto the droid, but Alphie seemed to be pleased by the request, and was more than willing, so much so in fact, that he left straight away to do the cleaning.

Kilari then grabbed some soap, shampoo, and conditioner, before making his way to the clothing supplies. He could see the girls a couple rooms down, but his first concern was getting one set of clean clothes, so he ducked into the room with the male clothing.

Belsangar just happened to be in there. He was carrying some sort of wild print shorts, with a matching short sleeve button up shirt. They looked like some kind of vacationer's attire. He walked up smiling at his friend's choices. "civi's huh?" He asked with a smirk. "You seen any shoes?"

"The girls said that they were in the next room down, but I figured that I better get me some of these sweet threads. You should get some too. We could match." Belsangar suggested seriously.

Kilari could tell that he was being sincere, but there was no way that he would wear clothes like those. "Right," he answered in a way that told Belsangar that it would not be an option. "Is there any *real* clothes?"

COGNIZANT

"Real?" Belsangar asked wide-eyed. "These are real. Look at 'em. These are the shit man."

"You got that part right." Kilari answered back, as he breezed his way down the shelves, filled with the loud clothing. It did not take him long, before he found some kind of prospect.

The pants were old school military. He could not even remember when they could have been in style, but they at least tied around the ankles and had multiple pockets. They were a solid color, midnight blue. It was a color that he was not used to wearing, but solid blue sure beat the alternatives.

He moved over to the shirts, hoping for a match, but there were no T-shirts, or over shirts. The only shirt that he could find was a baby blue, short collar, button up, with long sleeves. He cringed at the thought of having to wear such a thing, but at least it was not some type of crazy palm tree design that looked more like pajamas than street clothes.

He walked by another shelf and grabbed a pair of socks without being choosey. Then he turned back to Belsangar, who now was trying on different style hats. Kilari watched his best friend having fun playing around. "Are you sure that Ceilia is going to *let* you dress like that?"

Belsangar looked at Kilari with a crazy expression, not believing his ears. "What? Are you crazy? Chicks dig these threads bro. I'm telling you man. Don't be surprised if your girls don't ask you to be a little more like this." He said flashing his hands out wide showing himself off.

"Are you getting some shoes, or are you going to stay barefoot for the week, while you hang out in your pajamas?" Kilari asked with a grin.

"Yeah, let's go." Belsangar said taking the lead. Multiple types of shoe styles were available, but sandals were what interested Belsangar, while Kilari preferred the leather hi-tops.

"I've got everything that I need." Kilari said, as he grabbed a solid black pair of shoes off the shelf.

"That's good," Jezza said, "because we're ready too."

"Sounds good, let's go." Kilari said anxiously. "We'll catch you guys later, right?"

"Oh yeah, we'll be there my brother," Belsangar said flashing him a piece sign.

Kilari and his two young wives made their way to their room. Alphie had the bathroom and a large part of the main room clean. Kilari lit some incense and the candles that he had just picked up from the supply rooms. Then he started running water into the tub.

Kilari walked over to Alphie and praised him, saying, "Good job, the place looks great, but I have an errand for you to run." The droid soon agreed to get some food to prepare, for the guests that would be coming over later.

Marcia drew the curtains, and turned the lights out the very second that Alphie had closed the door. "Alone at last." She said with a sigh of relief.

"You're not worried about Alphie, are you?" Jezza asked, as she stepped into the hot tub, while it was still filling. She sat next to Kilari, who wasted no time getting in that hot clean water. He had even sprinkled some scent crystals into the water.

Marcia sparked a lefty, as she began to undress in the more private conditions. "Well, it's like this, my body is my body, and your body, so I don't choose to let anyone else look at me, unless we all consent." Then she inhaled deeply and handed the herbs to Jezza.

Jezza said, "Girl, it's just a droid. It doesn't have feelings." Then she paused to take a hit. She held it in and came back with, "At least not *those* feelings." She said laughing. The potent smoke rumbled out of her mouth as she laughed. The group passed the rolled herb cigarette around, as they sat back and just soaked in the soothing heat of the hot water.

"We do have to clue Alphie in on our situation, especially because this will be the first extended period of time that we'll have to be together." Kilari said, restarting the conversation, after a brief period of space out time. Kilari could not take the dirt anymore, so he grabbed the shampoo, and began to work it into his hair.

Jezza took over doing his hair, while Marcia began washing his body. He felt like he was a king.

"Oh," Marcia commented. "I guess our man isn't too tired for *other* activities. Jezza reached down checking for herself.

"You girls better watch out." Kilari warned. "I may not be responsible for my actions."

"Oh Kilari, we know that you're tired, but…," Marcia said out loud, before easing up close and whispering her intentions sweetly into his ear. "I just want to feel you close to me."

Jezza felt the same way. "How about, we get the washing part done first, and then we all can get close."

"I'm game for that." Kilari said as he dunked Jezza underwater. Once he let her up, Marcia just seemed to be laughing a little too loud, so he playfully dunked her too. He began laughing at his joke, but the girls decided that it was tag-team time, so they both dove upon him, which put him under the water, while still laughing. He sat up choking, the excess water from his lungs.

The girls started patting his back to help clear his lungs. "Oh baby, are you alright?" Jezza asked with a sweet-sounding concern.

Kilari had one hand over his mouth, the other one up in the air trying to open up his airway. He coughed harshly for a minute, and then began to laugh lightly. "You girls are tough," he said giving them their due. "But not *that* tough," he said as he stood flexing his pecks in a typical bodybuilder fashion. His chest and arm muscles puffed up like inflated balloons. He picked Jezza up in the air, and held her above his head.

"Excuse me sir." Alphie said, trying to announce himself, but he was not heard, so he blasted a short loud alarm, which about scared all three of the young adults out of their skins.

The girls each screamed. Kilari quickly brought Jezza down by his side, as Marcia jumped behind him.

"Excuse me sir, and ma'ams," Alphie said starting again to address his people.

"Alphie," Kilari said sounding relieved.

"Alphie!" The girls screamed, realizing that they were naked. They each quickly sat down in the water, trying to hide their bodies from the droid's view.

"What time would you like dinner to be served, sir?" Alphie asked, as if he had walked in on any ordinary activity.

"Dinner?" Marcia asked in utter embarrassment, after being seen, while nude. "We don't have any clothes on."

Alphie looked at them. "You don't usually wear them in the bath, do you?" He asked trying to process her statement.

Kilari started laughing. The girls gave him the look. "What? He doesn't have a clue. To him it's probably, no different than us looking at droids. They're never usually dressed, and we don't give it a second thought.

Alphie gathered what they were talking about and thought that he had better respond. "Droids do not have sex, or have the parts to do so. I was not programmed to judge human bodies or activities, just to serve. I can cook, clean, communicate, and can carry things. Your female caregiver has now taught me how to shoot, sneak, and cover, but your bodies do not spark any search engines."

"What?" Kilari asked. "Mary taught you to use a heater?"

Alphie responded. "Tessa Elliot is her new title, and her old title was Tessa last name unknown, but you knew her, as Mary Trenton, and then the Professor Mary Trenton. I was taught to shoot a gun."

"Wow," Kilari said all excited. "Are you a good shot?"

"I was used to be a scare tactic, and cover if need be, but I did not fire the weapon." Alphie explained.

Marcia became slightly less embarrassed, after talking with Alphie, and by seeing really, how unfazed, he was by their nudity, but she wanted to cut to the chase. "Alphie, you know that we will be together physically, right?"

COGNIZANT

The droid understood the ramifications of the mating rituals of living creatures, and answered affirmatively.

"Okay, is there a good way for us to have the privacy that we need. Can you shutdown, or turn off your sensors, so that you cannot hear, or see us?" Marcia asked, wondering if there would be some plans that they could put into place. "I don't want you to have to leave, every time that we decide to be intimate," she explained.

Alphie computed some alternatives, and then, made a suggestion. "I could hang a curtain, from this wall of the kitchen area, across to here, and then turn my audio receptors off," the droid said showing that the curtain would be angled away from the wall, and then passing the door.

ROC BLISS

Kilari watched the droid closely, and then asked, "Why would you hang the curtain all of the way past the exit?"

"I entered the room, unknowingly to the fact that I would walk in on three naked teenage humans, who did not want to be seen, or heard. What would you have done if, one of your parental units, or comrades would have walked in and saw you in such a condition. This way I can leave at will, and entering through the door will not necessarily give anyone an immediate view of the interactions that are transpiring." Alphie said explaining his reasons in detail.

Jezza shuttered at the thought that someone else could have just as easily walked in on them. "Alphie, you're a genius. I'll have to remember to talk with you more often."

COGNIZANT

Alphie did not understand the girl's logic, so the droid inquired.

Jezza explained, "The logic here Alphie is, the smarter the people that you talk to, the smarter you will become."

Alphie was puffed with pride. It was not that the girl had called him a genius, though it was nice. It was that she referred to him as, 'people'. "Thank you, Jezza, but we shall have to save that talk for a while. Right now, I have to get some things to make the room divider. I also must have forgotten a few things that I will need, to make dinner. I may be at least an hour," the droid spoke trying to be nonchalant, but in either case, the blunt hint was quite effective.

Kilari walked up out of the tub, and moving directly over to his friend, he said, "Alphie, I'm going to owe you one, but I need you to do me one more favor." He whispered in a voice lower than the girls could hear. They were somewhat interested in his whisperings, but they were even more preoccupied with the vision of their man standing right out in the wide open with no coverings, whatsoever.

Kilari, had asked the droid to go to check on Travis, and if possible, pick up some garments for Vail and her Queen. "You better pick up something very feminine and something a bit more masculine than most women would wear. Give them a couple choices. Tell them they are from us, and also, tell them, if they need any help, to come and see us tomorrow, and we'll talk." With that being said, the droid happily went forth to do Kilari's bidding.

The three young lovers finally found themselves alone. The moment that they all had been longing for had arrived. Kilari pulled the drain plug, and then he grabbed the girls, each, a towel, before helping them out. He moved to the bathroom mirror, and took a peek at his clean shave. "Smooth," he commented as he rubbed his fingertips across his face. He liked it smooth, he thought to himself, as he grabbed a brush and began working the remaining snarls from his hair.

Jezza and Marcia, had heard about his hair thing, so they marched right into the bathroom and pulled him out to the bed. "Hey, I got snarls still," he said.

"Oh, I don't mind, and I highly doubt that Marcia minds, so c'mon over here big boy, and let us tell you a *secret* or two." Jezza said invitingly, feeling the need for his presence.

Kilari laid upon the bed with Marcia to his left, and Jezza on his right. They each turned towards him.

The Way of Things to Come

Taking turns, first Marcia began kissing him, while Jezza whispered softly in his ear. She whispered saying, "Oh baby, I love you so much. Oh, I want you so close that we become one, together."

Then Marcia began to whisper, while Jezza began kissing Kilari deeply. She whispered loving words, as Jezza's kiss of unity, sent tingles down his spine. Feeling a sense of warmth resonating from his heart like ripples from a rock piercing into a still lake. The fiery glow reaching cyclically to his outer torso and slowly into his upper thighs and defined pectorals. With continuous flow it raised out into his upper arms as it crossed his knees. Before finally emanating out through his fingertips creating a violet light ringed with a golden aura. The hairs on his neck even stood up. He was beginning to feel a deeper, more passionate love, flowing between them.

Passion had settled upon them all, as thick as an impenetrable fog. The three had a natural flow that entwined them, keeping them bonded together with loving spirits.

When their tender loving souls had finished exploring the depths of their physical nature, the three laid back for a moment to reflect. "Do you realize how destined we are for each other?" Jezza asked to both of her wondrous partners. "Really, you two complete me. I'm not sure what I've done that was so right, but Yahiveh has certainly blessed me to have your love."

Kilari thought back to the moment, when they had first met, and how he had seen their beauty, striding across the grounds of the Crystal Academy. A divine vision emitting a metaphorical glow. He had never envisioned women in this way and yet it seemed, as though, he had known them forever. "We do seem to share a certain familiarity with one another. It has really, only been a few days, since we've first met, and when we did, it was love at first sight. You both seemed to be cool right away. We never had any anxieties about each other. I trusted both of you with my most personal thoughts and feelings. You are the only ones that I have ever been able to talk to, freely, without reservations."

At this point, the young ladies had tears in their eyes from the heavy emotional pull. Tears of love streamed down, as the three once again cleaved to each other and gave thanks to their God and father, Yahiveh.

After several minutes, the three had settled back down. Kilari walked across the room. He stopped at the mirror to see how his long golden hair looked. It was not only wet, but it was messy and snarled too. "Nice," he commented sarcastically, wishing that he had not been seen in such disarray.

"What's wrong?" Jezza asked, after hearing his tone.

Kilari said, "I'm surprised that you girls would even want to be seen with me. *Look* at my hair. It's going to take a lot of work to get it back into shape, and we've got company coming soon."

Jezza laughed. "See Marcia, I told you he's a pretty boy," Then both girls began giggling together.

Kilari did not appreciate the comment, but just seeing the girls laughing, and having a good time, brought a smile to his face. He grabbed a brush and began trying to force it through his thick, long hair.

ROC BLISS

The Way of Things to Come

"Here, let me help you." Jezza said holding her hand out for the brush.

"Let's get dressed first. Alphie could be coming through this door at any moment, and I think that it is the least we can do, since he is going to put up a privacy divider for us." Marcia stated.

"Oh, good idea," Jezza said in agreement. Kilari began looking for his clothes, but they were not where he had left them. Jezza noticed him looking around. "Your clothes are in the bathroom," she called out to him, to ease his search.

Kilari walked into the bathroom, looked on the counter top, in the closet, and pretty much everywhere, before calling out. "I can't find them. In fact, I can't even find my *old* clothes."

"Oh, we threw those things out. They were stinking up the whole place." Jezza told him factually.

Marcia walked into the bathroom with her choice of clothing in her hands. Kilari's eyes quit the search and began following Marcia. "There they are," she pointed out.

Kilari looked and asked, "Where? I don't see the clothes that I had picked up."

"Well, we sent those back, because *we* picked up an outfit for you to wear," Marcia said smiling happily. He noticed that she looked as if they had done him a good deed. "There they are," she said, pointing out the matching print outfit, which was sitting on the countertop.

Jezza walked in wearing a form fitting, slipover dress, which did not quite make it to her knees. Between Marcia being undressed, and Jezza in her cute little number, Kilari began to weaken in his attitude.

"Yeah, we picked them out special. We thought that you would look so hot in this that we just had to get it for you." Jezza coyly added.

Kilari's mouth hung open, but no words came out. His mind was in turmoil, not knowing how to react. The girls seemed so pleased with themselves, but he really did not want the clothes that they had picked.

"Just look at these." Jezza continued as she picked up the pants to the outfit. "Look, they tie at the ankles, just like all of the pants that you like."

"Well, put'em on." Marcia said urging him. Kilari kept looking around, first at Marcia, and then at Jezza hoping for a joking look. Their eyes were big like a puppy dog's. "What are you looking around for Kilari?" She asked pointblank.

Kilari was trying to make sure that this bad dream did not turn into a full-blown nightmare. Knowing that he had to come up with a plausible answer, "My shoes," he finally answered grasping at straws. "Tell me you didn't get me sandals to wear with *this*."

"What?" Jezza asked. "Why would we do that? We know what you like."

"So, my shoes are still here?" Kilari asked, trying to find some clarity amongst his panic.

"Yes, yes, I'll go get them. Is that all you're worried about," Marcia asked as she began to leave the room. Then she turned and looked back towards him. "I'm glad that is all it is, for a minute, I thought that you didn't like the clothes that we picked out."

The Way of Things to Come

"Well, you took my clothes away. I just really wanted to wear those shoes." Kilari answered, as he began pulling on the wild looking pajama pants.

"Here's your shoes and socks, hun." Marcia said as she re-entered the room. Then she spotted Kilari in the pants. "Ooh, baby, now that's what I'm talking about. Look at that." She grabbed his butt. "You sure were right, Jezza. He definitely has the beef cakes to fill these out."

Kilari reached for his shoes. "Thanks," he said giving her a peck on the lips, and then he decided that he better reach down for a squeeze of her sweet cakes, especially, since they were right there for his eyes to see. "Oh girl, the things that I could do with you," he said, as he gripped her lightly.

Jezza decided that she had better get him fully dressed, before things got

COGNIZANT

all started up again. "We do have company coming, or else you both might be in trouble. Now come on let us help you with your hair, and then it will be girl's time in the bathroom.

Kilari agreed wholeheartedly, and they whipped his hair into shape in no time, and he soon found himself helping Alphie hang the privacy border, while wearing the things that he did not want. Yet somehow, he still wore the smile to which all were accustomed to seeing.

"Sir," Alphie said, addressing Kilari. "When I was getting the curtain, I ran across these white garments and shoes. I thought you may want for later. They're in by the bed." Relieved that he would have an option to get out of these clothes at some point, Kilari thanked him graciously.

Kilari lit more incense to keep the room smelling sweet, so that when the girls had finished, they could enjoy the aroma. Alphie soon began cooking in the kitchenette, after the area had been sectioned off with a giant black drapery. Kilari sat watching Alphie, and asking him about how the island life was, when there was nobody there.

A knock sounded on the door. Alphie answered, "come in," before Kilari had a chance to get up.

The door opened, and the two invited guests walked into the room. "What's with the curtain?" Ceilia asked immediately.

"Oh, we have Alphie staying with us, so we put up a little privacy barrier." Kilari answered. "The girls are in the bathroom getting ready, if you want to go talk with them."

Belsangar gave her a quick kiss on the cheek, and then she eyed Kilari up and down smirking all the while, before quickly passing the curtain to find out how those girls got Kilari to wear that outfit.

The curtain swooped, as Ceilia past it. Belsangar knew that the coast was clear, so now, he let fly. "Nice pajamas man. I didn't know that you liked them so much. Couldn't wait to get'em on, could you?" He said teasing his friend with some of his own words.

Kilari's face turned red with embarrassment. "You should have seen the way that they looked at me. I just couldn't tell them, no."

"I'm telling you man. It won't be long and you may just decide that you like them." Belsangar said with a silly grin on his face.

"Yeah right," Kilari quickly retorted. "I just can't wait to wear them in public, so that everyone can get a good laugh. Heck, even ma will get a chuckle out of this one."

The Way of Things to Come

"Nah, ma won't laugh at you, at least not to your face, anyway." Belsangar said, beginning to feel at ease, for the first time, since their return. "You know man, this vacation thing is sweet. I mean, you know. I got a place with Ceilia. You and your girls are right here. We're not training, or studying, or running from fricken zombies either, for that matter."

"I know. I could get used to a little set-up like this," Kilari said in agreement. "Just think, I don't even exist right now. Maybe after this vacation is over, we'll decide to hang out here for a while." Kilari said just throwing out an open-ended idea.

"What?" Belsangar questioned. "We need you, out *there* man. You just can't up and quit on us."

"Dead men can't quit." Kilari stated bluntly. Then he decided to explain more in depth on the subject.

COGNIZANT

"It's not like I'd actually quit. It's just that I've made another choice that just might stir up some big trouble, but I had to."

"What could you have done? We were with you practically the whole time." Belsangar reminded him.

"I believe that the word practically is the key to your statement." Kilari retorted. "Look, I'm going to level with you." Kilari said aloud, but then he decided to speak very quietly, so that the girls could not hear him. "I went up to the place in the clouds again. I'm pretty sure that I had died for real back there fighting those zombies." Kilari stated in all seriousness. "I saw my real mom and dad up there, dude, they were still young looking, you know, maybe five or ten years older than we are, right now, and let me tell you, they begged me to stay. I saw Yahiveh, and he told me that if I were to stay, I would be guaranteed a place in paradise, but, if I chose to come back *here*, there would be no assurance of what would happen. I told him that I had to come back. I also told my mom and dad. I made a promise to them. I know this sounds crazy."

"No crazier than usual." Belsangar commented truthfully. Then he asked, "so, what did you promise them?"

"When I saw my parents, I had to ask them a couple questions. First, we talked about what happened when we were first taken, and they backed the Commander's story, but then I noticed the lack of people on their side of the gate, and they told me that most were being sent to the other side of the gulf, awaiting some type of retraining."

"Are you kidding me?" Belsangar asked forgetting to whisper.

COGNIZANT

"Keep it down man. I don't want to make the girls worry about this." Kilari reminded him. "Now look, Lucifer himself is behind the lack of good souls arriving to the afterlife. I told my parents that I'd be sending them some company, and I mean to keep my word."

"Maybe you *are* crazy." Belsangar whispered. "What do you plan on doing, killing the good people, so that your parents can get a few more friends?"

"Yeah, how did you guess?" Kilari joked, before answering seriously. "No, I plan on giving people something to believe in. I have to get the book copied and distributed around the whole planet of An'non."

"Printed?" Belsangar asked, giving his friend and brother of sorts a look that told Kilari that he was way off base. "Man, you get me a computer, and I could have that done quick."

The Way of Things to Come

Kilari was uncertain of Belsangar's look at first, but he really liked his explanation. "I kind of tried that route, in a round-about way. I sent it through the Z-Bank in hopes that Central Control would at some point, zap it into the minds of the people. You know in case the worst-case scenario happens, and Central Control *actually, is* trying to brain wash people, and we can't stop it. I figured. It was worth a shot. On the upside, Central Control could be a tool used to spread the word, right?"

"You did that?" Belsangar asked in a shocked tone. "I didn't even see you," he admitted to his brother agent.

Kilari began wondering, as his mind wandered through the recent events that the group had been through. "So, do you think that Central Control will actually send the words from our book into people's minds?"

COGNIZANT

Kilari asked, after thinking to thank Yahiveh for getting them through the long ordeal, and again, for bringing Jezza, Marcia, and all of the people that he knew, as family and friends, into his life. "Could you imagine an easier way to spread our father's word?"

"Kilari, let's not get involved in business talks, not now. We are on vacation. We'll have all of the time we need, after we get you to relax for a spell." Jezza said, after unintentionally sneaking up to overhear a small part of the conversation at hand. She really did not want to think about Central Control, and the possible mission that they would be facing, after vacation.

Kilari and Belsangar practically jumped from surprise by Jezza's unexpected entrance. "Dang girl, where'd you come from? You about scared me out of my skin." Belsangar quickly commented, trying to get the girl off the track of what she may have heard. Then he stood up and commented. "You look gorgeous. I'm telling you, Kilari is a very lucky man."

Kilari turned and stood speechless. There she was, standing in front of him, the woman of his dreams, with golden brown skin, jet-black wavy hair, and a perfectly sweet smile. She is his perfect beauty queen. He looked her up and down for a minute, until finally, he said, "Wow, you are beauty incarnate, sweetness. We were just talking babe. That's what we do, but you are right. We should relax for the week. There will be plenty of time for planning later."

The three made their way out to join the other two girls and have the dinner that Alphie had so expertly prepared. They talked about all the crazy things that they had been through over the last few days, while they ate. Once dinner was over, they decided that it was time to relax.

Jezza rolled a few herb cigarettes and fired one of them up. They began to pass it between them, when suddenly there was a knock at the door.

Alphie answered the door and invited in the new guests. None of them could have guessed that Travis and Vail would be stopping over. Jezza and Marcia, immediately closed in on Kilari, making sure that this woman knew, he was *their* man. Vail could see the move, as plain as day, but she did not let on.

Travis was the first to speak. "I hope that you don't mind that we showed up, but we just wanted to thank you for Alphie's help."

"No problem," Kilari said, as he handed the herb to Vail. "Try some of this," he said before taking a big drag, showing her how to smoke it, and then handing it to the Huntress. Jezza and Marcia looked a bit insulted by Kilari's move, but they did not mention it.

Vail looked at the two girls. She knew what they were thinking, so she turned and passed the herb to Travis. Travis was not interested, so he refused it, so after taking a couple more puffs not knowing what to expect, she walked over to Jezza and handed the herb cigarette to her. They looked into each other's eyes, each surmising the other's value. Vail spoke first, telling her, "you are a beautiful young woman. I just want you to know that Travis is my man. I do not want you too close to him. Is that okay?"

Travis and Kilari were both about to step into the situation, neither of them realizing what was about to happen, but before either of them could move, Vail stepped back and said, "I would just like to make friends, and you, I would protect as my own sister." This statement calmed the whole group.

Kilari whispered in Marcia's ear, as she took the herb cigarette from Jezza. Jezza did not know what to say, but she did say, "Thank you. I'm Jezza, and this is Marcia, and over here is Ceilia. We'd love to have you for a friend."

"My name is Vail, and I thank you for allowing us to enter your dwelling," the Huntress said holding her hand out to shake on the new beginning to a friendship.

Ceilia passed the herb back to Vail, saying, "Girl we'll have to hang out, so that we can get to know each other."

With that being said, Kilari and Belsangar took Travis aside, so that the girls could talk. "Hey, we're going over to the kitchen for a few to check on Alphie." Kilari told them, as the men moved around the curtain and sat down.

"Would you gentlemen like some refreshments?" Alphie asked. "I have some nice water, coffee, or tea. I'm sorry, but there aren't many choices in this place." In the end, Alphie made a couple of pitchers of iced tea.

In the other side of the room, the four women sat down together. "Vail, I see you are still wearing your cloak. Is that because you did not find any clothes that you liked?" Ceilia asked curiously.

Vail answered. "Kilari had sent the talking non-human over. Alphie? I think you call it. Alphie had selections of different thin cloth garments. Travis also picked, but I am not feeling very secure in these things."

COGNIZANT

"I don't understand. What do you mean secure?" Marcia asked.

Vail lifted her cloak a little, showing a strip of thin cloth dress material. "You see, if I was to walk in the forest with this thing on, I would have no protection from anything." Vail felt a true conflict of interest. She wanted to dress, as the women of this world, but she did not want to leave herself open for injury.

Jezza was beginning to understand. This woman was from a dangerous land, and lived in rough terrain. "Vail, we are in a world that is pretty much soft. The travel is easy. It would be unusual to have to hunt for food. Come over here." She said calling the blonde over to the bed. She pushed on it, showing her its springy nature. "This is the type of bed that we sleep in. The places with large wild animals are very few. We usually dress for our actions. In the cold we bundle up to stay warm, and in the summer, we wear light fabrics to help keep us cool."

"Yes, we have many furs also." Vail said trying to show that she was keeping up with the conversation.

Jezza thought again on how to explain further. "Our world is soft and living can be easy. Your world is hard, and you worked hard with your muscles to keep living." Jezza smiled with a small sense of accomplishment in the thought that she made a good example.

Vail looked through blood shot eyes. She was maybe, one toke over the line. She had a smile, which was not a usual expression for her, because of the serious nature of survival in Xibalba. She looked at the girls, who were all smiling a little too much, as well.

COGNIZANT

"Your world is soft. That is why the men do the fighting." She said, as she began laughing. "In my land, men are for cooking and sex. They are also good at cleaning, laundry and taking care of children. They are usually weak from lack of physical exertion. The women fight, hunt, and provide for the tribe.

The girls all began laughing, upon hearing Vail's explanation of men. "Women could have their man, or men, or they could choose from the group that were unspoken for. You," she began pointing at Ceilia. "You have one man?" Ceilia nodded affirmatively.

Then she looked at Marcia and Jezza and asked, "Is there a shortage of men? You two share one man?" They answered by nodding affirmatively that she was right. "Surely you must have some good teas, for one man to fulfill you."

Roc Bliss

"Tea? What does tea have to do with anything?" Jezza asked. Vail made a couple gestures with her hands, showing them the effect that this special tea would have on a man. The girls all laughed, blushing with embarrassment.

"I love Marcia, and Kilari. Marcia loves me and Kilari, and Kilari loves us both. It may sound strange to a woman like you, but we are very happy." Jezza explained.

Ceilia quickly decided to change the subject. "Let's see your dress Vail. I bet it looks wonderful on you. We could also do your hair, and get some make up on you."

"I've got some perfume too," Marcia added.

Vail looked around nervously, afraid to be seen in the strange clothing.

COGNIZANT

Kilari sent Alphie to go get Tanker and Sophie. He figured that they would help round out the group. Tank was always good for some laughs.

Soon the young couple made their way to the room. Tank took one look at Kilari and Belsangar and asked, "what's with the get-ups? You didn't say that this was going to be a pajama party". The big man's grin was enough to say it all.

"Oh Tank," Sophie sighed with embarrassment, as she walked through to go see the girls.

Kilari knew better than to allow the slur to continue, so before Belsangar could even start to give his take, on the matter, noticing something in Tank's hands, changed the subject. "So, what you got there, Tanker?" He asked pointing to the little box in Tank's grip.

The Way of Things to Come

Tank sat the box on the table. "Look what I found fellas. Check this out." He said, as he turned a switch. Music began to flow from the little box. "I knew that we had come unprepared, but heck, this little baby plays a few different types of music, so I thought that it would be good for some background noise." He hit another button and some old tune from long ago began to play. It seemed soothing, and Kilari liked it.

"Yeah, keep it there. I like the sound of that." Kilari remarked. "Hey, I know, we'll put the box over there out of the way, so we can still listen to it."

Belsangar being a tech, knew all about the box. "So, you guys really don't have a clue about the music player, huh. That thing looks so old; I'm surprised that it even works. It's a spin-off of a radio. They used to run on electricity." He began explaining.

COGNIZANT

"Okay, Mr. Smarty Pants," Tank joked, letting him know that he was not intent on receiving a history lesson.

Belsangar took the hint and asked, "so, what are we going to do?"

Tank whipped out a deck of cards that just happened to be in a drawer in his room. "I figured that we could play a game or something, so I brought the cards. 'Kilari of Chronos' can even pick the first game" he said with a playful bow.

"Ha, ha", Kilari answered sarcastically, as the rest of the guys were laughing. "Very funny."

"Yeah" Belsangar piped in. Does anyone know how to play, the 'Chosen One'?

After playing a few hands, Kilari suggested, "Let's go see what the girls are up to, maybe they'll want to play too." With that being said, the guys got up and moved around the dark curtain to check on the girls.

The night continued, and the group all became more acquainted with Vail and Travis, starting with how Vail seemed to shine, once the girls had cleaned her up. They styled her hair and applied make-up to her angelic face, and then they began to show her how to walk in a more feminine way. She learned how to move those hips by placing her feet in the appropriate locations. They also told her how women really did rule in An'non, but they just allowed men to think it was the other way around.

Vail sashayed across the room, as the girls displayed her to the men. She, however, did not like the attention that she was receiving from the males, who in her opinion were acting whorish. The way their eyes bulged sickened her, but she did however, like

COGNIZANT

the glow in Travis's eyes, not that he did not already glow with pride from her charms. It was not long, before she decided to wear her burgundy cloak. She felt it was necessary, as a cover-up, to keep the filthy men's eyes at bay.

All at once, a silence fell across the room. Nobody uttered a word. There was not a sound to be heard, except the sound of the still playing music box, echoing in the background.

An ominous feeling had crept upon the entire group, and then, suddenly, a light appeared from out of nowhere, hovering in the middle of the ceiling. They all watched, transfixed, upon the swirling, glowing, disturbance. Looking with more scrutiny, it seemed like a neon violet liquid plasma whirlpool.

"Wh-wh-what is that?" Travis's panic stricken voice asked in an utter state of shock. The influx of a magic

spell continued swirling, with a very foreboding essence. As the great disturbance grew, wind began to swirl, causing a greater feeling of dread to emanate over the young crowd. The three young agents and Vail, had already placed their loved ones behind them, in hopes to shield them from whatever this thing could be.

"It is the Black Mage!" Vail bellowed over the din of the great impending maelstrom.

TO BE CONTINUED...

COGNIZANT

ROC BLISS

BOOK IV

THE OMEGA WAVE

The captivating sequel to COGNIZANT

COGNIZANT

Chapter I

"Yes, what is it?" A groggy President Brague asked, as his com-unit beeped. The sleeping man began stirring into consciousness, slowly. "Huh… Hmmm… What is it? What is it?" Finally, after minutes of beeping, the seeping sound of the com-unit, which had invaded his dream, began rousing the man back to conscious thought.

Lucid thought, finally pryed its way into Brague's mind. He pressed a button saying, "President Brague speaking, and this had better be good." His rough voice spread, littered with fatigue.

"Pardon the disturbance Johnny, but this is Dr. Grimes, and since you would not wake-up, I have received horrible news."

"Well, what it is? Spit it out man," President Brague spewed grumpily, as he moved to a seated position.

ROC BLISS

"Johnny, we have received reports of multiple explosions on Flag Island, and I can't get in contact with Rudy, or anyone for that matter."

"What? Did you say explosions? Brague asked rhetorically, trying to buy some time for all of his cobwebs to clear."

Dr. Grimes felt as though Johnny Brague's post take-over extravaganza had been most excessive. "Look Johnny, we have some military issues that need handling," he said with consternation, trying to remind the big, blowhard of his function.

"Don't worry Doc. I got this," the semi-inebriated, hungover man stated solidly.

"Okay, that's more like it," Grimes stated with relief. "All, I ask, is that you keep me informed of your plans, and don't forget, we must send help. There is a plethora of important people and objects on that island. We need them."

"Yes, yes, we will soon enough see what is really going on, until then, stay close to your guards, and I will contact you soon." With that being said, President Brague ended the link, and moved over to his global map.

*   *   *   *   *

Amidst the blackness on a stagnant cloud filled night, four large military skiffs whisked silently across the smooth, slow rolling waves of the Blue Sea. They deliberately neared the shoreline of the southernmost coast of the Crystal Continent, loaded with merciless military men.

The small company of men is comprised of some of the most notorious, ruthless, military men, and mercenaries from all over An'non. Some of this crew have worked together prior to this escapade, but others only know of each other's reputation. They are all dressed in black unmarked uniforms, showing no affiliation to any military group, or country.

The small sea rafts held a steady course for a certain inlet of a certain small lagoon. Sgt. Gall, is a lone, dark silhouette, at the bow of the lead boat. His menacing form standing, searching, for the one, slimline opening between giant boulders, which not only, form the vast seawall, intended to keep massive tidal events from devastating the small coastal area, but also, to keep all larger vessels from the nearly hidden cove.

Sgt. Gull knows his critical objectives well. After making his way beyond the seawall, he is to hold position and monitor the suspect location, search for signs of life, and report status. His biggest wish, however would be to reach shore unseen, and then hunt down the traitorous criminals, who dared to kidnap a serving leader of the greatest and strongest continent of all An'non.

Even in the subtly rolling waves, the heavy dark water slapped at the large boulders, showing the brutal force of the Blue Sea, as it laps to, and fro. Finally, the old sea dog found his target point. He could see the calm of the inlet not more than a hundred feet to their starboard side.

"Starboard!" Sgt. Gall screamed out to the helmsman, as he pointed directly to the opening. The man, instantly turned the skiff and poured on the throttle, sending a few unwary souls off balance from the sudden thrust of the silent moleculitic motor. "That's it laddie, pound her in that hole and don't stop 'til she comes out clean." Sgt. Gull exclaimed, as he felt the nose of the craft lift.

The gap in the old sea-wall was thin. It was created by a blasting wave, which forced one of the upper boulders back, and once it was moved out of position, a minor shallow section was formed, directly over another very large rock, which lay slightly below sea level. Sgt. Gull knew that he had just saved, much needed, valuable time, taking such a risky route, but after the major storms that had recently rolled through, he had no doubt that the shallow depth would not be an issue. Each of the following rafts mocked the lead's maneuvers, and like a well-oiled machine. They zipped across the shallow spans of water, and immediately banked into an abrupt spin, which brought them quickly to a slow float. Each of the four skiffs anchored close to the inside of the

COGNIZANT

great sea-wall, utilizing it as
camouflage, against any unsuspected
eyes.

*   *   *   *   *

At 12 o'clock midnight, high, up in
an exclusive skyrise building, located
in Powder City, Anton, an influential
group made up of the most elite people
of all An'non, were meeting. They have
wealth beyond imagination, old money,
inherited. These are the descendants of
long generations of those, who have
controlled the ebb and flow of An'non.
Through direct ownership of central
banking, stock exchanges, and big
business, this highest echelon of power
does not rule, a government, or even a
continent, but instead they are all
members of a sect of secrecy. They
belong to An'non's most unknown sect,
Mammon. This entire group consists of
leaders of other secret societies, so

even though its membership is low, it brings forth the power of all of its groups.

This assemblage continues being clandestine by whatever means deemed necessary. For the most part, they meet in places where even the, so-called, rich people would not want to pay such exorbitant fees, but yet, for another fact, if they courted you to join, and you passed on the invitation, you would be erased by anonymous sources in one of a myriad of ways.

"Ladies and gentlemen, we have gathered once again, due to circumstances, which require our unique fortes," an older, balding, paunchy man said, as he stood facing his fellow clansmen, whom were all sitting at a large round table. "As we all know, there has not only been severe violence in the Crystal Continent, but there was also, just

COGNIZANT

recently, several explosions reported on Flag Island," he continued. "But what some of you may not know is; in the days and hours leading up to these events, there has been many strange power signatures." The elderly gentleman stood, wearing a long, draping, red tunic with a matching headdress both sacheted in black. "Madam Aria," he said, pausing, while holding his extended hand towards the woman, whom he was addressing, "would you care to take the floor, and explain what intel you have most recently discovered?"

A middle-aged woman dressed in her typical blue business skirt with matching dress jacket stood up. "Thank-you Otto, I do have a lot of information, in fact, it has been a long time, since we have had so much going on all at once." The lean, dark-haired woman gracefully whisked across the room to a podium. She picked up a remote control from a side holder, and clicked a button. The round table split down the middle and swiveled open, as did the pedestal on which the seating and table were fastened, creating two half-moons. Now, all eyes were upon her, and she was ready to commence with the debriefing. "Ladies and gentlemen, I have learned things in the last few days that seem unfathomable. As you all know, Central Control has upped their Z-Bank S.O.P.'s to absorb raw data straight from the minds of its subjects. This is where a load of new possibilities are now entering our grasp."

A man quickly shot a hand up in the air. It seemed way too soon for questions, but Aria gave him the nod. "Are you sure that this raw intel is trustworthy, being that this is all some

COGNIZANT

kind of a new phase for Central Control?"

"That is why we are here today, now. Isn't it, Hakeem?" Aria asked, holding a fake smile upon her lips. The truth is, she has subordinates, who run Central Control, and *they,* were even in disbelief of the recent divulgences.

"Yes Aria," Hakeem answered, as he stood. Hakeem is a very tall, slender man, wearing the tan tunics of his people. His skin is a dark tan color, and his mustache is thin and black. "I just want to go on record, as saying, I am sick of my people being massacred by the Crystal Continent's Death Squad, and I demand satisfaction in this matter, and I mean today!"

"Well Hakeem, I guarantee that your request is on record," Otto, the host of this meeting, stated matter of factly. He did not stand again, as Aria has the floor, but after speaking, he did give Aria the nod to continue her oration.

"As I've stated, we are in exciting times." Aria looked across all of the people in the room, as they faced her in anxious fervor. "Let us, first, go over the latest success of Central Control. As you all know, the Omega Wave project has been under way. We have been broadcasting into certain, observable locations. We have successfully altered thought patterns and beliefs of groups of people, including Aguanimos, which is where all kinds of information has turned up big." Aria sipped her water, before continuing. "Our broadcasts were not only able to penetrate the great depths of the Blue Sea, but we actually sent conflicting thoughts and beliefs, and they did cause general chaos. In one single stroke, we were able to test several modes of activity, which passed with flying colors."

The room broke into an instant applause, realizing the amount of control that they will soon be having over world affairs.

*　　*　　*　　*　　*

The four, anchored military grade sea skiffs were positioned approximately six hundred yards from the shoreline, leaving, maybe another twenty yards to the actual building to be surveilled. "Alright, it's time to break out the equipment," Sgt. Gall barked out, keeping his voice in balance between, loud enough to sound authoritative, but not so vehement as to be heard on shore.

Some men broke out long-range weaponry equipped with heartbeat monitors, showing the position of each, and every, living soul within the compound, while other weapons were equipped with infra-red scopes. These, shown heat signatures, of all objects and personnel within the compound, and still others carried high-tech telescopic sights. Most of the blasters were moleculitic arc blasters, which can penetrate most objects, and still remain accurate, via laser thin beams and minimal refraction. The down fall to this style of weapon is that you cannot use the infra-red sights due to the searing heat of the arc beam, and using the telescopic sights at night, one could check lit windows and other well-lit areas, but the weapons are definitely, more effective in the light of day.

"Okay, we need a body count, and location within the building. We need to get up on this and report status.

* * * * *

COGNIZANT

Kilari, standing in his room, encircled by his best, and closest friends and allies, faced the great unknown. A torrential maelstrom of bright clouded violet smoke. This swirling disturbance was growing by the second. The only one, who may have already seen such a thing, Vail, stood with her stone blade pointing towards the vexation, and her loved one, Travis, behind her, in his defense.

"The Black Mage!" Vail bellowed again above the din, causing Kilari, Belsangar, and Tank, to follow suit, and place their loved ones behind them.

At the sounding of Vail's warnings, each, and every, one of the nine souls, and one droid, were about to bolt for the door. They had no intentions of being trapped in the room by the Black Mage.

ROC BLISS

Then suddenly, all at once, at the climax of every heartbeat, as their bodies began to lean in movement, a shockwave sprung forth from the clouded whirlpool, paralyzing the entire group. Within another brief second, the swirling violet smoke transformed into a brilliant white light, illuminating a protective orb, until finally, it became clear as crystal.

Within the brilliance of the light, an enchantment nestled its embrace, and its power was emboldened, in a potion of calm. A soothing, tranquilizing effect, instantly saturated the worried minds of the immobile crowd.

A semi-translucent figure, arrayed in golden robes, appeared.

"Fear not. My name is Khana," A young woman's sweet voice, softly stated. "I've come to Thank-you." The dark-haired sorceress waived her hand, and the statuesque group, once again, held full mobility of their moving parts.

Kilari, instantly recognizing Khana, began looking around at his friends to see if they were cognizant, or perhaps, he had just somehow slipped into one of his visions.

"Fear not. I am a friend," the apparition explained.

"I've seen her," Jezza shared aloud, while pointing straight at the Sorceress.

Kilari tried explaining to his shocked friends that it was Khana, his spirit guide, who had been visiting him in his visions for some time.

"No, *my* dreams," Jezza said quickly reminding him that she was the one giving the information.

"We've *both* had dreams about her?" Kilari asked inquisitively.

"Yes, you both, have all been having dreams of me, and I of you." Khana said, once again soothing them with the sound of her voice. "I also know, Kilari, that you are a true follower of Yahiveh, as am I."

"I have come for two specific reasons; one, to personally express my gratitude." Khana continued. "Your actions in Xibalba created a chain of events, which freed not only me, and my people of Chronos, but also our entire plane, as well. Oblivion thanks you, because Xibalba is no more, and we have passed into the third world age of our plane. My people and I have been freed from an evil magic that had entrapped us in ageless bodies for centuries."

Vail, recognizing both Khana's name and Oblivion from folklore, shouted, "I must tell the Queen; the great sorceress has blessed us with her presence!" With that Vail flew from the room to share the good news, with Travis following hot on her heals.

The commotion of Vail and Travis running through the halls, brought all out to see what was going on. Travis signaled for Vail to run ahead, as he tried explaining the situation to Thomas and Tessa.

Within moments, every living soul within the safe house, had entered into Kilari's room. It was packed, standing room only.

The group staring in awe, watched as a man, with significant resemblance to Kilari, appeared from seemingly nowhere. He first whispered in Khana's ear, before settling beside her, with his arm around her waist. Another wave from Khana's magical hands, sent the protective orb back to its source, and the two Oblivionites stood before the crowd, in the flesh.

ROC BLISS

*   *   *   *   *

Sgt. Gall, sat low, while monitoring the equipment, when suddenly, he could see an ever-growing power surge on his grid. "What the fuck," he uttered in a near whisper, as he began peering up. He watched, all the while. A purplish light, gleaming from the top end of the compound, steadily grew brighter. After several seconds, the violet hue, instantaneously, flashed to a brilliant white.

All of his men, began pointing their weapons erratically, trying to follow the sudden swarming of every person in the compound, towards that very light.

"Ensign Zoo, I need a sit-rep., stat," snapped a semi-confused Sgt. Gall, assuring to be heard over the sudden commotion in the swaying craft. "As for the rest of you, sit tight and act like you've done this before," he added to defuse unwanted disturbances.

"Well sir, my heartbeat monitors shown two people fleeing the area," the ensign stated, never taking his eyes from the prize. As he continued focusing upon his monitor, the man continued. "Apparently, to gather everyone back to that upper room. A massive energized light source started the rapid movement. It could be panic, or perhaps, some type of weird ritual."

"Whatever that light is? It is using an exorbitant amount of energy, from seemingly out of nowhere," the Sgt. Added.

Just then, Ensign Zoo's eyes bulged in disbelief. "You're not going to believe this sir, but two extra heartbeats are suddenly present." The man's voice was flooded with nervous disbelief.

"So what, it seems plausible that if everybody is running to one area that more heartbeats would be showing up," Sgt. Gall stated peevishly.

"No, what I mean is; I've been showing twenty-seven hearts, and bam, when that light went out, I suddenly register twenty-nine."

"What? Are you sure that you are not confused? The Sgt. questioned, realizing that he was asking the man, whose opinion he trusted most on this little excursion.

"I've noticed the exact same thing," the lead man from another skiff stated," backing Ensign's unnerving story.

"If that is, in fact, true, then I'll be making that status-link earlier than I had ever hoped." The Sgt.'s face began gleaming from the satisfaction of thinking that they'll be moving in on their prey, within a very short period of time.

* * * * *

"I don't have to tell you what this means," Aria said, taking things from where she had left off. "Now, back to the Z-Bank situation. We have actually received data, which not only backs-up the power signature anomalies, but also, they explain the very reason for these oddities, and before you go thinking that this data has no merit, when I said they, I meant, we have several meshing accounts from different perspectives that all align. This is how we know that this is completely accurate information."

The silent room remained that way, as Aria walked away from her podium. Her hands were filled with files, one for every Mammon member.

She took her time handing them out, as if there was no hurry, or care in the world. After making her way back to her podium, she took a sip of water, and then faced the room once again.

"Ladies and gentlemen the reports in front of you have all of the details, which we have and will go over. I just wanted you to see for yourselves that what I am about to say, is all on the up and up."

Just then Aria's com-unit began blinking, alerting her to a message being sent. The slim woman paused, briefly, knowing that this had to be the status update. She checked her timepiece, thinking in her mind that it was almost, too early, for this report to be taking place without positive news, and without even giving the slightest hint that anything was going on, she continued.

COGNIZANT

"I need to motor through the facts, while giving you *all,* the chance to page through, and come up with your own conclusions. We have received these scans from the very people involved with the power surges. Here is a list of facts. Once again, the Crystal Continent has a new person in power, only this time, Blak is out, and instead of one, we have three new leaders, Johnathan Brague, Dr. Grimes, and Dr. Laforge. We all know Brague is no better than Blak, Grimes has been secluded for decades, but Laforge, he is a wildcard.

"Dr. Rudy Laforge is the man behind the power surges. He has erected a machine that apparently pulses people back and forth between dimensions." With that being said, the room became filled with murmurs, so Aria paused, waiting for the shock to hit home, and then subside.

ROC BLISS

Aria quickly utilized this time of interaction to her advantage, reading the message. The news hit her with a wave of introspection. Her mind raced frantically. She was told that all of the machines from Flag Island had been confiscated, and were now, on route to another facility. How could there be another so soon?

The crowd quieted, so she again, began speaking, giving no signs of the message's arrival. "Now, in case any of you had not realized, this could be a blessing of great riches." The room instantly filled with cheers and applause at the sound of even more extensive control and power. With a loud voice, Aria quickly hushed her fellow clansmen. "*However*, it could also bring *us* to *our* knees. This device will basically, morph our world, our pond, if you will, and transform it into an immense ocean, where we will no longer be the biggest fish in the sea. You see, the raw data shows powers, which we do not understand. These beings, significantly, control *worlds*, not *a* world, and not in secret. We have taken these machines from Flag Island, prior to the explosions, which kept certain key players hidden from most."

The audience began paging through the files, looking at pictures derived straight from the minds of the eight girls, and the woman now known as, Tessa Elliot. They could see the Black Mage, invisibly holding Kilari, upside down in the air. They could also see the three subordinate beings of Lucifer, and the Guardians of the wicked city.

After a moment of reflection, Otto raised his hand with a question. Aria allowed the question. "Just *who* are these key players of whom you speak, and can they be located?"

ROC BLISS

"Well Otto, I'm glad you asked. Do you know why? Aria asked pausing for a second, semi-excited by the news that she was about to share. She waited only briefly, before answering her own rhetorical question. "Of course you don't, but I am here to tell you. I know we all remember…, say about fourteen or fifteen years ago…, when we first started using the Omega Wave in small doses during brain scans and mind wipes. Soon after, we hailed the Crystal Continent with an astonishing revelation. They were going to allow an ethnic group of cadets to be brought up and allowed to compete, not only in the rigors of the academy, but also in the S.A.F. itself. Well, to make a long story short, these cadets have just graduated, the brain scans are from their girlfriends and their mother. They were sent by their Commander and father figure, and if that is not enough, they are in the company with the very scientists, who have invented this dimensional technology. They escaped Aguanimos in an A-Class submarine, which has recently become stationary off the southern coast of the Crystal Continent. In fact, I have eyes on the location right now, and it seems highly probable that this group still possesses some type of dimensional technology. So, now we're going to have to decide, just exactly what our next move will be."

*   *   *   *   *

"Blissful encounters, my name is Silbcor of Chronos, it is a true pleasure to greet those, who have saved our home of Oblivion, the place you knew as Xibalba".

Tank and Belsangar shot each other a look, after hearing the, 'of Cronos', title. Tank was the first to speak up saying, "Wait a minute, you look like Kilari, and more than once, he has been called Kilari, of Chronos, so, who are you, his big brother or something?"

Silbcor smiled at the overly large man's question. "Or something is closer to the truth."

Khana smiled, as she looked into Silbcor's eyes and interjected the man's teasing with, "Silbcor, they just want answers. It is not time to jest."

Agreeing, Silbcor began explaining saying "A spell was cast many, many, long times ago, in which our soul exists in every dimension of every time. In our time, Khana and I are that soul."

"So, you're saying you are soul mates, and in turn that means you actually share one soul?" Marcia asked.

"Yes." Khana replied, as she gazed upon Kilari, with his girls tucked into each side.

COGNIZANT

"So, what does that mean for Jezza, Kilari and I?" Marcia asked with a hint of concern.

Looking at Khana, Silbcor stated, "I've heard of a thirded soul, but never thought I'd see it with mine own eyes."

Silbcor, noticed the entire group looking at him inquisitively, so he explained. "In the beginning, Yahiveh created all souls. These souls are then split as they are awakened into worldly bodies. The term 'soulmates' has been coined to describe the lucky ones that have found their true and only counterpart. Occasionally, a soul splits into three beings, before taking mortal flesh. Typically, when this happens, due to socially accepted traditions only two of the three souls find each other, but never feel completely whole."

"We found each other", Jezza returned with a smile.

ROC BLISS

"Yes, you, and Marcia, are the split soul of, who I am, in my time. That is why each of you have resemblance to me but do not look as similar as Kilari and Silbcor." Khana replied reassuringly.

"I shall now tell you these small truths to put you all on the same page," the young sorceress continued. "Yes, Kilari is, the 'Chosen One', to all who have lived through and survived the time of Xibalba. Yes, Kilari, Jezza, and Marcia are of Chronos, through the supplication of our spell on, "Oblivion Night". Their soul is mingled with our blood. Yes, the prophecy of a thousand-year's toil has been fulfilled, leaving your own destinies to follow."

The entire crowd, all, stood staring at the magic wonder beholden before them. It also entered their minds that there was suddenly, much more to life than living for the day.

COGNIZANT

There was some eternal force behind all things, and they had all been utilized in some way by these empowering spirits, or Gods, to gain a favorable outcome for the sake of goodness itself.

Silbcor, once again, whispered into Khana's ear. "Silbcor has just reminded me of the second reason, in which we are here." Khana stated in a much more serious tone. "We have been watching your world, An'non. Even though your escape seemed flawless, and this out of the way place seems to have been forgotten. This is not the case."

Instant murmuring began, as many of the group began to worry of the next source of bad news. They had just barely finished the last ordeal, and now, another threat is looming in their murky futures.

"Don't worry, I've come to warn you of these foes." Khana said soothingly, which did calm the crowd.

"Yes, in an unknown, but seemingly brief amount of time, in this very position, in this very building, forces will come to find you, and yet even after that, the abolitionists will come, finding their stolen, underwater ship. I do not know more than that."

"But we had agreed to stay here for seven days," Cam stated to Layla whispering quietly.

"Yes, I know of this, as well, Cam, and that is why we came to warn you." Khana stated aloud, so that all would realize what was happening.

All around her. Every whisper, every murmur, and all actions, the young sorceress could perceive, as if they all had been stated plainly. She felt a responsibility to tell them of their consequences, if things would have gone unchecked. "You have until the stroke of midnight to prepare, rest, and be ready for our return. We may not be your only hope, but we owe you a debt that cannot easily be paid, so fear not. We shall return with help". With that being said, Khana spread her arms out wide, and the glowing protective orb had, once again, surrounded her and her soul mate.

Kilari, seeing his spirit guide about to leave, interjected saying, "Khana wait! We must talk."

"We shall talk Kilari, tomorrow, at midnight, until then, fear not, Yahiveh is with usss, always."

The entire group stared in awe, as Khana began casting her spell aloud. "Swirling currents, ebb of time, hold usss fast, with our binds, bring us back, to our home, through the swirling, rings of smoke, OBEY!" As Khana spoke the violet clouds formed around the orb of light. They began rotating, increasing their speed and turbulence by the second.

Thomas Elliot stood transfixed upon the scene in disbelief, and then, almost at once, the whirlpool appeared as though it was imploding, shrinking in upon itself. He took note of the fact that when Khana had exclaimed the final word, 'obey', the orb, Khana, Silbcor, and the swirling clouds, all, completely vanished without a trace.

Instantly, all of the people in the room, began discussing what had just happened. The clamor in the room rose to such a chaotic level that finally, Tessa put two fingers to her mouth and let out a shrill whistle. It took several seconds for the blasting whistle to take its full effect, but soon enough, silence filled the room. "Okay, now that I have your attention, I believe that we should bring this meeting to the lobby area, where we have more room and its shielded with anti-surveillance protection that we should test for functionality in case we end up needing it." Tessa then looked to her timepiece, and suggested, "at Four A.M., so in fifteen minutes in the main lobby, thank you."

*   *   *   *   *

Ensign Minga-Zoo's eyes rolled, as he watched two heartbeats vanish, once again, back into oblivion. Of course, he had no clue of the actual place of Oblivion. "Here we go again," he said with a sigh.

"I take it, you got that too?" The lead man from the second skiff called over.

Minga nodded, and then looked to Sgt. Stonewall Gall. With a sigh, he muttered, "you are going to have to

make another status report, Stones.
Two heartbeats missing again."

Suddenly, there were multiple sets
of whispers, amongst the four skiffs.
"What is it now?" Sgt. Gall asked
peevishly.

The lead man from the fourth skiff
settled his crew down and then turned
toward the lead vessel. "Well, all of
those people in the building made
another mass exodus from one room to
the main lobby of the compound, but
that ain't what's got my crew in a
ruckus. We all just wanna know, if the
names we are hearing are correct." The
man looked to be in a state somewhere
between fear and hatred. "We all
wanna know, if you're referring to the
fact that we have Minga-Zoo, and
Stonewall Gall over there?"

"And what of it?" Sgt. Gall quickly
snipped back, as he stood up

menacingly, looking as if he were about to pull out a short-range blaster.

Most of the rest of the men, those who have not already had the pleasure of working with the two infamous slayers from the Crystal Continent, sat back in their seats with eyes widened to every move that was being made. The head man on the fourth skiff, held one hand out in a motion of peace, while stating, "It's just that I personally knew at least two dozen men, whom you have slaughtered, and I swore that if I were to ever run across you two on the battlefield that I would personally see you two take your last dying gasps of breath."

Minga-Zoo instantly began to rise to the threat that was being laid out nearly within his grasp.

Sgt. Gall instantly had his side-piece out. "Fortunately for you, we are on the same side, or else, I would allow

Minga here, to have his fun with you. We have another mission, right now, and you are either with us, or you can go find your dead brethren on the other side. Make your choices wisely." Gall said threateningly with his blaster pointed straight for the man, who dared talk smack on his watch.

As the rest of the men sat back even a little further into their seats, showing their alpha-dog that he held the reigns, the leader of the fourth skiff, finally joined the men and said, "you are in command, and we'll have your back on *this* mission, but if the day comes, things won't be so pleasant."

"Well, now that your drama queen impersonation is over, maybe we can get back to business?" The cold and calculating Sgt. Gall added before, harshly calling for a Sit. Rep.

COGNIZANT

"Twenty-seven heartbeats, sir, all in the lobby of the compound. The other two just vanished, when the second occurrence of the power surge took place." The leader of the second skiff had no problem bringing the infamous Sgt. Gull up to speed, even though, he himself, may also have a few bones to pick with the man from the S.A.F., as well, but he knew better than to get on the bad side of this situation.

This time Sgt. Gall held no sway in his heart on the way things should go, so he direct-linked with Aria, so that he could persuade the woman that the time for action was now.

* * * * *

As the crowd flooded from Kilari's room on their way to the main lobby of the deserted motel, Kilari and his girls hung back to catch their bearings on what had just taken place. Belsangar noticed the stall, so he and Celia, along with Tank and Sophie, also remained to get a fresh take on the situation.

Kilari sat down casually. He was in no hurry to hear all of the plans that he felt would be just a waste of time. As he sat down upon the long couch, he noticed Alphie, standing at the door looking not unlike a sentry, which gave the young man an idea.

"Alphie, do you remember, back on Flag Island when you knew every move that we were making, when we were trying to sneak into the beach house?" Kilari asked trying to set the stage for what he wanted to know.

"Affirmative, master Kilari. As I recall, I placed all of your belongings from the front of the house to your rooms, while you and the other young masters here, walked very slowly around to the back door, and then I started making breakfast for you, until you finally..."

The girls, all began laughing at the sounds of Alphie's recant, and how the boys' plans were a flop. They imagined the look of failure on their faces, as a server droid foiled their extravagant entrance. This would have become more out of control, if it hadn't approached at such a crucial time.

"Okay girls," Kilari stated meekly, as he wanted to get on with his orders for Alphie.

"Yeah, you really cooked up a good one there, now didn't you?" Tank asked rhetorically, trying to get in on the fun.

"You too?" Kilari asked with a hint of redness on his embarrassed face. Tank grinned impishly, as he just, simply, shrugged his shoulders, holding no blame.

"Alphie," Kilari said, moving on with his original thoughts. "How far of a perimeter can you observe."

"I can perceive sounds, as low as one decibel, and see movements for approximately one hundred yards in the dark, but I can see much farther in the light of day." The droid answered informatively.

"Okay then, you stand over by the window, which overlooks the Blue Sea." Kilari ordered. As the droid moved over to the window, Kilari just thought of another question. "So, what types of alarm signals can you produce, and how loud are they?"

"Well, master Kilari, my volume can be up to one hundred and twenty decibels, and I have a myriad of sounds from voice, to beeps, or ringing, tornado sirens, air-raid sirens."

"Let's just go with that last one," Kilari blurted, before Alphie continued

COGNIZANT

with his list, which seemed never ending. "Make it at maximum volume, and you don't stop alarming, until I give the order."

"Yes, Master Kilari." Alphie replied. And with that said the group headed down to the lobby to meet with the others.

TO BE CONTINUED...

ROC BLISS

BOOK IV

COGNIZANT

ROC BLISS

Khana and Silbcor foreshadowed in the Oblivion Series, will be returning as main characters in the upcoming parallel series *Oblivion Night* authored by Lovey Bliss. Here is:

Oblivion Night Shades of Magic

Book I, Chapter I

COGNIZANT

Oblivion, a place that does exist, at least in the hearts and souls of most beings. A plane of existence, a realm, intact with all of the beliefs of magic, and folklore, intertwined with the powers of multiple religions, and legends.

The bold lands of this realm hold many races and creeds of people, each with its own very separate domain, however, there are also places where the many varied cultures have coalesced into one giant ethos, creating an amalgamation of all beliefs and peoples. Chronos is exactly this type of realm.

Silbcor, a young man, at the age of sixteen, an adult of these times, barely, is smallish for his tribe's male gender, standing five feet seven inches with long, golden blonde hair. A well-muscled sort, from all of his years toiling in the fertile soil at the fringes of Chronos. He has a genuine charm about him, which emits an aura of pure goodness, and engulfs all of those, who go near enough to feel his presence. He follows the many beliefs of spirituality, and his blood flows with the power of magic. Silbcor also has another charm, her name is Khana, his long-time love.

Khana, nearly the same age as Silbcor, is a taller girl of Chronos, with impeccable lineage, steeped in the magical façade of her parents, the high priest and priestess of the largest coven of Chronos. Khana stands at five feet, ten inches tall. For a leggy young girl, her hourglass body holds men at bay, with wonder of her splendors. Her midnight brown, naturally curly hair, frames an angelic face, built upon high cheekbones, and inset, piercing, deep, aphotic eyes. All of these things, added with her slightly tannish skin, make

COGNIZANT

her physical allure nearly incomparable.

Khana studied from ancient scrolls, in order to fully master, all of the spells and incantations, known by her coven. As her heritage suggests, she will someday be the High Priestess of Oblivion, and with it, will come all of the responsibilities, and expectations.

Khana and Silbcor, have known each other for many years now, and as fate would have it, their friendship has blossomed into full budding love. The better part of most days and nights, the inseparable pair strive to master their arts of supernatural origins, working high-end spells and incantations, together, for eternal purposes. Each of the two youths are feeling the effects of true love, and know that it is the ultimate power of all that is good.

ROC BLISS

Silbcor first met Khana when she came to purchase some apothecary herbs from his parents, Gwyneth and Archibald. She was studying the ancient ways with her mentor, Shelophis, a very wise and powerful sorcerer, while Silbcor studied her. The first time she came in, his soul was transfixed, and it didn't take long, before he began making every excuse, just to see her, as often as possible, if he has his way. On occasion, when he was younger, he would even go to the extent of telling her that certain herbs weren't available, and that he would be happy to *personally,* deliver any such needed merchandise, just as soon as he could obtain them.

Silbcor's deliveries, seemed to become more common than shopping. It was not unusual for Silbcor to stay a while, even if it was for no other reason, other than to watch Khana's

COGNIZANT

instruction, as she practiced spells and incantations from her coven's grimoire, with Shelophis.

Shelophis didn't mind Silbcor watching, he had grown up with his great grandfather, Aeneas, and had played a large part in the lives of Archibald's father, Archibald and now Silbcor.

Being naturally gifted in the magic of the ancients, Khana struggled with apothecarial magic. She would get so frustrated that sometimes when Shelophis would turn away she would cause the desired outcome using her ancestral magic, instead.

One particular day, Khana was struggling with a plant growth potion she was making. As usual, when Shelophis turned away, Khana enchanted the flower and it instantly grew filling in with lush foliage. Silbcor couldn't help but to laugh, at

Khana's sheepish grin when she turned to tell Shelophis she finally got it.

"Silbcor," Shelophis interrupted. "Can you please explain to Khana what the potion she just made is used for?"

"Um, yes Sir, we use that particular potion to prevent weed growth." Silbcor hesitantly started before getting lost in his explanation, knowing this one from frequent use. "It works very well, where we spread it, nothing gr…"

Khana, instantly clamped her hand, chanting something under her breath and with the glow of her eyes, Silbcor's voice faded to nothing but the movement of his lips.

Shelophis turned disciplinarily towards Khana, "Khana!" he sang out. "Do not be upset with Silbcor just because you were caught cheating. You may be able to make these small practice effects occur with your own magic, but you know someday you will need to master both, apothecarial and ancestral magic to protect and rule Oblivion."

With that being said, Khana released her fist, and Silbcor, who was holding his throat in confusion, began speaking once more mid exhalation, "ahhh ahhhhhhhh. Hey, my voice is back. I'm sorry if I offended you Khana. It was not my intent to do so."

"Silence, from both of you!" Shelophis interjected, as he walked over to the old wooden workbench and pulled out a small chain. "Khana, you have proven my suspicions." He continued as he walked back towards the young sorceress. "Now", he said as he held out the chain, "let us see how you do *without* your magic". With that, he held out the chain above her wrist and as he released it, it wrapped itself around and solidified into a solid unbreakable shiny metallic binding, that appeared delicate with intricate symbols, befitting a princess. "Your lessons are complete for today Milady, I shall see you tomorrow."

"You are just going to leave this on me?" Khana asked in astonishment. "How am I supposed to… What am I going to… Seriously?"

"Yes Khana, perhaps maybe you and Silbcor could use the remainder of your instruction time to try to actually make the potion assigned you today." and with that Shelophis turned and walked away. "Oh, and Silbcor, I'm off to visit your parents. I will let them know you will be returning later this evening."

After watching Shelophis turn out of sight, Khana turned and glared, at this know-it-all, little, apothecarian, want-to-be warlock.

COGNIZANT

"Khana," Silbcor started with hesitation, "just come for a walk with me."

"As you wish." Khana patronized.

As Khana and Silbcor entered the palace gardens, Khana thought to herself, that she wasn't, really mad at Silbcor, only herself, it was just easier to redirect her frustrations.

Silbcor darted across in front of her and picked some young foliage, this is the turquoise Aplicia bush, not to be confused with the Bush of Will, to which is flowerless. Then, he plucked one of its full blooming, rich, fuchsia flowers. He placed both items on the stone bench along the path. "Hey, this is a fun one I learned when I was a little boy," Silbcor chuckled to the now, guilt ridden, but to ashamed to admit it, sorceress.

"Watch." Silbcor said excitedly as he rubbed the Aplicia leaves upon the evergreen, beside them and chanted "In is out, out is in, make this bush mirror its friend." Instantly the evergreen was as vibrantly turquoise as the Aplicia.

"That's awesome!" Khana exclaimed forgetting she was still trying to be upset with him. "And what, does that, *gorgeous*, flower do?"

"This stunning flower basks plainly in the glow of the most beautiful girl in all the realms." Silbcor said, as he tucked it behind her blushing left ear. "It can also prevent the slumbering effects of the Deception Willows, but we don't have to worry about them around here."

"I guess, I just never had interest in apothecarial arts, since I can just conjure the same effects. But I would never have thought to change a bush's color." Khana offered honestly.

"Try it." Silbcor encouraged. With that being said, Khana mimicked

COGNIZANT

Silbcor's actions and changed a Golden Dragonflower turquoise.

"I did it!" Khana exclaimed as she pointed towards the flower.

"Yes, you did. The Aplicia is a conductor. Not only of itself, but can also conduct other flora, watch." He took one of the Aplicia leaves and a petal from a Golden Dragonflower, and again rubbed it on an evergreen with the same incantation. Again, the evergreen transfigured, only this time into a glowing bush with golden leaves. "The evergreen is the most commonly used apothecarial ingredient due to its natural longevity, which acts like a preservative. However, many spells require other ingredients. By using the Aplicia the evergreen is not only changed in color, it is infused with any number of plant life ingredients for potions, tinctures and spells."

"I'm impressed." Khana answered with intrigue.

"The only drawback," Silbcor started, "is there is no way to harvest or preserve the Aplicia, or the evergreen. The Aplicia leaf must be fresh and it only can be infused into the living evergreen bush. The bush itself will return to normal in a few brief minutes, as you can see in the two bushes I turned, and the cutting must be added to a mixture within an hour."

"Then, what do you do in the winter when the Aplicia is dormant?" Khana wondered aloud.

"We can't do many things in the winter. That's where you come in." Silbcor continued. "You see, I've been watching your studies, and I believe that if you enchanted the evergreen with your ancestral magic, and I infused it with some of the most common, and powerful vegetation, we could provide our people with the resources that many go without, for extended periods of time."

"Oh, so your interest in *me*, is so your family can increase business in the winter." Khana stated with disappointment.

"No, not at all." Silbcor stated, as he held out one hand, motioning Khana to again walk with him, and the other, ever so gently across her back, in the proper, escorting fashion. "Most of our business is helping people, and honestly most are unable to pay. We provide the necessary supplies that ease the symptoms and discomfort from incurable diseases, infections and occasionally, provide the potions and tinctures for everything from infertility to coagulation of war injuries. With the help of the evergreen infusing method, we can make some of them last for a longer time than without, but we lose patients every year, because we cannot provide relief year-round." Silbcor finished with a heavy heart.

"As soon as Shelophis releases the binding on my magic, I will try to help you Silbcor. It's still fairly, early in the spring, so we should have no trouble perfecting it by winter. I bet one of the binding spells would work," Khana said sincerely. "I knew you sold supplies that we used in studies, I guess I never realized the importance they had for everyone else."

"Oh, thank you, Lady Khana." Silbcor said, with his hand in hers, and a bow. "I knew I could count on you."

"I'll try Silbcor, I can't make promises on something I never attempted before. For right now, let's start by going to see if Girardus, the cook, has any snacks. I'm famished."

COGNIZANT

Khana admitted, with her arm across her corset. Without disagreement, the two headed for the kitchen.

Meanwhile, Shelophis did in fact visit Gwyneth and Archibald, and the three of them decided that it would be beneficial, for Silbcor to officially attend daily instruction with Khana. As he entered the courtyard, he noticed Khana and Silbcor, walking up the path, 'if they weren't only a decade in age, one might have thought they were courting with such smiles and giddy behavior', he thought to himself.

Grinning at his own cunningness in getting the two to work out their differences he approached them. "Silbcor, your parents, and I, have decided that you will start attending instruction with Khana, to help her with her apothecarial arts.

"Does that mean you will remove this binding?" Khana asked with a hope filled smile.

"No, the intent will be to learn without your ancestral magic." Shelophis softly explained.

"Shelophis, Silbcor, and I, wish to combine our knowledge, and abilities, to provide patients with year-round treatments from seasonal ingredients." Khana said, almost too eagerly.

"That is an excellent idea Khana!" Shelophis exclaimed. "I will release your bindings during instruction, for the time being. Depending, on the subject of course."

"Thank you, Sir," Silbcor chanted. And with that they parted ways and went about their day, after the kids obtained their snacks of course.

Then one day, a few years later, it happened, Silbcor had time enough, to stay past their usual wrap-up of one of

COGNIZANT

these sessions. Upon the young sorceress's release, they snuck off together, for several hours.

"Come this way," Khana said, as she excitedly took Silbcor by the hand. Her glowing smile resonated with inner anticipations. These new feelings of young budding admiration for Silbcor, saturated her very essence. She seemed to be suddenly swooning, not just from the touch of his skin, as she clasped his warm, strong, hand. It was not just from the instant friendship that had been growing into more, or his sheer magnetism, which drew her to him, ever so soothingly, nor was it the golden aura that she swears to see, every time that he smiles, but it was, all of these things, and a myriad of more, and some, she doesn't even realize yet.

As this tide of emotions swelled up inside of her like a cresting wave, her heart began to pound, causing her to quicken her usual pace. She extended her gate, making their secretive escape, seem riddled with danger, and urgency.

The rather brisk cadence, wound them down, and through, many dark, almost forgotten hallways, until finally the two young companions bled their way out of the further most reaches of the palace grounds. All of the while, Silbcor found himself engulfed in the fervor of Khana's posturing's. To him, what he thought would be a relaxing, casual walk, transformed into what seemed to be a very clandestine departure.

As the blackness of an old tunnel faded away unto the light of the setting Betelgeuse, the two stealthy youths forged out into the vicinity of the nearby, Sweet Forest.

The Sweet Forest, was filled with perfect apothecarial flora. The smell of the trees alone, were said to have intoxicating effects, but if the wood were to be burned along with the proper herbs, the effects would become much, much more than just a simple relaxant.

Silbcor knew this forest well. With his family delving deep into the apothecarial arts of potions, tinctures, and other various elixirs, he has travelled and searched the Sweet Forest often. "My turn to lead, I know of a place. 'Tis the most beautiful place that I have ever seen," Silbcor stated with all of the confidence in the world. "I have never had the chance to show it to anyone, so you'll be the first."

Khana drew even closer to Silbcor, under the backdrop of the Sweet

Forest. The golden-haired spiritualist youth, immediately eased the walking pace back to that of a relaxing stroll, which is exactly how the young man had envisioned their journey.

"Oh, that's quite alright. I haven't been out of the palace much," Khana stated agreeing that he should take the lead. "You won't get us lost, right?" The young dark-haired girl asked nervously.

"Oh, you don't have to worry," Silbcor answered reassuringly. "I have been through the forest so many times, that I probably could find my way blindfolded."

"Well, let's not try it," Khana joked with a big smile.

"Oh, with the beauty in this forest today, I wouldn't even want to," Silbcor stated matter-of-factly. "I mean, this place holds all of the wonders in all of Oblivion. It's nature at its best, and now that you're in it, the beauty is incomparable." With that being said, both Khana, and Silbcor, began blushing.

"Oh, such a sweet talker. I'd bet you used that line before, on other girls." Khana quipped in her own sweet way, while trying to get any past-history of her new suitor.

"Other girls?" Silbcor asked inquisitively. "I've never noticed any other girls, only you."

"Well, you are really, quite a charmer, Silbcor," Khana blushingly admitted. "So how far is this place that you are taking me to?" Khana asked, being anxious to see this mysterious place of which he had spoked so highly.

"Don't worry, it's just beyond the fringe of the forest gulch." Silbcor said, answering quickly. He continued his casual stroll through nature's bounty, down the widest areas that he could find, so that he could continue to casually hold the hand of this tan-skinned beauty.

"Gulch?" Khana inquired. "I've never heard anyone talk about a gulch in the Sweet Forest."

"It may be a ravine, or some kind of ancient sink-hole, of that I am unsure, but I'm telling you, once you see this place, you'll fall in love," Silbcor said in all honesty.

Khana had a thought, and then her grin began beaming, showing Silbcor that she was indeed thinking of some witty remark.

The young man stopped in his tracks, directly in front of his bronze sorceress, and with the simplest turn of the hand that held Khana's, he spun her into position, facing him eye to eye, much closer to him than envisioned. At first, he had fully intended to find out what she was

COGNIZANT

thinking, but once their eyes, transfixed upon one another, he forgot everything. Staring directly into each other's souls through their eyes, the two stood there motionless, their bodies instantly fevered, as they found themselves lost in the overpowering adrenaline, which was ripping through their veins as Betelgeuse's final rays painted the backdrop of this enchanting moment, with reflections glimmering upon their bodies.

Without a word, moments passed that felt like decades. Like statues in the palace courtyard, the youths were frozen in time. Here they were, without the required chaperone, far from home, out past curfew; breaking all of the rules of their people. The magnetism was overwhelming and each of them fought every breath in restraint.

Slowly, their heightened senses regained a foothold in the conscious realm, starting with their hearing. Flowing water in the nearby distance, began to ease into their minds, as they could also hear the scampering of small woodland creatures scurrying home to take cover for the night. Then, a sudden gust of cool night air, began sweeping across their burning flesh, not only keeping them from being overtaken in their fervor, but also making Khana's robes dance seductively in Silbcor's eye, which made him need the cool breeze all the more. Silbcor could feel the sudden static nipping him from the air itself, as the magical influences of their coalescence, began to intertwine, all on its own.

As Khana adjusted her footing, she noticed torches approaching, and with them came the sudden realization of the situation, which struck her like lightning.

COGNIZANT

"There she is! You may all return to the palace." Bonigo, the palace's central guard called out to his men in relief. Khana took a step back, slowly, with her gaze still entranced into Silbcor's soul, as Bonigo rode up to the young pair. He reached down, as if to lift her upon his horse, and carry her home, but Khana would have none of it.

"Bonigo, wait." The young sorceress pleaded, while quickly side stepping the guard's advance.

"Wait! Wait for what?" The guard's rough voice shot out, showing the consternation that he was under. "Do you want me to wait for your mother or father, to discipline me for not keeping my watchful eyes upon thee. Or to have this young man hung for attempted courting outside of his station"

"No Bonigo, I just hoped to see the beautiful place that Silbcor wanted to show me, that's all." Khana looked up at her old friend, giving the man, her lost puppy-dog eyes.

Bonigo, instantly shifted his gaze over to Silbcor. "So, this boy here has promised to show you a very scenic place, did he?" The guard's eyes stared upon Silbcor hard enough to bore holes in the lad. "Well, what have you to say on the matter."

Silbcor cleared his throat a little. The young man's nerves were racing into overdrive.

"Well? Spit it out sonny. I don't have all night to get the young miss back to the palace." Bonigo not only sounded agitated, but he also looked it.

"Sir, you see, we did not mean to cause any trouble," Silbcor stated, as a wind-up for more useful information, but before he could take a breath and continue, the palace guard cut him off.

COGNIZANT

"Stop, stop right there. I know your father, and well, I know better than to let you come off with some magical pretext, and soothe me into doing whatever it is you would talk me into."

"Bonigo," the sweet young voice of Khana sang out. "Will you please allow me to explain?"

"No. I will tell the both of you. Seeing that I don't know this young man's true intentions, he will show the both of us this wondrous place of his, and if it turns out to be a ruse, then we'll both know the value of his intentions."

"So, then we can go? We don't have to leave for the palace?" Khana's voice was filled with excitement. "Thank-you Bonigo, I knew you were a friend, and not just a guard."

"Don't thank me yet, young miss. Silbcor here," the guard pointed, "had better be honorable."

"Well sir, to put your mind at ease," Silbcor finally stated, jumping into the discussion. "Shelophis suggested that I may be of help to the young miss with some of my apothecarial skills, and where we are going is only a few minutes away."

The guard gave the youth one more, stern look, just for good measure, and then motioned for the lad to lead the way.

Khana breathed a sigh of relief, and briskly grabbed Silbcor's hand. Silbcor drew her close to his side, and asked, "Do you know how I can tell that we are almost there?"

The guard rolled his eyes a little and sighed to himself saying, "because you know the way."

COGNIZANT

Just as Silbcor was about to point out a certain vibrant bush. He overheard the guard and began to chuckle.

"Oh, don't mind him, he's just grumpy, because he'll be late for dinner," Khana said with a smile.

Silbcor was ready to get back to the subject at hand, so he nodded his agreement with Khana, and went right back to pointing out the turquoise bush. "When you can hear the water flowing, and the Bush of Will is at hand, you are drawing near." Then he looked back to Bonigo, and after giving him a wink, he stated, "And because I know the way, I will walk straight passed the bush," he continued walking for several paces, "and then around this rocky mound," he continued as he pointed out the thirty-foot diameter, twenty-foot high pile of boulders, which did have green foliage growing forth, "And behold! Isn't that the most beautiful sight that you have ever seen," he said, as his hands were held out, presenting an impressive scene indeed.

Khana looked down, into the deep crevice that had somehow been torn into the very fabric of Oblivion. She found herself standing upon a shelf, if you will, and as she began looking downward to take it all in, she realized that it was a sheer rock wall beneath her. The view was immense. She could peer easily three-hundred feet down, over trees and bushes, boulders and bluffs, but then, that's when the true magical sight shifted its way into her sightline. Betelgeuse was beginning to set, but its shimmering rays glowed upon a rather sizable body of water, making it appear to glow. "Is that a lake, Silbcor?" She asked in perfect awe of this spectacle of nature.

COGNIZANT

"Yes, and that's not all that's down there, "Silbcor added. "If you look straight down, just before the ground, there is a cave that overlooks the Ancient Lake."

Khana began to peer downward, but their angle was not the best for views of the cave. The majestic beauty of the lake near the mountain on which they stood, with the glistening of Betelgeuse lapping in its waves drew Khana's spirit towards it.

"I can take us all down there on the wings of a spell, so we can get a closer look," Khana touted reassuringly.

"I think, you may be forgetting about something," Silbcor stated, as he held her wrist out to remind her of the magic shackle that Shelophis had used to restrain her.

A look of disappointment crossed the eager girl's face. "Oh yeah," she said disconcertingly.

"Don't worry, I know a way, and it doesn't take that long. Maybe only twenty minutes," Silbcor said in a soothing voice.

Khana quickly looked over to Bonigo for approval, and she could see by the look in his eyes that the gears were beginning to grind. "Can we go?" She asked point blank.

Bonigo loved the young miss, being that she has been under his watchful eyes for several years now. "Let me strike a bargain with you, being that Silbcor here," he paused to point towards the young man, "definitely did have a wondrous place to show you." Then the guard paused again, striving for the right words, but none came simply, so he decided to cut right to the chase. "Honestly Khana, it

COGNIZANT

seems, as though you are growing up right before my eyes, so I am going to cut you some slack. I don't want to go down there and be in your business, especially when I have other things to do, so I will be back here in a couple of hours, when I'm ready to wrap up the days business, and I will be expecting you to be right here and ready to go."

Khana couldn't believe her ears, not only could she go and check this mystical place out, but Bonigo was trusting her to be alone with Silbcor. "Thank-you Bonigo. I won't let you down. I promise," the young sorceress vowed with a gleaming smile.

Bonigo nodded accepting Khana's promise, and then the guardsman looked over to Silbcor, saying, "You better take care of her, or it'll be both of our backsides at the whipping pole. If you know what I mean?"

"Nothing to worry about here, sir. I've spent months working up here, and have never seen another soul," Silbcor stated, trying to ease Bonigo's mind. It did not seem to have the effect that he was hoping for, as he swore to have seen the guardsmen grimace a little, upon hearing his statement. "Oh, and I was wondering, if you would not tell anyone of this place. I was rather hoping to keep this, our little secret."

"Don't worry about that sonny. I think this whole arrangement needs to be kept under wraps, and as long as you can behave, I believe it will," Bonigo explained cunningly, as he smiled at the fact that he put all of the responsibility, right back onto Silbcor. With that the guardsman turned his stallion and rode off through the forest. "Two hours!" He yelled from the distance, before picking up his pace, and disappearing, from sight.

COGNIZANT

Silbcor waved to Bonigo, saying, "Bright Blessings," as he watched the guard fade into the forest. Then, the young apothecarian turned his attention back to Khana. "We better get going. We don't have a lot of time, but I seriously believe, that once you see all of the possibilities, you will be wanting to practice here."

"I don't know how much practicing we'll have left, Silbcor. As you know, in a few days I will embark upon my spiritual journey, and *if* I return, my rite of passage will be shortly there-after." Khana stated as if these facts were not already weighing on both of their minds.

TO BE CONTINUED...

Roc Bliss

COGNIZANT

Roc Bliss

About the Author

Roc Bliss's abiding love for fantasy and science fiction only shadowed by his undying love for his wife Lovey, inspired him to begin writing shortly after high school. The loving support and indescribably jubilant marriage with Lovey and their five inspirational children has led to launching his first set of novels with the 2017 release of the *Oblivion Series* including the first three books *The Test, Xibalba* and *Cognizant* with many more to come. The breathtaking dramatic landscapes of their native Michigan inspired the visions depicted throughout the series.

You can find out more about Roc, Lovey and their books at www.oblivionnight.weebly.com.

Made in the USA
Lexington, KY
11 October 2017